Lord of Gold and Glory

Fae Isles - Book 2

Lisette Marshall

Cover design: Saint Jupiter

Editor: Erin Grey, The Word Faery

www.lisettemarshall.com

www.facebook.com/LisetteMarshallAuthor

www.instagram.com/AuthorLisetteMarshall

To W.,
who always comes back to me.

CONTENTS

CHAPTER 1

ALL OF TIME AND space was squeezed into two everlasting heartbeats.

With an odd tugging sensation just below my midriff, Tared's magic pulled me out of Faewood and into a sickening maelstrom of colour and sound, dizzying flashes of impressions whirling around me faster than my drained mind could follow. A cold winter breeze and a gust of clammy warmth. Screaming, singing, a wolf's howling. Glimmers of gold and a sweep of purple deep enough to swallow me.

Into emptiness – into some place I didn't even know – and I could no longer bring up the energy to care. All that counted was ...

We were out.

Away from the Crimson Court. Away from the Mother. Away from the hounds, the mockery, the need to watch my every word and movement ... My body refused to believe it even in those dazzling moments of nowhere and everywhere at once; my muscles wouldn't loosen. I clung to Tared's slender hand so tightly it hurt, as if the slightest slip might send me sliding back to that cursed island, back to suffer the consequences of the Mother's wrath.

I didn't expect her to receive me with much affection after that burst of red I'd sent into her eyes.

But my hand didn't slip, Tared didn't let go of me, and the world cleared as abruptly as it had blurred into nothingness.

The whirling darkness turned solid around me, and the colours slid back into shapes and patterns my eyes could recognise. Chairs. Bed. Desk. We had faded into a dusky room with a low, vaulted ceiling and stone walls blacker than anything I'd ever seen – a smooth, shiny surface, like solidified pools of ink. Little balls of light hovered in the corners, not the glasslike orbs that illuminated the Crimson Court, but spheres of fire, miniature suns small enough to fit in the palm of my hand.

They were the only source of light. There were no windows, not even the faintest glimmer of daylight to be seen.

And not even the quietest whisper to be heard.

I'd never heard a silence as deep as the one pressing against that vault-like room – no rustle of the sea in the distance, no wind or footsteps or birdsongs. The ominous quiet was broken only by Tared's curse as he yanked his hand from mine and staggered back, away from Creon, until he collided with the wall and sank onto the floor like a rumpled rag doll. Then there was just his heavy breathing and Lyn's near-in-audible fidgeting, a surreal sense of peace beside the shouts and the howls and the trembling mountains of the Crimson Court still echoing in my ears.

I swallowed and glanced at Creon's motionless body, curled up on the rough woollen carpet. There was nothing surreal about those tears in his wings, and it took a moment for my lips and tongue to agree to even the most basic of questions.

'Where ... where on earth are we?'

'Home,' Lyn said, an apology in her amber eyes as she gently lowered Creon's arm to the floor and stepped back as well. With a quick glance at Tared, she added, 'Eat something, will you?'

He pulled a face but grabbed a small leather bag from his pocket, tore it open with trembling fingers, and shoved three dried apricots into his mouth at once. For a moment, the sound of his vigorous chewing was all that held that utter silence at bay.

Home.

Which meant that Tared hadn't moved us into some prison cell. Which meant he believed me on the matter of Creon's current loyalties. Which meant we were …

Safe?

Nothing about that word seemed to be even distantly related to reality. As far as my buzzing limbs were concerned, the Mother herself might come bursting through the room's rune-covered wooden door any moment, ready to melt our flesh from our bones with a flick of her hand and decorate her throne hall with the remains of our corpses. Hell, perhaps she wouldn't even need to find us. If she had mauled Creon badly enough in the past few hours …

A rush of red-hot alarm scorched my dazed bewilderment to the ground. Zera help me, what was I doing, staring sheepishly at walls and pondering matters of geography? He needed a bed. He needed a healer. He needed time and rest and loving care, and if *I* didn't make sure he got all of those things …

Who would?

I sucked in a breath, ready to plead or threaten or whatever else would shake the other two into movement. Tared was faster.

'Patience, Emelin,' he muttered, still chewing. 'Give us a moment.'

'A moment for what?' My voice came out too loud for this low room. Around me the walls reflected the glow of the small suns in iridescent flickers, like the light shimmering in bubbles of soap. 'Are we waiting for something?'

'Wisdom.' He rubbed his hand over his face, then gestured for me to take a seat in one of the two worn armchairs in the corner, which were covered in vaguely recognisable floral patterns. 'I'm trying to figure out what we should do next.'

I blinked. 'It seems clear enough that he needs a healer, yes? Or were you planning to leave him like this and—'

'Emelin,' Tared interrupted, closing his eyes. 'Sit down.'

'Not if you—'

'Sit *down*.' There was a sudden edge of steel in his voice, something razor-sharp cutting through the usual casual nonchalance with unnerving ease.

Enough for the words to freeze on the tip of my tongue. Enough for my trembling knees to finally give in and buckle. I plopped down on the carpet like a badly balanced sack of grain, more grateful for the firmness of the floor than I liked to admit.

Lyn followed my example, albeit more gracefully. 'The problem is, Emelin ...' She faltered, exchanging a reluctant look with Tared.

I bit my tongue so hard it hurt. It was all I could do not to lash out and have them lose the last of their patience. 'The problem?'

'Not all of our healers will be happy to tend to him,' she said, closing her eyes. 'More specifically, a majority of them would be tremendously happy for a chance to stick their scalpels through his heart as soon as we turned our backs on them.'

I stared at her. Only then did the realisation hit my tired brain, hopelessly late – that the two of them would be far from the only ones who knew Creon in this place.

Worse, that they would be far from the only ones harbouring a grudge against him.

'Honestly,' Tared said, swallowing his last bite, 'I doubt they would wait for us to turn our backs. So if you want him to live ...' His face twitched as he sat up straighter, shoved the empty apricot bag into his pocket, and met my eyes. 'We need a little patience. And more than a little politics. Trust me, I'm as unhappy about both as you are.'

I forced myself to attempt a laugh, eyes swerving back to Creon's lifeless face. In this bright, yellow light, the sickly sheen of his forehead looked even more ominous, the abrasions and bruises even more painful.

'So what are the options?'

'We should probably keep it in the family,' Lyn said, glancing at the door. 'Ylfreda won't do anything rash, at least. The problem ...'

'Yes.' Tared let out a groan. 'How is your use of blue magic, Emelin?'

'My ... what?'

'His wings.' He gestured vaguely at Creon. 'Ylfreda is good, but I don't think she can stitch those holes up without leaving permanent damage. So?'

An abrupt wave of nausea twisted my stomach into knots. *Permanent damage.* Oh, no. I'd never trained my blue magic much. What if I messed it up? What if I blew his wings apart the way I'd destroyed the pavilion over and over for days?

'I don't think I should try if I can avoid it. My magic tends to ...' I swallowed. 'To over-perform a bit.'

Lyn threw me an intrigued look but turned back to Tared without probing. 'Do you think Cale would keep his mouth shut if Ylfreda asked him to?'

'If we're lucky.' He didn't sound particularly hopeful. 'At least for a few hours, probably. Which sounds better than ...'

'Yes.'

'Well.' He sighed. 'In that case ...'

'Better than *what*?' I said, bewildered by whatever age-old jumps their brains were sharing.

Lyn seemed genuinely surprised as she turned back to me, as if every simpleton should have drawn the right conclusions from three quick words and a look. 'Better than waiting for him to wake up and heal himself,' she clarified. 'If the tears start healing like this ... Well, that would make it damn hard to fix them. So ...'

'Cale will have to handle it,' Tared said grimly, hauling himself to his feet. I stiffened, but he knelt next to Creon without punching him in the face, even though the way his jaw clenched suggested it took an effort. 'That's all, then?'

Lyn nodded, and he lifted Creon's limp body with surprising ease. I bit my lip to hold back a gasp at the way his dark wings folded back, twisting in ways I'd never seen them twist before.

'Oh, dear,' Lyn said, her voice choked. 'Perhaps you should ask Naxi to give a hand, too.'

Tared nodded as he carried Creon to the bed and lowered him onto the thick blankets with surprising care. The next moment, with a last look of unfathomable dread, he was gone.

Lyn cursed.

The expletive came out like a bolt of lightning, so heartfelt and abrupt that I suspected she'd held it in for minutes. When I jerked around, she'd pulled her knees to her chest and rolled over on the thick carpet – a little red-haired ball of frustration, brighter than anything else in the room.

'What ... what is it?' I said, my last grasp of the situation unravelling rapidly.

'There's a couple of things you need to understand.' She spoke fast, staring at the ceiling with exhausted eyes. 'You did the right thing, don't get me wrong – you did the only thing you could do – but he's in a damn dangerous place here, yes? Quite a few alves consider themselves honour-bound to kill him, and trying to argue with an honour-bound alf ...'

She hesitated, the thin line of her lips evidence that she'd tried it often enough and never enjoyed it much.

I stared at her, my stomach turning all over again. So much for my dream of safety. 'But then why—'

'We're in Tared's family home now,' she interrupted, speaking even faster. 'Which is good, because it would *also* be a grave breach of honour for alves of another house to fade into this place and kill someone who's technically a family guest. But the Council – that's the group coordinating most of what the Alliance does – the Council could probably overrule house sanctuary, and then Creon would be in trouble. So we need to convince the rest that we need him. Still clear?'

I nodded, even though my brain was spinning, hanging desperately onto any word she spoke. I hadn't slept in twenty-four hours, for hell's sake. I'd played diplomatic games for weeks; I was too tired for politics. But Creon ... If I delivered him to a horde of rabid alves now, I might as well have left him hanging in the Mother's bone hall, and I wasn't, *wasn't* going to let him die on me.

To hell with the safety, then. To hell with the peace.

'What do you need me to do?'

Lyn gave me a small, joyless smile as she sat up again. 'First priority is to watch your words. Ylfreda is Tared's cousin, and she won't go blathering to the rest of the Alliance if we ask her to wait a few hours – but that's not to say she doesn't *strongly* dislike Creon. Don't try to defend him. It won't win you anything.'

'Alright.' I swallowed. 'And the rest?'

'Let's talk about that after you've had some sleep. We can spare a few hours, and you shouldn't—'

With a shimmer of light, a tall, blonde alf female appeared by the bed.

Lyn abruptly shut her mouth and jumped to her feet, leaving me on that rough woollen carpet in the middle of the room. 'Oh, Ylfreda. Thank the gods. Did Tared tell you ...'

'He did.' There was a firm sort of disapproval in her voice, but she turned towards Creon without elaborating, shaking a bulging leather bag from her shoulders. 'Well. Not looking too healthy, is he?'

My stomach turned again, but I thought of Lyn's warning and bit my tongue. Begging her to save him probably wouldn't be the best start at showing the right priorities.

'She apparently hung him by his wings for a full night,' Lyn said, and the alf clucked her tongue with that firm, resolute demeanour of a healer who's seen too much to still get upset about banal things like perforated guts, bones sticking out of limbs, or in this case, torn wings.

'Ah. So much for his attempts to please mommy-dearest.'

I sucked in a breath, then caught Lyn's warning glare and slammed my mouth shut again. Not the moment to object. Not the moment to defend him.

Not the moment to feel that violent, painful rush of gratitude whenever my eyes slid over his battered body in that unfamiliar bed.

I tried to keep track of the conversation between the two females – something about Cale and Naxi who would be here soon, something about warm water and magic and security measures – but no matter how hard I tried to pay attention, my mind refused to absorb more than shreds of sentences. I'd held myself up by nothing but panic and anger ever since I'd stepped out of the Labyrinth and into Ophion's waiting arms. Now that there was, at least for a minute or two, no war left to be fought, the last of my clarity came crashing down with alarming speed, reducing the world to mingling voices and iridescent light and Creon, so very familiar and yet strange with no trace of the arrogant, almighty fae prince left on him.

I couldn't help but stare as Ylfreda unbuttoned his torn shirt, revealing rough, abraded skin, marred by bruises and the occasional cut. A testimony to last night, his body telling the story of whatever he had endured more eloquently than any witness could.

Whatever he had endured – for *me*.

Invisible hands squeezed my throat, tighter and tighter, until it took all I had not to squeak with every breath I wrestled into my lungs. Every wound Ylfreda cleaned with the pungent-smelling liquids she pulled from her bag, every swollen bruise, every broken bone ... he must have known they were coming. He must have known the Mother would take her revenge slowly and painfully. Hell, if he hadn't expected me to come back for him, he must have prepared for worse.

And yet ...

After I'd accused him of magical manipulation, after I'd thrown the names of his old enemies into his face to hurt, he hadn't even doubted.

At the bed, Ylfreda bent over to examine his wings, running her practiced, herb-stained fingers over the tatters. Before I could regain control of myself, a pained sound escaped me, something between a sob and a wail. Those *wings* – Ophion with those gods-damned *hooks* ...

Ylfreda abruptly glanced over her shoulder. Her eyebrows shot up her forehead as she caught sight of my face.

'Orin's eye. He kept you prisoner, didn't he?' The cold in her words was unmistakable. 'I wouldn't waste my tears crying about him, if I were you.'

I swallowed, and my voice came out as barely more than a pathetic squeak. 'He saved my life.'

'Did he.' She turned back to the bed, still less than impressed. 'Well, don't worry too much. If he could die from a simple hook to the wing, we'd have killed him centuries ago. He was in worse shape last time we captured him, and he seems to have survived that too.'

I swallowed. The catch in my throat wouldn't go.

Lyn threw me a look of concern but just said, 'Tea?'

I didn't want tea. I wanted Creon to be alright. I wanted all of these people to understand what he'd done, what he'd sacrificed all these years they believed him a traitor. I wanted them to stop thinking I was a hapless little victim they'd saved. I wanted him to wake up so I could hold him and promise I'd never abandon him again.

'Yes, please,' I said numbly.

Lyn stepped back from the bed and held out a hand to help me get up. I grabbed it, even though she was no taller than my elbow and didn't make it *that* much easier to stand – but my trembling legs needed all the help they could get.

With a gesture at the two floral armchairs, she said, 'Make yourself comfortable. I'll be back in a moment.'

I fell into the padded seat as if I'd never get up again. She exchanged a last look with Ylfreda, who was cleaning yet another nasty cut just above Creon's hip, and slipped out of the rune-covered wooden door.

A quick glimpse of the corridor outside suggested it was as dark as this bedroom, a narrow, winding tunnel with not a spark of daylight to be seen.

Where the hell were we?

Some cellar or impenetrable fortress? My exhausted thoughts turned too slowly, as if dragging through mud. The room didn't *look* like a fortress room, massive stone walls notwithstanding – not with these worn armchairs and the broad bed with its piles of rough linen pillows. A weathered, unrefined sort of comfort, but comfort nonetheless, and much more welcoming than the frighteningly flawless beauty of the Crimson Court.

Ylfreda stoically worked on, cleaning wounds and inspecting bruises as if I wasn't in the room at all. Before I could work up the courage to ask about this strange, buried world, knuckles hit the bedroom door and a dark-skinned young man stuck his head inside. At first glance, he looked rather human for a place like this, but Ylfreda didn't seem in the least surprised.

'Oh, Cale. Good. I need your magic for his wings.'

Magic? I blinked at the healer crossing the room to her side, carrying a tub of steaming water, two bags, and several dark blue towels. Only as he put down his load and raked a tense hand through his hair did I notice the clue his chestnut curls had hidden from me so far.

His ears seemed round at first glance. But in the warm light of the room's hovering miniature suns, their shape was just *off* – too elongated for human ears and strangely ragged at the upper curve. Or not ragged, but rather ...

Scarred.

Oh, no.

A violent nausea slammed into my stomach as the realisation hit. Someone had *cut off* his ears. Mutilated him in some desperate attempt to hide the truth of his nature ...

Half fae.

I clawed my hands into the rough linen of my chair, unable to take my eyes off him as he exchanged a few curt words with Ylfreda and went to work. He was *half fae*. Which meant he was like *me*. Bound, perhaps, and likely raised by parents who hadn't hidden his fae blood from him – and yet ...

Not alone.

The words hummed through my thoughts as I watched the two healers work, hypnotised by the circling motions of their hands. *Not alone. Not alone.* I'd spent so many weeks unable to trust anyone, so many years unable to feel like I belonged anywhere at all, and all of a sudden there were *others*? Others who hated the fae male I desperately needed to be safe, others who might scoff at me if they knew what exactly he meant to me, and yet ...

The last hole in Creon's wing membrane had just grown closed under Cale's careful sparks of blue magic when the door slammed open and smacked me from my drowsy contemplations like a hammer to the head.

'Ylfreda!' A melodious, girlish voice. Its owner bounced into the room, green skirts fluttering on some invisible breeze, tight blonde curls with pink tips dancing around her blushing face. 'Tared said you needed me! For Creon! Is he *back*?'

Ylfreda closed her eyes as she turned around, visibly suppressing a groan. 'Oh, morning Naxi. If you could ...'

I choked on my own tongue.

Anaxia whirled towards me, ignoring the rest of Ylfreda's sentence on internal damage, blue eyes fixing on me with bright, unnerving sharpness.

That gaze, the piercing, ruthless force of it, was the only thing spoiling the air of softness she carried along. The rest of her ... She looked so painfully small and painfully fragile and most of all painfully *innocent* that it was hard to believe she was the same female who'd battled Thysandra for two full days and barely let her escape alive.

This was the demon fighting on the Alliance's side? I had, admittedly, no idea what demons without fae blood were supposed to look like, but she resembled Creon less than anything or anyone I'd ever met.

'You're surprised,' she cheerfully told me, eyes flashing over me with more interest than I liked. Her loud, bright excitement was a jarring assault on my drained senses. 'How intriguing! Did he tell you about me?'

'He ...' I managed a bewildered laugh. 'He did, yes.'

'Such a sweetheart,' she said, turning to the bed with an affectionate smile. 'Oh, dear, he doesn't feel too well, Freddie. Lots of pain. Lots of ... *oh*.' She cocked her head, then threw me another glance, blue eyes twinkling even brighter. 'How very interesting.'

I sat frozen, convinced she would blurt out every single secret I'd so stubbornly tried to hide from Lyn and Tared and everyone they knew. But she looked away without another word, waving at Creon's bare chest with that disconcertingly innocent smile still on her face. 'Sixth rib is broken. On the left.'

'Missed that one,' Cale muttered, grabbing another blue towel. 'Anything else?'

'Something in his right wrist. And ...' She closed her eyes, face contorting into a grimace as she stepped closer to the bed. 'Zera have mercy, he's so *dramatic*.'

'There's no need to start evaluating his entire emotional state of being,' Ylfreda said, sounding slightly annoyed. 'Physical issues are the relevant part for now.'

'Hard to separate them, Freddie. Ankle is sprained. And you might want to look at that broken finger one more time. That's all I can make out under the layer of' – she groaned – 'other issues. It'll be easier when he's awake and more in control of himself.'

'If he's awake,' Ylfreda said, all but rolling her eyes now, 'he'll probably be able to tell us himself where he's hurting.'

'Oh, yes!' Anaxia beamed at her. 'Well, that's solved, then. Do you need any other help? I could tickle him a bit, see if he wakes up?'

'No one is tickling my patients,' Ylfreda snapped. 'Not even this one. Go tell Tared we're almost done, will you?'

'So annoyed,' Anaxia said dreamily and skipped out of the room with a last devilishly broad grin at me.

I realised I was still clutching my armrests like a madwoman, and sheepishly pulled my fingers from the upholstered wood. Zera help me. These demon powers ... I hadn't taken much time in between the danger and rescue missions of last night to fully consider how unnerving it was for someone else to be aware of every emotion stirring within me – but by the time Creon woke up, we would need to have a good chat about that part.

Several good chats, perhaps.

Tared and Lyn appeared a moment later – he without his sword, she with a mug the size of her own head clenched between her small hands. Their simultaneous glances at me made me sure they'd been talking about me, but I was too tired and too grateful for some familiar faces to make a point of it.

'Almost done,' Ylfreda said without looking up. 'Cale fixed most of the wings.'

Lyn muttered a thanks as she tiptoed towards me, careful not to spill the hot tea. Tared didn't say anything, but he did throw me something like a smile, which I supposed was enough of a win for the circumstances.

'You're alright?' I said, and it wasn't even all diplomacy.

'Alright enough.' He sank into the chair next to me with a muffled groan while Lyn settled her tea mug in my lap, dropped to the floor, and tucked her legs below her body. In a lower tone, he added, 'Naxi just told me not to worry about Creon. No idea why she thinks I was particularly worried, but in case it reassures you ...'

'Oh.' I tried to be relieved, but something about Anaxia still had me feeling all kinds of unpleasant. 'Look, do you mind if I ask – what exactly *is* she?'

'Half demon, half nymph.' He raised his eyebrow at my expression. 'I thought Creon told you about her.'

'He didn't mention the nymph part,' I said weakly. 'It explains a bit. Is everyone half something in this place, or does it only seem like that?'

'It's more that most of the half-somethings end up here,' Lyn said, brushing her hair from her face. 'The whole-somethings tend to make a fuss about them. Down here, even the fullbloods are generally deviants, so ...'

'I heard that,' Ylfreda said loudly from the other side of the room, sounding somewhat amused for the first time. She was packing her things again, leaving a handful of jars and bottles behind on the bedside table. Next to her, Cale had already hoisted his own bags back onto his shoulders.

Lyn gave a joyless chuckle as she turned to the bed. 'Done?'

'He should be stable. I expect he'll wake up within a few days at most.' She nodded at Cale, who grumbled the quickest of greetings and hurried out as if he couldn't wait to wash Creon off his hands. Sitting down at the foot of the bed, Ylfreda sighed and added, 'Should I assume you have a plan to deal with this madness, or would that be terribly optimistic?'

'Have you ever known me to make plans?' Tared said wryly.

'An alf can hope, Thorgedson.' She gave him a sour smile, rubbing her herb-stained hands over her face. 'Does the rest of the Council know about all of this?'

The deadly silence that fell was enough of an answer. Ylfreda closed her eyes and muttered a curse in some language I didn't know – and only then did the full meaning of that sentence get through to my weary thoughts.

I blinked. 'Did you say the *rest* of the Council?'

Another abrupt silence. Tared looked like a man forced to confess to murder. Lyn looked like a child caught with her hands in the cookie jar.

'Oh,' Ylfreda said, sending them looks of pale amusement. 'I don't suppose these two told you about that part, no.'

'About *what* ...'

'The part where they manage most of the Alliance.' She nodded at Tared, who glared back at her as if he'd be glad to commit that murder. 'Or at least, alves make up half of the Council, and my lovely cousin here is generally considered the leader of the—'

'I'm not a *leader*,' Tared interrupted, a little too loud. 'They tend to listen to my suggestions, but that's mostly because I usually don't suggest housing fae murderers in the Underground. So—'

'In the *what?*' I said.

'The – oh. The Underground.' He swung a hand at the room. 'Welcome below the earth and all of that. Listen, Freda, *I'm* not even mad enough to spring this on the rest of the Council without preparation and hope they'll just agree. I'm not even entirely sure what I'd like them to agree with, frankly.'

She pressed her lips into a thin line, glancing at me with that scrutinising healer's look in her eyes. 'Perhaps that's something to discuss while the girl sleeps.'

'I don't need to sleep,' I blurted, even though the room was admittedly spinning at the edges of my sight and every word they spoke came through to my aching brain a fraction later than it should have. But if Tared was still doubting – if *anyone* was still doubting – I couldn't afford to be away from the world for hours on end. 'If you're going to make decisions, I can—'

'Ylfreda is right,' Lyn interrupted, wiping yet another stubborn curl from her face. 'We can keep this silent for a few more hours. That should give you some time to take a nap and prepare to see the Council while we figure out how to go forward with all of this.'

'But ...' I hesitated, trying with all I had not to glance at Tared. But what if he decided in an hour he didn't want Creon here after all? What if those honour-bound alves Lyn had mentioned didn't wait for the Council's decisions and showed up here anyway to kill him? 'Are you sure that's ... safe?'

'It'll be fine, Emelin.' Lyn's look was a little too meaningful. *I know what you're thinking,* that look said, *but did you forget I'm trying to help him, too?* 'Ylfreda can stay with him while you sleep. He'll be alright for a few hours.'

I swallowed, glancing at Creon again. Bandaged and clean, he at least no longer looked on the brink of death – but the thought of leaving his room and abandoning him yet again made me feel like roaring at them.

'I'm staying here.'

Lyn blinked. 'Emelin ...'

'I'll just sleep in a chair.' Old Emelin, I realised, might have given in at that first spark of disapproval. But Creon had told me I should want more, and if there was one thing I wanted now, one thing I needed, it was just a few quiet minutes with him during which no one was trying to kill us. 'Or on the floor. I don't care. As long as we aren't entirely sure it's safe, I'm not leaving him alone.'

'I'm not in the habit of stabbing my patients through the heart when no one is looking, girl,' Ylfreda said curtly. 'And if a horde of alves would be mad enough to violate house sanctuary and burst in here, I doubt one little half fae will be enough to stop them.'

I clenched my fists. 'Wishing them good luck.'

'Good gods,' she said but got off the bed with a tired glance at Tared. 'I'll let you deal with this, then. If you need me for anything else, let me know.'

She was gone before anyone could object. Tared gave me a single glance, muttered something about stubbornness and better ways to spend his time, and got up from his chair with a slightly exaggerated groan.

Lyn appeared tempted to try convincing me again, but something about the looks the two of them exchanged seemed to change her mind.

'Anything else you need then, Emelin?' she said instead.

Even shrugging was a struggle for my worn-out body. 'I could sleep on a wooden plank now. I'll be fine.'

She looked unconvinced but nodded. 'We'll come pick you up in a few hours, then. With breakfast. If you need anything, just—'

'*Lyn.*'

'Alright, alright.' She gave me an apologetic grimace as she jumped up and wrapped her fingers around Tared's wrist. 'Sleep well.'

'See you. Oh, and please knock when you come back. Don't want to accidentally kill you.'

'You're too kind,' Tared said dryly, and then they were both gone, leaving me all alone in a quiet, dark room with the silence and the shimmering lights and ...

Creon.

Creon.

He lay motionless as I got to my feet and staggered towards the bed, didn't so much as stir when I whispered his name. His battered face was strange and familiar at once in the rough, worn pillows. Against the pallid bronze of his skin, his inked scars seemed even darker; his full lips, those lips that had kissed me with such unbridled desire in the Labyrinth, were bloodless and grey. Surrounded by the earthy cosiness of the Underground, he looked like he'd been torn from some pretty nightmare and cruelly dragged back into the confines of reality – an overwhelming, incomprehensible reality I couldn't possibly make sense of yet.

I brushed my fingertips over his cheek, his sharp jaw. Hell, I couldn't even fully make sense of *him*.

'Who are you, really?' I whispered.

I knew the answers – knew far too many answers. Creon Hytherion. Demon and fae prince. Lover and liar. Nightmare and saviour. Mine, and yet ... a mystery.

It had taken me weeks to find out the truth of his magic powers, and not because he had opted to tell me. For good reasons, or at least for understandable reasons ... but how many other untold stories were hiding behind that impossibly beautiful face?

Not a question for now. I pulled back my hand, suppressing a curse, and squashed my useless brooding back on the pile of worries for later. Once he woke up, we could talk. Once we'd talked, I could figure out what exactly we were to each other, if the answer wasn't allies by necessity.

Today, I just needed to keep the both of us alive.

I turned away from Creon, made a quick round of the room, and found an extra quilt on the bottom shelf of the sturdy wooden wardrobe. A little dusty, but fine enough. It was easier to drape this over him than to pull the woollen blankets from under his body.

I carefully tucked him in. Then, with a last glance at the door, I slipped out of my dusty blue dress, put it within reach in case of emergency, and slid below the quilt, careful not to put my weight on Creon's wings as I snuggled up between his arm and torso.

Head on shoulder. Skin on skin. All thought evaporated from my mind as I wrapped my arm around him and my limbs moulded to the familiar firmness of his body. My brain seemed to sputter and shut down; muscles that hadn't relaxed since sunset abruptly unclenched. Had my skin not held me together, I might have melted into a boneless puddle of relief and exhaustion against him, drowning in his familiar scent of sun and autumn sweetness.

Safe, finally.

And suddenly, nothing seemed so complicated anymore.

I was going to sleep. I was going to wake rested and ready, or at least no longer on the brink of collapse. And then I was going to figure out what this mysterious Underground was, give the Council whatever answers they needed to keep Creon safe, and start preparing for the next time I'd look the Mother in her damaged eyes.

A child could do that, couldn't they?

Sleep stole over me in seconds, heavy yet soft as down, and I drifted off into a dark and dreamless world where even lies and broken hearts couldn't follow me.

CHAPTER 2

Arguing voices woke me.

They came out of nowhere, just outside my door – at least three of them, rattling in some language I didn't recognise, let alone understand. I shot upright, blankets tangling around my hips and legs, and needed a moment to remember where I was.

Underground.

Creon.

Council.

With a curse, I rolled out of Creon's arms, snatched my dress off the floor, and yanked it over my head. Knuckles hit the door in the same moment, sounding like the hollow booms of drums announcing an execution.

'Emelin?'

Tared. He kept his promises, at least.

'A moment!' I shouted, combing my fingers through the brown mess of my hair to create a semblance of presentability. Had I covered all my tracks? Creon's blankets – I hastily tucked them in closer, erasing the impression my body had left. Good enough. If it looked even half convincing, they probably wouldn't go out of their way to assume I'd spent the last few hours in the Silent Death's arms.

I was his poor little prisoner, after all, the innocent little half fae he had abducted and used for his own ends, and quite possibly subjected to treacherous demon magic. How could they ever accuse me of liking him, let alone *desiring* him?

With a quiet snort, I stepped away from the bed and stretched the stiffness from my limbs. On the other side of the door, Lyn and an unknown male voice continued their argument, with short interruptions from Tared.

Well. If they were keeping themselves occupied anyway ...

I turned back to Creon. Perhaps it was the few hours of rest, perhaps it was my own clearer mind, but he looked infinitely better than before my nap – his skin the usual deep bronze again, his breath steady and regular. Like he was just sleeping, rather than recovering from a night of torture. Like he might wake up any moment.

I bent over the bed and brushed a knuckle over his jaw, his sharp cheekbone, his temple. Did I imagine the tremble that ran through him, or was it truly a sign of life?

'I'll be back soon,' I whispered. 'Just a quick meeting. I need to employ some diplomacy for a bit. Absolutely no way that can go wrong, in other words.'

Even now, part of me still expected him to laugh, to give me that cautious smile of shared secrets. My heart sank a few inches when he didn't react.

I pressed a quick kiss to his forehead, tucked in his blankets more tightly, and repeated, 'I'll be back.'

Then I turned and walked. Looking back at him, even if I knew I was leaving him behind for his own good, made my stomach feel stuffed full of nettles.

The voices in the corridor abruptly stilled when I nudged the door open.

There were three of them, indeed. Tared stood leaning against the doorpost, in a clean, moss-green shirt, but with his sword on his back again – as if he was wary of fae ambushes even in this buried place. Behind him, Lyn was pacing the winding corridor, a flaming silhouette of wild red curls and bright yellow linen and murderous glares at the third member of the company.

The object of her ire resembled Tared too closely for them not to be family. Same grey eyes, same slender features, similar sword on his back. But with his long blond hair and his weathered leather overcoat, something about this other male seemed strangely wilder – or perhaps it was the expression on his sharp, handsome face, a scowl suggesting he'd feel much better about the world if he'd been allowed to disembowel a few fae before breakfast.

He jerked around to face me the moment I appeared, aiming a steel grey glare at me that told me I should consider myself a prime candidate for disembowelment.

'So there she is.' No greeting. No introduction. He spoke a dialect pretty close to Cathra's language, although with a heavy northern accent. 'You're the one who brought our traitor princeling back, then?'

He was lucky Lyn had told me to be diplomatic. I might have blasted his pretty nose off his pretty face right there and then if she hadn't.

'Nice to meet you, too,' I said, glaring back at him. 'The name's Emelin, in case "the one who brought our princeling back" gets unwieldy. Yours?'

He gave me a skewed grin. It was not a very friendly grin. 'Proud of it, aren't you?'

'Edored,' Tared said sharply. 'Knock it off. Emelin is not the one who made the decisions or faded into this place – so perhaps you could do us all the extraordinary pleasure of acting civilised for once?'

'The problem with acting civilised,' Lyn grumbled before the other alf could reply, 'is that it requires him to possess at least a modicum of civilisation.'

Edored scoffed. 'I'm a fucking *pinnacle* of civilisation, Lyn darling. At least I'm not the one regularly burning children at the stake, as opposed to your beloved traitor with his sob stories and his pretty—'

'*Edored,*' Tared snapped.

'What?' The alf's voice rose again. 'Just because you don't want to see—'

Tared muttered a curse and grabbed my shoulder, pulling me into yet another whirlpool of deep drums and shades of soot. We didn't travel far this time; another room took solid shape around us before I had the chance to worry where the hell he was taking me.

This new place was larger and far messier than the bedroom I'd just left behind. Tapestries in walnut brown and pine green covered the walls, lending a warmer glow to the shine of the miniature suns that hovered near the vaulted ceiling. A long table stood in the middle of the room, pillow-covered benches on either side. My eyes slid over a half-finished knitting project, a pack of cards, a small pile of leather-bound books – signs of simple daily life.

'Apologies for that pinnacle of civilisation,' Tared said, sounding mildly exhausted as he took his hand off my shoulder and stalked over to the table. 'My cousin. Bit of a handful at times. I'm afraid we don't have a lot of time, but would you like to eat something?'

Only then did I notice the bread and marmalade at the far end of the table. I wasn't particularly hungry, but a moment of objective consideration told me I hadn't eaten for at least twenty-four hours. Confronting a horde of rabid alves on an empty stomach might not be the wisest of ideas.

'Yes, thank you,' I forced myself to say. 'And what do you mean, not a lot of time?'

'Well.' He paused while he quickly cut two slices of bread. 'We were planning to calmly inform the Council a few hours after you woke up, but Cale told his sister about the news, and his sister is apparently an old ... friend ... of Edored. Whose sense of discretion is not the greatest of his qualities.'

Somewhere behind us, a door slammed, audible even through the massive stone walls; a voice suspiciously like Edored's shouted something, then vanished abruptly.

'Ah,' I said, grimacing.

'So the rest of the Council found out fifteen minutes ago and is throwing a fit that we didn't inform them immediately. We're meeting in five minutes or so.' He shrugged. 'Cheese? Marmalade?'

'Marmalade is fine,' I said, collapsing onto one of the long benches as he spooned a blob of bright orange marmalade onto my bread. A pit was opening in my stomach. 'So what am I supposed to do now?'

Tared shoved the bread towards me on a linen napkin and sat down on the bench opposite me. 'Not too much. If we had more time to discuss strategies, I would probably ask you to make a few points at that meeting, but as it stands … just let Lyn and me do the talking. We know our audience better.'

'You're saying I have to trust *you* to keep Creon alive?'

A shadow slid over his face. 'Don't forget to eat.'

I groaned and took a bite of bread, scarfing it down despite my revolting guts.

Tared stared at the table in silence for a moment before he sighed and met my gaze again. 'I won't deny I'd have preferred to never see his face again, but if it's true he never left our side, we need him too much for me to make a fuss over our personal issues. I had a word with Lyn while you were sleeping. It should be …' He contemplated the next word a moment too long. 'Manageable. So if the rest of the Underground can accept his presence here, I won't be causing trouble.'

Not entirely reassuring – but then again, at least he was being honest. I tore off my next bite a little too violently, swallowed it, and said, 'So what exactly are those personal issues you—'

The door slammed open behind me.

I whirled around just in time to see Lyn stomping into the room, looking like a tiny volcano about to burst. The red of her hair seemed even brighter than usual, and little flames played over the skin of her hands and forearms like fire licking at a log about to ignite. I reflexively flinched. A few weeks of Creon should have prepared me better for the sight of murderous-looking company, but something about this explosive, sizzling fury seemed far more dangerous than even his cold, calculated darkness.

'Solved the situation?' Tared said, sounding impressively unimpressed.

She flung the door shut and sent him a withering glare as the flames sizzled out. 'You owe me several weeks of laundry duty for leaving me to deal with *your* unhinged family members, Tared.'

He chuckled. 'Fair deal. How did you get rid of him?'

'Played the Nenya card,' Lyn grumbled, climbing onto the bench next to me and planting her elbows on the table with remarkable force. 'Came up with some stupid message to pass on to her. Turns out he won't turn down an opportunity to bother her even when he has fae to kill.'

Tared rolled his eyes. 'Useful to know.'

'Quite.' She groaned again. 'Anyway. Slept well, Emelin?'

'Fine enough,' I said cautiously, wondering how fine I should believably have slept folded up in a chair. To prevent any necessary lies, I quickly added, 'Who's Nenya?'

'One of the vampire representatives on the Council,' Tared said and grinned when he saw my face. 'Don't worry. She only bites with permission.'

'Not sure if she got permission from that fellow whose head she gnawed off,' Lyn muttered, and Tared's grin broadened.

'He really was a solid bastard, though.'

I gulped down my bread too loudly, wondering whether the average vampire would consider Creon a solid enough bastard to justify some non-consensual chewing. Not a very fruitful line of thought, I knew. I'd be better off focusing on changing their opinion of him. But it was hard to scrub the image from my mind's eye now that Lyn's words had planted it there, some pale, grisly creature bending over him, bearing bloody fangs to ...

'Emelin?'

I jolted at Lyn's voice and realised I had frozen mid-bite. Stuffing the rest of my bread into my mouth, I mumbled an apology and said, 'Anything I absolutely shouldn't do if I want to keep my own neck safe?'

'Don't kill any alves,' Tared said cheerfully, which placated me slightly, because at least he apparently considered me capable of it. 'Don't call anyone a liar, either. We tend to take that poorly. *Definitely* don't call anyone dishonourable – we take that even more poorly. That said, challenging someone to a duel and blowing their head off is perfectly honourable, so if push comes to shove, that's the best way to go.'

Lyn threw a chess piece at his face. 'Please don't start any duels.'

'I'll try,' I said, not entirely reassured. 'What about the others?'

She shrugged. 'The nymphs will be fine. Don't cut down any trees if you ever set foot on a nymph isle, but there's little to ruin here in the Underground. The vampires ...'

'Don't call them pretty corpses,' Tared said, aiming his eyes at the ceiling with an expression like an exasperated teacher. 'Don't ask them if they smell something dead nearby, don't inquire after their bowel movement, don't call them "leech" as a cute nickname, don't ask them if teeth size corresponds to ...'

I sniggered despite the nerves drawing my guts into unpleasant knots. 'Why do I feel like you're drawing from lived experience here?'

He grimaced, getting up from his bench. 'I've dealt with Edored and Nenya for centuries. If you manage to insult her worse than he's ever done, I'll be impressed. So.' He looked at Lyn, who nodded. 'Ready for battle?'

I was further from ready than I'd ever been in my life, my mind still grasping for every little clue the conversations had offered me – what to say, what not to say. But if the Council was already displeased about the delay, waiting was likely the worst possible strategy, and if Edored's welcome was anything of an indication, getting them to approve of Creon's presence would require more than a few pleasant smiles and a promise that I knew what I was doing.

'I'm ready,' I said.

'Wonderful.' Tared faded to my side of the table, appearing out of nowhere two feet away from me. I shrieked despite myself, and he gave me a slightly apologetic grin as he extended a hand. 'Let's go.'

I grabbed his wrist without allowing myself another moment to think. He scooped Lyn from the bench with a practised motion and pulled the both of us into yet another storm of nothingness.

The room – no, hall – emerging around us didn't resemble anything I had imagined.

I'd expected some formality, a certain amount of *stature*, for the heart of the last resistance against the Mother. Some marble. A dozen pillars or so. At the very least, a couple of heavy velvet curtains and some imposing portraits of the kind my father used to paint. But the Council hall in which we had arrived just looked like the rest of the Underground, smooth black walls and not a sliver of daylight to be seen ...

Except the ceiling was higher.

Much, *much* higher.

I forgot to take note of the rest of the room as my eyes drew to the hollow space above us – hundreds and hundreds of feet up, the ceiling so far removed from us that I couldn't quite make it out in the distance. Galleries and balconies clung to the dark walls, some with people on them, watching the scene below. Little suns hovered around the balconies, too, and strings of faelights and dancing flames that seemed to crawl over the stone all by themselves, with no fuel or fuse to keep them burning. They shrouded the lower half of the imposing room in a dozen different shades of white and gold but left the upper parts dusky, making it impossible to see how deep we were.

'It's a lot, isn't it?' Lyn said next to me, and I forced myself to glance down again. She was still looking up, but perhaps that had more to do with our relative heights than with the emptiness towering over us.

'So what's above this place?' I said weakly. 'Sea? An island? Some mountain?'

'You have an uncanny talent for asking exactly the most forbidden questions,' she said, shooting Tared a glare when he chuckled. 'We'll tell you if you ever need to know. For now ...' She tugged at my sleeve. 'Time to take our seats.'

Seats.

Right. The Council.

I followed her gaze to the other side of the hall, to a meeting place not nearly as grand and imposing as I had expected. The Council gathered around a wide circle of some two dozen mismatched seats, from stiff wooden chairs to the occasional plush sofa. Despite the apparent urgency of the meeting, only about a third of the seats were currently occupied. A handful of alves, swords in their laps. Anaxia, swaying back and forth in a giant rocking chair. A petite girl with grey-blue hair, small black horns and what looked like silvery fish scales covering the back of her hands. A suspiciously pale, white-haired gentleman in waistcoat and high leather boots, a heavy velvet cloak over his shoulders.

Rhudaki fashion, Miss Matilda helpfully whispered in my memory. Rumours said the vampires still lived in the north of the island, far away from the bustling trader cities.

I tried to look as bloodless as possible.

An odd sense of déjà vu washed over me as I followed Lyn and Tared and tried not to notice the many eyes following my every step – my memory returning to that first night in the Mother's bone hall, Creon dragging me in as his little human captive. This group was different, admittedly, no rainbow of shirts and dresses, no glimmering, glittering decadence, but calloused hands and worn weapons and shades of grey and black and green. But the looks were similar, sharp and curious, waiting for yet another game to play.

'So.' A hook-nosed alf broke the silence, and although his voice lacked Edored's raging fury, there was nothing friendly about it either. 'Finally decided it was time to show up, Thorgedson?'

That pulled me back into the here and now faster than a bucket of ice water to the face would have done.

'Very sorry to have kept you waiting for ten whole minutes, Oskil,' Lyn said, falling into the most comfortable-looking fauteuil on our side of the circle with a glare at the offending alf. 'Next time you spend a full day in battle, we'll just skip your breakfast the following morning too, shall we?'

Tared sniggered quietly behind me, nudging me to take a seat as well. I perched on the edge of a padded leather stool as Oskil gave some sharp retort about urgent news and how perhaps they should have thought of the logistics *before* dragging the bloody Silent Death into their only safe refuge. His point was met with several hums of agreement and a nodding head or two. Only Anaxia kept smiling that eerily cheerful smile, rocking back and forth on the other side of the circle.

Lyn's suggestion to delay this discussion until the rest of the group had arrived calmed matters down, but judging by the grim murmurs as conversations were resumed around us, it was a delay of execution more than anything else. Still, Tared didn't seem particularly concerned as he shook his sword from his shoulder and settled in the chair on my other side, which was high-backed and decorated with swirls of fake gold that hadn't been stylish since the War of the Gods.

'What are the chances someone challenges *me* to a duel before the hour has passed?' I muttered from the corner of my mouth, and he raised an amused eyebrow.

'You're safe as a newborn babe. No one's going to harm an unbound mage.'

'Even though I just dragged some fae murderer into your home?'

Tared shrugged. 'That was my decision, wasn't it?'

I stared at him, speechless. He gave me a quick grin, turned away, and smiled a calm, icy smile at a newly arriving alf female on the other side of the circle, ignoring her look of obvious displeasure.

His decision.

Emelin is not the one who faded in here, he'd told Edored – and not just Edored, then? As if I hadn't strongarmed him into any of this. Leaving me free of the blame, free of the backlash that might follow in this very hall.

'Your highly civilised cousin didn't seem to care much about the distinction,' I said weakly.

Lyn snorted on my other side, leaning over the armrest to follow the conversation. 'Edored is a little protective of the family.'

'*Protective*? He about bashed your head in!'

'That's what protective looks like for alves,' she said sourly. '"Take care of yourself or I'll kill you" summarises it, really. Best to – oh, hello Valeska.' She abruptly turned to the female taking the chair to her left, who was purple haired and sported a pair of small antlers curling elegantly from her skull. I glanced back at the horned girl with the scaly hands next to Anaxia. This was what fullblood nymphs looked like, then?

Lyn lowered her voice to a hushed volume as she began some conversation in a language I'd never heard before. I didn't interrupt; she knew her audience best, after all.

Around us, the last seats quickly filled up. Tared muttered concise commentary for my benefit with every new alf to arrive – 'Thorir always takes snacks to meetings, definitely a good one to sit next to – Valdora is head of the house of Svirla, expect her to make an issue of Creon's demon powers – best to feign a heavy coughing fit when Hreidar opens his mouth, because he won't shut up for hours ...'

Behind us, a husky female voice said, 'I'm most curious to hear what you'd tell her about me, Tared.'

I spun around. The speaker stood just behind us in a black velvet-and-lace Rhudaki dress, her skin mortally pale, half of her long dark hair bound into two tight buns on top of her head. Deep scars ran over her face, as if some monster had forcefully dragged its claws over her forehead and cheeks – one cut running from her eye to her chin, one splitting her bright red upper lip in two. Wounds no mortal woman would ever be able to survive – but what were the chances she was mortal, in this place?

Next to me, Tared didn't blink as he leisurely turned around. 'Oh, hello Nenya. Nothing but praise, obviously.'

She grinned, revealing two razor-sharp fangs. 'Right answer. You were always the sensible one of your house.'

'Way to stab me in the back, Nen,' Edored sputtered as he appeared out of nowhere by her side, still looking like he'd been pulled from a battlefield two minutes ago. I began to suspect he would look ready for war even if someone dragged him out of bed in the dead of night. 'I'll have you know I'm the most sensible alf in existence since Skirnir the Sensible got himself mauled to death by—'

'Might start showing it, then, arsehole,' Nenya interrupted him, turning back to me without waiting for a reply. 'And good afternoon, Emelin. I'm Nenkhet – Nenya for friends, Nen for arseholes. Lovely to meet you.'

'Pleasure,' I said feebly; the sight of those fangs did some unnerving things to the structural integrity of my knees. 'Just to be sure, what's the preferred form of address for half humans who shove fae murderers into your home?'

She chuckled as she stepped around Tared's chair and installed herself in the next seat, casually rearranging her skirts around her voluptuous backside. 'Not a category I've had to deal with all that frequently, but if it's true you blinded the bloody Mother, consider yourself a friend. Which is not to say ...' She lowered her voice, glancing at Tared. 'Which is not to say I'm exactly happy about any of this.'

His jaw tensed. 'Trust me, we agree.'

Nenya sighed, nodded, but left the matter at that, glaring at Edored as he crashed into the chair beside her. At the same moment, on the other side of the Council floor, a yellow-eyed, furry-eared nymph even shorter than Lyn took the last free seat.

Every single muttered conversation around the circle stilled at once.

The weight of two dozen pairs of eyes hit me like a sledgehammer – the eager, impatient looks of people who had spent every last crumb of their self-restraint on their attempts to appear deep in conversation for two whole minutes. I almost flinched, then recalled that flinching wasn't going to make me look any more reliable, and steeled my shoulders instead.

'Good afternoon?' It came out sounding *almost* confident.

A few mildly amused greetings came back, although most faces didn't soften. Even if I had blinded the Mother, even if I might be the weapon they desperately needed, even if Tared had told them to hold him responsible for Creon's return ... I was still the girl who had spent weeks in a demon's close company. Still the girl who had risked her life to save the Silent Death, after all he'd done to them.

They had no reason to trust me.

And as if she'd read my mind, Valdora, the thin-lipped head of the house of Svirla, brusquely said, 'First of all, are we sure we want to keep a child under demon influence at this meeting?'

Gone was the silence of tense anticipation. Before I could even open my mouth, the disconcerted grumbles were everywhere, eyes narrowing at me from all sides and curt voices demanding to know what in hell Lyn and Tared had been thinking to be so careless with their hard-won security ...

'Oh, don't be like that, Dora,' a pensive voice said, cutting effortlessly through the cacophony. 'There's not a trace of demon magic on her.'

The hall abruptly fell quiet again.

Anaxia sat beaming in her rocking chair like a child at her birthday, watching me with those knowing blue eyes. Only when every head in the hall had turned her way did she add, still equally dreamily, 'No need to be so surprised, all of you. I told you ages ago that you were underestimating him.'

'I wouldn't dare to underestimate him,' Nenya said grimly. 'Which is exactly why I'm less than excited to have him walking through my home, if you don't mind. How certain are we he's not going to blast us all to pieces the moment he wakes up?'

'Emelin says he made a bargain regarding his intentions to kill the Mother,' Lyn said, and that revelation sent another wave of confused murmurs through the gathered company.

Nenya glanced at the red gemstone on my wrist, considered that point for a moment or two, then stoically raised her perfectly drawn eyebrows at me. 'He's been spectacularly successful at hiding his true loyalties, in that case.'

'Speaking unwillingly in his defence,' Tared said, crossing his legs, 'if he hadn't been successful, he'd be dead by now.'

She huffed a laugh. '*You* believe this story?'

I stiffened, but Tared didn't even blink. 'Do you think I'd have brought him here otherwise?'

'Hm. Unexpectedly wise.' She fell back in her chair, throwing a quick glance at the circle of frowns and scowls around us. 'What convinced you, then?'

'I strongly considered the possibility it was all demon influence until this morning,' he said and threw me a glance that was more apologetic than the rest of the circle likely noticed. Even without the full story of the last day's events, he had to suspect that his revelation of Creon's powers might have something to do with the abrupt escalation of my mission. 'But you didn't see the Mother breaking down the court at his escape – hell, I'm pretty sure a couple of walls went down. She wouldn't lose her mind like that for anything less than her son betraying her. That, combined with the state he was in—'

'What about the state he was in?' Edored snapped, his voice a freshly sharpened blade. 'All it tells you is that he displeased her for some reason. Might just have given her the wrong look, for all we know about the bitch.'

'He displeased her by throwing a knife at her face,' I blurted out, unable to bite my tongue for a moment longer, and Nenya's eyebrows shot up until they nearly disappeared below her hairline.

'*That* sounds like a monumentally stupid idea.'

'It was my fault.' Even now, knowing he was alive, knowing he was out of that place, it hurt to speak the words aloud. 'I was careless and got myself caught near the Labyrinth. He took the blame. Then she kept him there and let me go, and ...'

Nenya fell back in her chair, blowing out her cheeks. 'And you threw a blast of red into her face. Gods have mercy.'

The displeased mutters of the Council had become mumbles of confusion, of people slowly losing their grip on convictions they'd have preferred to hold on to. The fury on Edored's face could have sent a blind man running for the hills, but before he opened his mouth again, Lyn hastily said, 'And there's more. We've been looking into this since Emelin first told us about it – the people of Cathra didn't die in that fire. Took a while to get the confirmation – you know how they are in the White City – but it seems that they all arrived unharmed and in possession of enough money to buy their way inside.'

'Gods have mercy,' Nenya repeated, and this time she wasn't the only one. Even several of the alves appeared doubtful, exchanging nervous glances with their neighbours as if to ask whether honour and pride allowed them to change their minds on their righteous fury.

Valdora, on the other hand, sat staring at me with wary eyes, probably trying to figure out whether I was lying through my teeth despite Anaxia's assurance I wasn't a walking bonfire of demon magic.

'So,' Lyn said, and there was a sense of finality in her voice that made my heart leap against my ribs. Was it going to be this easy, then? 'All of this taken into consideration, I would say—'

'I have one more thought to add,' the grey-haired vampire in waistcoat and cloak said, speaking for the first time. He had an unnervingly smooth voice, like the darkest, sweetest honey. 'Did you consider that the Mother might start looking for us once she realises the Alliance could have played a role in this escape?'

An abrupt silence fell.

'She hasn't found us in the past thirteen decades, Gish,' Tared said, but his voice came out a fraction less nonchalant, and his shoulders tensed as he sat up straighter. 'I don't see why she would suddenly manage now.'

'She doesn't seem to have looked for us very thoroughly,' Gish retorted. 'We've never been enough of a danger for her to make the effort. If she suspects we now have an unbound mage and the Silent Death at our disposal, who knows what she'll do? If she attacks the communities above to provoke us, we won't be able to—'

'So what else would you suggest?' Nenya said sharply, drowning out the disconcerted mumbles around us. 'To kindly send the only advantage we have back into her hands? That hardly sounds like a winning strategy to me.'

The other vampire spread his hands, a soothing expression on his pale, angular face. 'I'm not suggesting anything – just pointing out it's an illusion to think we'll be safe forever if they stay. The Mother isn't going to let an unbound mage walk around freely, and once she has excluded all other options, it will occur to her sooner or later that the

Alliance could be involved. So will we be ready for battle by that time? Will the girl be ready?'

The girl.

At once, all eyes were back on my face, examining, estimating – noting, no doubt, my youth and my striking lack of weapons and battle scars.

I opened my mouth, felt myself hesitate. *I'll be ready*, I wanted to say. *Of course I'll be; what other option do we have?* But in this company, surrounded by the people who had fought the Mother for centuries and still didn't have a victory to show for it, who had been through hell and back again only to lose yet another battle, yet another war ...

I had no idea what I was talking about, and they *knew* I hadn't. I may be the only person in this hall – in this world – who could use magic against the High Lady of faekind, but what was the use of that if the Mother killed me with a flick of her hand the moment we met again?

'Valid concerns, Gish,' Lyn said next to me, with a spectacularly polite impatience that didn't fit her young voice at all, 'but I don't see how that relates to the question of what to do with Creon. As Nenya said, sending him back seems—'

'Well,' he said mildly, 'I suppose if Creon were to wash up dead on her shores in two days, she might conclude he and Emelin both drowned at sea in an attempt to escape. Which *would* give us more time to—'

'*Wash up?*' Too loud. Too sharp. All my hesitation crumbled to never be seen again; so did my last resolve to keep my mouth shut and let the adults do the talking. 'Good gods, there's no need for *that*. I'll be ready. I—'

Gish looked even milder. 'You've been training for a few weeks, haven't you?'

A mere few weeks. Against a mage who'd honed her magic skills for over a millennium, a near-goddess who might burn down half the world in her quest to find me. Would I be ready? A ludicrous, laughable thought. But the alternative ...

Wash up. The bloody *nerve.*

'A few weeks of training were enough for me to free her prisoners from right below her nose,' I said, clenching my nails into my palms.

'Allow Creon to train me for a few more months, and I'll be where I need to be.'

'Creon again,' Valdora said, her voice dangerously sweet as she squinted at me. 'I'm starting to suspect she's just telling us whatever she needs to save his life, honestly.'

Oh, fuck.

I forced a puzzled laugh over my lips. 'I've told you nothing but the truth. I wouldn't—'

'But is it the full truth?' Her words turned sharper and sweeter at once. 'You seem very damn troubled about the thought of using him to cover your traces. Gish's plan *would* keep you safe, do you realise that?'

'Good gods,' Lyn interrupted before I could open my mouth, in the exasperated tone of an adult pulling her fighting children apart. 'Silent Death or not, it's hardly a pleasant idea to sacrifice others for your own life. Let's not start looking for trouble just because a girl of twenty summers isn't entirely happy to play that game.'

'A girl of twenty summers who just outwitted the Mother herself,' Valdora corrected coolly. Her gaze brimmed with heavy suspicion – worse, suspicion I knew to be justified. 'So who's guaranteeing that we're getting the full story from her? Because you *are* trying to save his life – aren't you, Emelin?'

The silence drew out for a fraction too long, and every single person at the Council heard it. *No*, I had to say. *No, it's not about his life at all – what makes you think I would care?* But then who knew what other cruel ideas they might come up with, and how was I going to talk them out of those without admitting I had lied through my teeth?

But telling them that I *did* care, that I'd rather blow half of the Alliance to pieces than sacrifice him to their plans and strategies ... They would doubt every word of my story forever.

'Valdora—' Lyn started.

'Wait a moment, Lyn,' Nenya said, eyeing me with watchful curiosity. 'I would like an answer to that question, too. What exactly is it that you want, Emelin? His safety or ours?'

What did I want?

And at once the frantic mist of my thoughts cleared – at once I knew what to say. I might not be ready for battle, but I knew *this* game - hell, I'd played it since I was old enough to talk, learned its rules before I learned to stand on my own two feet.

What do you want, Emelin?

A test, time and time again. A challenge to find out what *they* wanted and follow those wishes to the letter, to keep the peace, find that sweet spot where everyone but me was happy, a necessary sacrifice to avoid yet another week of cold looks and one-syllable answers. *Rather impressive*, Thysandra had said, *how often you managed to say exactly the right half-witted things ...*

The parents who raised me may not have taught me how to use my magic, but I realised in that very moment I owed them the one other skill that had kept me alive so far: the talent to tell people exactly what they needed to hear.

'I tried to kill him the first time I saw him,' I said.

Ten chairs away, Valdora had already opened her mouth to claim the victory, then froze as the words came through. 'What?'

'I tried to kill him,' I repeated, my voice loud in the puzzled silence. 'On Cathra. Swung a few flares of red at his face and was very damn disappointed he didn't break to pieces on the spot. It definitely wasn't for lack of trying.'

Tared gave a near-inaudible chuckle next to me, the most reassuring hint of approval I'd heard in my life.

Valdora glared at him and then back at me, struggling for words. 'So what's your point? That we can indeed kill him, as far as you're concerned?'

'No,' I said slowly. 'Just that I understand where you're coming from. Just that we would have very much agreed a few weeks ago. But I've learned a thing or two about him since then, and ...' I drew in a deep breath. The right words, now. The right businesslike considerations. I was not his little fae whore, desperate to get him through this place alive. I was the Alliance's perfect unbound mage, ready to follow their every strategy, just like I'd tried to be my parents' perfect daughter, just like I'd been the Mother's perfect witless toy. 'He knows so much about her. Her magic, her plans, her weaknesses. He's been working out ways to get rid of her for such a long time. And honestly, that's the only thing I really want – to get rid of her.'

The lie fell from my lips so easily, and with all eyes aimed at me, no one seemed to notice the grin that flashed over Anaxia's face. My apologetic shrug contained just the right dose of regret, just the right dose of *I don't like it much either, but don't we all know that sacrifices must be made?*

'I figured I needed allies more than pleasant company,' I said flatly. 'So I stopped trying to kill him. And unless you value your perfectly clean morals over a chance at winning this war, I'd honestly recommend you do the same. That's all.'

Valdora stared at me as if she'd just swallowed a lemon whole.

'That,' Nenya said, 'is an answer.'

And at once, everyone was talking again, voices growing louder as the meeting fractured into a dozen separate heated debates. Gish chewed on his bottom lip with a single razor-sharp fang. Anaxia giggled uncontrollably at something her nymph neighbour was saying. Next to me, Lyn sat frozen in her pale pink armchair, her feet dangling a few inches above the floor, her calculating gaze shooting over the row of wildly gesticulating Council members. Counting, I realised. Estimating chances, estimating votes.

To my right, Tared leaned over with a gleam of tired satisfaction in his eyes and muttered, 'Liar.'

I threw him my most oblivious smile, the smile Emelin the little fae toy had been so fond of employing. 'But a good one.'

He grimaced. Exchanged a single glance with Lyn. Threw a last look at the Council circle, sat up straighter, and loudly said, 'I vote he's staying. Who is with me?'

And as the discussions stilled, seventeen of the twenty-four hands hesitantly rose towards the soaring ceiling.

CHAPTER 3

'TARED, YOU CAN'T BE *serious*,' Edored lamented for the fifteenth time, pacing back and forth through the family living room with wide, furious gestures at every piece of furniture he encountered. 'Either you've gone mad or you've gone suicidal – why would you even *consider* keeping him here after everything he—'

'Did you even notice the last five times we answered that question for you?' Lyn said coldly from her place next to me at the table. 'At some point, it gets a little tedious repeating the same thing over and over again.'

'I wasn't talking to *you*, Lyn sweetheart, and—'

She shot a burst of fire at him. It missed him by a hair's breadth and left a scorch mark on the tapestry behind his slender back; not the first one, I realised as I scanned the green and brown forest imagery more attentively. The pungent stench of burning thread followed a moment later, mingling with the fragrance of the fresh bread on the table.

Edored gave Lyn an indignant eyeroll but dropped down on the bench opposite us and threw Tared another look of despair. 'You're not even going to stop her? She could have *killed* me!'

'For Orin's sake,' Ylfreda said, appearing next to the table with a steaming pan of soup in her hands. 'Wouldn't it be glorious if you could all get through a *single* family dinner without killing each other?'

'I didn't start it!' Edored protested.

'He definitely started it,' Tared said dryly.

'The relevant question is who's stopping it,' Ylfreda said with a glare at both of them. I couldn't suppress my chuckle, and she sent me an apologetic look as she planted the soup in the centre of the table. 'I'm sure Emelin would like to talk about something other than Creon after that bloody Council meeting of yours.'

Hallthor faded into the room after her – the alf male Tared had introduced to me as Ylfreda's husband on our return from the Council hall. He was tall and taciturn and somehow managed to look slender and broad-shouldered at the same time. 'Good gods, are we still talking about Creon?'

'Not entirely voluntarily,' Lyn said sourly, 'but Edored darling won't shut up about—'

Edored snorted so violently he might have breathed fire. 'You should be the *last* person to complain about my concerns, Phiramelyndra dearest, and—'

'*Phiramelyndra?*' I said.

Tared stifled a chuckle. Lyn sent him a glare so foul it could have left scorch marks on his face and grumbled an impolite request for everyone to shut the hell up.

It didn't work.

'She's a bit touchy about that name,' Edored told me, his conspiratorial look rendered useless by the fact that he was speaking loud enough to stir a sleeping volcano. 'No idea why. I mean, it's a bit of a monstrosity, but at least it's not ...' He faltered, momentarily overwhelmed by the daunting task of producing a worse name than Phiramelyndra. 'At least it's not Shithead or something.'

Tared burst out laughing. I glanced at Lyn, who glowered back at me, the sparks in her amber eyes daring me to engage in this conversation for one more heartbeat.

'I don't know,' I said, looking back up at Edored. 'Shithead *does* have a nice sort of ring to it.'

From the corner of my sight, I just saw the chess piece Lyn flung at me. My fingers reacted in a mindless reflex, instilled in me by hours and hours of training on the porch of Creon's pavilion – left hand to the purple pillow I was sitting on. Right hand in a wide swing up. An instinctive draw of magic, a bright burst of red—

The black pawn disintegrated, only a flutter of dust left where polished ebony had been a moment before.

Tared abruptly stopped laughing.

I blinked up to find five pairs of eyes gaping at me – Hallthor still standing, Ylfreda halfway through the motion of sitting down, the other three snapped from every last childish argument between them. The grins were gone. The dramatic glowers were gone. Just wide eyes and lips parted in baffled, breathless silence.

Oh.

Fuck.

I felt myself shrink under those looks. *Shrivel.* Back into hiding. Back into the little girl on Cathra who could not have used magic if her life depended on it. 'I ... I'm so sorry.' The words were a blur on my tongue, the heavy, metallic taste of shame clogging my throat. 'I didn't realise ... If you'd rather not have me use fae magic around here—'

'Emelin,' Lyn interrupted me, her eyes still too round.

I flinched. 'I get it, I really do, I—'

'Stop apologising!' She let out a dazed laugh, planting her elbows on the edge of the table. 'And you don't get it at all. You ... Inika help us, Emelin, how long have you been practicing that magic, exactly?'

I stared at her, my thoughts turning over that question three, four times before I realised it was not at all what I had expected. 'What?'

'That was *excellently* measured,' she said, flapping a hand in the direction of the obliterated pawn. 'No leftovers, no explosion. Most fae I've known need months or years to reach that level of—'

'What?' I said again.

'You didn't know?'

'I ...' No. Hell, what *did* I know about my magic? Relatively powerful, but even that sounded so very meaningless now that I repeated it to myself. Relative to what? Relative to who? 'I suppose I've been training for pretty much every hour of the day for a while, but ...'

'Good gods.' The look she exchanged with Tared said a lot more than those two words. 'That is ... helpful, I suppose.'

Helpful. Because they, too, had doubted whether I would stand even the slimmest of chances by the time the Mother decided to crack down on the last resistance in her empire.

'It's not going to stop me from putting a sword in her hands,' Tared said dryly, and Lyn let out an impatient laugh, slumping back onto the bench. On the other side of the table, Ylfreda finally sat down as well.

'A *sword*?' I said, glad for something else to focus on than my looming disastrous defeat.

'Of course,' Lyn said, throwing me a wry look of warning. 'Basic Alvish education – nothing but death is going to change his mind on that. So if you were still thinking of murder, this would be the moment to—'

'Food, anyone?' Ylfreda interrupted.

There was a steely undertone to those few words, and we all wisely shut our mouths as she distributed bowls and slices of bread. For a few seconds, no sounds broke the silence but clattering spoons and chewing jaws and Edored's muffled curses as he burned his tongue on a scorching hot sip of soup.

Then a faint voice behind me said, 'I'm just in time for dinner, I see.'

I strained several muscles jerking around. These bloody alves with their bloody spontaneous appearances would end up giving me a neck injury.

The newly arrived alf female was shorter than any of the others I'd met, although still taller than me; her hair was so blonde it looked almost silver, her skin tanned, her eyes the lightest shade of blue. She wore leather trousers and high boots under a knee-length grey coat, and on her back ...

Two swords.

I blinked. Most alves I'd seen so far had been armed, but none of them had carried more than a single blade.

But before I could figure out what to make of that anomaly, Lyn exclaimed, 'Beyla! I hadn't expected you back so early?'

Beyla smiled as she quickly unbuttoned her coat. It was an odd smile, kind but hollow – a smile that reached her eyes but did not go any deeper, like a layer of pleasant wallpaper stretched over her features. It faded in the blink of an eye while she took off her weapons, leaving nothing but mild colourlessness behind.

'I hadn't expected me back so early either,' she said. Her voice fit the strange emptiness of her expressions, flat and eerily light, like pale morning mist strung into words. 'I found the Crimson Court in absolute disarray when I took a look a minute ago. Somehow I suspected you two might know more about that? And either way, I could hardly stay there with a pack of rabid hounds on my heels.'

'Ah,' Tared said wryly. 'Yes. Apologies for that. We found an unbound mage, it seems.'

The revelation barely seemed to surprise her; those pale blue eyes slid to me without so much as a blink. 'Really. Half fae?'

I managed a nod, and she gave me another one of those superficial smiles as she shook her coat off her shoulders. 'Pleasure.'

'Mutual,' I said weakly. I wasn't sure whether it was entirely true, but in this place where most of my allies were only allies by the grace of my lies, diplomacy seemed the safest way to go. 'I'm Emelin. Are you—'

She faltered. 'Emelin?'

It was not the interruption that made me fall silent. It was the tone of her voice – a sudden spark of interest, of *life*, piercing through the pale fog of her appearance. I must not have been the only one who noticed. Behind me, the sound of clinking cutlery abruptly stilled.

'Yes?' I said slowly.

'Of Cathra?'

I stared at her.

'Twenty summers old?' She still spoke so softly, so carefully, that it took a heartbeat for the weight of her words to come through. 'Born in the first week of hay month? Raised by a childless painter and his wife?'

'How in hell ...' That didn't sound diplomatic at all; I forgot to care. 'How in hell do you know anything about—'

'Orin's eye,' Tared said with a joyless laugh. 'Was she one of yours?'

'What are you talking about?' Too shrill. Not my problem. 'How did you—'

'We've met before, it seems,' Beyla said slowly. Although her smile at me was not unfriendly, there was still no warmth in it. 'You were just a few hours old on that occasion, though. I was the one who brought you away from the court.'

'Away from the ...'

The rest of the sentence drifted from my grasp before it could reach my lips. I sat paralysed, staring at her inscrutable face, her words rolling over me like an avalanche of more and more unpleasant implications.

Away from the court.

A few hours old.

'Are you saying I was born *there*?' The room cooled down around me, a chill that drew deep into the marrow of my bones until even the thought of moving became a laughable fantasy. Born at the Crimson Court. Which meant that at least one parent, my human parent, must have been there too. But humans were bound to the island. Which meant ...

'You were, yes.' A joyless smile. 'And before you ask, no, I don't know who your parents are. I tend not to ask questions.'

The air rushed from my lungs so abruptly I saw black spots. 'Oh.'

'You must understand' – she faded to the other side of the table and sat down next to Edored, throwing her coat over the bench beside her – 'there's a network we have on that island, some of the human captives spreading our food and medicine across the villages. Which is dangerous work. Most of the humans only know the names of their direct contacts, and I don't press for any information I don't absolutely need.'

I swallowed, glancing at Lyn and Tared. *Looking for humans in need*, they'd said the first time they found me in Faewood. Was this what it meant – quietly supplying the human population of the court with whatever could help them survive?

'We don't get a lot of children,' Beyla said, picking a single braided bun from the nearest pile and examining it for a moment before tearing off a bite with her slender fingers. 'A handful every year at most. Most parents need a very good reason to hand their newborn over to a stranger.'

I swallowed thorns and nettles down my throat. 'Do you know ...'

'My contact told me your mother gave you up because your father abandoned her and it would be too dangerous for her to raise a child alone. I didn't realise at the time ...' She sighed, tilting her head as she slid her gaze over me. 'You look human.'

Human, yes. No wings. No pointed ears. And so she hadn't realised the full extent of the story, some fae male leaving the human woman he'd seduced to fend for herself as soon as matters turned complicated.

I tried to pick up my spoon again and found my hand shaking so violently I might have knocked my bowl off the table if I'd tried to take another bite.

My mother. No longer just a hypothetical soul moving somewhere in the world, barely more than a figment of my imagination, but a real human woman, locked in that hell of a place, caught between two desperate options and making the choice that would keep at least one of us safe.

That would at least keep *me* safe.

Some sort of syllable fell from my lips, not yet a sob but nothing near a sensible word, either. So she'd smuggled me out. And she ... she was still there? She still had to be there, if she was bound to the island – but that meant I'd been so very close until a few hours ago. That she might even have *known* who I was, if my name had spread as quickly as my reputation as Creon's little fae whore.

Lyn was talking to me. I barely registered it.

And my father? The bastard who'd left her, who'd left *me*? He might have been there, too. He might have been in the hall when Creon dragged me in for the first time, or – gods help me – when we'd all but fucked against the Mother's bone walls, or when ...

Small hands wrapped around my shoulder. Lyn, saying my name. I tried to focus, tried to make sense of words that seemed to come from a hundred different sides around me, the conversation taking place on the other side of the table.

' ... go back to ask around?' Tared was saying.

'Under normal circumstances, I would,' Beyla said, grimacing, 'but the few glimpses I caught a moment ago ... They'll be turning the island inside out for weeks. Far too dangerous to—'

Edored scoffed. 'Since when do you care about risks?'

'We would endanger the humans in the network, and I *do* care about—'

'Emelin,' Lyn muttered, squeezing my shoulder. 'We'll figure this out. We've found people under worse circumstances. If she's still there—'

Still there.

Because even if she couldn't leave ...

She might be dead.

I swallowed, opened my mouth, closed it again. The smell of dark bread and salty pumpkin soup clogged my nostrils until I felt like gagging. She might be dead, killed by that black- and blue-eyed horror on her throne, and I might never even know her name. Might never hear her voice, might never know what she looked like and if she'd loved me and how she'd managed to smuggle me out of the Mother's clutches without anyone noticing ...

Creon. I needed Creon here.

My mind latched on to that thought with desperate force – a need so frantic that just the absence of him was enough to make my skin ache. All of this would be so much easier to bear with his strong arms around me, wings embracing me, a shred of that safety we'd shared at the pavilion ... He would have solutions, wouldn't he? Or the right words of encouragement, or else the right infuriating remark to make me think of a solution by myself. Hell, what would he say? *Sounds like we may still have one decent parent in between the two of us ...*

I squeezed my eyes shut, clinging to the image of his ink-scarred fingers dancing the shapes of words between us, to the memory of that familiar smile that was part challenge, part reassurance, part dangerous shared secret.

He wasn't that far. Still in the same house, at least. Could I just get up and find him?

But Lyn or Tared would come after me and ask questions and offer advice – helpful advice but advice I didn't want nonetheless. Not when all I needed was the one person I could be entirely honest with, the one person who made me feel safe despite all sensible objections.

I'd have to wait a few more minutes. Get through this meal without falling apart and excuse myself in a slightly more coherent way when we were done. *Then* I could find him and hold him and pray to every dead god that he would wake up soon, that he would have the thoughts and plans and comforts I so desperately craved.

I willed myself to sit still. Forced that aching need back to the shadows of my mind, a jarring sense of absence chafing against my heart, and opened my eyes.

The alves had resumed their meal, casting me concerned glances in between bites. Lyn had pulled up her knees to her chest beside me, making good attempts to pretend she wasn't monitoring my every movement as she stared at her plate.

'Thanks for telling me,' I said to Beyla, and my voice only wobbled a little. 'I'll ... I'll think about it. Perhaps if everything's calmed down a bit—'

The room lit up in a sea of red.

Crimson. My brain screamed alarm as I snapped around, my hand already back on the purple of my pillow – had the Mother followed us? Found us? Sent an army of fae into this underground realm to retrieve us and kill whatever members of the Alliance they found along the way? My right hand flew up, the magic tingling up my arm as I turned towards the door ...

Or towards where the door had been.

The heavy, rune-covered wood had vanished without a trace, gone up in smoke in that blast of red magic. Behind it, in the narrow corridor with its flickering little suns and its iridescent black walls ...

Creon.

He stood slumping against a curving wall, his left hand pressed against the inky black stone for support as much as for magic. Shirt unbuttoned and unable to conceal the bandages on his arms and shoulders. Face contorted in that grimace of suppressed pain I knew all too well, breath shallow and irregular. But his dark eyes were bright and alert as they swept over the gathered company once, then returned to my face with all their usual lethal intensity – scanning me for wounds, for hurt, for a trace of damage to avenge.

Awake.

Alive.

Behind me, the silence was deafening.

It was a silence I could *feel* even if I didn't hear a thing – a deadly quiet of hands on sword hilts and muscles tensed to the point of tearing. A dazed moment of deadlock, like the frozen instant before a scale tipped one way or another ...

Death or peace?

I didn't trust Edored to make the right choice. Not in this silence like an oil-drenched fuse about to ignite.

My body moved for me, driving decisions before my mind recovered. Off that bench. One uneven step away from the table. Stilted, staggering motions, but they broke the spell; I heard slow breaths sucked in behind me, the rustle of a sword sinking back into its sheath. Creon didn't move. With those intoxicated eyes fixed on my face, I wasn't fully sure if he even noticed.

'Creon?' I whispered.

'I gather,' Beyla said behind me, her eerie, gossamer voice nowhere near enough to shatter the breathless tension, 'that I'm still missing some parts of this story?'

A huffed laugh – Edored. 'Oh, you absolutely missed—'

'Edored.' That was Tared's voice, cold and sharp as iron. 'Get out.'

'Oh, really?' Another one of those shrill laughs. 'You can't honestly expect me to leave you alone with—'

'Get. *Out.*' He had to feel it too, that heavy promise of violence in the air, like a storm gathering above us. 'Hallthor, go notify the Council. Ylfreda, explain this to Beyla. *Elsewhere.*'

There came no word of protest, not even the quickest of questions. When I hesitantly turned a fraction, Tared and Lyn were the only two still standing behind me at the loaded table. He had faded to her side, his sword not yet drawn, but his fingers clawing into his thigh as if it was a struggle to restrain the reflex.

I turned back to Creon. He had finally torn his eyes away from me, the full force of his gaze now aimed at the two people behind me.

I looked back again. Lyn had gone wide-eyed and white-faced, more seven-year-old than I'd ever seen her before. Tared ... I couldn't identify the look on his face, a flawless match to the unbendable steel that had snuck into his usually casual voice. The light swirled around him in a fickle, restless glow, as if even his alf magic was straining to withstand the shadows gathering around Creon's frozen figure.

'So,' he said.

I hadn't known a single word could contain so many shades of hatred, so many shimmering layers of fury and dread and cold, bottomless hurt. I swallowed and glanced at Creon again, feeling like an unwitting participant in some game of which I didn't know the rules, the stakes, or even the participants themselves.

'Evening, Creon,' Lyn said, her voice small. 'Welcome back, I suppose.'

He didn't move, leaning heavily against the wall. His narrowing eyes were the only evidence he'd even heard them; no nod, no smile, not even the faintest attempt to soften the blow of this strained reunion. Around us, the alf lights flickered, dimmed, shrouding the room in an ominous glow of bloodshed to come.

'Well,' Lyn added, and I turned just in time to see her glance up at Tared. 'Time to go, then?'

He released his thigh in a flash of movement, clenching his fingers around her shoulder instead – so fast I could only assume *that* was the reflex he'd tried to suppress, not his impulse to draw a sword and go to battle. His knuckles strained white as he nodded, but the spinning light around him calmed.

'Don't cause trouble,' he said, and before I could determine whether he was speaking to me or to Creon, they were gone.

Leaving me on my own with a table full of food and the sputtering lights and the fae male I had risked my life to save – looking like a stranger, suddenly, his face hard and emotionless in the shadows of the Underground.

I stared at him as he stared at me, his dark eyes brimming with some bitter emotion I couldn't even begin to name. This was the moment to speak. The moment to throw myself into his arms and sob with joy. But there was no relief in his gaze, not the smallest flicker of affection, and I stood there like I'd taken root, the distance between me and his battered body suddenly a gap of centuries.

Last time we'd exchanged a word, he had sacrificed his life for me.

The second-to-last time, I'd accused him of heartless manipulation and vile magical games and thrown the names of his old enemies into his face to hurt him.

It hadn't seemed to matter in the last twenty-four hours, not while he was still in danger, not when I was all that stood between him and torturous death. Now, in the absolute quiet of the Underground, the air hummed with all we hadn't told each other, all we should never have said. Every unspoken word, every unanswered question. Every lie, every accusation.

That was *distrust* in his eyes, sharp and venomous.

I staggered half a step forward, then stiffened when he didn't move. Even on the brink of collapse, damaged and dishevelled, he was still so painfully beautiful – a study in black and bronze, his scars and rigid muscles a warning as much as an irresistible lure. Still the male who'd sacrificed himself for me. Still the male who'd made mind-shattering love to me and held me in my sleep.

Mine ... or at least, he had been mine.

'You're awake,' I breathed.

Safe, undeniable truths. I didn't dare to say more, didn't dare to tread into the quicksand of what had been and what still was for fear I'd hit just the wrong spot, would pull the one loose thread that could set this fragile webbing unravelling.

He didn't release the wall supporting him. But his right hand rose a fraction, the motions uneasy on his fingers. *You needed me.*

Needed him?

Oh. The memory rose too slowly and brought an overwhelming sense of alarm with it – my parents, Beyla's revelations, and those few moments of almost unbearable yearning for his safe arms around me.

'You ... you *felt* that?' The words came out helpless and awkward. Yet another reminder of how pathetically out of my depth I was, how ignorant of his magic and all the consequences that came with it. A reminder of all he should have told me but hadn't.

The wrong thread. Something seemed to lock shut behind his eyes, settling a new layer of stiffness over his shoulders.

I opened my mouth, shut it again. 'Creon—'

His fingers interrupted me, faster and brusquer now. *What happened?*

Right. Reports. Explanations. He deserved to know how he'd passed out from the pain on the floor of the bone hall and woken up alive in the home of people who apparently wanted him dead just as much as the mother he'd betrayed.

I took a step back and sucked in a breath, a hopeless attempt to soothe the anxiety tying knots in my guts. 'Shouldn't you sit down? You don't look like you've fully recovered yet.'

More accurately, he looked like he'd dragged himself out of the grave, flung his torn shirt over his shoulders, and struggled out into battle – because he'd felt my want for him. Because I might have been in danger. And yet he didn't meet my gaze as he cautiously, unsteadily stepped away from the wall and staggered towards the nearest stool, wings flaring to keep his balance until he collapsed into the seat.

I stood motionless, torn between the painful desire to hold him, touch him, ensure myself that our perfect fairy tale wasn't lost yet and the equally agonising fear that I would find no such reassurance.

There was a frostiness about him, a tightness in his movements and the lines of his face. A distance between us that I had not the faintest idea how to cross. I knew how to deal with the Mother's arrogant murderer. I knew how to handle the scarred, broken soul hiding below. But the fae male sitting before me now, his face cold and empty, eyes so painfully detached it seemed he was barely even here ... This was a different monster entirely.

I shrunk back, sat down on the bench where I'd started my meal, and whispered, 'How much do you remember?'

Hall. The gesture came with a disparaging sort of shrug, as if to suggest a night of torture was not much to worry about. I wasn't sure what would be worse: for him to be lying, or for it to be the truth after a life of violence. *Hooks.* His wings shuddered as he spelled out the word. *Then nothing.*

'She kept you in the hall for the night,' I said, unable to keep the tremble from my voice. 'I'm so sorry I left you there – I couldn't think of ...'

He shrugged again. No understanding in his eyes, no trace of care for the choice I'd made or what it had cost both of us. Just that single motion, brusque and indifferent, and an impatient gesture for me to go on.

I swallowed down the pit opening in my stomach. 'I got my hands on a horse. Brought it into the Labyrinth. Sewed a new pocket into my dress, lined it with red fabric. Walked back into the hall, told her I had a gift for her, blew her eyes from her face. Then I broke your chains and escaped into the Labyrinth with you by breaking a hole in the floor.' I hesitated, then added, 'You know, someone trained me well for that.'

No smile, not even the faintest ghost of one.

I wanted to shake him, shout at him, plead for him to come back to me. But I couldn't imagine it would help even the tiniest bit, and the damage it might cause ...

Don't cause trouble, Tared had said. A furious outburst from either of us wouldn't help to secure our place in the Underground.

'You woke up for a moment, down there,' I managed. 'In the Labyrinth. I don't know if you remember?'

He hesitated, then shook his head. No recollection of the way his lips had mimed my name or of that kiss, that fierce, glorious kiss that had promised me all would be fine, *we* would be fine ...

No sense in lingering on that memory. No sense in reminding him of something he might not even wish to remember. 'I carried you out on that horse. Had a chat with Thysandra, convinced her to let us go – I still have a message to deliver to Anaxia, now that I think of it. Then I found Lyn and Tared and convinced them to take you, too. That was this morning. Ylfreda and a few others took care of your injuries, and I think I convinced them that you never truly betrayed them. They're letting you stay, in any case.'

His lips had tightened at the mention of Thysandra and Anaxia; they did again as he glanced around the living room, pausing at the lights, the tapestries, the food. *What is this place?*

'You haven't been here before?' I had assumed this was where the Alliance had held him captive all those decades ago, but he shook his head.

'Oh.' I hunched up my shoulders. 'They call it the Underground. I'm not sure what's above us – some island, I presume. As far as I've seen, most of the Alliance is living here.'

A single slow nod; he didn't stop scanning the room, looking for clues or weak spots. Not a single glance at me. Not a single word of appreciation for saving his life from the Mother first and a horde of furious alves second, not a trace of concern or the quickest enquiry as to how I was doing. He *knew* how I was doing, presumably – had to feel I was not in urgent pain or fearing for my life. But if he knew that, he had to know I was dying to hold him too, and he made not the slightest move to bring me closer.

'Creon,' I said hoarsely.

He had to feel *something* as he turned to meet my gaze, his eyes dull and cold. These were the same eyes that had clung to me with such predatory fierceness after he'd destroyed a door in his hurry to find me, the same eyes that had watched me like I was a living marvel in the multi-coloured darkness of the Labyrinth. But I wasn't a demon, and the blank canvas of his face didn't betray the slightest hint of whatever was living behind that inhumanly gorgeous façade.

'I – I found your letter. Last night.'

The grim shadow of regret that slid over his features didn't do my composure any good – as if he wished he'd never written the damn thing. *I'll be here*, it had said. *Yours.* Words he'd written after I'd thrown my accusations in his face, words he still *had* to believe. Because if he'd changed his mind in the meantime, if he'd decided he'd rather be rid of me ...

'I'm so sorry,' I blurted out, unable to tolerate that train of thought for a moment longer. 'I was so very confused and so very hurt, but I should never have thought you would actually ... I should never have said ...'

He sat frozen – an unbreachable wall of muscle and magic, hiding something that might be cold fury as easily as broken-hearted agony. I clenched my fists and forced myself to continue, to soldier on despite the dreadful urge to crawl away into a shadowy corner and hope everything would simply solve itself. None of this would get easier if I let it fester.

'Creon ...' Damn the crack in my voice. Damn my trembling hands. 'I'm just trying to say ... can we talk about whatever it is we've both been doing all these weeks? Because I have so many questions and I want to know ... I need to know ...'

Words. What were words? The world had seemed so very clear in his arms mere hours ago. Now, under his numb gaze, the very concept of language seemed to have melted from my mind.

'I just want to understand you,' I managed. 'I just want to understand what in hell we are. So if you—'

His fingers twitched in his lap – involuntary and meaningless, the smallest loss of control. I abruptly shut my mouth, frightened to interrupt him, to stifle even the most minimal signs of life.

'Creon?'

He averted his gaze, long locks falling over his face with that jerky movement. But his hand came up, the motions of his fingers rushed and unrestrained.

Clear enough you'd rather not be anything.

'I ... What?'

Another violent twitch. *You were happy enough with an excuse not to want me, weren't you?*

'What?' I stared at him, the knots in my guts drawing tight enough to hurt. 'Wait, no, that's not what—'

Drew your conclusions before you asked a single question. His gestures grew wider, like a rising shout. *Just assumed it must have been magic messing with your heart and I must—*

'Creon! Creon, please, I—'

—have been manipulating you, because who in her right mind would ever fall in love with gods-damned demon brood like me?

'That's not what I said!' Now it was my voice rising, echoing back at me from the mirror-smooth walls. 'You're putting words in *my* mouth now! I never meant—'

He got up with an abrupt, erratic motion, jerking away from me as he made for the open doorway.

'Creon!' I jumped up before I could stop myself, a blaze of anger breaking through the shock. 'Don't start doing that again. Don't start avoiding me again. You know I hate it when you—'

His wings drew taut, as if preparing for flight. *Just hate me, then.* Snappish, violent gestures. *Spares you the effort of finding another reason to shove me aside.*

'Oh, for fuck's sake!' I snapped, staggering after him like a sleep-walker. This couldn't be real. This couldn't be happening. 'Are you just looking for reasons to throw a fit? What in the world has gotten into you?'

Why don't you just ask Lyn and Tared? I hadn't known finger signs could look so bitingly venomous. *Since you seem to like listening to them more than—*

'Creon, *stop* it!'

He yanked his hand down in a last frustrated gesture and vanished into the shadowy corridor without looking back.

I stood frozen for a moment, then bit out a curse and stormed after him. No. No, this was not the game we were going to play. He wasn't going to tell me that I was to blame for taking offense at his lies; he wasn't going to deny how much I'd still wanted him even in those moments I'd thought him a heartless monster.

'*Creon!*' My heart pounded in my fingertips. I could explain myself. I could explain everything, if he'd just shut up and *listen* for a moment. 'I'm not asking them anything, for hell's sake! I have no desire to hear this story from anyone else, so stop this nonsense and—'

He barged into his guest room without looking back and slammed the door behind him. A flash of yellow lit the chink between the hinges; when I grabbed the handle a moment later and tried to push it open, the wood didn't give way.

Yellow.

He'd changed the door somehow – sealed it shut. Sealed me out.

I stumbled backwards, the world spinning too fast, my thoughts moving too slow. This didn't make sense. None of it made sense. I only wanted answers, and instead ...

Just hate me, then.

Was this the same male who'd written me that he'd be there for me, that I was a first for him, that he was *mine*?

Because who in her right mind would ever fall in love with gods-damned demon brood like me?

He had spelled those words, *demon brood*. As if he was throwing my literal words back at me ... but I hadn't been *that* venomous, had I?

Had I?

I sank down onto the smooth black floor, wrestling to control my jagged breath. Where had I gone wrong? All I'd ever wanted to do ... find friends. Find the truth. Save his life. Kill the Mother. And here I found myself small and defeated in some underground realm I barely understood, surrounded by allies who might be enemies as soon as they figured out the truth, sitting close to tears before the door my lover had slammed shut in my face.

My former lover? Were those the words I should use, or should I interpret that blast of magic in any other way?

Yellow for change.

A sob broke from my lungs at last. The world was shifting, straining and tearing, and I felt like any moment, the cracks might open up below my feet and swallow me whole.

CHAPTER 4

'CREON?'

Quite as I'd expected, no reaction came from the room behind that closed wooden door. There hadn't been a reaction for the past five days.

I suppressed a curse and added, more calmly than I felt, 'It would be helpful if you let me in so we could discuss how we're going to keep you alive in this place. Edored's friends are still loitering around the front door. Haven't started looking any more cheerful about your existence since yesterday.'

An understatement, really. They claimed they were merely being upstanding citizens guarding the Silent Death, the dozen or so alves who took turns keeping an eye on the entrance to Tared's family home. Entirely in accordance with the Council's ruling, they insisted they wouldn't lay a finger on their captive unless he came out and started blowing the Underground to shreds. But their sharpened blades and equally sharp glares told a different story, and what I understood of their ominous murmurs behind my back sounded not nearly as peaceful either.

My Alvish wasn't good enough to make out any specific plans. But the language was closely related to the human dialect of the White City, which I spoke fluently, and there was too much bloodthirst in the stories they told each other when they thought I couldn't understand a word of what they said.

It seemed unusual for mere guardians to gleefully anticipate the moment their captive would finally have to come out of his cell, too.

'Lyn and Tared keep telling me not to worry,' I told the door. 'Good news for you: I'm not listening to them this time. But I'm not sure if can solve this bloody mess by myself. If they get tired of waiting ... well, I don't know what they'll do.'

The door didn't move.

I muttered a curse and glanced down at the tray I'd put at the threshold: buttered bread and goat cheese and a bowl of fresh dates. 'I brought you lunch, too.'

Not that he ever touched the food; I'd likely end up returning it to the kitchen, as I'd done with every single meal over the past five days.

'And there were visitors yesterday.' Again, I had to push away a spark of raw, hurt anger. I'd lain awake until long past midnight, the argument between Lyn and Tared and their nameless friends replaying without mercy in my thoughts. Creon had to know. He must have felt my misery, must have known I needed his help, and still he hadn't bothered to come out. 'I ... I listened at the living room door, admittedly. Some people want to attack the Crimson Court as soon as possible. The Mother has apparently cancelled every public appearance she had planned this week – the Council thinks her eyes are worse than she wants the world to know, and they're trying to take advantage of that.'

No reaction. Of course there was no reaction. What had I thought – that he'd spontaneously give a damn about me and my problems again?

'Tared kept telling them I'm not ready for any of it,' I continued, unable to stop talking despite the hopelessness of it. That repeated argument, sharper and more impatient the longer the discussion lasted, had returned to my feverish mind most often of all. 'But sooner or later they'll want me to do *something*, Creon. So I need your help with training – *please*.'

Nothing.

Damn him, why did my tears still make the effort of burning behind my eyes?

It was hard to accept, the damningly simple conclusion that he just didn't care about anything I did. He *had* to care. He'd been prepared to die for me, had woken from unconsciousness for me. But if he cared, then why wouldn't he come out of that bloody room and *fix* things?

Was he waiting for me to apologise for every non-existent crime he'd accused me of? While *he* was the one who'd been keeping secrets since the day I arrived at the Crimson Court?

'Well,' I told the silence, my voice inadvertently sharp, 'I'll leave you to your wallowing, then. Once you've figured out how to unlock a door again, I'll be glad to—'

'Emelin?' Lyn said from the other side of the corridor.

I jolted like a thief caught stealing. She'd emerged from the living room, leaning against the wall in an admirable attempt to pretend she hadn't found me talking to a door with no intentions of opening anytime soon.

'Oh,' I said gloomily. 'Hey.'

'I was looking for you,' she said with just a tad too much brightness. And she'd known exactly where to find me, of course – back at my delusional attempts to be optimistic, to fool myself into believing there was something to be salvaged of whatever the Silent Death had been to me at the Crimson Court. 'Thought you might want to join me on a short trip through the Underground? It's really a crime that you've only seen Council rooms and training halls in all this time.'

She knew as well as I did that I'd been the one to refuse all invitations – that I was the one who hurried back home after every sword training session with Tared and spent my spare hours holed up in the small but cosy bedroom they'd given me. The quiet of this house was much more attractive than the cold politeness that most members of the Alliance employed towards me, and what if anyone tried to break into Creon's room while I wasn't around?

'Perhaps tomorrow,' I said weakly. 'I'm a bit ...'

I hesitated. I had quoted tiredness as a reason to stay at home for my first three days, feigned a headache when that lie began to sound formulaic, and made good use of the start of my period yesterday. I was running out of excuses, and judging by the way Lyn's smile grew joyless, she knew it as well as I did.

'Those idiots outside really aren't going to break into his room, Emelin. House sanctuary isn't shoved aside so easily.'

Tared told me the same thing every morning when we passed the group of watchful alves on our way to the training hall. Similar reassurances had also been brought forward by Beyla and Ylfreda and Hallthor, who all seemed unnervingly determined to treat me kindly despite the murderous company at their front door I was responsible for. But no matter how often they repeated their arguments about honour and tradition, it seemed to me they were placing a lot of faith in the common sense of people who mused out loud about torn wings and amulets of dried fae ears whenever I walked past.

'Thanks,' I said anyway, because she was going out of her way to be pleasant and it wasn't her fault I was feeling miserable as a wrung-out rag. 'Look, I really appreciate your concern, but I'm not—'

'Come to the library with me,' Lyn interrupted, firm in the way only seven-year-olds could sound firm. The way she folded her arms over her flaming red dress suggested objecting wouldn't be a very fruitful course of action. 'You'll feel better if you don't spend all day loitering around here.'

The *library?* I hadn't been aware there was a library down here; it sounded better than the parties and dinners she'd invited me to before. Books knew when to keep their mouths shut, for one thing. 'Well. Perhaps I could join you tomorrow? I'm a bit—'

'Beyla has been making a list of powerful fae males,' she interrupted, her words too measured to pretend this wasn't some calculated reveal. 'You know, to see if one of the bastards roughly matching your magical abilities might be your father.'

I stared at her. She gave me a small smile, looking just a little smug.

'That's shameless manipulation,' I said.

'I know.' Her smile turned wry. 'I've been trying to drag you out of here in more ethical ways for days now, Emelin. It's time for the ugly strategies. So ...' A shrug. 'Are you coming?'

Hell take her. I glanced at the food before Creon's door, resolve wavering for the first time. I didn't want to leave him alone with a group of potential murderers lounging around nearby. I really, *really* didn't want to leave him alone. But my parents ...

I suppressed a curse. If Beyla found anything useful, I damn well wanted to be the first to know.

'Proud of you,' Lyn said as I turned to follow her.

We navigated in silence through the living room and the hall on its other side. It was at that point that I faltered, unwilling to confront our pack of unwanted guardians once again, but Lyn stamped on without slowing down.

There were five of them today, males and females sitting in the broader and higher corridor I'd come to think of as our street. They were all blond, tense, and heavily armed and conversed loudly about that time one of them had managed to tear a fae male's wings off his shoulders with her bare hands.

'Of course,' Lyn said as she locked the door behind us and shot them a narrow-eyed scowl, 'the lot of you could spend your day counting lentils instead. That would be significantly more useful than this nonsense.'

The wiry alf male who went by the name of Njalar scoffed in a way that suggested he'd spent too much time with Edored. 'Just looking out for your safety, Phiramelyndra.'

She rolled her eyes, but grabbed my elbow and pulled me to the right without setting him on fire. 'This way, Emelin.'

I swallowed and pretended not to hear the continuation of their violent talk behind our backs. Lyn still seemed entirely unconcerned about their bloodthirst, but perhaps that was easy when you were their leader's ... well, whatever she was to Tared.

'Are you really sure—'

'Creon isn't a fool,' she interrupted in a hushed tone, leading me through a winding corridor I'd never seen before. Tared usually just faded me wherever I needed to go. 'He's not going to look for a confrontation with these idiots. To the left, here.'

I didn't point out that these alves seemed determined enough to bring about a confrontation by themselves; she'd counter that Creon wasn't coming out of his room to be confronted by anyone, and I didn't want to think about the painful truth of that argument.

The next corridor we walked into was even broader and higher, the left wall covered in long runic inscriptions, the right wall overgrown with many-coloured mosses and succulents. To my surprise, there was not a soul to be seen here; no one to glower at me or whisper about me.

I couldn't keep in a quiet sigh of relief.

'So,' Lyn said, pretending she hadn't noticed, 'time for some Underground geography. This tunnel is the border between Orin's quarter on the left and Zera's quarter on the right. Did anyone tell you they created the Underground during the War of the Gods?'

I blinked. 'Who?'

'The gods. Four of them, that is – Korok was busy screwing High Ladies, so he wasn't invited.' She grimaced at me. 'It was supposed to be a safe haven for humans caught in the crossfire. Then the Mother wiped out all five gods at once, and most people forgot about the place. We've been using it to hide since we lost the Last Battle.'

She stayed quiet as I studied the corridor with new eyes, suddenly understanding the clues around us – Orin's runes to our left and Zera's flowers to our right. That did make sense. Orin was the god who'd given magic to the alves, so of course they lived in his quarter. Zera ... She'd been the patron goddess of the nymphs. Anaxia and her family would likely have their homes in that section of the Underground, then.

Before us, a familiar room loomed up – the Council hall I'd seen during my first day here. This was the heart of the Underground, then; indeed, three other broad corridors sprung from this central place, separating the four quarters. With no Council meetings in progress, it was as good as deserted. Only a handful of vampire females stood chatting and laughing at the farthest wall. They stiffened as they noticed me.

'That's Etele's quarter,' Lyn said with a nod at the section behind them. 'Poor Etele was patron goddess of the fae – do they still teach that part at school these days?'

I blinked. 'I thought Korok was—'

'Korok gave the vampires their power before he got himself all tangled up in fae wars. They lost their god; Etele lost her people. The vampires are living in her quarter now.'

The vampires waved at us – or more likely, at Lyn – as we walked past. She rattled off a greeting in some language I didn't know, then tugged me into the corridor that separated Etele's quarter on the left from the fourth Underground section on the right.

'So that's Inika's quarter,' I said, glancing at the small flames playing over the walls, 'who was patron of the phoenixes.'

'Very good.'

'Are you living there?'

'I used to.' She shrugged. 'But there aren't that many phoenixes in the Underground, so I moved most of my stuff to Tared's place. It's good to have some company.'

Tared's company specifically, perhaps – but I wasn't sure how to ask that question. After a few days in their home, the exact nature of their relationship was still unclear to me. They slept in separate bedrooms, which didn't suggest a romantic entanglement. Then again, I rarely saw them away from each other for longer than five consecutive minutes, which seemed unusual for a mere friendship.

'Most of your stuff?' I said after a moment of hesitation, because asking about her love life seemed unwise when I was very much hoping no one would pay attention to mine.

'My books stayed here.' She nodded at the corridor emerging on our right. 'I wasn't going to put those at the mercy of an alf household.'

'Ah,' I said, unable to suppress a joyless chuckle. 'I have to admit Edored doesn't strike me as the greatest of readers.'

'I doubted for years that he actually knew the alphabet,' Lyn said dryly. 'But I found him writing an elaborate threat on a wall with the blood of a dead enemy one day, so that answered the question. To the right, here – we could also walk on and go right just before the fields, but this route is shorter.'

'The ... fields?' I said.

'Oh, yes. Where did you think we got our food?' She vaguely waved at something in the distance. 'You'll see.'

Farmland in an underground city? I hobbled after her, more intrigued than I'd planned to be, and for a moment, the thought of Creon didn't sting as sharply. Perhaps she had been right to drag me out of the house. Staring at the same closed door for hours on end, mulling over my own failures and waiting for some alf ambush that never came ... it wasn't a great way to soothe that persistent fear eating away at my heart.

Lyn guided me through a maze of corridors, left and right and left again, past houses that had to be smaller than Tared's, going by the distance between the doors. No large family homes for phoenixes, then? It struck me I had no idea of the way any of these magical peoples lived. They'd been pushed to the edges of the empire after the War, surviving out of sight of humans. During all my etiquette lessons on Ildhelm, no one had ever mentioned the proper way to greet a vampire, or the ten rules to keep in mind while dining with a nymph.

Perhaps I should ask Lyn if she has any books on magical manners. It might reduce the chance of tragic death by enraged alf.

The door where we eventually stood looked like any other we had passed in this quarter: blood red wood and elaborate brass knockers shaped like lizards and salamanders. But the hall that opened up behind ...

I stood stunned and silenced in the doorway, all thought of murder shoved into the farthest shadows of my mind.

There were rows and rows and rows of books, more than I'd ever seen in one place together, meticulously ordered over dozens of heavy bookcases. Other writing was displayed on the shelves too, wood tablets and inscribed clay and scrolls made of something that looked like tree bark; all of them were covered in signs I couldn't even recognise, let alone read. Long tables stood between the aisles, and vampires and nymphs sat bent over books or manuscripts in progress, barely looking up to greet us as we entered.

But it wasn't the sight of those books that made the breath stop dead in my lungs for a moment, or the earthy smell of ink and leather and parchment washing over me. It wasn't even the sound of the library – a never-ending rustle of pens and pages, like the slow breath of some immense creature of knowledge and curiosity.

It was the *light*.

Falling bright and buttery throughout the room, drawing long shadows behind the pillars and the book cases, it looked nothing like the artificial fire that illuminated most of the Underground. It didn't resemble the glowing orbs of the fae either. If I hadn't known we were standing hundreds of feet below the earth, it would have looked like *daylight*.

'And that,' Lyn muttered as she closed the door behind me, 'is alf magic in all its glory.'

A laugh escaped me. 'What is it?'

'The fields.' She trotted forward, bright red curls dancing over her shoulders. Only as I stepped from the low portal where we'd entered did I see the high windows on the other side of the library hall, open and arched and dazzling with light.

We climbed two winding staircases to the second gallery, where we could look out. Stretching out below us, at least half a mile into the distance, lay the fields.

At first glance, they were not unlike the farmland on Cathra, where I'd worked whenever my father didn't have anything useful for me to do: rows of grains and vegetables, interrupted by some stretches of messier, weed-covered earth where the farmland was recovering until the next crop rotation phase. But the plants grew larger in this place. They smelled sweeter. The leaves and flowers seemed brighter and more colourful, reminding me strangely of Miss Matilda's cloth inventory.

Perhaps the light was to blame. It seemed to come from everywhere and nowhere at once, filtering from the inky black ceiling of the cave in vivid rays of nearly-sunshine and flooding the growing crops with life. Even *I* felt more invigorated at the sight of it; the eggplants and barley below may feel the same.

Or perhaps ... I squinted at the slender figures moving in the fields, some of them weeding and watering, some of them lounging around the plants as if they were spending time with friends. Nymphs, if I could go by the bright rainbow of their hair colours. Their magic was related to nature, wasn't it? That might also explain a thing or two.

'The fields run in a circle around all of the Underground,' Lyn said next to me, resting her arms on the windowsill. Standing on her toes, she could just glance over the edge. 'This side is where we grow crops. We keep some animals as well, behind Etele's quarter.'

'With the vampires?' I had trouble imagining Gish and Nenya as cowherders, but Lyn shrugged.

'It's a blood reserve for them. And they tell me blood tastes better when its donor is healthy and happy, so our herds tend to be in excellent shape.'

'Oh. Right.' I hadn't thought about the logistics of keeping an army of vampires alive. Really, I hadn't thought about the logistics of *any* life in this place. 'And water?'

'There's an underground river running around the outer rim,' Lyn said, waving at an invisible point in the distance. 'Inika created quite an inventive water supply system when the Underground was built. I still don't fully understand the technology, but I suppose being a goddess is helpful at times.'

I rubbed my face. 'I thought Inika was supposed to be a fire goddess. Why was she the one handling irrigation?'

'Fire *and* water,' Lyn said, clucking her tongue like an exasperated mother. 'Don't they teach you children anything anymore?'

A laugh escaped me, the lingering fear lifted for another brief moment. 'Please fill the gaps in my knowledge, ancient creature. I'm all ears.'

She shook her head, chuckling. 'The gods were dual in nature. Inika was a goddess of both fire and water; it just so happens that she gave us her fire powers. Orin was the god of both earth and sky, and the alves received his powers relating to daylight.'

I blinked. 'So when they taught us Korok was the god of death ...'

'Death and life.' She moved back from the window, sending a smile up at me. 'He forgot about the life part at some point, unfortunately. Let's go see Beyla. She should be somewhere in the Wanderer's Wing.'

'Whose wing?' I said.

She was already walking. 'Wanderers are alves who go out and travel across as much of the archipelago as possible. The thing about fading is that they can only fade to places they've seen before, did we tell you about that? In ancient times, wanderers were helpful to reach remote islands and deep parts of the continent and other unlikely places.'

'And since the War ...'

'They make for excellent spies and scouts. Beyla is one of our best when it comes to current affairs.' She looked over her shoulder to check if I was following, then dove between two book cases, into a narrow corridor. 'Which is why she's highly annoyed to have missed the birth of an unbound fae mage.'

'I'll cry a little harder next time,' I said, and she laughed out loud.

The next library hall looked out over the fields as well, but was smaller and lower. To our right, a low doorway led to a dusky, cellar-like room – 'Best to stay out of there,' Lyn told me – and in the far corner, a winding staircase led to a higher floor. Lyn hurried past the towering piles of parchment and the filing cabinets and the occasional nymph tiptoeing around, in a straight line to a rune-inscribed door looking suspiciously similar to those in Tared's house.

Voices washed over us as she pulled it open.

I heard Tared somewhere, dry and casual as usual, Nenya, her low timbre easily recognisable even when she was speaking Alvish, and Edored, ranting to no one in particular about nothing in particular. Gods help me – *Edored*. Some strict words from Tared were probably the only reason the bastard hadn't yet invited his friends into the home to break in Creon's bedroom door, and even Tared's strict words couldn't keep his cousin from complaining about the household's unwanted fae guest at every meal we ate together. His face was about the last thing I wanted to see in between mealtimes, and Lyn should have known that much.

Which was probably why she hadn't warned me.

I glared at her as I stepped into the room, my pride all that kept me from turning and running. She patted me encouragingly on the elbow as she walked in after me.

'Oh, Emelin!'

The conversation stilled mid-sentence at Nenya's interruption, all heads snapping towards me. Only Beyla did not look up, engrossed in the lists spread out on the table in the middle of the room.

'Morning,' I said awkwardly, following Lyn towards them. Below piles and piles of parchment, I recognised a map of the archipelago in the table surface, the familiar shapes of the sea, continent, and islands created from different shades of wood. Other maps covered the ink-black walls of the room, some of them mere sketches, others elaborate pieces of art. The bookcases were filled with atlases and carved tablets and notebooks that looked like they'd survived weeks at the bottom of traveller's backpacks.

Nenya and Edored greeted me, then continued their heated bickering over something related to Midsummer celebrations and vampire traditions.

Tared seemed glad enough to turn away from them as I sat down between him and Beyla. 'Lyn finally lured you out, I see?'

I glowered at Lyn, who returned a dazzling smile as she clambered into her chair on his other side and said, 'You should be glad you got me. Tared's suggestion was to grab you from your room, fade you into the library, and let you find your own way home.'

'Which would have worked,' Tared said dryly.

She threw a pen at him, then hastily inserted herself into the conversation between Edored and Nenya, which sounded like it was about to turn into a fight.

'Did she tell you about Beyla's study?' Tared said, watching the scene with a little too much amusement. 'We're trying to make a selection—'

'—of possible fathers.' I stole a glance at the dozens of names Beyla had scribbled down. 'She told me. What exactly are you looking for? Just fae males with strong magic?'

'That's the basis,' Beyla said with one of those empty, lifeless smiles. Her voice barely rose above the discussion on the other side of the table.

'It's hard to make an exact estimate of how strong your magic is, of course, because you're still developing mastery of your powers – but Lyn and I suspect your father should be in the upper five percent of the fae population. Which still leaves a lot of candidates, obviously ...'

'But at least the stronger mages tend to be more visible,' Tared said, 'so there is a better chance we actually know him.'

Beyla nodded. 'So I'm selecting on the basis of additional characteristics. Skin colour should not be too different from yours. He must have been at the court nine to eleven months before your birth – I'm taking both fae and human pregnancies into account, since length seems to vary with half fae. And ...' She tapped the list with a tanned finger. 'I'm excluding the more law-abiding ones, too. Most of them would have informed the Mother the moment they took a mistress, and I doubt anyone would have been able to smuggle you out in that case.'

'Good gods.' I rubbed my eyes, then let my eyes glide over the lists – dozens and dozens of names, all of them equally unfamiliar. 'You've put a lot of thought into this, haven't you?'

'Oh, I'm absolutely enraged one of the bastards escaped my notice.' She hardly blinked as she spoke the words; her voice sounded about as enraged as a whispering spring breeze. 'Just out of curiosity, did you ever get stung by a bee?'

'Um.' That was not the question I had expected. 'Not that I know of?'

'Shame,' she said, shaking her head. 'The house of Haimon is terribly allergic to bee stings. Would have been useful to know if you inherited that.'

'We could let a few bees loose at her?' Edored suggested, turning away from his boisterous conversation with Lyn and Nenya on the other side of the table. 'If we rub a little honey on her face, I'm sure—'

'Helpful as always, Edored,' Beyla said, granting him the smallest of empty smiles. 'Any other suggestions on this paternal mystery?'

Tared's cousin looked indignant about her lack of enthusiasm, but gave me a probing look nonetheless as he ran his fingers through his long hair. 'How about Megander? The one with the nose, I mean, not the bastard from—'

'Died sixty years ago,' Beyla said without looking up from her list.

Edored frowned. 'So?'

'Emelin is twenty years old, Edored.'

The alf stared at me in stunned confusion for at least three heartbeats before finally a spark of understanding dawned on his face. 'Oh. Orin's eye, I hate mathematics.'

I snorted a laugh; I couldn't help it, violent bastard or not. 'Thanks, though. And I'd be happy to hear if my nose reminds you of anyone else.'

'I never paid much attention to fae noses,' he said with a skewed grin. 'My favourite thing about them is when they're no longer attached to the fuckers' faces. Did you consider Iorgas, Bey? At least he's been screwing around with humans before, so ...'

'Can't be Iorgas,' she said, browsing to another page of notes. 'The Mother caught wind of that unregistered daughter five years ago and forced him into a bargain to either kill all his living children or die a painful death. Since he's still alive ...'

'*All* his children?' I blurted out, and Beyla looked up with an apology in her pale blue eyes.

'Oh, yes. Six of them, as far as I know.'

'But the others were all registered and bound?'

'It wasn't about those children,' she said, her voice even flatter. 'It was about punishing their father and warning the rest of the world not to follow his example. Iorgas didn't come out of the whole ordeal very well, and if he hadn't been so important to her administration, she would have thrown him to the hounds without any second chances.'

I swallowed. 'Right.'

'So.' She sighed. 'Not Iorgas. Tared, I've been thinking ...'

I sat beside them for some fifteen more minutes as they exchanged names and theories, the exercise not as exciting as I had hoped. I didn't know the people they knew, their histories and activities of the last decades; even if one of them was my father, his name was as meaningless to me as any of the others. What had I hoped for – that one of these strings of syllables would spark some flash of recognition and I would magically *know* which bastard had abandoned my mother at my birth?

My thoughts wandered off. Back to the house on the other side of the Underground. Back to the pack of alves waiting to take their revenge; back to that damned door Creon had melted into the wall and never opened again.

What in hell had gotten into him?

Staring at the books and maps around me, a new idea bubbled up.

Just before he'd cut me off, I'd told him I wouldn't ask Lyn and Tared for more information about his past – and I intended to keep that promise. Uncovering more secrets behind his back could only make things worse. But there were a damn lot of books in this place, and if I were to accidentally stumble upon any helpful shreds of knowledge ...

Who knew if that might tell me why he had reacted so unpredictably to that last conversation?

'Lyn?'

She whipped towards me, rubbing a rogue curl from her cheek. 'What is it?'

'Where do I find the history department?' I said, trying to look like an innocent half fae who could safely be left alone with valuable books. 'I was trying to learn the basics at the pavilion, and I'm thinking I should continue—'

'Oh, of course!' She brightened at once, so delighted with my interest I didn't have the heart to elaborate on my lies. 'Most of it is in the main hall where we came in, but the books on the wars are in the room behind that one. Door is on the first gallery to the left. If you need me to show you ...'

'Oh, no, I'll be fine.' I managed a smile as I got back to my feet. 'Thanks for bringing me here. And see you later.'

CHAPTER 5

I WANDERED BACK TO the main hall more slowly than we'd come, taking a few minutes to examine the shelves I encountered. It would have been helpful, after all, if there were any books to be found with titles such as *Ten Ways To Quietly Get Rid Of Murderous Alves* or *The Lady's Guide To Dealing With Dejected Demons*.

Disappointingly, most of the collected literature discussed more boring topics. An entire bookcase was dedicated to vampire biology and the nutritional value of blood; another contained iron-plated tomes on the magical properties of phoenix fire. The dark room Lyn had told me not to visit was filled to the brim with works on divine magic. A half-finished manuscript on the writing table described some experiment that had ended with several fatalities, or at least, that was what I could decipher from the long Faerie sentences.

I carefully backed away and went to look for War history books instead.

The door on the first gallery was easy to find, and the brightly lit room behind was deserted. I allowed myself three deep breaths to feel intimidated by the packed shelves full of leather-bound volumes, then scraped myself together and went to work.

The bookcases were sorted chronologically, it turned out. A helpful start. The Alliance had captured Creon near the end of the War, which meant I had to search just before the Last Battle.

It didn't take me long to find the shelves I was looking for. I dismissed books in languages I didn't know, taking only those in one of the two human languages or Faerie into consideration. Then most of the works were still useless. I wasn't looking for a study of economic shifts during the last years of war, or a memoir of some alf house that had been particularly honourable in that period ... But the chronicle with an overview of the entire decade looked like it may be a helpful start; surely the Mother's son and the leaders of the Alliance would be mentioned once or twice in a history book as thick as my fist?

I dragged the thing to the nearest reading table and settled myself there, basking in the almost-sunlight. The final pages of the book contained the index I had hoped for.

Creon Hytherion. I found him within two glances.

The sight of his name, penned down in a small, regular hand, brought something thorny to my throat that I couldn't swallow down so easily. Just one of the many in this endless list of people and places. Just another murderer, just another traitor. And yet those deceitful letters, combined with the familiar scent of parchment and leather, evoked entirely different images in my mind's eye – of his scarred hands browsing through books and scrolls at the table in the pavilion, of the conspiratorial smile that slid over his lips as we discussed the secrets of the Labyrinth, of the light that broke through in his eyes whenever one of my jokes or jabs hit just the right spot ...

The letters on the pages turned misty. I shut my eyes and tried not to think about the motions of his fingers.

There's nothing small about you.

Just hate me, then.

'Oh, here you are!' a chipper voice said behind me.

I shrieked as I whirled around. Not even an alf – I would have been excused for not noticing someone fading into the room. But the small, blushing figure that emerged between the bookcases ...

'Oh dear,' Anaxia said, pursing her lips as she cocked her head at me. 'You taste of heartbreak *and* anger today. How fascinating!'

Piss off, I nearly said. *I already know I'm being miserable; I don't need some demon to remind me of it.* But her smile told me she knew exactly who my heart was breaking for, and I wasn't going to antagonise her to the point where she might let the secret slip and give those damn alves another reason to swoop in and rescue me from Creon's dastardly wiles. I wasn't even sure what I had done to deserve her secrecy so far.

'Morning,' I said feebly. 'Anything I can do for you?'

'Oh, I just wanted a chat with you.' She dropped down on the edge of the next writing table and folded her legs under her skirts, revealing an amount of thigh that would have my mother pressing her lips together in a most disapproving way. 'We don't have newcomers in the Underground *that* often, you see? Very exciting! Creon's still being an idiot, I take it?'

I stared at her.

'Don't look at me like that,' she said, waving my confusion aside with a fidgety gesture. 'He must have been an utter buffoon to upset you like that. What did he do?'

'Just ... not want me, I suppose,' I said bleakly. Little sense in keeping secrets from her, and it was oddly relieving to say the words out loud, even if it was to a little half demon I didn't trust entirely. 'I'm not sure, really. He—'

Anaxia snorted. 'Don't be daft.'

'Don't ... what?'

'He's utterly consumed by you,' she said impatiently. 'It's the main reason I knew we had little to fear from him this time. He may be displaying some of his usual dramatics, but—'

'He locked me out!'

She chuckled. 'Of course he did.'

'What are you talking about?' I fell back in my chair, my heart thumping painfully against my ribs. *Consumed by you.* She had known, indeed, the moment she laid eyes on him – but how in hell was I to fit that with his almost wilful attempts to tell me I hated him? With his refusal to open his door to me even in times of lethal danger? 'But then why would he – why would he …'

Anaxia waited, piercing blue eyes shooting over my face, noting every fleeting expression, every flare of emotion.

'I just don't *understand*,' I burst out, too bewildered to hold on to my secrets. 'Listen, he wrote me this letter, back at the Crimson Court, told me he would be there if I ever came back, told me he understood why I was leaving – and then he woke up and suddenly he was blaming me for ever thinking the worst of him? Telling me I hated him?'

'Ah, yes.' She shrugged. 'That makes sense.'

'It doesn't make sense at all!' My voice cracked. 'Why would he change his mind like that? All I did in the meantime was save his life!'

'Yes,' she said patiently, 'and you moved him.'

'What?'

'He wrote that letter at the court. He woke up here. That's the difference.' She gave me a broad smile as she slid off the table again. 'Well, nice to have had a chat with you. Let's—'

'Wait!' I interrupted, barely suppressing the urge to grab her wrist and keep her here. Moved him? What in hell was that supposed to mean? 'Wait. I still don't understand – could you explain this in a little more detail? Please? Because I really don't see …'

'Sorry, Emelin.' She sounded genuinely sorry even as she beamed her broad, pearly white smile at me. Her small teeth were too sharp for her blushing round face; I suppressed a shiver. 'That's against the moral code. But I do hope you figure it out, honestly.'

'What moral code?'

'My moral code,' she said, slinking back towards the door. 'I know so many secrets, Emelin. I could start a civil war just saying a few wrong things to the wrong people. The only way to keep things fair is to only give advice using the obvious facts everyone already knows. You can ask me to tell you a secret, but I'll be sharing it with everyone else who asks, too, and that—'

'I have a message for you,' I blurted out.

'A message?' She whirled around, eyes widening excitedly. 'Oh, how fun. Are we going to bargain? I could have known you'd pick the fae way to—'

'From Thysandra,' I added.

She froze.

For a heartbeat or two, there was nothing bright about her, nothing joyful; gone were the restless motions of her fingers, the lights in her blue eyes, the blushes on her pale cheeks.

Then she took a single step back and folded her arms, leaning cautiously against the bookcase behind her. 'Ask away.'

I blinked. 'Is the moral code that easily ...'

'Moral code?' She grinned – a wolfish, sharp-toothed grin – and suddenly there was nothing childlike left about her. 'What's that?'

Zera help me. Thysandra wasn't the only one betraying principles and loyalty for the sake of whatever had happened between them during that bloody battle. But I wasn't going to complain, not with Creon still locked away in some prison of his own making, so I sucked in a deep breath and said, 'What is the relevant difference between the Crimson Court and the Underground, exactly?'

She shrugged. 'People with opinions.'

I must have looked particularly stupefied, because she clucked her tongue and added, 'He's a demon, yes?'

'Yes,' I said weakly, 'but—'

'We sense feelings and emotions. When the emotions are aimed at us, we feel them even more clearly. He's currently surrounded by a few hundred people who loathe him from the bottom of their hearts.' A chuckle. 'That's bad for anyone's mood.'

I stared at her, feeling like someone was lighting a bonfire of sudden sense in my brain.

'More questions?'

'I – I have a thousand questions.' The words couldn't leave my lips fast enough. 'Good gods. Is this why he felt it when I needed him, specifically – because that made the sensation much stronger for him than if I had been thinking of anyone else? Strong enough for him to wake up?'

'Oh, I suppose so,' she said, all but rolling her eyes. 'That's what woke him, you say? Zera have mercy. Seems like he's still as ridiculously poorly trained as when he—'

'Poorly trained – *Creon?*'

'Terribly so.' She saw my question before I asked it, and impatiently added, 'Not when it comes to murder and violence, of course. The Mother had him educated well enough about demonic warrior tactics. The problem is there's so much more to this magic than simple destruction, and he's never learned any of that.' A fluttery gesture at her own chest. 'I can shut out the feelings of others when I have no need for them – it's a basic skill we all need to learn as children. He's never been able to do that. Which means he's constantly drowning in the moods of his company.'

A baffled laugh escaped me. 'But that's ...'

'Unbearable? Yes.'

'But ... *oh.* Wait.' I swallowed. 'Is that why he was living in that pavilion, so far away from the palace itself? Because he'd go mad if he had to be around the court every minute of the day?'

She gave me a grim smile. 'Exactly.'

'Oh. Oh, gods.' That peaceful home at the beach, covered in roses and twisting vines ... Not a luxury retreat, but a necessity, a safe refuge on the quietest side of the island. No wonder my constant company had been so overwhelming to him, with the relentless shifts of my feelings about him – from anger to sympathy, from hate to lust. No wonder he'd preferred to avoid me for a week, rather than subject himself to the torment of my indecisive heart whipping him in the face. But there was no avoiding the members of the Alliance in the Underground, no avoiding that small army of alves that had installed itself on his doorstep ...

'So,' Anaxia said, watching me closely. 'You can see why he's not exactly in his sanest mind at the moment.'

'Because he's being flooded by their hate.'

'Yes.' She had a mysterious way of sounding cheerful and gloomy at the same time, as if she was optimistically dancing towards her downfall. 'At some stage it becomes hard to separate your own feelings from those of the world around you. If enough people hate you to death, you'll start hating yourself, too.'

Who in her right mind would ever fall in love with demon brood like me? I swallowed a wave of nausea – oh hell, the room he'd walked into moments after waking, barely able to stand on his feet and unsure of where he'd even ended up ... Edored had been ready to kill him. Tared had likely been ready to do worse if he hadn't considered himself a male of some civilisation. And then I had exploded at him, too.

I'd stood in front of his door angry and bitter a moment ago, adding my own poison to the venomous hate from the alves outside.

'Is there a way to solve this?' I no longer cared how desperate I sounded. I *was* desperate; if she knew it anyway, I might as well focus on being rational. 'You said you can filter people out, didn't you? Can't you teach him to do the same?'

She flung up her hands. 'Of course I can! Do you think I never offered?'

'But then why ...'

'Did I mention he's an idiot?' She let out a long, dramatic sigh. 'Look, Emelin, he hates demons – hates them with a passion, hates himself with a passion, hates his powers with a passion. He'd rather go insane as an untrained martyr than accept he has this bloody magic and learn to deal with it in a sensible way. I frankly don't know what made him turn away from his own blood so staunchly, but the consequence is he is currently turning his own heart inside out. Like an idiot. Now what did you say about that message?'

Message? It took a moment to remember what she was talking about through the whirl of her revelations – oh. Thysandra.

Yes. We'd made a deal, and letting an impatient demon wait seemed foolishly unwise.

'She ... well ...'

I hesitated. Only now did it occur to me that Anaxia would likely not be too grateful for the specific contents of the note. What was I going to tell the others if she cried her eyes out for the next three days? Hell, what would I do if she took out her anger on me?

'She?' Anaxia repeated, and the warning in her voice made me give up on my attempts to find a more diplomatic way of wording things.

'She almost stopped us when we fled the Labyrinth,' I hastily said. 'Thysandra, I mean. Then let us go, on the condition that I'd tell you ...'

Anaxia watched me like a starved animal about to lash out, her hands balled into fists, her lip curled up to reveal those small, sharp teeth. It took all my self-control not to put my left hand on the nearest red surface.

'She asked me to tell you she should have slit your throat when she had the chance.'

Anaxia gaped at me in stunned silence.

Then she threw her head back and laughed out loud – joyous, victorious laughter, shaking through her slender body until she almost toppled over at my feet.

'Um,' I said, even more concerned now. 'I'm glad you're happy, but ...'

'So she *does* think of me.' Another triumphant burst of mirth. 'Thank you very much, Emelin. I've heard enough – more than enough. Now go deal with your own idiot, will you?'

She danced out of the light-streaked room without looking back, leaving me flustered and bewildered between the books.

Deal with my own idiot.

My idiot.

It was preposterous to draw so much hope from a few words – but as I carefully put my unread book back where I'd found it, my heart finally seemed to be beating at its own pace again. At the very damn least, this meant I wasn't the root of the problem after all. And if all of this was just a matter of the wrong place and time, of poorly chosen words and unfavourable interpretations, I *might* be able to fix it in the end.

I told Tared to fade me back home. I didn't trust myself not to kill Njalar and his comrades, now that I fully understood how much they were already hurting the object of their hate.

Creon's food had remained untouched, the bread and cheese and dates still on the tray before his door. In the past five days, that observation had sent me spiralling into bitter resentment and self-loathing every time. This time ...

I needed to be stronger than that.

So I sank down on the floor opposite his closed door, rested the back of my head against the smooth stone wall, and let the memories flow through me.

I recalled the first time his fingers had spoken to me. *What can I do?*

I recalled the first time he'd smiled at me, *truly* smiled at me, imagined that genuine, vulnerable expression that softened the hard line of his jaw and revealed the crinkles around his eyes. The way his face came to life when he laughed, doing away with all traces of the lazy, arrogant fae prince and exposing the male who'd so much rather joke about books and cacti than play the Mother's murderer for a single day more. The dresses he'd given me, his tender arms around me as I woke in his bed, his practiced, graceful motions as he cooked me dinner.

The sudden flash of anger on his face, that one morning. *There's nothing small about you.*

I shut out all other feelings: my grief, my anger, the paralysing fear that every single one of those memories belonged forever to the past. Opened the floodgates and allowed that nameless emotion to wash over me, fill me until I could feel it tingling in the tips of my toes and fingers – until I was nothing but the desperate, violent need for him to be well again. For him to be *happy*. For him to be safe and loved and seen for what he was – not a monster, not a traitor, but a male who'd give his life and sanity for just a chance at fixing this broken world.

His door didn't open in the hour I sat there, curled up on the floor, focusing on nothing but whatever it was that I felt for him. It didn't open when I finally crawled back to my feet and retreated to my own bedroom, oddly exhausted and yet calmer than I'd been in days.

But when Ylfreda called me for dinner a few hours later and I passed his door again, the plates on his tray were empty.

CHAPTER 6

'YOU'RE SLIPPING BACK INTO a rhythm,' Tared told me for the twentieth time, helpfully poking me between the ribs with his training stick before I could slap him away with my own.

I stifled a growl of frustration as I stepped back, interrupting the sequence of training motions. Slipping back. *Again.* How many times had he stopped me already this morning – how many times had I lost focus because my thoughts kept straying to that cursed closed door a few hundred feet away?

Far too often. That was all I needed to know.

I lowered my training stick and rubbed the spot just above my midriff where he'd hit me. 'You could have let me know *without* breaking my ribs, bastard.'

Tared grinned, easily flicking his own stick around. 'If I'd wanted to break your ribs, they'd be smashed to smithereens by now. You need to let go of that cadence. It makes it far too easy to see when your next move is coming.'

I muttered a curse. 'Fine. Let's try again.'

'We said this would be the last one,' he said, raising an eyebrow.

I shrugged and gripped my stick more tightly – as long and as heavy as an average alf sword, but blunt and unlikely to accidentally decapitate my training partners. Not that I had ever gotten it near anyone's neck, of course, except perhaps my own whenever I managed a particularly poorly aimed swing.

The thought nearly made me curse again.

'Well, it wasn't good enough yet, was it?' I said defiantly.

He quirked that eyebrow up another fraction. 'I defined "good enough" as ten rounds for today's training. You did eleven. I think we can consider it a glaring success.'

It was even more annoying that he was being reasonable about it. 'But you would still have killed me if this had been an actual fight.'

'Of course,' he said dryly. 'Which is why I'm not sending you into any fights yet.'

Was he deliberately missing the point? His unhurried, unworried nonchalance only heightened my frustration, making me feel like swinging my stick at his head just to make him share some of the urgency buzzing in my veins. But of course my stick wouldn't make it farther than whatever lightning-fast defence manoeuvre he'd put in its path, and either way, I doubted he'd blink an eye even if I were to hit him square in the face.

'Tared ...' I averted my eyes, sucking in a deep breath. 'This is going too slow, isn't it?'

'I'd say you're going faster than the average human I've trained.'

'Yes, but that's not what this is about!' I burst out. *Will the girl be ready?* Members of the Alliance had been discussing me again last night, unaware of my ear pressed to the living room door – had been arguing for fast action again, for an attack I would never be able to pull off without Creon's help and advice. 'The average human isn't supposed to ... to ...'

To be available for whatever suicidal strategies the Council came up with, preferably tomorrow. Nothing I could tell Tared if I didn't want him to know about my clandestine sources of information, but ...

'Ah,' he said, raking a hand through his blond hair. 'You've been listening at the door?'

Oh damn it, then. 'What else do you expect me to do when people are making all sorts of plans for me and no one even tells me—'

'I didn't tell you,' he interrupted me, unfazed, 'because nothing is happening yet.'

'Because I'm too slow.'

He shrugged and turned to put his own stick away in one of the large chests along the walls of the training hall. Somehow the place was always suspiciously empty around this time, despite clear traces of use between my training sessions. I suspected he'd told the others to let me blunder in privacy, and right now, that didn't improve my mood in the slightest.

The girl wasn't ready. The girl was less and less ready with every day flying by, every day of murderous whispers and solitary magic practice and useless pleas before that gods-damned door.

'So I need to do better, yes?'

'If you say so,' he said, examining me with a small smile on his lips. 'Sorry, Emelin. In that case – how dare you not have grown ten pounds of muscle in the past week? And it's frankly humiliating you still haven't beaten a single age-old warrior in combat. Consider yourself an abject failure, and tomorrow's homework is to gain two centuries of experience overnight.' A grin. 'Was that what you had in mind?'

I stood there, clutching my stick in the middle of the empty training hall, and felt like an abject failure indeed. Six days had gone by since Creon started eating again, and I had not the faintest idea why he still wouldn't come out of that bloody room and talk to me. A couple of scouts had informed the Council yesterday that the Mother was summoning troops to the Crimson Court, strengthening her defences, preparing for war. I needed to hone my skills, needed to figure out how I would ever take down a mage with over a millennium of experience ...

And I couldn't even finish a single damn training sequence without letting my guard down.

So what did I have in mind?

I cursed and muttered, 'I suppose it doesn't sound too reasonable when you put it like that.'

'Stop agonising, then.' It was infuriating how easy he made it sound. 'You can't do more than you're doing. And keep in mind, as soon as we start mixing your fighting skills with magic, things will get interesting very quickly.'

I considered that. It sounded slightly more promising than waiting until I found myself on par with alf warriors who had been training for five centuries or longer.

'Could I beat you now if I used magic?'

He chuckled. 'No.'

'Bastard,' I said, unable to hold in another laugh. A challenge at least got my blood flowing a little faster than undeniable failure. 'Why not? It's pretty powerful magic.'

He picked up his sword from the bench where he'd left it during our training and easily buckled the sheath over his shoulder. 'I know, little brat. I've dealt with some pretty powerful mages in my life.'

It was easy to forget that when I hardly knew him outside of these casual, domestic contexts, just like it was hard to imagine Lyn as anything but the cheerful, overly considerate seven-year-old who dragged me around the Underground and shoved two new books into my hands every night. But I needed to remember that the Tared who joked around with me during training, who taught me card games in the evenings and slipped his glass of honey mead into my hands whenever Ylfreda wasn't looking, was only a single and rather deceptive side of him. The ease with which he handled that sword should be reason enough to know better.

Then again, I was fed up with myself and the world in general, and nettling him back at least brightened my mood. So I scoffed my brattiest scoff and said, 'You seem to forget I blinded the Mother a few days ago.'

'The Mother was unprepared,' he said, disappointingly unimpressed. 'And don't bother trying to surprise me. Your face is screaming murderous intent.'

Damn it. 'Try to stop me, then.'

'Ah. It's one of those days.' He threw a glance at the door, then turned back to me and gave me the grin of an older sibling momentarily shaking off his parental responsibilities. 'Don't tell Lyn I'm letting you do this.'

I laughed and dropped my left hand to the dark dress Ylfreda had lent me, firing a burst of red at him.

He had disappeared into thin air before the magic hit, and the beam of red slammed into the floor instead, drawing a deep furrow through the dark stone. I whirled around and found him mere feet behind me, his sword in his hand now. My next attack was nowhere near as measured as it should have been, a flash of panic as much as strategy, aimed at roughly his person rather than any more sensible target.

He didn't dodge.

Instead, his sword came up, a flash of silvery white, and caught my magic straight from the air.

I shrieked a warning, cowering reflexively against the shards of steel that would surely burst from the impact ... and then nothing happened. No violent explosions. Not even the slightest dent in the gleaming metal. My flash of red was gone, as if it had been swallowed whole by his blade, and he faded again before I could recover from the surprise.

An arm locked around my shoulders from behind. That damned sword followed next, settling against my throat with the flat side pressed against my artery.

I froze. 'Fuck.'

Tared chuckled behind me, not even slightly out of breath. 'Excellent work, Emelin.'

'You call that excellent?' I squeaked. Something about the sensation of cool metal against my throat made it hard to keep breathing or speak at full volume. 'I didn't even *scratch* you.'

'You found me after that first fade and aimed fast enough to attack me again,' he said, still not releasing me. 'Pretty impressive without training.'

It had taken him less than half a minute to defeat me. Nothing about that seemed even close to impressive to me – but at least the rush had taken the sharpest edge off my gloomy despair, and at least I had a few new questions to keep my mind distracted.

'But your sword ...' I tried to glance down at the weapon without cutting myself open. 'It didn't break.'

'No.'

'How?'

I felt him shrug. 'Make a guess.'

This was getting on my nerves. Much as it was my own bloody fault, I didn't look forward to spending the rest of this conversation worrying about the state of my windpipe. 'Would you mind releasing me first?'

'Depends,' he said dryly. 'We might as well make it a training exercise, now that we've gotten to this point anyway. How would you deal with this if I weren't your most trusted friend and all that?'

Friend. What a ridiculous moment for my heart to jump at that word – to realise no one had called me a friend since I'd left Ildhelm two years ago.

To set myself straight more than anything else, I clawed my right fingers into his sword hand and drew another spark of red through the hand I still had resting on my skirt.

Or at least, I tried to.

The magic always came to me effortlessly, a power I had to constrain rather than force. But now, with a blade against my throat and my life theoretically at stake, nothing happened.

Not even the weakest, most pathetic flicker of pink.

I blinked and tried again, more consciously now. Nothing. How did I even do this, normally? It was such an unthinking reflex, as natural as breathing and blinking, but now that I actually *tried* to pull the colour out ...

Nothing.

My pulse quickened, a sudden sense of panic washing over me. 'Tared, what did you *do?*'

'Not much.' His arm let go of me, but his sword remained in place; I didn't dare to pull away from it. 'Take your hand off your dress.'

I did. Only then did he pull back his blade, spinning me around to face him with a steady hand on my shoulder. His smile was a little too satisfied as he slid his sword back into its sheath and said, 'Alf steel.'

'Alf ... what?'

'It blocks fae magic.' A nod at my throat. 'Skin contact is enough to make wielding colour impossible. That myth about iron didn't come out of nowhere, you see – the humans of these days just got the metal wrong.'

I blinked at him, then at my right hand, and pulled an impulsive blast of blue from my dress. The colour sparked from my fingertips, bright and reassuring; the damaged floor grew shut at once, although the surface remained more uneven than it had been before our training.

'You could have *told* me that.'

He shrugged, clearly amused. 'I'm not above the occasional dramatic reveal.'

'So it turns out,' I said sourly. 'Good gods. Look, if we have this stuff, then why are the fae still ruling anything? Can't we arm the humans with alf steel and—'

'Lofty ideas,' he interrupted, sauntering back to the bench at the wall. 'The problem is alf steel is mined from the mountains in the north.'

'The north – on the continent.'

A wry grin. 'Yes.'

'You mean ... Oh, hell. You can't reach the mines anymore since the plague?'

He nodded, took a few sips from his leather water bottle, then handed it to me. 'We had somewhat of a hoard, of course, and there's some of it left scattered over the archipelago. But the supply is very much limited.'

'Well.' I groaned and took a sip as well. My throat was drier than I'd noticed. 'Glad we at least still have that sword of yours.'

'You sound positively overjoyed.'

I threw him a glare. He grinned and affectionately ruffled my hair, which mollified me slightly, although not enough to make me forget about the torturously slow progress of my training efforts.

Perhaps, I finally admitted, my sword fighting wasn't the problem. Perhaps it was just another failure to underline that greatest disaster of all: the undeniable fact that my possibly former lover was currently suffering the hate of his own dubious allies and didn't even want to see me, let alone teach me the magic I desperately needed.

Tared took the bottle from my hands and narrowed his eyes. 'You're still worried.'

'Are you a demon too, now?' I grumbled.

'Mere immortals have eyes too, brat.' He fell down on the bench and crossed his legs. 'More doubts on your progress? Or is it still about Creon?'

'*Still* about Creon? He's been locking himself in a room for over a week!'

Tared seemed genuinely surprised by that perspective. 'Ylfreda said he's eating again.'

'Is that how alf medicine works?' I said sharply. 'All is well as long as someone's eating?'

'Not inaccurate,' he admitted with a small grin. 'Sorry, Emelin. Keep in mind he didn't talk for months the first time he joined us either, so this is quite what I expected. I've never known him to be a great conversationalist, even before ...' He hesitated, then sighed and slumped back against the wall. 'Never mind. You still don't want us to talk about that, I presume.'

As miserable as I felt, that brought a small smile to my lips. They had been painfully respectful of my request not to tell me more about their history with Creon. 'Thanks.'

'You're very welcome,' he said. 'Always happy to assist when people are determined to make life harder for themselves.'

'*I'm* not making anything harder! If those bastards around our front door could just stop soaking the entire place with their hate, that would be—'

'The Underground as a whole hardly likes Creon any better.' His smile had dulled. 'And no, don't ask me to do something about it. I have no authority to send the fools away as long as they're not strutting into my living room.'

'They're openly planning murder!'

'They're *talking* about murder.' He grinned at me. 'Which is a traditional Alvish pastime. Doesn't mean they'll actually do anything.'

I scoffed. 'And if they do?'

'We'll see,' he said, shrugging that point off with maddening calm. 'Until there's more than boasting and glowering to warn us, I'm not going to pick a fight with the other houses for the minor difference it will make if they move two streets away. If Creon wants to get rid of the hate ...' He groaned. 'Coming out of that room and actually doing something useful would be a better start.'

'Thanks,' I said ironically. 'How silly of me not to think of that. Perhaps I should start asking him to come out.'

Tared pulled up an eyebrow, unimpressed. 'I'm not telling you what to do. Just sharing the alf perspective, but you know well enough I'm hardly an expert on fae princes.'

I suppressed the urge to slam a few more holes into the floor. I'd thought myself an expert on fae princes once, and then this one decided to avoid me for reasons I still couldn't figure out – even though he had to know I wanted him, even though Anaxia had assured me there was no way he'd suddenly gotten sick of me.

Restraining myself, I muttered, 'The expert would be Lyn, wouldn't it?'

There was an unusual, although not unexpected, curtness to his voice as he closed his eyes and said, 'Yes.'

'If I asked her to make an attempt to get him out, would she do it?'

'No.'

Too terse; there had to be more to that answer. 'Did you ask her not to try?'

'She suggested she wouldn't try,' he said slowly, looking back up at me, 'and I gladly accepted the suggestion.'

I examined him for a moment. He didn't shy away from my gaze, lounging on that bench with such casual calm ... and yet ...

It had only been a little over a week since he'd panicked, honestly and genuinely panicked, at the thought of bringing Creon into the Underground. And somehow Lyn had talked him into acceptance. Had this promise been part of the deal?

I settled on the bench beside him and rested the back of my head against the wall. The cold of the stone was a welcome relief against my sweaty shoulders.

'Tared?'

'Hmm?'

'What *is* the thing between Lyn and you, exactly?'

For a moment the hall was entirely quiet, in that overwhelming, ominous way only the Underground could be quiet. Then he groaned, sat up straighter, and said, 'You're not the only person who insists on making life complicated for themselves.'

I blinked. 'That's not an answer.'

'I'm well aware.' He held out his hand to me. 'Coming to the library?'

I opened my mouth to object, then caught his look and faltered. There was no challenge in his grey eyes this time, no invitation to the usual playful back-and-forth. Just cold, earnest hurt, and a flicker of something ruthless, something unbendable and unbreakable as alf steel, mirroring that edge of stone I'd heard sneaking into his voice a handful of times.

There were not many lines I couldn't cross with Tared, these first days in the Underground had taught me. Alf humour came hard and fast and sharp, and his patience ran deep; I had little need for diplomacy around him. But for all my testing and challenging, for all my juvenile grumbles and complaints, it had never been my intention to actually hurt or provoke him – and that look, that shimmer of old agony, told me this was a topic where anger and pain lay dangerously close to the surface.

I retreated. There were better ways to fight this battle.

'Fine. Let's go to the library.'

He smiled, the coldness gone ... but even as he faded us home for clean clothes and then into the library for Lyn's language lessons, I could tell by his unusual quietness that he was brooding on something.

Lyn had a private study above the Wanderer's Wing, a small room furnished with a desk, two comfortable velvet couches, and several bookcases making brave attempts not to collapse under the weight of the collected literature on the shelves. It was in that room that she worked on her own research, which revolved around a concept she called "involuntary magic" and which, on this particular morning, apparently required strings of complex calculations on fae wing spans.

'The gravity issue again?' Tared said as he dropped me off, and she looked up from her sketches and formulas with a pained sigh, rubbing several wild red curls from her eyes.

'It just doesn't make *sense*. I don't know why Stasia keeps arguing it's a matter of muscle power when ... Anyway, morning, Emelin.' She sent me a bright smile. 'Miraculously survived Tared for another few hours, I see?'

He casually threw a pencil at her. She dodged it, stuck out her tongue at him, and jumped up from her chair at the desk. All the usual light-hearted taunting ... but her eyes rested on him for a fraction longer than I expected, and I knew she, too, noticed the way his smile slid off his face too quickly.

She turned to me without hesitation, though. 'I found a text on the Mother's Conquest that should be relatively easy to read, and it has some information on the construction of the courts. I think you asked about that last week?'

I had asked about a hundred things last week, but this was probably a topic that had come up once or twice. 'Sounds wonderful.'

She chuckled. 'Liar.'

'Sounds better than most texts in Faerie,' I corrected myself as I fell onto our usual couch at the window overlooking the fields. She was an excellent teacher, which made this a lot easier than my attempts to figure the language out by myself – but it would likely never be one of my favourites.

Most days, Tared left us alone with our discussions on grammar and vocabulary. Today he sat down on the other couch, however, and mindlessly thumbed through some of Lyn's recent reads while we discussed the text on the Conquest. It was a fairly readable summary, and it contained numerous verbs with amusingly specific meanings such as "to burn a city down to the ground", "to break a dam with the explicit intention of flooding a settlement", and "to steal a village's goats but not its sheep".

But it was hard to stay focused when Lyn's eyes kept flashing to Tared's figure on the other couch, and I was almost relieved when she finally said, 'Would you mind handling the next sentence on your own, Emelin?'

'Oh, no,' I said faintly. 'That's fine. I'll just ...' I waved at the parchment, pretending not to notice Tared's sharp eyes on me. 'I'll see what I can make sense of and ask you about the rest.'

'Excellent.' She slid from the couch, careful not to step on the small pile of parchment rolls that lay on the floor, and exchanged a single look with Tared. 'A word?'

He nodded, smiled at me, and followed her into the next room.

I tried to ignore their soft voices just behind the door; eavesdropping was impolite, after all, and they were being so damn kind to me that it would be the height of ungratefulness to come barging into their personal business. But browsing through Faerie dictionaries was a poor distraction strategy, and I couldn't help catching shreds of words as they drifted into the room.

And my name.

Tared was saying my name.

I flew to my feet, attempts at politeness forgotten at once. It was hardly their personal business if they were talking about me. And if they were discussing me in relation to Creon, I *certainly* wanted to know their opinions.

Their conversation was clearly audible as I tiptoed closer. They were speaking in Alvish, but my education in the language of the White City had been solid; after a week and a half in an alf household, my grasp on this dialect was strong enough to understand most of the words.

'... suppose that was a matter of time,' Lyn said, sounding tired. 'Honestly, I'm pleasantly surprised she asked you and not ... well, anyone else.'

'Could hardly give her a decent answer, though.'

'Why? I'd rather have you tell her the basics than wait for Edored to give her his version of events, or—'

'I'm not saying I don't *want* to give her a decent answer,' Tared interrupted, a fraction louder now. I almost jumped back from my spot near the door. 'It's just ... how are we supposed to tell her a single thing about this mess if she doesn't want to hear about Creon?'

I stiffened.

On the other side of the door, Lyn was silent for a moment, too.

Creon.

'Right,' Lyn said, her voice muffled as if she was rubbing her face. 'I see how that complicates the matter.'

A joyless laugh from Tared. 'Yes. He does have a habit of complicating matters, doesn't he?'

Oh.

Fuck.

I shrunk away from the door, my heartbeat so loud in my own ears I feared they would hear it and come to check I wasn't dying.

Complicating matters. A habit of it ... which meant ...

And at once, I understood. *Everything.*

CHAPTER 7

CREON'S DOOR WAS STILL locked when I finally reached the family home, out of breath from my sprint through the Underground, knees shaking from the stairs I'd climbed and descended at breakneck speed. I pounded my fist against the wood once, waited with admirable patience for a grand total of one and a half heartbeats, then gave in to the restless fury in my veins and drew a good splash of red from Ylfreda's borrowed dress.

The door burst to splinters.

Strong magic, strong father; for once the thought of my overenthusiastic powers didn't register as I shrugged the wood dust off my dress and stepped through the gaping hole where the door had been.

Nothing in the room had moved since I'd last left it. The tea mug still stood beside my armchair, Ylfreda's herbs still lay on the bedside table. Only the unconscious body on the bed was gone; my eyes found nothing but meticulously made blankets as I came to a panting halt inside the wide circle of wood fragments.

Something moved at the edge of my sight, and I snapped around.

Creon sat a few feet away from the ruined door, closest to the spot where I'd waited so many hours for him. Something about his posture suggested he'd spent days in that same place – wings wilting, head sagging powerlessly against the smooth wall behind his back. But his eyes were wide open, staring back at me with unmoving, unblinking blankness, as if he'd barely noticed the explosion that shattered his bedroom door a moment ago.

Watching me numbly, the way he had watched me after he killed himself seven times over in Rhudak.

There was too much anger in me to leave room for that paralysing feel of worry. Anger and this newfound, razor-sharp clarity, insight upon insight unfolding inside me so fast it left me dizzy.

There was nothing paralysing about it. It felt like fire. It felt like *magic*.

'Was it Tared?' I said.

Creon didn't move, empty eyes drinking in my presence like parched earth at the first rain.

'Don't you dare ignore me.' My voice could have cut steel. I knew what I was doing, finally, knew what I wanted, and those convoluted twists of his hate-soaked mind weren't going to stop me. 'Who told you that? That no one in his right mind would fall in love with demon brood? Tared? One of the other alves? Edored?'

He shook his head, a motion too minimal to shift his eyes away from me.

'Who *was* it, Creon?'

His fingers twitched in his lap. Stiffened, twitched again. Then spelled, with staggering, uneasy motions, *Tared*.

The air left my lungs so fast it was a miracle I didn't faint on the spot. 'Because of Lyn.'

Creon froze again.

'Because you fell in love with her.' It all made sense – so much sense I no longer understood how I could ever have missed it. 'Because you sat in that cell for months and she talked to you and she was the only living soul you had left to cling to. Of *course* you fell in love with her. Is that why you changed sides at first? Not out of some grand concern for ethics and morality, but because of her?'

A shudder ran through him, violent like a fever twitch.

'Even your *mother* knew.' My brain was turning inside out, going over every memory, every word, every glance, finding more and more pieces of the puzzle to put into place. 'What was it she said, that night you introduced me to her? *Remember what happened last time some girl amused you a little too much?* That's what happened, isn't it – you betrayed the empire?'

I fell silent, still out of breath. He remained frozen, staring at me as I stared at him – watching, perhaps, whatever feelings had my heart pounding so violently in my throat, had my hands clenching at my sides so fiercely.

Then, abruptly, he moved.

A flash of blue lit up the room, faster than I could blink, and at once the splinters were gone from the floor at my feet. I whirled around and found the door whole again, not a trace of violence left in the mahogany wood.

A rustle of movement broke the silence behind me, and I snapped back to find Creon leaning towards me now, wings tightening behind his shoulders. His hand came up slowly, as if he hardly dared to speak.

Why are you here?

'Why *am* I …' I faltered, breath quickening. 'Oh, for fuck's sake. I'm here because I need you to stop this bloody melodrama, Creon. I need you to scrape that clever brain of yours together and help me deal with a bunch of allies who are trying to kill us. I *miss* you. Should I spell out in any more detail what the words "I want to talk with you" are supposed to—'

I mean … His fingers stiffened again. *If you know …*

I stared at him.

About Lyn, he bleakly added.

Another burst of clarity barrelled through me.

'That is why you were avoiding me? Because you didn't want to tell me you were turned down by someone else a gods-damned *century* ago?' I let out a baffled laugh. 'What in hell did you think I would do – storm off in dramatic fashion and declare you an adulterer and a heartless monster for daring to have lived a life before I was even born?'

The flicker of self-consciousness in his eyes told me I wasn't that far off.

'For the love of the bloody gods, Creon, you *are* a horribly dramatic person.'

Didn't want to give you another reason to hate me. The motions came fast now, his eyes wide and panicked, his fingers desperate to explain. *You were so fast to assume the worst last time, you—*

'Not because I was happy with an excuse to hate you!'

But—

'Creon, listen to me!' I sucked in a breath, willing my voice not to crack, willing my tears not to well. 'I was in shock. I didn't understand why you never told me about your powers. I drew my conclusions too fast. But then I spent the entire day hoping you'd come back, hoping you'd somehow convince me you never manipulated me. And then you didn't, and I couldn't think of any reason why other than a guilty conscience. You understood that at the court, when you wrote me that letter. Can't you understand it again?'

His eyes went empty at the mention of the court – as if the person he'd been at the pavilion, the person who'd set those words to parchment, didn't even exist in his mind anymore.

Numbly, he signed, *You'd be right to hate me.*

I stared at him, lost for words.

The darkness in his eyes ... I'd seen it before, a whirlpool of power and death, of memories no one should ever be forced to carry. But it had always been a darkness that spread outwards, a pain that might one day flood the world and drown every soul in it. Now, in this dusky, buried room, it had turned inwards – a festering wound poisoning him from the inside out, eating him alive.

Right to hate me.

Surrounded by alves, their loathing pressing on his shoulders every minute of the day, it was easy to assume that I, too, would turn against him at the slightest inconvenience. Not because I was an opportunistic turncoat, but because I was reasonable, and he was a monster.

Something sank in my chest, the sizzling outburst of my anger melting into something entirely different.

'Stop listening to them.'

He stared up at me, lips a hard line of doubt, thoughts awhirl behind his eyes. Unable to understand why I was still standing here, why I was still trying, why I would care enough to try.

'Creon.' His name felt like a prayer on my lips. Was it even possible to pull him out of this? 'I don't hate you. You *know* I don't. Shut out the rest of this place, shut out those arseholes outside, and focus on how I feel about you. Can you do that?'

You …

He faltered, his fingers frozen halfway through that single gesture. The vulnerability of him was jarring, almost incomprehensible. He still *looked* the part of the world's most dangerous mage, the Mother's dark god of death and destruction, every perfectly defined muscle of him honed to maim and kill … And yet here he sat, tense and defenceless on the floor of a stranger's room, losing his words at the sight of me.

'Creon.'

He flinched. *You're angry.*

'Yes, of course I am! But not because you're half demon or because you committed the horrible crime of having loved someone else in your life!' I bit out a laugh. 'I'm pissed you're still underestimating me and avoiding confrontations instead of *talking* to me when you're in trouble. Which is good news for you, because while you're stuck with those powers, you can perfectly easily stop being a coward and fix this mess. Unless you actually don't give a damn about me and—'

He shot to his feet so swiftly I flinched, his limbs and wings moving in a single burst of perfect, purposeful harmony. Towering over me even from six feet away, there was nothing pitiable left about him, about the furious snaps of his fingers. *Never say that again.*

My knees were going to give in – relief or frustration, I couldn't tell. 'Then why aren't you bloody *trying*?'

I'm nothing but trouble. I'm nothing but hurt. There it was again, that starless night in his eyes, the self-loathing seeping out from the very marrow of his bones. *You shouldn't be wasting your time on—*

'Didn't I tell you to stop listening to the rest of the Underground?' I said sharply.

His lip curled up. *I betrayed every single one of them, do you realise that? Didn't fight at the Last Battle, didn't do a damn thing to save this world until it was far too late. You shouldn't forgive me for that reason alone.*

I narrowed my eyes. 'Did you stay away because of Tared?'

Yes. No. His lips parted a fraction, then pressed to a thin line. *Partly.*

'The other part was Lyn?'

For a moment too long, he stared at me, wings taut and face tight, the look of a male caught between fighting and fleeing. Then he whipped around, strode to the bed on the other side of the room, and settled himself on the edge with all his usual catlike grace.

Every fibre of me itched to follow him, but I didn't dare to – was afraid that one wrong bet, one rash motion would snap this thread I'd spun between him and the world of the living. I stayed where I stood, two steps away from the door, watching him as he drew in a deep breath and gestured, *What do you want to know?*

'They captured you.'

Yes. He didn't look at me, the movements of his fingers short, curt gestures. *Few months before the end of the War. They attacked the Mother, me, some others. I managed to get her to safety. Not myself. Last thing I heard was her command to leave me there.* His fingers paused; then, slowly, he added, *Served my purpose.*

'Those were her words?'

He nodded, closing his eyes.

I folded my arms, stepping back to rest my back against the door. 'The bitch.'

A small grin flickered around his lips – just an eyeblink, but I clung to it nonetheless.

I thought I was dead, he added, still slower than usual. *Then woke up in chains. Couldn't make sense of that. Couldn't make sense of Lyn asking*

questions without torturing me. Couldn't make sense of – again that pause
– anything.

Two centuries of life as the Mother's beloved prince, faekind's most
celebrated warrior – and when it had come crumbling down, his enemies were the ones showing mercy. I didn't have to be a demon to feel
the utter incomprehension.

'So you changed sides.'

He nodded.

'And they eventually let you out of that cell.'

Another nod.

'And then Tared told you that you were an unlovable monster?'

Not ... A shadow slid over his face. *Not immediately. Things were just
tense. Think Lyn convinced him to keep the peace while we had bigger things
to worry about. Then the night before the battle ...* He sat up straighter
but averted his eyes, his gestures rushed and restless. *We collided. I said
stupid things. He said stupid things. Then he threw that in my face – that I
shouldn't hope to ever be more than a sympathy project to her, because ... well.*

'No one in his right mind ... and so on.'

He nodded, the motion strained. I swallowed down the bitter taste of
betrayal at the thought of Tared – a friend, I'd believed ten minutes ago,
and now?

I'd have to think about that later. I'd have to think about *everything*
later.

'And then you didn't even kill him?'

No. His shoulders tensed. *I asked her.*

'Asked her what – if you were just a sympathy project?'

He nodded again.

'But you *knew*, didn't you?' My voice cracked. 'You're half demon. You
had to realise that whatever she felt for you, it wasn't ...'

Em ... It looked too meaningful, the shape of those two letters on his
fingers. *How was I supposed to know what love felt like?*

I stared at him, my stomach not so much turning as numbing.

It's like learning a new language. He still didn't look my way. *At first, all
sounds seem alike. Takes a few years until you fully understand the difference,
and then you no longer understand how you ever confused them. I'd never*

dealt with honest, selfless affection before. It all felt the same to me at the time – friends, family, lovers.

'So she had to very sympathetically tell you there was a difference ...'

And I threw a fit.

'You mean ... you didn't fight.'

No. Just wallowed in self-pity until I realised we were losing. Now he finally met my gaze, his eyes brimming with age-old agony – a hundred and thirty years of regret. His hands didn't falter. *They could have won, Em. I could have ...*

Changed the course of history. He didn't finish the sentence, and I didn't have the heart to do it for him. The tributes, the murders, the starving children ... Had that battle not been lost, how would the world have looked today?

Unforgivable, indeed, but then again ...

Demon brood.

That wasn't a slap in the face. It was a knife stab in the gut with an extra twist of the blade, ice-cold, deliberate cruelty aiming for the sorest spots. Wallowing in self-pity, he might call it, but from what Lyn had told me that day in Faewood ... he'd fallen apart at the Mother's betrayal. Stitched himself back together to leave his blood-drenched past behind – for Lyn, perhaps, but not for her only, if he hadn't returned to the Mother's side when she rejected him. And then for all his attempts to become someone better, someone *good,* Tared had kicked him down for that one, most loathed part of him. That one part he couldn't possibly get rid of.

I didn't think it was self-pity that had left him incapable of fighting on that fateful day. He might have been on the brink of ending himself, convinced the world would be better for his absence after all.

And yet, when he'd realised the battle had been lost ...

He hadn't.

'So then you tried to kill her,' I said quietly. 'The Mother.'

He blinked – having expected, it seemed, a long and winding monologue on how he was indeed the most revolting coward to ever have seen the light of day. *Yes.*

'And that didn't work?'

She was suspicious about the lack of carnage I left behind at my alleged escape and had me put in alf steel before she saw me. I didn't dare fight back. Would give me away. His hands twitched. *Then it was dying or allowing her to bind me.*

'Oh, gods.'

I didn't expect it would take this long. If I'd known ...

Again he didn't finish his sentence. Those few words said enough – a hundred and thirty years of playing her murderer, of killing himself time and time again. Had he known ...

Death would have been the sensible choice.

'But you kept going,' I whispered. 'All those years.'

After a decade, it seemed like such a waste of effort to end it. I kept thinking, what if I find a way next week? What if I give up just before the victory? So I kept pushing myself for one more year, one more decade, because someday it would have to end. And then after all that time ... He gave me a helpless, powerless shrug. *You.*

I tried to swallow. My mouth was dry as ash. *Me.* That day in the garden, the stunned, blank look in his eyes – an end to thirteen decades of torture, and I'd had not the faintest idea.

'Imagine torturing yourself to death for more than a century,' I said, my voice too hoarse, 'and then getting some pesky little half fae who can't even keep her mouth shut.'

And finally a true smile built on his face – not yet laughter, but a prelude to laughter, a cautious lightness that washed over his features and curled the corners of his lips into something that made my insides swim and wobble. *I'll admit you were not what I imagined.*

'No.' My chuckle came over my lips too brusquely, too close to a sob of relief. 'Neither were you. Didn't expect you to fall for me with a single glance into my pretty ditchwater-coloured eyes, if I'm honest.'

His smile broke into an incredulous grin. *Overestimating your own charms. It took at least two glances.*

I snorted. 'Bastard.'

I know. He rubbed his eyes, the amusement dwindling. *Em, you shouldn't be here. You shouldn't still feel this way about me. You're too sensible to—*

'Oh, stop doing that!' A flare of frustration burned through me; on the bed, Creon winced. 'I've been saving your life for weeks, for hell's sake! Don't you dare go back to treating me like a child after—'

How am I supposed to stop? he interrupted, signs growing sharper with every word. *I've never wanted anyone to be happy the way I want you to be, and you're telling me to let you walk straight into the arms of some murderer with a monster's heart?*

'Yes, because I can think for myself, you self-castigating idiot!' I staggered half a step forward, away from the safe support of the door behind my back. Who was I fighting now? Him or the hate of others? 'Because you're supposed to respect my wishes, and if my wishes are to throw myself into some murderer's arms, then who the hell are you to think you know better?'

His lip curled up. *So what else would you have me do, then?*

'Focus on what you want?' I suggested sharply.

I want you to be safe.

'Don't be obtuse. You know that's not what I mean.' I took another step forward, and he tensed, as if my very nearness might be enough to break him. 'You'd die a torturous death to keep me safe, but don't pretend that would make you happy. What do you *want*?'

He hesitated, his dark eyes trailing over me – that focused predator's gaze, wild and so very restrained at once. *Nothing I should have.*

'Not what I asked.'

Stop asking me the damn question, then.

I bit out a laugh. 'No. What should I do to make you talk – spend another two weeks shouting at your door? Cry and whine? I don't care, Creon; I'll do it anyway, so if you want to spare me the effort, you might as well just—'

In a flash of slamming wing and straining muscle, he lunged forward, an inhuman reflex so fast I didn't see him coming until his hands were already around my shoulders. My body obeyed instinctively, stumbling backwards at his unspoken command. Two uneven steps and I bumped into the wall, caught between cold stone and his tall body, his fingers digging so hard into my skin they might leave bruises. Suddenly his face was mere inches away from mine, the lines and shadows of his features contorted into a grimace of crumbling restraint.

Only then did I gasp, hopelessly late. 'Creon ...'

One scarred hand released me, hovering between us, his signs sharp and rushed. *Why do you have to push me like this?*

'Has it occurred to you I might care about your happiness?' I forced out. I couldn't think with his scent rolling over me, that sweet, woody fragrance of honey and hazelnut. Couldn't get my thoughts to focus on anything but the nearness of his lips, the memory of their softness, their warmth, their hunger. 'That I need you to get what you want as much as you—'

I. Want. You. Measured, razor-sharp signs. His jaw twitched – as if it took all he had not to bury his teeth into me. *Is that what you want to hear, then? All this time. All these weeks. You have not the faintest idea how much it cost me to stay away from you – how even when you hated me ...* He drew in a slow, shuddering breath. *You hated me like a person. Not like a monster. It's so gods-damned easy to get drunk on you, Em – on the way you feel about me. As if maybe I'm a soul worth saving after all.*

I clenched my fists so hard it hurt – all I could do not to bury both my hands in his hair and yank him into a kiss. 'So why won't you take what you want?'

He closed his eyes. *Don't. Please.*

'You know I want you. You can *feel* I want you. What's stopping you from—'

I don't want you to want me against your better judgement. Or against my own. His throat bobbed. *You make a mess of me, do you understand that? I'm constantly torn between needing you with me and needing to protect you from myself, between—*

'You're not a threat to me.'

There's a thousand different ways I could hurt you. His fingers were all but shouting now, brusque, hurried gestures. *I'm frightened I'll lose control of myself, frightened I'll disappoint you, frightened you'll wake up one day and realise I'm not worth any of these feelings you've wasted on my sorry person—*

'That's not you talking,' I snapped. 'That's an Underground full of people who hate you getting into your head, telling you you're not worth the slightest bit of affection.'

And what if they're right?

I scoffed. 'What if they're wrong?'

He averted his face, chest rising and sinking too fast, wings quivering restlessly against his back.

'Creon ...'

You need to understand there's nothing gentle about me, he interrupted, the signs so urgent now I could barely read them. *Nothing tender, nothing kind. Do not mistake me for something moral just because I'm trying to keep the monster down for you. You're courting darkness, and I'm so very frightened of eclipsing your light—*

'Did I not make it clear enough,' I said sharply, 'how much I want the monster, Creon?'

He stiffened.

'You could understand that at the court. Without hundreds of people rubbing their hate into your thoughts.' I leaned over as far as his hand on my shoulder allowed me to. The last empty inch between our lips became a battlefield, feral lust mingling with desperate constraint. 'I've known who you were from the start. If I'd wanted sweet and loving, I would never have lost my mind over you.'

He didn't move away but closed his eyes, as if the mere sight of me was too much for his heart to handle. His fingers digging into my right shoulder tensed and un-tensed. Uncontrollable twitches, conflicting instincts tearing at his self-control – have me or protect me.

Hell. Why was this even a question?

'Stop making this so hard for yourself,' I whispered, raising my hand to his face. 'Forget about monsters. Focus on me.'

He sucked in a frantic breath, squeezing his eyes shut as I trailed my fingertip over his face, along his scarred eyebrow, over his high cheekbone, all the way to the lips he'd pressed into a thin, barely restrained line. His body was tight as a coil against me, every muscle and tendon fighting for control, fighting for sanity.

All that inhuman strength, all that boundless power ... Warmth flared in my lower belly, and Creon shuddered, his hand on my shoulder an iron vice now.

Oh.

He felt that, too, of course.

Oh.

A tingle of dangerous, wicked triumph ran through me – that thrill of terrible ideas and irresistible power. Watching him closely, I drew my finger down over his chin, his vulnerable throat, his collarbone, studying the way his long lashes fluttered against his cheeks with every jolt of his muscles. So close to the edge. So close to breaking. If I could give him just that last little nudge ...

A laugh rose in me. Creon's eyes flew open, narrowing warily at my face.

Em, his lips said.

Was it the sight of my name or his fraying self-control that made my heart flutter so violently in my chest? Euphoria burned through me like a burst of powerful magic, the certainty of a nearing victory.

Dropping my hand, I let my head fall back against the wall and repeated, 'Focus on me.'

Wait. With a jerky movement, he grabbed my other shoulder too, as if any touch would constrain the stirrings of my body. His lips said, *You*
...

I let my memories take over.

His hands on my body ...

I remembered their teasing over my hips, my thighs. Remembered the way those same strong fingers had kneaded my breasts with such merciless tenderness, thumbs circling my nipples until they screamed for his touch. Remembered how those fingers had found their way between my legs, how they had spread me open and filled me deep ...

Hot, heady arousal flared below my navel, and I allowed it to wash over me, allowed myself to sink into it like I would lower myself into a steaming bath.

Creon's eyes flickered alarmingly.

'Believe me yet?' My voice came out rough and broke into a near-moan as his hands gripped me even tighter. 'Or do I need to be more convincing?'

Em. Tight lips, gritted teeth. Sweet, savage loss of control. Last time I'd seen him like that, holding on to his self-restraint with the last shreds of his willpower, he'd fucked me into oblivion a minute later – and that thought alone was enough to let the memory flow through me, the overwhelming sensation of his broad tip stretching me wide, his rock-hard cock slamming into me ...

The fire burning in my lower belly turned liquid, a molten ache sliding down, down, down. Creon gulped in a lungful of air, pressing me back against the wall, holding my gaze with dazed, spellbound eyes. Enough sensation to drown out even the lingering hate. Enough to forget what he'd been afraid of. The sound of that gasp, the sight of his quivering wings and his straining shoulders, was enough to make my body clench tight around the emptiness at my core where I wanted him, *needed* him ...

I saw the restraint snap in his eyes.

With a soundless snarl, he yanked me into his arms, dragged me to the bed, threw me facedown onto the blankets. I hardly had time to lift my head from the soft wool before he was upon me, pinning my arms to my back – trapping me against the mattress with a single hand around both my wrists no matter how hard I thrashed and writhed in his hold. My fight for freedom was entirely futile. He had me caught and contained, utterly at his mercy, as he yanked up my skirt with his free hand and slid a single demanding finger below my underwear.

Every muscle in my body abruptly gave in.

I wilted in his hold, my cheek pressed into the tickling wool of the quilt, and surrendered myself to that raw, purposeful touch. His fingertip drew a long, lazy slide over my slippery flesh, leaving my body burning and clenching in its wake ...

And vanished again.

I let out a hollow moan of disappointment. Creon breathed out hard above me – half-laugh, half-groan – and ran his fingers over the inside of my thigh, delicate, feathery caresses, far too gentle for the abandon

I needed. I tried to shift, tried to move closer, anything to get his hands back to those hankering places between my legs. It was no use. The brushes of his fingers only turned more careful, more unfulfilling, the harder I wrestled. *Your just reward*, they seemed to tell me as they trailed their excruciating circles over my skin. *This is what you get for challenging the Silent Death himself.*

'Creon, *please*—'

He flicked a finger over my drenched lips once – a single, almost indifferent touch – then moved his attention back to the vulnerable insides of my thighs. Creeping just a little higher, inch by inch by inch, closer and closer to where I needed him and yet somehow never close enough.

'Don't tell me this is all you want.' Whispering was an effort. There seemed to be no air left in my lungs no matter how deep I tried to breathe. 'Don't tell me you're happy torturing me if you could be fucking me senseless instead.'

He didn't release me to answer; his fingers on my thigh didn't falter. The burning, yearning ache building at my core could have set the blankets on fire – every single nerve of me so excruciatingly aware of his absence, so excruciatingly alert to each twitch of his fingers, that even the shifting linen of my underwear almost drove me to release. I gave up on escaping. Gave up on persuading. Closed my eyes and delivered myself to his torment with a sob of surrender.

As if that was all he'd waited for, his fingers returned between my legs.

There was no mercy to his touches now, no patience. His thumb rushed along my slippery lips and flicked over the bundle of nerves in between so roughly I saw stars; every next stroke sent another bolt of lightning into the very heart of me, the sensation dancing on that razor-thin edge between pleasure and pain. Agonizing tension rose in me as he held me down and worked me, a looming eruption swelling through me like the rising tide ...

I was going to break. I was going to shatter into a thousand little pieces and sew myself back together for just another heartbeat of this insufferable bliss.

And just when ecstasy was about to turn into agony, just when I opened my mouth to *beg* him for mercy, he pinched that most sensitive spot between thumb and forefinger and sent me spiralling into oblivion.

Thank the gods he had repaired that door, or my moans might have reached into every alf household in Orin's quarter.

My release swept my mind clean of every rational thought, every festering fear; I was nothing but sizzling power under his hands, defeated and yet entirely victorious. Perhaps it lasted a single heartbeat. Perhaps it lasted three hours. I found myself in Creon's arms when the ripples of pleasure finally faded, giddy with triumph and drunk with desire, moaning quietly with every brush of his fingers through my hair.

'You ...' I managed, and then words failed me again. 'You ...'

He held me tight against his chest as his hand vanished from my scalp and hovered before my face. *Consider that your reward for saving my life.*

'Oh, gods.' A lightheaded laugh escaped me. 'Let me know if you're ever in need of saving again.'

He breathed a chuckle and tugged my dress over my hips, stripping it off me with quick, practised motions. My underwear followed it onto the floor. Only then, as he gently lowered my naked body into the blankets, did he allow me to meet his gaze again, his eyes hooking onto mine with dark, insatiable intensity.

Consumed by you, Anaxia had said, and he looked like a male consumed indeed – like I was a wildfire raging inside him, reducing all but my name on his heart to ashes.

Heat pulsed in my veins as if it had never been gone, my body demanding more of this, more of him. His eyes narrowed dangerously as he studied me, the gleam in his gaze a little too knowing.

Oh.

He'd *known* exactly how far he could take me, how to torment me without driving me over the edge, and when to release me.

I couldn't keep down another breathless laugh as I let my gaze trail over his fingers, the inked skin still glistening with my pleasure. 'I think I might end up liking these powers of yours.'

His smile turned sharper, almost predatory. Keeping his eyes on me, he quickly unbuttoned his shirt and pulled it off his torso and wings, revealing the chiselled planes of his chest, the slender muscle of his shoulders, and his ink-scarred forearms – watching me as I watched him, feeling every rush of admiration, every thrill of eager anticipation that ran through me. By the time he lowered his hands to the band of his trousers, I was trembling, so very ready and yet not even close to prepared for the full, merciless beauty of him.

I gasped when his cock finally broke free, a ruthless weapon of the smoothest, silkiest bronze. Perhaps I shouldn't have. The grin that curled around his lips as he disposed of his trousers and leaned over me was a grin of merciless victory, shimmering with that familiar arrogance of the invincible prince I'd known.

Enjoying what you see?

I huffed a laugh. 'All show and no substance until the contrary is proved, Your Highness.'

He lowered himself between my thighs, supporting himself with one hand beside my shoulder, and rubbed his tip over my drenched sex. I bit my lip to keep a next gasp down. Somehow even my feverish dreams had underestimated the sheer size of him, the delicious pressure of his girth as he positioned himself against my entrance ...

And waited.

I whimpered despite myself. A shudder ran through his wings as he pressed a single, feathery kiss to my forehead and slowly sank into me – just the first inch. Just the first two. Enough to make my body stretch and strain around him, nerves drowning me in the overwhelming sensation of *fullness.*

He paused again. Came up a fraction, lifted his hand to his chest with a devilish twinkle in his eyes, and signed, *Enough substance for you?*

'Bastard,' I managed, wrapping my legs around his hips to pull him closer, deeper. He didn't move the slightest fraction – an unmovable rock of solid muscle and velvet wings. 'What do you want me to say? That I'd probably prefer you to a cactus? That—'

He pinched my nipple between thumb and forefinger, a wordless reprimand firing another burning sting of need through every fibre of me. I clenched all the way to the tips of my toes with a cry of frustration, his cock a sizzling brand inside me. Again his wings shivered with the restraint it cost him to stay still. And yet ... no movement.

'Fine!' I groaned, too far gone to fight now. 'You're utterly gorgeous, if you want to know! And stupidly irresistible! And insufferable, too! Is this—' Another gasp escaped me as he tweaked my other nipple, then leaned over and flicked his tongue over it. Silk strands of dark hair brushed my breast, my throat. I let out a desperate laugh and managed, 'Is this what I get for saving your life, then?'

With a chuckle, he looked up, watching me closely as he slid a fraction deeper. His free hand brushed over my hip, my side, before he raised it between us and signed, *You got your reward for saving my life. This ...*

He paused, trailing his eyes over our entwined bodies, my limbs wrapped around him – pale gold meeting deep bronze, soft curves meeting hard muscle. When he met my gaze again, something in the night of his eyes had turned impossibly gentler.

This is for saving my sanity.

My breath hitched. 'Creon ...'

He slammed into me without warning, every glorious inch of him, with enough strength to shove me backwards over the rough wool. My hoarse cry shattered the stifling silence of the Underground. He gave me no time to adjust, no time to recover; clasping a hand around my hip, he pulled me closer, locked me tight against him to meet his thrusts. I clung to his shoulders for dear life, back arching from the blankets in some desperate attempt to get him harder, deeper, as he filled me again and again and again ...

Finally. *Finally.* I let my head fall back and surrendered to his fingers squeezing bruises into my hip, to his cock stretching me relentlessly. Pain did not exist in this feral, forbidden world of ours. Just hunger. Just instinct. Just the Silent Death fucking me, every inch the invincible warrior again, every inch *my* invincible warrior again. I let the sight of him wash over me. Allowed myself to drown in the blur of sensations, gleaming muscle and straining wings and the delicious friction of our bodies melding together, until far too soon my release rose in me again.

A flicker of triumph glinted in his eyes as he slipped one hand between us and found that little knot of pleasure with his thumb.

The first rough stroke had me shattering. I clenched around him as my climax washed over me, moaning his name, begging him to join me. He rammed himself home one last time, then pulled out with a soundless curse and erupted, spilling hot seed over my breasts and belly.

I grabbed his cock and milked him to the last drop, unwilling, *unable* to let go of him. Only when the last of his pleasure was spent did he collapse into the blankets beside me, long locks a rumpled mess, eyes blazing with life. No more room for hate. No more room for guilt. An easy, satisfied grin played around his lips, so much like his old grins, so much like *him*, that it took all I had not to throw myself at him once more.

He cleaned the mess off my belly with a casual flicker of red magic and pulled me into his arms. I buried my face so tightly against his shoulder that I couldn't breathe for a heartbeat – drank in the scent of him, the familiar sensation of his heart rattling below his ribs. His wings wrapped around me, a soft, safe embrace of black velvet.

And then suddenly I was crying.

The relief cracked through some iron layer I'd built around my heart over the past days – oddly soothing sobs, tearing out of me as the world finally returned to a manageable state. The Mother was still hunting us. I was still lying to my only allies, and I still wasn't ready for whatever the world needed from me. But he was here, he was talking, he was *mine*, and I cried for all the times I could have lost him, all the times I hadn't known if I'd ever see him smile again.

One scarred hand released me, hovering before my face as I blinked open my eyes. *Em ...*

I sagged against his chest and cried even harder.

I'm sorry. I'm sorry. He spelled out the words again and again. *I should have trusted you, I—*

'You *should*, you idiot.' I barely even understood myself, bawling and blubbering as the words wrestled from my lips. 'And I should have trusted you too, and—' An uncontrollable sob cut through whatever

I'd wanted to say. 'Oh hell, will you please just be honest with me from now on? Because I don't think I can get used to that demon magic of yours if you won't even tell me ... won't even let me know ...'

His fingers moved back into my sight, every sign a cautious, meticulous venture. *You're saying you do want to get used to my magic.*

I blubbered a chuckle. 'It seems to have its advantages.'

Laughter shook through him, but the tension didn't melt from his arms. *You could enjoy the advantages by just fucking me every now and then.*

The flow of tears finally abated. I scrambled out of his embrace to meet his gaze, red eyes and runny nose be damned; he didn't move, but the small twitch of his jaw proved it was not a matter of indifference.

An honest offer, a simple way out. Easy pleasure without obligations, sparing me the trouble of his demon magic, sparing me the opinions of our allies. I could accept it and he wouldn't hold it against me. He'd probably agree I'd made the wiser choice.

The problem ...

'But that's not what you want, is it?' I breathed.

He slumped in the pillows, his lips hesitating on words that would never be sounds. Two infinite heartbeats dragged by before he finally drew in a strained breath, averted his eyes, and signed, *No.*

A single gesture, but it hovered between us like a judge's final verdict. 'No,' I echoed.

My heartbeat was a dizzying flutter in my chest, my mind a tangle of conflicting instincts. This ... this was what I'd wanted, wasn't it? *He* was what I wanted. I'd spent days sitting before a closed bedroom door, desperately wishing for this very moment, for him to come back and tell me he was still mine ...

But I parted my lips and not a word came out.

All those days. All those endless silent hours.

I know, Creon signed, demon eyes untangling the mess of my emotions before I could make sense of it myself. *I haven't exactly given you a reason to trust my pretty words.*

I swallowed down a sudden bitterness in the back of my throat. 'No, but ...'

He waited, motionless.

Oh, hell take me. I hadn't had a decent night of sleep since he'd locked me out of his room. I'd been sick with heartbroken worry every minute of the day. And if this thing between us became anything else, anything more ...

The deeper I dug my heart into this mess, the more devastating a next time would be.

'Is this going to happen more often?' I managed, wiping my cheek with the back of my hand. 'If we have to stay around this place for longer, is there any risk you'll be sinking back into ... that? That you'll lock me out again?'

I honestly don't know. A shiver trailed through his wings. *I'll try, Em. I'll really try. But ...*

But he couldn't control his powers, wouldn't *learn* to control his powers. Which meant he had about as much influence on his own state of mind as I had, perhaps less.

And how many other unpleasant surprises would emerge along the way? How many magical powers I hadn't even imagined, how many past hurts no one had told me about?

You don't have to deal with this, he hurried to add, his signs too brusque now. *You're not obliged to—*

'I know! I know, but the problem is that I ... that I ...'

I stopped myself there, just before that sentence could turn into a confession of something I wasn't sure I dared to reveal yet. I didn't *have* to deal with this, no, but the thought of leaving him to figure it out by himself ... it made me feel cold to the core in a way that both thrilled and frightened me.

'That I like you a little too much,' I finished weakly.

His eyes were bottomless pools – noting what I'd said. Noting, far more dangerously, what I hadn't said.

'Listen, it's been *weeks*.' I sat up straighter, a spark of frustration lending new strength to my voice. 'We've only ever been allies by necessity, and it's occurred to me that I technically barely know you. So perhaps this is not the moment to make any grand promises about eternity. I mean ...' I huffed. 'For all I know, you're one of those people who leave their dirty socks under the bed.'

The unexpected grin that quirked up his lips was so familiar I almost cried again. *There are lines of depravity even I won't cross, Em.*

I chuckled – damn him, of course I chuckled. Because that was how we worked, wasn't it? No matter the lines he'd crossed, no matter the objections of sense and propriety, his mere presence made the world seem easy. Safe. *Fun.* Keeping my hands off him had been a hopeless effort from the start. Keeping my heart out of this ... I may be well on my way to losing that battle, too.

So I had to be rational now. Rational and very damn careful.

'We can give it some time,' I said, weighing my words one by one as I allowed them over my lips. 'By the time I've observed your sock management for a while ... well, gods know where we'll be. We might understand your powers better. Things might be clearer.'

Creon didn't smile, fingers hesitating for the shortest of moments. *That sounds –* another small pause – *very wise.*

'But?'

But I feel like you're already sacrificing too much of your sanity for me. He closed his eyes and let his head roll back onto the blankets. *I'll make everything so much harder for you.*

'Probably,' I admitted and fondly patted his softened erection. 'To keep matters even, I'll make some things harder for you, too. Does that solve the issue?'

He choked on his soundless laughter, slapping my hand aside as he came up on his elbow. *For the love of the bloody gods, Em.*

'Look, I tried to resist you,' I said, swatting back at him. 'I really did, and you know where that got us. It would be recklessly optimistic at best to hope it'll work better this time. Why not see what happens if I actually allow myself to like you?'

His hard breath was, presumably, a groan. *Yes.*

'So.' I rubbed my eyes. 'Anything else we need to discuss before I stop being sensible for the rest of the day?'

He wrapped his left arm around my waist without a reply and pulled me back into his embrace, entangling our naked bodies in the blankets until I couldn't tell where I ended and he began. My cheek snuggled against his chest. My arms moulded to his muscular torso. And as his wings folded around me, the last of that painful tension finally melted from my shoulders, leaving me free to breath for the first time in what felt like ages.

I stopped being sensible.

'I'm glad you're back,' I whispered.

I'll always come back, Em. He buried his face in my hair, his breath faltering for a moment as he kissed the crown of my head. *I'm sorry I made you doubt that. I'll always come back for you.*

CHAPTER 8

So, Creon signed, sitting shirtless and cross-legged on his bed, chewing away on one of the sweet cardamom rolls I'd nicked from the kitchen before the rest of the household was awake. *What's the matter with those murderous alves?*

'I'm starting to think *murderous alves* might be a pleonasm,' I said.

He chuckled. *I couldn't tell you. The world always seems rather murderous around me, but I suspect that's just something my pretty face brings out in people.*

I laughed and leaned back against the wall, my bowl of yoghurt and fresh berries balancing dangerously in one hand. Over the past hours, in between attempts to sleep and interludes of far more pleasant activities, I'd finally given him a more elaborate report of all that had happened since the night that nearly killed him – Finn the stable girl and Wilfred the horse, my strategic needlework, Thysandra and her message. He'd been appropriately impressed at half of it and thoroughly amused at the other half – an amusement that lingered on his face even now, with no trace of the darkness of the Underground slipping back in.

As if we were back at the pavilion, just the two of us in quiet, delightful secrecy, exchanging strategic gossip and flirtatious jabs over a meal on his bed.

'Most of the Alliance is being reasonable,' I said a little more seriously, or at least as seriously as possible while sitting in my underwear on a winged fae prince's bed. 'It's just … These idiots *say* they're just guarding you, but I've heard them speculate about how many swords it would take to bring you down. Which—'

He chuckled. *How many did they guess?*

'Must you?'

Please stroke my ego a little, Em. It's good for my poor tortured soul.

I rolled my eyes, unable to keep my laugh down. 'An optimistic one thought five. The pessimistic ones thought twenty. I considered telling them to bring a cactus instead, but I didn't want to give them a head start.'

He burst out laughing. *I could handle five swords. Not sure about five cacti.*

'Yes, but if they show up with half an army …' I sucked in a breath. 'Look, they've decided you need to go. I'm afraid they'll try to simply stick a sword between your ribs and tell the Council you attacked them. It's not as if anyone will believe the opposite when there are no other witnesses.'

With characteristic Alvish subtlety, he signed wryly.

'Ah, yes.' I rolled my eyes at him. 'Feeling homesick for the Crimson Court, where they would rather make amiable jokes with you while attempting to poison your wine and blame it on someone else?'

He sniggered, tearing another bite off his cardamom roll. *Surviving at the Crimson Court has always been easy for me. The trick is to find a knife you can trust and then trust no one else.*

'I can find you a knife here?' I said sourly.

I'm not entirely harmless even without one, Em. His smile came down a fraction. *But I doubt I'd make the situation better by killing any of them. The rest won't be more inclined to leave me alone if matters escalate.*

I muttered a curse. 'So what do we do?'

I avoid them. He shrugged. *I can't think of a better strategy for now. Unless the bastards were the ones who upset you so badly the evening I woke up, in which case I might have to slit their throats anyway.*

'The ... oh.' I'd forced myself to forget about that matter; Beyla's list hadn't led to any specific suspicions, and with the military forces at the Crimson Court growing fast, an exploratory visit to the island would be far too risky. 'Oh, no. That wasn't them. I got news about my parents – blood parents, that is.'

He settled back against the headboard, raised eyebrows urging me to go on.

'I was apparently born at the court,' I said, shoving my yoghurt bowl aside. 'Beyla was the one who smuggled me out.'

Creon stared at me, frozen halfway through the motion of raising his hand before his bare chest.

'So I was surprised,' I said weakly. 'And frustrated. And a couple of other things.'

He blinked once, twice, then averted his gaze with a soundless, joyless chuckle. *Hell. That's ... not what I expected.*

'You did expect something?'

Spent some time thinking about it. He nodded at the bargain mark at his wrist as if I needed a reminder of the demand I'd made. *Although I may have forgotten to tell you that.*

I snorted a laugh. 'You may have.'

He at least had the good sense to look a little embarrassed. *I didn't want you to get your hopes up for nothing, but I don't suppose that's an excuse.*

'Not at all,' I said, 'but I might forgive you if you have any sensible thoughts about the matter.'

I had some sensible thoughts. Like how you must have been born on some more remote fae island to have escaped her notice. He rubbed his eyes, frown deepening. *This doesn't make sense at all. Did Beyla know more?*

'Father was fae, he abandoned my mother, and she was the one who smuggled me out.'

The look in his eyes turned colder, darker. *Bastard.*

'Yes.' I swallowed, tendrils of that numbing fear slipping back into my thoughts now that I could no longer push the subject away. 'And I figured ... if my mother is human, she must have been bound to the island, yes? Which means she's either still there and I can't reach her through the mess, or she's ...'

Creon closed his eyes and nodded.

'You don't have any ideas either?'

Wish I had. He was quiet for a moment, motionless except for the restless shifts of his wings. *There were rumours of fae rebels at the Golden Court in the weeks around your birth. The Mother didn't send me after them, so I'm not sure how much of it was true, but that could be related?*

'You mean one of those fae could have helped her?'

I'm not sure. They're a small group at the Golden Court, just a military outpost to control the eastern islands. I don't recall if any of them visited us in those months. With a sudden, frustrated gesture, he sat up straighter, uttering another soundless laugh. *It doesn't make sense. I must have been at the court for most of your birth week. How did I miss you?*

'Quite disappointing, truly,' I said primly, and he sank back into the pillows and sent me a glare that made me chuckle whether I wanted to or not.

I'm trying to recall whether anything else happened on the island around that time, he added, slower now. *She made some noise over human slaves conspiring against her a few weeks before you were born, but she had them all executed, so your mother can't have been one of them.* The shadow that slid over his face made me wonder if he had been the one executing them. I decided not to ask; none of the possible answers would make anyone happier.

'No other big events? You didn't spot any women sneaking around with baby-sized bundles?'

He shook his head with a thoughtless grin, raking a hand through his long hair. *It would have been helpful to have this information before I checked the archives of the other islands.*

I blinked. 'You did?'

He made it halfway through the gesture for *Of course*, then thought better of it, hesitated, and sheepishly signed, *I should probably have told you that, too.*

'Good gods,' I said, unable to suppress a rather desperate laugh. 'You're surprisingly dense for someone so clever. I take it you didn't find anything useful?'

Would have told you that. He frowned. *But I didn't look for developments at the court itself. It didn't seem likely that ... well. Your mother must have been somewhat of a genius to get you out.*

The little thorny thing in my throat wasn't a full catch yet, but swallowing was unpleasant nonetheless. 'Yes.'

For a few more moments, he was silent, staring at the ink-black wall on the other side of the room, visibly stewing in his thoughts. Then, with a heavy sigh, he shrugged and signed, *The good news is at least one of us may still have a decent parent.*

I burst out laughing.

He blinked at me rather bewilderedly. *What?*

'I *knew* you'd say that.' I let myself drop sideways into the messy blankets. 'You're so predictable sometimes.'

A grin grew around his lips as he wrapped a hand around my ankle and dragged me closer. *And you claim you don't know me?*

'Perhaps I know you better than I think,' I admitted, making fruitless attempts to kick his hand away with my free foot. He pulled me into his lap as if he hadn't even noticed my efforts, the scarred ridges of his bare chest suddenly dangerously close. 'Or perhaps I just know you extraordinarily well in the contexts of banter and bloodshed. We should probably expand our shared horizon and go on some proper dates.'

He chuckled. *Didn't we yet?*

'We ... no?'

Day trips to admire the magical scenery of the island? His eyes were twinkling when I turned in his lap to face him, his lips about to curl into that mischievous smile that somehow brought the taste of his kisses straight back to the foreground of my memory. *Lunch parties and festival events?*

I snorted. 'Do you mean "exploring potentially murderous Labyrinths and visiting decidedly murderous High Ladies"?'

So what were your suggestions for this place? he signed, smile souring. *Going out for dinner and slapping the alves off ourselves in between courses? Because they don't feel like they'll …*

His fingers faltered. A disconcerting stiffness tightened around the corners of his lips, and for a heartbeat, his eyes no longer seemed to be seeing me, no longer seemed to be aimed at anything visible to mere immortal eyes – as if his mind had slid straight back to his would-be attackers camping outside our front door, conversing about the colour of fae blood, waiting for an excuse to draw their swords.

My heart stopped dead in my chest for a single moment of undiluted panic.

Was that enough to start him slipping back? A mere mention? A mere thought? Because if it was, then what in the world would happen whenever I had other obligations to attend?

'Creon?'

His eyes snapped back to me, the glassiness gone. As if nothing had happened, he shrugged and finished, *They don't feel like they'll happily leave us alone for a romantic walk around the gardens.*

'Rude,' I said weakly, trying with little success to calm my rattling heart. Distraction, then. I could figure out later how I would ever safely leave him alone. 'But fine. If dates aren't an option, let me ask questions.'

Creon raised an eyebrow, waiting.

I clambered over his thighs until I straddled him. 'The apprentices at Miss Matilda's had this joke about secret magical powers. As in, odd talents most people didn't know about. One girl could write with both hands at the same time, that kind of thing.'

A grin grew back on his face. *They asked you about your secret magical powers?*

'Yes, and I died seven and a half deaths before I realised what they were talking about.' Even with the worry clawing through me, it was hard not to smile at the memory. 'Then I told them I'm really good at picking stuff up from the floor with my toes. Which is the full truth and an entirely useless skill. So, what is your secret magic power?'

My unrivalled charms, he gestured dryly.

'Ah, yes. You're being immensely secretive about those, indeed.'

He shook his head, laughing. An honest laugh again – bless Zera's merciful heart. *I always know where north is. Not entirely useless. It made charting the Labyrinth easier.*

'Excellent secret magic,' I said, poking him approvingly in the chest. He was back, wasn't he? Now all I had to do was keep him here. 'Your turn to ask a question, then.'

He tilted his head, considering that. *Your favourite book?*

'The socially acceptable answer or the actual answer?'

Another raised eyebrow was the only reply I received. I cleared my throat and said, 'Officially it's *Queen of Roses*, which is a very moving, very heartfelt, immensely boring epic about some woman who takes care of a garden. It's probably symbolic? I always made sure to be reading it when Father's patrons were around. He liked that it made us look like an intellectual family.'

Had I not known his opinion on the man who'd raised me already, Creon's scoff would have told me all I needed to know. *And the actual answer?*

'A terribly theatrical drama called *Breathing in the Dark.*' I grinned. 'It has ridiculous duels and midnight pursuits on horseback, and the last quarter or so is just the heroine screwing her handsome pirate lover in flowery but rather explicit language. Very instructive. We all read it on Ildhelm. Yours?'

He was laughing openly now. *A Divine Age treatise called* On the Night Sky, *but I'm starting to think I might like your pick better.*

'A male of exquisite taste,' I said brightly. 'I'll try to find you a copy. Favourite animal?'

Cats.

'Cats?'

He shrugged that slow, lazy shrug of his. *They mind their own business and kill something every now and then. I can sympathise with that.*

His expression was just too careless, his posture just too languid, his overall air just too close to the Mother's arrogant fae prince. I narrowed my eyes and said, 'That's not the only reason, is it?'

His slight hesitation was enough of an answer. *They were Etele's sacred animals, too. That might be part of their appeal.*

'Ah.' Etele, who had lost her people when their High Lady decided she'd rather ally with another god. 'Just like I started sewing my own blue dresses because my mother kept telling me pink was such a terribly cute colour?'

Painfully accurate, he admitted with a grimace.

I sniggered. 'Why did the Mother turn her back on Etele in the first place? Was Korok easier to seduce?'

From what I've understood, Etele mostly didn't support her warmongering plans.

'No?' I frowned. 'Wasn't she supposed to be a goddess of war?'

He gave half a shrug. *Partly so, yes.*

'Partly ... Oh.' Lyn's words of a few days earlier returned to me. 'If she was dual in nature like the other gods ... What's the opposite of war? Peace?'

Depends on the source and the translation. The phrase commonly used is "beauty and war".

'Really?' I said, fascinated enough to forget about murderous alves for a moment. 'Are we supposed to conclude war is ... pretty much everything that isn't beautiful?'

According to Etele. A bleak grin. *So I suppose a High Lady looking to conquer the world would have no choice but to find another god to support her. How about your favourite animal?*

'Doves,' I said. 'When I was five or so, my mother told me that myth about Zera sending white doves to bless people. I spent a lot of time running after birds, hoping one of them would happen to be white.'

He chuckled. *Typical.*

'What?'

If the gods won't bless you, just get the damn blessing for yourself. Excellent strategy.

'Thanks,' I said and stuck out my tongue at him. 'I feel there's some metaphor here about stupid fae males who won't talk to me. Zera should be happy I didn't knock down her front door to demand my blessing.'

Should she? His grin grew dangerous – an expression that pleasantly reminded me I was currently perched on the kind of thighs that could crush a skull, that his chiselled and eminently kissable chest was not even half a foot removed from my lips, and that the fingers signing those words at me had made me come hard enough to forget my own name several times over the course of the night. *I don't have any complaints about your demands so far.*

It was infuriating how easily he stirred those smouldering embers of my desire into flames again; I hadn't thought there was any fuel left to burn after these sleepless hours. In a hopeless but heroic attempt to deny the undeniable, I jutted up my chin and gave him my most indignant glare. 'I don't see you doubting the grand and terrifying force of my wrath, do I?'

I wouldn't dare. His eyes flashed with a little too much daring.

'For the bloody gods' sake,' I said, and my voice came out too husky to sound properly exasperated. 'If you go on like this, I'm not sure we'll ever leave this bed again.'

The glimmer in his eyes became a smoulder, the smile on his lips a smirk. *Could go with the wall, if you prefer a change of scenery.*

'You're not helping at all!'

His left hand moulded to my waist and slid down from there, tracing the soft curve of my hip. I let out an overly dramatic groan and wilted against his chest, pretending I didn't feel the chuckle that shook through him. If I felt that chuckle, I'd have to object some more for reasons of personal pride, and I frankly didn't quite feel like objecting.

The trail of his touch made it to my bare thigh and lingered there, his warm palm unbearably soft against skin that had far from forgotten his previous torments. For a moment, neither of us moved; then he pulled away and gently wrapped his fingers around my chin, tugging my head up a fraction.

Releasing me, he signed, *I shouldn't keep you away from training.*

Training? It took me a moment to figure out what he was talking about – sticks and swords, endless breathing exercises, Tared.

Tared.

Something withered below my heart. *Demon brood.*

'Might have to find someone else to teach me,' I grumbled, resting my cheek against Creon's chest again. Gods be damned. It had to be about time to show up at the training hall, indeed, and I'd been so occupied by rogue demon powers that I hadn't even begun to figure out how to handle this mess with Tared. 'I'm really not in the mood to see him at the moment.'

Creon's fingers stiffened. *Em.*

'What – do you want me to keep exchanging pleasantries with him now that I know what he did to you?' I shot upright to meet his eyes, uttering a bitter laugh. 'He went out of his way to hurt you over some stupid jealousy? While there was no chance of her running off with you in the first place? How am I supposed to—'

It would be helpful, he signed slowly, *if you learned how to handle a weapon.*

I rubbed my face, suppressing a curse. 'Can't you teach me?'

No. That gesture came out with too much sharpness – as if it was a ridiculous idea to ask the Mother's most feared warrior to disclose some of his secrets.

'Why not? It's not as if you don't know how to—'

Em, he interrupted me, closing his eyes as he rested his head against the wall. *The only way I've ever been trained is with pain and fear.* There was no anger in his motions, no plea for sympathy, just plain, exhausted facts. *I have no idea where I'd start if I'm not supposed to break any of your bones. Work with Tared. He's better at these things.*

I threw myself sideways into his blankets and released a long, dramatic groan. 'Don't be so bloody magnanimous if I just want to be furious on your behalf. You're supposed to tell me I should shove his own sword up his arse next time I see him.'

He chuckled, sitting straighter to hold my gaze. *Not saying I wouldn't find that amusing.*

'But?'

But just because I hate every gods-damned breath he takes doesn't mean he's a bad person, and I want you to be safe more than I want to punch his teeth from his face. He hesitated, then added nearly apologetically, *We don't have infinite time. You need to be prepared when everything goes to hell again.*

When. Not if. I closed my eyes for the shortest of moments and only saw Gish more clearly in my mind's eye – *Will the girl be ready?*

The Council was waiting. The entire damn world was waiting. I wasn't prepared to face a single damn battle, and Tared's stupidities of over a century ago didn't deserve enough weight to compromise our fight against the Mother.

Training meant leaving this room, though.

My mouth turned dry again as I shoved to the edge of the bed and snatched my dress from the floor. 'Will you be alright? It's usually an hour at most, and I could miss my usual meeting with Lyn, if—'

His shoulders tightened, wings stiffening with them. *Don't you dare. I'll be fine.*

'But—'

Not knowing your thoughts made it easier to sink into it, he interrupted, the gestures wide and rushed. *I'm prepared now. Take your time. Finish your training. I'll be here when you're done.*

Barely reassuring, with the shadows seeping into his smile already. The sting of dread returned without warning, too strong to push away this time – that sensation of the earth shifting beneath my feet. He'd be here, and in the end, he'd always come back for me ... but how much would it cost him?

How much would it cost me?

Em. His jaw twitched as he watched me. *Don't start panicking before you have a reason to.*

Right.

We might just be fine, I reminded myself as I pulled my dress over my head and kissed him one last time. He might get used to his new surroundings after a few days, get less susceptible to that merciless alf hate. He might revert to the male I'd known at the Crimson Court, the unfaltering ally who would always be there to keep me safe.

And I'd no longer have to be sensible.

But surrounded by the pitch-dark, empty silence of the Underground, doubt wouldn't stop gnawing at my guts.

CHAPTER 9

THE FOUR ALVES PLAYING card games on the tunnel floor outside looked up as I slipped out of the house, expressions hardening as always when they identified me.

'Looking for Tared?'

I faltered as that question sunk in, confusion briefly trumping the itch to chase them all out of Orin's quarter with a much deserved shower of red. 'Yes. Why?'

The alf female who'd spoken shrugged. 'He said he'd wait for you inside.'

Damn it. I was late, then. A night of little sleep and a morning of too much distraction must have distorted my estimate of the hours; in between the brightening and the dimming of the alf lights, I missed the sun to tell me the time in this world below

'Thanks,' I said curtly, slammed the door behind me, and went to look for Tared.

The living room was empty, except for the breakfast someone had left on the table for me. So was Tared's bedroom, a sparsely furnished place full of old wood and even older leather. The only other sensible option ...

I tiptoed to my own bedroom, which lay deeper into the house than Creon's, and pushed the door open. Before it had swung even halfway, I was greeted with a rather bored, 'So there you are.'

That solved the problem and created several others at the same time.

I stepped inside, steeling myself. Tared was sitting in one of the chairs at the right wall, book in his lap, legs nonchalantly crossed, sword on the seat of the other chair. As if he'd been lounging in the same spot for hours, waiting for me. Judging by the smile he gave me, just a fraction cooler than his usual smiles, he might have been.

'What in hell are you doing here?' I said sharply, and he shrugged.

'Having a chat with you.'

'Did you have to break into my bloody bedroom for that?'

'It's my house,' he said dryly. 'Where you don't appear to have shown up for a single meal in the last twenty-four hours. Also, you seem to have forgotten our training. So I—'

'I didn't forget anything,' I said, shutting the door with more force than I should have. 'Just a little delayed. I was somewhat distracted chatting with demon brood, if you must know.'

He didn't even blink. 'So it worked? Good.'

'So it ...' I came to a befuddled standstill in the middle of the room, the retort I'd planned to throw at him sizzling out before it could reach my lips. 'Worked?'

Tared shrugged, cautiously folded the book in his lap shut, and sat up straighter, watching me with patient grey eyes.

So it worked – my thoughts slammed into a solid marble wall. That conversation behind a poorly shut door. His careless use of my name, guaranteed to draw my attention. His voice, rising slightly as he spoke those dangerous, all-revealing sentences ...

'Wait,' I said, staring at him. 'You deliberately dropped that information for me to hear?'

He shoved the book next to his sword on the other chair and leisurely folded his arms. 'Yes, of course.'

'You ... What?' I let out a sharp laugh. 'What kind of a stupid plan was that? You should have *known* I would be unhappy with—'

'You should know by now I don't make plans,' he dryly interrupted. 'I do things, and then they work out. I was getting tired of you making everything so bloody complicated for yourself, so I thought I'd do something about it. That seems to have worked.'

'Well, yes, but—'

'So then the next step is to figure out how I'm going to appease you again.' He gave me a skewed grin. 'Looks like that might be somewhat of a challenge. Interesting. I promise you he's not in need of protection *that* badly, Emelin.'

'It's not about protection!' I burst out. To hell with the civility, then. If he wanted a chat, he would get his bloody chat. 'It's about you being a cruel bastard and throwing the worst of his fears into his face to hurt! And about you acting like you have some bloody *claim* on Lyn, picking fights with anyone who might potentially take an interest in her, which is frankly pathetic at best and downright—'

Tared still didn't even flinch. 'Does it mollify you at all that Lyn has told me the same and worse a few hundred times at least?'

I scoffed. 'I bloody well hope she did.'

'Glad to reassure you, then.'

'Is this why everything is so utterly unclear between the two of you? Because she's equally unhappy about you turning into—'

He briefly closed his eyes. 'Mind if I keep that between her and me, Emelin?'

'That's a yes,' I concluded bitterly, dropping down on my bed. Thank the gods I hadn't neatened the blankets after the last night I'd slept in it; at least it wasn't obvious I hadn't set foot in the room since yesterday. 'Well. Making things bloody hard for yourself, indeed. Is that what's supposed to placate me? Some sob story about your unfulfilling love life?'

For a moment, he was silent, utterly unfazed, not a trace of yesterday's cold regret in his eyes. He'd been prepared, I realised – prepared for me to fling all of this and worse at him, prepared for me to give up on training I might need to save the world.

And yet he was here. Patient and unbendable, like the still surface of a lake that would never show more than a ripple no matter what you threw at it.

It took most of the satisfaction from my anger, I had to give him that. And it did admittedly make me wonder what in hell had happened all those years ago to make *this* male lose his composure to the point of cruelty.

As if to answer that thought, he slowly said, 'You do realise this had been going on for months before the mess exploded, don't you?'

I snorted. 'That doesn't make it sound any more heroic.'

'Fuck's sake, Emelin.' He let out a laugh, rubbing his hands over his face. 'I'm well aware there's nothing heroic about anything I did. I'm mostly hoping to convince you not to stab me to death at dinner tonight, and it would be helpful if we could resume your training soon, considering your astute observation of yesterday that time is not exactly on our side. So?'

I glowered at him, torn between an overwhelming desire to shout at him and an equally dangerous desire to listen to what he had to tell me.

'There's a lot I could say about this,' he continued, voice flat. 'But to keep it short ... Creon was strutting around her for weeks looking very fucking pleased with himself. And he's a bloody *demon*, Emelin. Which seemed to mean that either Lyn was lying when she told me she didn't care for him that way, or that he knew she didn't care for him that way and was brooding on some plan to change that. So I panicked. For weeks on end. Nothing heroic about it – just plain, stupid fright.'

How was I supposed to know what love felt like? I closed my eyes and tried not to curse, not to blurt out every detail Creon had entrusted me with, not to demand we walk into his room right now so I could shout at the both of them.

'And so you solved the matter by taking the one thing you knew would hurt him most and throwing that in his face?'

He sighed. 'Yes, that's about it.'

'Damn unpleasant thing to do.'

'I know,' he said with a bitter chuckle. 'That's why I did it, I'm afraid.'

A joyless laugh escaped me as I sagged back against the wall and wrapped my arms around my face. *Panic* – which I might have thought an exaggeration, if not for the mortal dread I'd seen in his eyes that morning in Faewood.

Perhaps I should have known better than to assume that verbal kick in Creon's face had been a calculated attack.

'These arseholes camping outside,' I said, talking to the inside of my elbows. 'Are you allowing them to stay there because you agree with them?'

'First of all,' Tared said, a spark of sour amusement in his voice, 'I have no authority to allow anyone anything. But even if I had ...' He hesitated. 'I'm not sure if I agree with whatever they think they're achieving there. But I do understand the urge.'

'To kill him, even though he could win you this war?' I said sharply. When I lowered my arms to throw him a look, he hadn't moved, lounging in that chair like we were chatting about the weather. 'Is honour and revenge really worth that much to you?'

He didn't move. Didn't tense. Didn't so much as raise an eyebrow. But his voice had gone cold when he finally said, 'I'm not sure how to put this kindly, Emelin.'

I blinked, taken aback by that turn of the conversation. 'What do you—'

'You're undeniably a tough little fighter,' he said. Somehow it didn't sound like a compliment at all. 'And rest assured, I'm growing rather fond of you. But you'd be wise to keep in mind you're also twenty years old and, at the current moment, utterly clueless regarding what you're talking about.'

'I ...' My heart stuttered. 'Wait, Tared, I didn't mean to—'

'You didn't live through five centuries of war and defeat,' he interrupted, voice sharpened even though he didn't sit any straighter. 'You don't have the faintest idea of what we've survived, what we're still surviving. And as clever as you are, as much as *you* decided to forgive him or like him for whatever unfathomable reason, you're in no position to tell us how to cope with that history or with the remnants of it currently staying in my house.' A glass-edged laugh. 'I'm not judging you. Be so kind as to return the favour.'

I stared at him. Few lines I couldn't cross, and only then did it occur to me that I *had* crossed them this time – that he was furious, calmly but utterly furious, and I had no one but myself to blame for it.

'Tared …' The words got stuck somewhere in the back of my throat. Fuck. *Fuck.* Got a little too comfortable, forgot to mind my words for the first time in my life, and look what came of it. 'I'm sorry, I—'

'Good.' He got up with a quick, fluent motion, snatched his sword from the chair, and held out a hand to me. 'Let's take a little trip. I'd like to show you something.'

I blinked at his hand, heartbeat quickening. 'What … what kind of something?'

'Consider it a different sort of training,' he said, lips tight. 'Since you seemed rather fixated on the concept of real fights yesterday.'

An ominous kind of surprise. But I didn't suppose he'd drag me straight into a battle just for the pleasure of seeing me beg for help, and anything else he came up with …

I wasn't ready. And I needed to be.

With a quick glance in the direction of Creon's room, I shoved to the edge of my bed. Would he notice my absence if we faded away from the Underground? If so, he might be worried. He might be hurt by the stewing emotions of this place. And then again …

He'd told me not to panic without a proper reason.

I muttered a curse and grabbed Tared's outstretched hand, expecting to be sucked away at once.

Nothing happened. He nodded at me and said, 'Cover your eyes. The daylight can be painful after you've spent a while in the world below.'

We were going back to the surface, then? I wanted to ask if that was even safe, with the Mother hunting us – but the world blurred around me, and all I could do was squeeze my eyes shut and hope he had a semblance of a plan for whatever we were about to do.

The sun hit me like a sledgehammer even through my closed eyelids – a stab of pain sharp enough to make me wince the moment I felt solid earth below my feet. I cursed again, clutching my hand over my eyes, desperately blinking away the tears.

'Apologies,' Tared said, sounding thoroughly unaffected as he released my hand. When I finally managed to look up, half a minute of adjusting later, he stood examining the scenery without a trace of discomfort on his slender face.

I sniffed away the last of the tears. 'Does it get better if you do it more often?'

'No. Alf eyes.' He smiled joylessly. 'I'd prefer to have the Underground far brighter, too, but the vampires started complaining when we tried to adjust the lights. You'll get used to it after a minute here.'

I threw a look around at what turned out to be a surprisingly nondescript landscape, not too different from the inland of Cathra I knew so well. Dusty green hills, the stretches of half-dried grass interrupted by the occasional oleander bush or olive tree. The rustle of the sea in the distance. The smell of dry earth and briny water and a trace of citrus.

I drew in a long breath, sucking that familiar fragrance deep into my lungs – expecting the hollow sensation of homesickness but finding no such thing, even when I tried to call it from the pits of my heart. I'd forgotten the human islands were so colourless, even the greenest leaves and the brightest flowers oddly drab compared to the brilliant colours of the court where I had spent my last few weeks above the earth. Had forgotten that weight on my shoulder, those unspoken rules that had dictated my every movement at home.

Don't be visible. Don't be difficult. Don't be *you*.

Just a few weeks ago, yet already the girl bending under the pressure of those impossible expectations seemed another person entirely, someone who didn't yet know how soon nothing in her life would ever be the same again.

'Ready?' Tared said next to me, and I jolted from those peculiar realisations, remembering a moment too late that he hadn't brought me here to wallow in the past.

'Where are we?'

'Sevrith.' He threw a quick glance around and up at the blue sky, checking for unexpected bystanders. 'You may know it as the isle of ruin.'

I froze. 'The battlefield?'

'Yes. Just behind the hills.'

Those hills, looking so innocent and peaceful in the light of the early afternoon ... I suppressed a sharp bite of dread as I followed him over the winding path to the south, little more than a narrow goat trail through the wild grasses.

The island wasn't as silent as the Underground, but a heavy atmosphere hung over it, a gloom that even the surf in the distance and the buzzing of insects nearby couldn't lift. The location of the Last Battle ... How many people had set foot in this cursed place in the last hundred and thirty years?

Something splintered under my shoe as my foot landed a few inches beside the path. Just too late did I see what it was – a bone.

Long and thin and, it turned out at the crack, hollow. Not human, but I was still wracking my brain to figure out what it could be when Tared calmly said, 'Wing bones.'

'Oh.' Oh, fuck. 'Didn't they bury the bodies?'

'There were quite a lot of them.' His voice still held that unnervingly level tone, a self-restraint too steely to be real. 'I don't think they had time to clean out every bit of shredded wing before it all started to rot.'

Shredded wings and rot. The buzzing of the insects suddenly sounded too loud to my ears, reminding me of the flies around the butcher's shop on Ildhelm, dragging the smell of blood and dead meat from the depths of my memory. I swallowed something bitter and sour and whispered, 'Why in hell are we here?'

'I'm not trying to shock you.' There was a trace of apology in his eyes. 'But I don't think I can explain the reality of what we were fighting those days if I have to rely on words alone. Let me know if you want to go back.'

I sucked in two deep breaths, then nodded. They hadn't been given breaks either, those fateful days over a century ago. They hadn't been able to turn back. Whatever was waiting for me behind those hills, it could hardly be worse than the horror they had faced.

It could hardly be worse than the horrors I might have to face far sooner than I liked.

We walked on in silence, through the grass and up the nearest hill, the afternoon heat a stifling blanket on my shoulders. Now that I knew they were there, I found the traces of the battle wherever I looked – maimed skeletons and rusty weapons, crudely inscribed bits of wood on heaps of earth I presumed were hastily dug graves. Tared didn't look away from the narrow path before us, as if even the trees and the shrubbery might show faces he wasn't able to forget, echo sounds he wasn't ready to hear again. Only as we approached the top of the hill did he slow down, gesturing for me to walk on beside him for the last part.

Close enough for him to grab me and vanish at any given moment. There was no lowering our guards in this place.

Walking shoulder to shoulder, we reached the top, a small expanse of browned grass and dead trees from where we could look out into the plain below.

The plain ...

It was *white*.

Stretching out at least a mile before us, the battlefield was a landscape devoid of all colour – barren alabaster earth with only the occasional brave blade of grass breaking through the emptiness, scorched trees whiter than any birch I'd ever seen. Even the weapons scattered across the field had more often than not lost their colour, white steel rusting dismally in the burning sunlight, the magic sucked out of every last inch of their surface.

'They were using the blood of their fallen comrades to fight,' Tared said next to me, his voice far away. 'Sucking the colour out of the corpses, too. I've wondered at times how desperate they must have been to dishonour their friends' bodies like that.'

I heard a dazed curse fall from my lips. Tared sat down in the dry grass without reply and crossed his legs, staring out over the white desolation with an unusual emptiness in his eyes.

'Did you feel sorry for them?' I whispered.

'Not as much as I should have, perhaps. They effectively started the war by slaughtering my family.' A small chuckle. 'There's the sob story you asked for.'

I didn't want sob stories, didn't want to hear any of it – wanted to flee back home and forget I'd ever seen this hell of a place. But he might still be seeing it in his mind's eye every single day, and one day I, too, may not have a choice.

I sat down beside him, pulled my knees to my chest, and wiped my clammy hands on my dress. 'I shouldn't have worded it like that.'

'No,' he agreed, uncannily mildly.

We were both silent for a while, until I scraped myself together and said, 'What happened to your family?'

He seemed to have been waiting for the question. 'It was a little over a century after the War of the Gods had ended. The archipelago was unstable at the time – thousands of human refugees had escaped the plague and were looking for a new place to live, flooding the islands, causing small fights all over the place.' He hesitated, then added, 'Some of us tried to help them. My uncle, for example.'

I hadn't heard any uncles mentioned by the family. An unpleasant gut feeling said the nameless alf had paid a high price for his helpful intentions.

'They clashed with the inhabitants of some small fae isle when a couple of humans tried to build a village there,' Tared continued, still with that hollow, detached tone to his words. 'There were fatalities on both sides, but some of the dead fae were of importance to the Mother. She found the name of the alf who'd killed them and sent a small army to his home on Skeire to get her comeuppance. He wasn't there. So they killed most of the family instead.'

Anger or not, I was momentarily overcome by the urge to throw my arms around him and hug that emptiness from his voice. But under the gloomy atmosphere of Sevrith, I couldn't bring myself to move, to speak.

'We used to be a large house,' he said quietly. 'After that day ... well, Edored and Ylfreda survived. So did my mother – more or less. My father and little brother died, as did my uncles and aunts and great-uncles and great-aunts and cousins and nephews and nieces and ...' A weak, directionless gesture. 'Everyone. The house of Skeire consists of five alves now, if you count generously.'

'You, Edored, Ylfreda ...' I faltered. 'Your uncle and mother – are they ...'

'My uncle devoted himself to the war against faekind and was killed in battle a few decades after. My mother ...' He drew in an unnaturally level breath. 'Alves bond for life. After my father died, she was ... a shell. Such an empty husk of herself that we were all honestly relieved when she eventually fell on her sword after a few years and ended the ordeal.'

I flinched. 'Oh, gods. I'm so sorry.'

He gave me something in between a nod and a shrug – that gesture that said, *thanks, but there's damn little any sympathy can change about it.*

'So it's the three of you,' I said faintly. 'And Hallthor because he's with Ylfreda, and ... Beyla?'

'Beyla was visiting us that day. Visiting my brother, really.' He looked away, avoiding my eyes and the stark white battlefield. 'They were ... courting, I suppose. Nothing official yet. He died trying to keep her safe.'

I tried to swallow. A small, painful sound escaped my lungs instead.

'She tried to go back home,' Tared added, his voice no louder than a whisper. 'But the rest of the magical world ... they ignored what had happened. Told us it was an unfortunate isolated accident, that there had admittedly been provocations, that keeping the general peace in the archipelago was more important than mindless revenge – you know, all the things cowards say.' He rubbed his face, then looked back at me. 'The Mother had obliterated five gods at once a few decades earlier. They were frightened of what she might do if we drew her attention to the other magical peoples. But for the few of us who'd been there ... it wasn't a day you could forget in order to blissfully go on with your life.'

'So Beyla came back to you.'

'Yes. I consider her my sister in every way that matters.'

I wondered if it was her lover's death that had left her so painfully colourless, a slightly lighter form of the alf grief that had cost Tared's mother her life. I didn't dare to ask. The memory of his brother seemed to be even more painful to him than the rest of the story.

'And then what did you do, if the rest of the world didn't want to take revenge?'

'Looked for revenge anyway,' he said with a sour grin. 'I'm an honourable alf, Emelin. And frankly ...' A sigh. 'I didn't have much else to live for.'

Again we were both silent for a while.

'I was a bit of a mess,' he said eventually, and it sounded like an apology. 'It was just a handful of us for a few years – the ones who survived, some ideologists from other houses. And everyone kept telling us we were mad for thinking there might be more behind that day, for doubting whether the peace could be salvaged at all. I was just existing and trying not to die. And then ...'

'You met Lyn?'

He sighed again, still staring at the battlefield before us. 'Yes.'

An uncanny talent for saving people, indeed, I wanted to say, but kept my mouth shut once again. Wherever this story was going, I wasn't forcing the subject of Creon upon him during the history of his family's murder.

'She was dealing with a mess of her own at the time,' Tared said after a short pause. 'Which turned out to be related to our mess, so we ended up working together, and then we didn't solve the mess at all, but ...' His face didn't seem to know whether it should be smiling or crying. 'I didn't really care that much anymore, to tell you the truth.'

'And then the war came?'

'The war was already there. Skeire was the first battle – we just didn't know it at the time. But yes, the other peoples got involved, and that turned into two centuries of bloodshed, building to ... ' He sighed, a nod at the plain before us. 'This.'

I turned back to the stark white battlefield, a weight sinking into my stomach.

'Here's what you should understand, Emelin,' he said quietly. 'I devoted my entire damn life to that war. So many of us did. So many of us were born after it started – never knew a day of true peace. And so many of them died before they could ever know a day of peace, too – in this hellhole of a place, or in the decades after, when she was putting down everything that was even *rumoured* to lead to rebellion.'

He paused. I knew what was coming – knew and couldn't help but understand it.

'So call us vengeful and violent and unreasonably stubborn.' There was a stiffness to his smile – something that was not a smile at all. 'Call us proud bastards. Call us bloodthirsty idiots who stab before they ask questions. We *are* all those things, but don't think for a moment we are because it's what we like to be. We protect what's ours only because we don't have much left.'

Like the safety of the Underground. Like the friends and family who'd somehow survived to this day and age, through battles and famines and torturous stretches of war.

I didn't dare to breathe. 'Yes.'

He was silent next to me, staring out over the pale remains of the Last Battle. Behind us, a particularly loud fly came buzzing closer, then wandered off into the distance again, leaving us in tense, doubtful silence.

'I don't know what he ever did to earn your loyalty,' Tared finally said, and although he didn't look aside, didn't mention names, the tone of his words told me all I needed to know. 'And if it means he bettered his life in the past few months, I'm glad to hear it. But you should understand that all these decades while we were scrambling to survive and mourning a new bloodbath every other month, he was sleeping in his princely bed and gorging on the banquets humanity starved for, and ...'

His voice caught. I bit my lip so hard it hurt as he drew in a torturously slow breath, avoiding my eyes.

'I've seen the bodies he leaves behind,' he finally said, voice hollow with age-old fury. 'We all have. Innocent people, slaughtered like gods-damned dogs – hell, even dogs get to go with more dignity. And perhaps he was on our side all that time, and perhaps he'll win us the war in the end, but don't tell me we're stubborn for remembering every gouged out eye and every flayed corpse, that we're fools for mistrusting a male who inflicts that kind of pain on his allies as easily as—'

'They never felt it,' I said.

The words were over my lips before I could think. *Slaughtered like dogs* – which was true, but then again ...

Such a lie, too. Such a filthy, deadly lie.

Tared blinked, turned towards me. 'Beg your pardon?'

'The people he killed. Creon.' Now I was the one to avert my gaze – not my secret to share, and at the same time, why hadn't I told him before? 'He's been using his powers to take their pain. For all his victims, all these years. It's why he kept doing it, executing her orders – because no one else would have—'

'Wait. Emelin, what?' He had gone pale as morning mist beside me. 'Are you ... What?'

I gave a stiff shrug. 'I was awake when he returned from Rhudak.'

The way he tensed to the very tips of his fingers told me I didn't need to elaborate about that mission. 'Oh, fuck.'

'I genuinely thought he was dying.' My voice came out too small. 'And then he told me he'd been doing it all this time, taking their pain when he killed them – he felt all of it himself, all that torture you've seen. I just didn't realise he was describing demon powers until you—'

'No,' he said, and there was a helplessness to his voice I hadn't heard before. 'He ... No. No, that can't ...'

'The Silent Death, Tared.' I swallowed. 'There's a reason for the lack of screaming.'

He stared at me for two thunderous heartbeats, then abruptly looked away and repeated, '*Fuck.*'

'Not that I really expect it'll make you hate him any less,' I added, forcing a mirthless chuckle over my lips. 'But ...'

'But at least I could try to hate him a little more respectfully?' He threw me a bewildered, almost panicked glance. 'Orin damn us all, Emelin. Why in hell have you been keeping this quiet?'

'He prefers not to talk about it.'

'Speaking of people making life difficult for themselves.'

'It may have helped if no one had called him fundamentally unlovable for having those powers,' I said sharply, and he winced, turning away from me with a groan that sounded like a confession.

'Yes. Admittedly.'

I had expected to feel anger at that acknowledgement. The empty gleam of misery in Creon's eyes was still there in my mind's eye, the desperate way his fingers had signed at me not to bother with demon brood. But then again ...

If I could forgive Creon for being an idiot due to past hurts and general misfortunes, perhaps it would be unnecessarily demanding to hold the rest of the world to different standards.

'Tared?'

His eyes were still too wide, and his answer came too slowly. 'Yes?'

'If I promise I won't stab you to death in your sleep ...' I hesitated. 'Could you promise me something, too?'

'Depends on the request,' he said with a joyless grimace. 'I know well enough not to make blind deals with fae.'

I huffed a laugh. 'Half fae. And it's nothing outrageous. Just ...' *Just keep him safe. Just get those bloody friends of yours to make peace with his presence before anyone gets killed.* Hell, somehow my allies would have to stop hating each other to death; why not start here? 'I was wondering, could you – if the occasion arises – could you try to have a normal conversation with him for *once*? Without talking about Lyn or about how happy you'd have been to see him die a violent death a few decades ago, I mean?'

Tared opened his mouth, hesitated, closed it again. It took a few heartbeats of visible deliberation before he finally said, 'He'll have to come out of that bloody room first.'

'He will.'

'I ...' He groaned. 'Orin's eye, Emelin, I'll see how civil I can find it in me to be. That's the best promise I can make you right now.'

Better than nothing, and I'd first have to convince Creon, too. 'Fine. I appreciate the effort.'

He smiled faintly, looking more relieved than I'd expected. 'Does that mean I'll see you at training tomorrow?'

'I'll be there,' I said, rolling my shoulders. 'And I'll even be merciful and try my best not to accidentally kill you.'

'The day you accidentally kill me is the day I can declare my teaching a success,' he wryly said as he rose to his feet and held out his hand to me. 'Nonetheless, I appreciate the sentiment. Time to get out of this cursed place, then?' He glanced at the sun without narrowing his eyes. 'Lyn is probably waiting for us.'

In that peaceful library room, without bones and blades and graves wherever I looked. I jumped to my feet and grabbed his hand a little too eagerly. Below our hill, the white earth lay shimmering in the sunlight, telling its silent story of death and despair and utter destruction. Soon, far too soon ...

'Let's get out,' I said.

I still had time.

I would be ready.

Chapter 10

Bickering voices echoed through the corridors as I walked back into Orin's quarter a few hours later, louder and louder the closer I came to the Skeire family home.

Whatever optimism an hour of Faerie reading had left in me abruptly evaporated.

The differences between furious alves and festive alves were subtle but noticeable enough to the trained ear, and nothing trained the ear as fast as a week spent in the same house as Edored. These alves did not sound festive at all. Quite the opposite: by the vehemence of their shouting, it was a miracle no swords had been drawn yet.

And they were undeniably standing around my front door.

'... but see,' an alf male whose voice I didn't recognise snapped just before I rounded the last corner, 'is it really a violation of house sanctuary if we're doing it for their own good?'

I skidded to a halt just out of view, stumbling over my own feet from more shock than the bastard deserved.

House sanctuary.

Oh, *fuck*.

'What he says!' another one yelled. 'Remember that time Brodir was down with the flu and we bashed in his bedroom door to bring him food? Nobody made a fuss about house sanctuary that time!'

'Well, he could have died,' someone else pointed out.

The first speaker huffed triumphantly. '*Exactly*.'

An uncomfortable silence fell. I stood frozen behind the corner, heart racing in my throat – oh, gods help us all. Was this the moment to warn Tared that his cousin's friends may be about to get truly unpleasant? The moment to involve the Council? But if I walked off now and these idiots decided to act on their convenient interpretations of their own laws the next minute ...

Who would stop them?

'Lyn would be pissed, though,' someone warned, and a breath of relief escaped me. Yes. *Please*. Let them listen to that one. Let them realise that even Creon's head couldn't be worth a phoenix's eternal wrath ...

'She can hardly burn our heads off if she doesn't know which of us went in,' the first alf said smugly.

For fuck's sake.

I stepped from my hiding place without thinking any further, moulding my expression into the most innocent of doe-eyed smiles. The group was bigger than usual. Not a good sign. I noticed Njalar, a few other familiar faces, and some I'd never seen before – eleven of them altogether.

They jolted at my appearance, then slumped back against the walls as they recognised me. 'Oh, hello Emelin.' My native language, this time. They still weren't aware I could understand most of their Alvish. 'Where's everyone?'

What did they expect me to say? *Miles away, so you have plenty of time to commit bloody murder in their home?* I forced a careless shrug and said, 'Not sure. I think Tared should be back here soon.'

A lie, but at least it might keep them from acting for a few more hours, and in the panic of the moment, that was all my hammering heart could care about. Keep them out. Warn Creon. And then ...

Then what were we going to do?

I slipped into the house, shut the door behind me, and triple-checked the lock with trembling hands. The living room was deserted. I tip-toed through the corridor like a burglar, nonetheless, throwing several glances over my shoulders before I opened Creon's door and slipped into his room.

A knife whooshed right past me, slamming into the wall behind me with a sickening thwack.

I shrieked, whirling around.

Creon chuckled silently on the other side of the room, twirling a second knife around his fingers as he gestured for me to move aside. He still hadn't put on his shirt; I was welcomed by an alluring display of rippling muscle and ink-marked skin, a faint sheen of sweat empha-sising every hard line, every bulging ridge. A few long locks had slipped from the bun at the back of his head, fluttering softly with each shift of the wings behind his shoulders.

But it was the expression in his eyes that caught my attention most of all – stark, savage focus, a look as sharp as the blade in his hands.

'For the bloody gods,' I said, my voice too feeble. 'Are you preparing for your imminent murder, or is this some happy coincidence?'

He pulled up an inquiring eyebrow and flung his second knife at something behind me, a fluent motion too fast for my eyes to follow. All my senses registered was a flash of silver, a hiss of steel splitting the air. I expected the loud clatter of metal against stone, but instead, the knife hit its goal with another dull thud, like a blade sinking into soft wood.

I snapped around. Ah. It *was* wood.

The smooth, iridescent stone wall had changed into a provisory training surface, pale birch wood with targets marked in charcoal crosses. Creon's two knives were sticking out from the centre of one such cross, less than half an inch between them. Deep gashes around the hearts of the other targets showed he'd been at his training for a while and that a few days without practise hadn't been particularly harmful to his condition.

Zera help me. Perhaps I should have been a little less concerned about his health and a little more worried for the alves plotting to attack him.

When I turned back around, I found him studying me, his eyes unreadable. *What did you say about my imminent death?*

'Edored's damn friends,' I said bitterly. 'They're telling each other they might as well just ignore house sanctuary because it will all be done with good intentions.'

A sour grin curled around his lips. *That's all?*

That and the sight of the battlefield he had so catastrophically avoided ... but this probably wasn't the moment to bring up that second subject. I gulped in a breath, wrestling to keep my heartbeat down. 'Do you need more than death threats?'

He shrugged. *They're hardly surprising.*

'Is that why you took up training again?' I glanced at the knives jutting menacingly from the wall. 'Just in case they broke into the house after all?'

His fingers faltered, then briskly signed, *Hoped it would help to keep myself straight.*

The last of my optimism died a swift and merciless death. I squinted at him to examine that fiercely focused look in his eyes more carefully – Zera help me, how long had I been gone to Sevrith and Lyn's reading lessons? No more than two hours, a mere two hours in which I wasn't so close that he could easily concentrate on me over the simmering hatred of the Underground, and yet ...

'How quickly does it get worse without me?'

Could still be rational about it. If it was supposed to be a reassurance, the slow, overly cautious motions of his fingers undermined the intention entirely. *Don't worry. I'm not sinking back.*

'Yet.'

A shadow drew over his face. *Em ...*

'I'll be back earlier tomorrow,' I said, blurting out words too rapidly now. If I spoke fast enough, at least I wouldn't have to think, wouldn't have to ask myself how in the world I was ever going to handle this mess. 'Tared can probably teach me plenty in half an hour, and I'm—'

Em, don't. He stepped back, jaw and wings tightening. *You have meetings to attend. I'm not going to hold you back that way.*

'You're not holding me back at all! I can decide for myself that I'd prefer not to see you torn to shreds by your own powers – there's no need to—'

You're not going to lock yourself away for me, his signs interrupted, curt and sharp. Too sharp. There was a loss of control there, an alarming sense of agitation. *Don't even try. I'll run off and hide myself until you've gone about your day like a sensible person.*

I bit out a laugh. 'I don't want to go about my day like a sensible person if the consequence is you getting swallowed by self-hate again! Don't tell me you're allowed to dramatically sacrifice your life for me while I can't even cut training short for you.'

His lips moved around a soundless curse as he slipped past me and stalked to the perforated wooden wall. I plopped onto the edge of his bed and sucked in two, three deep breaths to calm my pounding heart. So much for the safety of the Underground, again. Perhaps no one would even need to break into his bedroom and skewer him on an alf sword after all – perhaps they did all the damage they dreamed of simply by feeling.

And would that ever pass? Or were we doomed to continue like this, him hanging onto the last threads of his sanity, me dragging him out of that dark hole time and time again?

Worries for later. I yanked myself out of that useless spiral of thoughts, ignored my crumbling heart begging for attention. This was not the moment for lovesick fretting; we had to survive this day first of all. 'Creon ...'

He pulled both the knives from their target with his left hand, then tucked his wings in tight, sank down in the nearest chair, and hesitated, his fingers hanging motionless for a moment too long. *I'll be fine.*

'I'll be a flying goat,' I said with a scoff.

He closed his eyes, the palest ghost of a smile trembling around his lips. *It's better already, Em. You're very pleasantly concerned about me.*

'But it can't go on like this forever!' I could have punched him – could have punched the bastards outside, could have punched these gods-damned walls, if only it would have *helped*. 'That's no life to live, Creon. You can't just ... sit here, falling apart half of the time. You'll go insane.'

He gave a brusque shrug. *What else do you propose? For you to shackle yourself to me every minute of the day?*

A curse fell over my lips. No, that wouldn't solve anything either. I had work to do, lives to save, and if I spent months staring at these bedroom walls, I would go mad as quickly as he would. But if I didn't stay near, if he was forced to hide here without my anchor to keep him stable ...

I closed my eyes and saw that empty look on his face again, the detached rigidity that had crept up on him over days of isolation. *Why are you here?*

As long as his demon senses kept soaking up every shred of emotion, he would keep sinking back. I didn't want to think any further, and did it anyway – imagined the light in his eyes sizzling out day by day, imagined his smiles growing duller and duller, until there was nothing left but torturous memories and all-consuming loathing.

A sword to the heart would be the more merciful option.

'We could leave?' I said bleakly, looking up. 'At least in the world above we could find a quieter place to stay, even if we'd still visit the Underground?'

I know how the Mother goes about finding people she wants dead. Something twitched around his lips. Memories, again – how often had he been the one finding those people? *She has eyes and ears everywhere, and no one is going to risk his head to save my life. You wouldn't be safe for a minute there.*

'No, but ... Oh, for hell's sake.' Going insane or walking back into his mother's arms. There had to be better choices. 'What else can we do? We're not going to change everyone's minds about you with a quick charm offensive either, are we?'

A joyless laugh. *Oddly, alves appear mostly immune to my unrivalled charms.*

'Terrible taste,' I said wryly, rubbing my eyes. 'So if they'll keep hating you and you have no other place to go ...'

He watched me, eyes too dark. Was that the influence of the Underground, oozing in despite my presence? Or was it merely that core of guilt and shame and hatred that had always been there, even back at the Crimson Court?

Layer within layer within layer of hurt, like a thorny, ink-black rose, every row of petals another shade of age-old agony.

'Could you shut it out?' I whispered. Anaxia's voice echoed in my ears – *He'd rather go insane as an untrained martyr.* 'Is that something you could learn?'

He stiffened in his seat, every last trace of his smile evaporating. *Don't say that.*

'But it has to be possible, yes? Not every demon is spending his time—'

Em, stop. His wings strained behind his back, as if attempting to escape the confines of that padded chair. *I'm not going to* ... His fingers clenched and unclenched, their motions as rigid as the hard line of his lips. *I'm not going to indulge these powers.*

'It's not about indulging!' My voice echoed too loud through the silence of the Underground. 'Those bloody powers are killing you! If you can learn how to mute them, if Anaxia can teach you to—'

He jerked to his feet so abruptly I flinched, his knuckles clenching white around the hilts of his knives. *Don't.*

'But—'

Don't! His gesture was a sudden, uncontrolled swing of his hand. *I'm. Not. Training—*

'Creon, it would *solve* things!'

He turned away and flung both knives into the wooden wall with a single unrestrained motion, the smack of metal into wood a more elaborate reply than any gesture his fingers could produce. For a moment he stood frozen, his back towards me, his wings quivering against his shoulders, his rough breath all that broke the suffocating silence of this place. Then, his gestures too sharp and too measured, he signed, *So would killing all of them, and I don't hear you suggesting that either.*

Zera help me. 'You know that's not the same.'

You have no idea. He didn't meet my gaze as he knelt and yanked his shirt from the floor. For a moment, his hands were occupied with pulling the cloth over his wings and shoulders; then, untying his hair with his left hand, he signed with his right, *There's more to these powers than the part you're having fun with. The part that makes a man kill himself at a twitch of my hand ...*

'You could use your magic to take the pain of others,' I said, ignoring the disconcerted shudder that ran through me. 'Would it really be so horrible to take away some of your own struggles, too?'

He fell back into his chair with his shirt unbuttoned, elbows on his knees and face in his hands, the veil of his dark locks obscuring every glimpse of his features. No answer, not even the slightest inclination he might be thinking about one. For a long, frustrated moment, I found myself wishing that I was the demon here, that I'd at least understand what storm of emotions was raging behind his eyes.

'Is it because this would be for your own benefit?' I added, biting that exasperation away. Lashing out wouldn't help. More anger was the last he needed now. 'Because when you were tormenting yourself with the pain of others, at least you were punishing yourself for using those bloody powers, too?'

He didn't move, but his wings seemed to *shrink* as I spoke – drawing in so tight that I almost expected the taut membrane to crumple before my eyes. Oh, fuck. Too blunt, too direct; this wasn't going to convince him, let alone help him. I wrapped my arms around myself and tried to focus, tried to be *rational* about the shreds of thoughts and ideas crowding me. Fine, dimming his powers was out of the question for now, and so was leaving. Which meant ...

'How far do you need to be removed from people to no longer sense their feelings?'

He cautiously lifted his face from his hands, as if he expected that question to be some dastardly trap, the wrong answer a straight road to ruin. When I gave no signs of dastardly scheming, he slouched in his chair and gestured with tight fingers, *Depends on how strongly they're feeling.*

'Do numbers make a difference?'

He nodded. *One or two I can ignore from a short distance. A few dozen will be annoying, but not painful. At the court ...* His sharp jaw clenched. *Half an island between me and the palace was just enough.*

'Right.' I let out a slow exhalation, ordering my thoughts. 'In that case ... even if we can't leave the Underground, would it help if we moved to another part of it? We're currently sitting in the middle of Orin's quarter, closest to the alves. And I know the others won't particularly like you either, but they might be a little less ... aggressive?'

His throat bobbed, but he nodded again. The restraint seemed to gradually return to him now that I wasn't suggesting training anymore. He could deal with solutions, then? Could deal with discussions, as long as they didn't force him into any acceptance of his powers?

Not for the first time, I found myself wondering, with a pang of horror, what in hell his father had done to him all those years ago.

But that was not a question for today either. Today I was going to figure out how I would keep him alive and well without spending every minute of the day in his vicinity. So I smiled my most determined smile, even though I knew he'd pick up on the anxiety behind it, and said, 'How about a library visit, then?'

He blinked. *I doubt they want me at the library.*

'Lyn is not kicking you out.'

He considered that for a moment, a thin line between his brows. *Perhaps.*

'She's not kicking you out,' I repeated, more firmly now to convince myself, 'and most others there are nymphs and vampires, who will at least not throw a fit because their honour obliges them to hate you until the end of time. Also, not even Njalar is going to kill you straight under Lyn's nose. So it might be better. We won't know if we don't try.'

How far is it from here? he gestured slowly.

'A little under a mile, I think. It was about fifteen minutes of walking.'

This time his silence was not that explosive, anxious silence of his mind breaking in on itself, but rather the thoughtfulness I knew from our time at the court, that lethal focus that suggested he was looking for the most efficient way to end someone. Balancing risks, estimating benefits. Leaving the house meant leaving the theoretical safety of Tared's home, facing the alves waiting for us outside. Which was a risk. But then again ... so was staying here for days or weeks on end, and this home might not be so safe after all.

I knew his conclusion the moment he rose, his gestures carrying that smooth, purposeful air of a decision made. *When?*

Thank the gods. I hunched up my shoulders and said, 'Are there any advantages to waiting? We could ask someone to fade us to the library so we can avoid the welcome committee outside, but ...'

There was a spark of amusement in his grin, a glimpse of something that said, fine, it's time for another adventure. *None of the Skeire alves are going to fade me anywhere close to Lyn if they can help it, Em.*

'Oh, come on.'

He shrugged, quickly buttoning his shirt as he swept his gaze over the room. Now that he was moving, now that something was *changing*, a brand new restlessness seemed to come over him – an impatience itching below the perfect control of his movements. *Don't worry about it. I never did well with help.*

Like a cat minding his own business, indeed – a solitary killer even before his own people ostracised him.

And then I had demanded he'd start working *with* me. I stifled a wry chuckle. Damn it all; we'd handle it ourselves.

'In that case ...' I got to my feet. What had Tared said? *We protect what's ours.* 'Might be better not to take those knives with you. They might see it as a threat.'

They might see it as theft, too, he signed dryly, then gestured at something deeper in the house. *Got them from their weapon room of sorts.*

How typical, I wanted to say, for an alf household to have an entire arsenal steps away from the living room – and then I recalled Tared's story, the massacre of his family, and pressed those words very, very far away. It would be a miracle if they weren't all sleeping with an extra set of blades under their bed.

'Let's leave them here, then. Unless you think you'll need them, in which case ...'

He shrugged. *By the time my magic is no longer sufficient, we'll have greater issues to worry about.*

A fair point. We left the knives behind.

I slipped into my own bedroom to put on clean black clothes, weighing my options to appease Edored's friends regarding this trip. Then I stepped out, found Creon lounging against the doorpost, and decided that nothing I could say would bring any honourable alf to accept this pinnacle of merciless fae beauty prowling through their home.

'Let's be a little fae about this,' I said, making my decision in the blink of an eye.

Scantily clad and prone to wanton debauchery?

I snorted. 'Will you think of Tared's poor heart?'

He laughed as he followed me into the living room and the entrance hall, eyes noting every weapon, every coloured surface, every lock and emergency exit. I gestured for him to wait out of sight as I slipped into the corridor, finding Njalar and his entourage where I'd expected them. They were heatedly discussing the advantages and disadvantages of killing a hypothetical enemy in his sleep over facing him in open battle.

'Oh?' I said, staggering to a halt in feigned surprise as they snapped around to face me. 'You're still here?'

That shut them up amusingly quickly.

'What?' Njalar said, scanning me with narrowed eyes. Behind him, two of his friends habitually grabbed for their weapons. 'You didn't think we'd let the fucker out of our sight, did you?'

'Oh, no, no.' I giggled a little helplessly. 'No, but that's exactly why I'm surprised that ... Well, if they didn't tell you, perhaps you're not supposed to know—'

'Tell us *what?*' one of the others snapped. 'Did they fade him elsewhere?'

'Well,' I said and cleared my throat. 'I mean, the news will probably spread anyway? He's ... um ... he's in the hospital wing, after he—'

They were gone before I got to my tale of Creon's non-existent injuries.

I whirled around just in time to see him emerge from the doorway, tall and gorgeous, biting his lip to keep his laughter down.

Never mind about the wanton debauchery. His gestures were tight with suppressed amusement. *Could probably get off just listening to you playing tricks on alves.*

'I suggest we conduct that experiment another time,' I said with a grimace, unable to stop scanning the corridor around us. Even the laughter in his eyes was not nearly enough to slow my pulse. 'They won't need long to be back.'

But we were around the corner before Njalar and his company returned, and no one stopped us before the next bend either. Creon strolled along next to me, looking deceptively unconcerned with wings tucked in and his hands deep in his pockets. Only his eyes told another story, examining every crack in the wall, every shadowy passage and shallow niche.

We just reached the tunnel separating Orin's quarter from Zera's quarter when he faltered and whipped around.

I followed his gaze, grabbing reflexively for the black, rune-covered wall. The corridor behind us was empty, not a living thing to be seen but the mosses and succulents covering Zera's side of the tunnel.

'What is it?' The words came out on a whisper.

Felt someone. Slow, vigilant gestures. His wings flared, prepared for lightning-quick movement. *Just a flash. But if they saw—*

And in a flicker of light, there were five of them.

Ten of them.

More of them, and I stopped counting, stopped seeing anything but their unsheathed swords and the feral gleam of bloodlust in their eyes. From a far and useless distance, I heard myself cry out a warning. A sturdy alf female whirled towards us, blade whooshing up for attack. Voices yelled in encouragement, shouted at me to get out of the way, and another sword gleamed white in the corner of my eye.

Creon shot forward.

A lightning bolt of yellow crackled through the tunnel.

And the swords diving at him, ready to kill – they halted abruptly.

Cries of bloodthirst turned into cries of confusion as two, three alves staggered backwards, their weapons still raised over their heads. They *kept* their weapons there, in that unnatural half-swing position, and only then did I realise where that flash of magic had gone.

Their shirts were no longer made of pliable linen.

Instead, a sheet of grey iron lay wrapped around their arms and torsos, following every crease and fold of the cloth it had once been. Fit snugly to their skins, the metal held their limbs trapped in place, unwilling to bend to the mere force of muscle and anger.

Rendering them useless in a fight without harming a hair on their bodies.

The surprise tempered the fervour of the attack more easily than a burst of red to the throat could have done. Alves faltered and jumped back around us, their passionate cries stilling at the sight of their friends caught in those unnatural positions. A single moment of hesitation, and I jumped on it without thinking.

'What in hell do you idiots think you're *doing*?'

Creon stepped back, ending up beside me – away from the alf steel around us, black wall within reach. He still hadn't even pulled his left hand from his pocket. Somehow, circled by their wolfish fury, he looked even more coldly indestructible – like a polished obsidian dagger, every honed edge promising the taste of blood.

As soon as the first alf steel blade reached him, though ...

He'd be entirely unarmed.

'Emelin,' Njalar said between clenched teeth. I found him to my right between two of his friends, gripping his sword with two hands as others pulled back the alves in the iron shirts. 'Get out of here.'

'So you can do what?' I refused to allow a tremble in my voice. Refused to consider their numbers – more than twenty of them now, twenty-five perhaps. 'Kill a guest the Council has explicitly allowed to stay?'

He snarled a curse. 'Get *out*.'

They were slinking toward us again, like growling dogs surrounding their prey. Next to me, Creon didn't waver, watching their advance with the distant amusement of a male who's wondering what fly he'll squash next.

Killing them, he'd said, would make everything worse.

And yet, if they insisted on this madness ... would we have a choice?

'You should realise' – my brain was turning so fast it left me dizzy – 'that if you let me go, the first thing I'll do is warn the Council. Do you really want Tared to come walking in while you're slaughtering his guests?'

'As if Tared cares—'

'Or Lyn?' I added briskly.

They faltered at that threat, the circle moving back like a loosening noose. Creon breathed a chuckle but didn't attack at their hesitation – nothing to provoke, nothing to ignite this fuse.

'Well, what do you want, then?' a female whose name I didn't know sneered. 'For us to kill you too?'

My rib cage seemed too small for my lungs, but my voice didn't waver. 'Would you kill me?'

They didn't seem to have anticipated a question that direct. Looks flew back and forth as they hesitated, swords ready for attack, unsure what their non-existent plan had to say about this complication.

Like a wave pausing at its highest point just before breaking.

'You'll probably have to kill me,' I added breezily, folding my arms but keeping my hands from the black of my dress. 'Really, that's the only way you can avoid me informing the Council of all of this – you know, you attacking an ally without any provocation and—'

'Well,' Njalar said, lowering his sword a fraction, 'if we just tell them he *did* attack us ...'

As they'd planned. If not for my presence ... I shrugged that thought off and said, 'After you've been shouting about your murderous intentions for days? Worst case I'll make a bargain of honesty with someone and allow them to interrogate me – that should do the trick.' I beamed a smile at him, and somehow my knees didn't give way. 'So I'm afraid killing me is really the only option you have. You'll have to tell them I attacked you, too. Perhaps I was some nasty fae spy all along? Goes to show you really can't trust people, even if—'

'But you're not a fae spy,' Njalar sputtered.

'Oh, I know,' I said, rolling my eyes. 'I'm telling you you'll need to lie. To cover your arses for killing me. Which you'll need to do if you want to get away with this madness.'

He stood gaping at me, sword hand sagging down, thoughts spinning frantically behind his pale green eyes. 'But we can't kill *you*. You're an unbound mage!'

'Fair point,' I admitted, nodding gloomily. 'Bit of a conundrum, then, isn't it?'

Swords were sinking on all sides of me now, their owners gaping at Njalar and me, throwing unsettled glances at Creon in between. The Silent Death leant against the wall with that unconcerned hand in his pocket, almond eyes fixed upon my face, the smallest of smiles playing around his full lips.

'But ...' Njalar started.

'We can just *not* kill him,' the sturdy female said triumphantly, as if she'd had the scientific breakthrough of the century. 'She can't rat on us if no one harms him.'

'But ...' Njalar stammered again.

'Bad news,' I said brightly. 'Creon just froze three of you in perfect attack position, if you'll recall. Good luck denying you tried to harm him even if you let him escape unscathed now. Can't wait to hear what Lyn has to say about—'

'Look,' Njalar interrupted, voice rising to a shrill timbre, 'there's no need to tell Lyn about any of this, is there? This is just between him and us. Would be pretty damn childish to go running to her to complain.'

'Oh, you know what? You're right.' I cocked my head at him. 'Let's keep it between you and us, then. Give me your word you'll give up this ridiculous guarding guise, that none of you will try to kill him again, and we can leave the Council out of it.'

He blinked at me. 'But ...'

We protect what's ours. I risked another smile and quickly added, 'Of course, if he actually *does* attack any of you, you're free to do whatever you like. But until that time ...' I shrugged. 'Your word?'

They stood stupefied, the momentum of their attack lost, their plan reduced to a pathetic pile of reckless guesses. They shouldn't have struck with witnesses around. They shouldn't have struck with nothing but a stroll around the Underground as their provocation. Now, unless they wished to subject themselves to Lyn's wrath and whatever authority Tared had ...

'Oh, go to hell,' Njalar spat. 'My word.'

Creon merely lifted a hand. Yellow light filled the corridor, and the three alves in the back let out a cry of relief as their arms finally fell down again.

'Lovely,' I said, and spite was all that kept my knees from buckling. 'You don't mind if we continue our walk around the block now, do you?'

Clearly they minded. But they'd given their word, bound their honour, and taking that back ... They may as well have chucked their swords into the ocean.

The first two to leave faded hesitantly, throwing dubious looks around as they dissolved into thin air. But the next few went faster, and so did their neighbours, until no one but Njalar was still standing in that broad corridor, green eyes flashing with fury, knuckles white around the hilt of his sword.

'Don't think we're done yet,' he growled, '*Hytherion.*'

And then he was gone, too.

CHAPTER 11

HAD CREON NOT GRABBED my arm as the last flash of alf steel disappeared, I might have toppled over. Ten minutes of fear hit me all at once, turning the bones of my legs to pulp.

Stay on your feet. He slipped a muscular arm around my waist as if we weren't standing in a very public space, potentially close to people desperate for an excuse to think ill of him. His signs were calm, but his eyes had a hawkish air to them as they shot back and forth along the corridor. *It's bad form to break your skull on an innocent floor moments after talking down half an army.*

A watery laugh escaped me. 'Thank the gods for your good manners.'

Thank the gods for your clever brain. His left hand tightened around my waist, then released me and tucked a loose lock of dark brown hair behind my ear. His gaze flashed over my shoulder one last time before it settled on my face. *I'm glad to see you're ordering alves about as easily as fae. Go on like this and you'll be ruling the world next year.*

'Flatterer.' They did get me back on my feet, though, those words and the flicker of pride in his eyes. I threw another glance around, found the corridor still empty, and added, 'I doubt this solved anything. They'll be more furious, if anything.'

Creon grimaced. *Yes.*

'Oh. Right. You felt that.' I rubbed my face, unable to keep in a groan. 'What do we do? We could tell Lyn and Tared anyway and leave it to them to sort out the mess. I'm not terribly concerned about my honour.'

Could, he signed absently, rolling his shoulders like a cat preparing for the hunt. *But once you break your word to them, they'll never trust you again. Not helpful.*

I grumbled a curse.

I doubt they'll be back today. He combed a hand through his hair, black locks and black scars forming a grotesque spider web against the bronze of his skin. *Still want to try the library?*

The cowardly part of me wanted nothing but to run back home and hide before any of the bastards could figure out a way to circumvent the promise they'd made. I knew better than to think they'd call it bad luck and make their peace with Creon's presence after this one misguided attempt.

But on the other hand ... the next few hours should be safe.

'It's that way,' I said, sucking in a deep breath. Damn them all to hell and back, then. We'd have to survive their next try somehow.

Somehow.

I pushed the sting of worry away.

We reached Inika's quarter without running into a single person, just a few quick glimpses of movement on the far end of halls and tunnels, faint sounds of footsteps in the distance. I wasn't sure if we were being avoided or if luck was simply on our side for once, but neither seemed a reason for complaints.

Creon didn't take his hands from his pockets until I eventually stood still at that red door with its salamander knocker. Only then did he throw a last look around and sign, *Not a lot of life in this part.*

'Lyn said there weren't too many phoenixes around,' I said, and he sighed and nodded for me to go first.

Had I not known he'd never seen this library before, I might have assumed he knew the place like the back of his hand. He didn't falter at the light falling in from the fields, didn't falter at the sight of the towering bookcases, didn't falter as every nymph and vampire at the long writing tables looked up and froze above their work. One unhurried glance around, and he turned back to me, one eyebrow raised slightly in a wordless inquiry. The faint smile around his lips was one I knew from the Crimson Court – that smile that radiated effortless invincibility, a pleasant reminder that bystanders might do themselves a grand favour by letting him go about his day exactly as he wished.

As if he hadn't scarcely avoided bloody death by alf sword mere minutes ago. As if he hadn't crumbled under the force of his own magic for weeks.

Whether it was that smile or my presence by his side, I didn't know, but none of the scribes and readers objected when I said, 'First gallery and then to the left.'

He nodded, manoeuvring past the tables and up the stairs with the supple, unhurried grace of a dark panther. The flutter of his wings as he glanced out through the high windows didn't escape me – how long had it been since he'd flown?

'There's a door behind that third aisle,' I said quietly, painfully aware of how loud even my near-whisper sounded against the backdrop of rustling parchment and scratching pens. 'Perhaps you should let me go first.'

He sent me a nod of understanding and stepped aside so I could pass him by. I pushed the door ajar, listening sharply for a moment. The room had always been deserted over the past few days, but who knew whether a horde of hot-headed alves had decided today was the perfect day for some history reading?

It didn't seem to be the case. I opened the door entirely and slipped inside, double-checking the empty desks and window seats before I glanced back over my shoulder and gestured for Creon to follow me. His shoulders abruptly loosened the moment he shut the door, the smile plastered on his face moving over for a far more genuine expression of both exhaustion and slightly dazed wonder.

She's been expanding.

I blinked. 'Lyn?'

He nodded as he crossed the room to my side and threw a longer glance at the fields behind the arched open windows. Turning back to the dozens and dozens of books, he signed, *Last time I saw these, the entire collection more or less fit into a single hall.*

'She mentioned she collected a lot in the decade after the Last Battle,' I said, wondering how big exactly that single hall had been. 'Just to make sure the books would be safe.'

Creon smiled faintly, an odd expression of regret as much as affection. *Of course.*

A flicker of some entirely new feeling lit up in my chest as I watched him saunter through the nearest aisle, pausing every now and then to examine a title or browse one of the volumes. Not the feeling I had expected. We were alive. He gave no urgent signs of demon trouble in this place, the look in his eyes no longer so full of desperate focus. I ought to have been mortally relieved. And instead ...

Seeing him here, mentioning that library of old, I could far too easily picture him and Lyn at one of these working tables, browsing through rare manuscripts together, discussing theories I wouldn't understand and linguistic oddities in ten different languages I'd never even heard of. And then there was that smile, that expression of painful nostalgia – or was it something else?

He snapped around as the anxiety flared through me. *What is it?*

'I ...' Hell. What was I *thinking?* All of this happened over a hundred years ago, and he had tried to sacrifice his life for me two weeks ago. Shouldn't that put things into perspective? 'Nothing. Just a little nervous. Are you—'

Em.

I clenched my jaw. 'Yes?'

He studied me for a moment with those all-seeing eyes – that demon gaze so strangely like Anaxia's bright blue stares, cutting straight through every defiant scowl, every pretence of indifference. Then, with a small sigh, he turned and walked over to the nearest writing table, kneeling to pull ink, pen, and parchment from the drawers.

We were going back to writing? I hurried after him, too intrigued to keep up my unsuccessful pretence of composure. By the time I reached him, he had already sat down on the single stool, smoothing the parchment with a scarred hand. I leaned over his shoulder to read, and his wings wrapped around me as by instinct, keeping me pressed against his slender back while he dipped his pen in the ink.

He scribbled down a single sentence, in a messy, hurried hand.

I meant it when I said you were a first.

I stared at those words for two paralysed heartbeats, anxiety mingling with an almost fearful embarrassment.

His letter at the Crimson Court had told me, indeed. Why was I forcing him to repeat himself, even if I was doing it involuntarily? He'd been clear enough, and *I* was the one who didn't dare to want more from him – so wasn't it a bit childish, really, to—

Em, his fingers signed, dropping the pen, *stop that.*

'But ...'

He sighed, picking up his pen again. *I also meant it when I said I wasn't used to being treated like an equal. Lyn and the others didn't treat me like half a god, but the result was the opposite. It was me feeling less than others for the first time in my life.* He underlined the *less.*

'Oh,' I said numbly. 'Alright. I see how that might be unhelpful.'

I didn't fall in love with her, he continued, faster now. *I put her on a pedestal as some epitome of perfection. Took me a few decades to figure out the difference, but now that I'm there, I have not the slightest desire to go back. I still think highly of her, I'm very grateful for all she did for me, but I promise that's all there is to it.*

I swallowed, wrapping my arms around his shoulders to bury my face in his hair. 'That ... thank you.'

And you ... He hesitated, his pen hovering above the ink pot for a moment too long before he dipped it in. *You're a fierce and utterly uncontainable little cactus hugger, you make me feel like the world's biggest idiot and the most brilliant of souls at the same time, and I'm well aware neither of us is anywhere close to perfect, but every time you shatter my doors and windows, I can't help feeling we might just be quite perfect together. So don't ever worry about Lyn or anyone else – there's no comparison. You're incomparable. And tell me if you ever doubt that, because it will be my pleasure to remind you a hundred times more. Clear?*

My knees might be giving in – hell, my heart might just be giving in. I clung to his shoulders so tightly it was a miracle he could still breathe and whispered, 'Clear.'

He squeezed my hand on his chest, quickly and lightly, then shoved pen and ink back where he'd found them and cautiously folded the sheet of parchment. Only as he handed it to me over his shoulder did the understanding dawn on me, with a sensation like the abrupt brightening of the alf lights in the morning.

'Did you ... did you deliberately write that down for me?'

He folded his wings back to release me, then turned when I stepped away from him. His shrug was not the usual careless shrug at all; this one looked almost bashful.

Just in case I'm not around to tell you.

'You ... *Creon.*' I swallowed something prickly; if I wasn't careful, I'd burst out crying. 'Good gods. Don't ever try to tell me again how there's nothing kind about you, because I'll ... I'll ... '

He raised an amused eyebrow. *Be unkind about it?*

'Yes. I'll slap you in the face with this thing until you agree with me you're terribly and embarrassingly wrong about yourself.' I glanced at the folded parchment a last time, then shoved it deep into the pocket of my dress. 'And ... and thank you.'

He didn't reply as he rose to his feet, but the quick brush of his fingers over the back of my hand said all he didn't put in signs. I stumbled after him like a sleepwalker, my mind three-quarters occupied by the lines now sitting safely in my pocket.

Perfect together.

Words that rang true far too easily, sense and reason be damned; I had to pull myself back into more rational territory with what felt like a physical effort. What was I thinking? Pretty words, indeed, but I'd known him for weeks, and half of that time, I'd known him through the unforgiving wood of a door he wouldn't open for me. I had no idea if the real Creon was the male who'd save the world for me or the male who'd rather fall apart than save himself, and if I wasn't careful, I might just spend the rest of my life fighting the deadly pits of his mind.

Even if the mere thought of the parchment in my pocket made me burn with giddy joy.

For the bloody gods' sakes. Time to give myself something else to fret about, like staying alive and fighting wars. Hurrying after him to catch up, I shoved the thorny questions of feelings and commitments back into the shadows of my mind and said, 'Creon?'

He turned around at the window, the gesture of a male bracing himself. He, too, had noticed the whirlpool of my emotions, and the stiffness of his shoulders suggested he was as unsure what to make of it as I was.

And yet something in his eyes was just a fraction softer than before – no, a fraction *calmer.*

'It's not as bad here, is it? The hate?' Focus. This was what we were here for: keeping him from crumbling. More waffling about feelings wouldn't improve anyone's day. 'You do look ... better.'

A grin crept over his lips. *Even better?*

'Oh, go to hell,' I said, which would have sounded more convincing if not for the undeniable chuckle lacing my words. 'I'm dead serious. Do you notice any improvement?'

He sank into the window seat with that easy, deadly elegance, a small frown on his face as he thoughtlessly rearranged his wings against the backrest. *I think I do. I feel suspiciously uninclined to remind you that you should stay away from me before I dramatically ruin your life, at least.*

My thoughts unhelpfully swirled back to the parchment in my pocket. 'Ah.' My voice croaked a little. 'I noticed that.'

He sent me a wry smile but mercifully refrained from commenting. *It's not entirely gone, but it's different. More like ...* He hesitated, then shrugged, a nearly forgotten twinkle dancing in his eyes. *Different types of storm winds probably don't mean much to you.*

'Not at all,' I said and dropped down next to him on the pillow-covered seat, pulling my knees to my chest without bothering much to keep my thighs covered. Something about that look on his face made chastity seem like an utterly ridiculous concept. 'But I think I under-stand the idea. It's not like a hurricane in the face here?'

He nodded slowly, wings shifting behind his shoulders. *More like flying against a strong current. It's annoying, it takes more energy, but I don't think it'll drive me mad.* A long, unusually focused exhalation – as if he was figuring out how to adjust to the change in the emotional landscape. *Remind me to take you for a storm flight one day.*

'What – for fun?'

His grin broke through in its full, dangerously dazzling capacity, laced with that tinge of recklessness that somehow made him look impossibly more alluring. *Can go pretty fast on storm currents.*

'That sounds like a terrible idea,' I told him, even though the warmth welling in my lower belly told me in no uncertain terms my objections would be powerless if the occasion arose. The idea of soaring through the skies in his arms, clouds swirling and winds roaring around us ... Perhaps it would be worth a few broken bones. 'Makes one wonder how you survived to this day and age, frankly.'

I rarely crash. He looked even more amused as he watched me, waiting for the exasperated groan that was sure to follow – or perhaps rather for the mixture of amusement, fascination, and very justified concern that rolled through me. Odd, how his gaze alone made me so much more aware of every twinge of emotion I felt. *And as long as I'm conscious enough to use magic, it's not a problem.*

'You and I have very different ideas of what constitutes a problem,' I said wryly. 'What do you use magic for – healing your broken neck?'

He waved at the floor. *Softening my landing.*

'You ... oh. Yellow?'

Yes.

'You just change the earth into a giant pillow? Like that wall you turned into wood a few hours ago?' I rubbed my face, considering that. 'Is it me, or does yellow magic seem rather ... limitless?'

Creon raised an eyebrow, leaning back against the windowsill. *Why yellow specifically?*

'Red has a specific function,' I said with a nod at the bargain mark on my wrist. 'It breaks stuff. Blue is even more specific, because it can only restore things into a state they were in before. But yellow is so ...' I made a wide gesture at nothing in particular. 'So general. *Change*. That could be pretty much everything, couldn't it?'

He closed his eyes. *Did I mention I'm a worthless teacher?*

'You're no such thing,' I said, swatting at him. 'Lyn said I was making ridiculously fast progress with my magic.'

You are. Which I think I also forgot to tell you, to support my point. He looked up, his glare enough warning to smother my attempted objection. *I can give myself very little credit for your talent. Growing up around a painter's workshop gave you a much better sense for colours than most of us have at the start.*

I glanced at the golden oakwood of the window seat. Even miles and miles away from Father's paints and palettes, the proportions came to me without so much as a thought – roughly equal parts blue and red, and double the amount in yellow.

'Right,' I said slowly. 'I see your point.'

He gave me a small smile. *So the most I do as a teacher is forgetting over and over again how little you know about the basics. No one ever told you about the rules for yellow magic?*

'Oh, there are rules?'

His expression turned sour. *As I thought.*

I chuckled, sitting up straighter. 'Tell me about them, then. Are they rules that can't be broken or rather rules that we would be strongly advised not to break?'

Bit of both. First rule is you can't change colour. The power can't affect its own source. People have tried and gone mad trying – it's impossible.

I'd never even thought of making an attempt; it had always seemed intuitively problematic. Then again ... 'But colours can change with a change of material, can't they?'

He smiled. *Yes. That's the workaround.*

'So if I need red ...' I pulled a fluffy green pillow from under my knee. 'I can't change this into a red pillow, but I could change it into a block of cinnabar and suck the colour out of that?'

He raised his eyebrows. *Cinnabar?*

'The basis for red dye.'

Didn't know that, he admitted. *I usually pick some red type of wood.*

I huffed a little too smugly. 'Amateur.'

He barely raised his hand in reply. Yellow flashed between us, and suddenly the pillow in my hands had become a particularly slimy blob of glue, slithering from my grip and hitting my half-bared legs with a wet, mushy splat. I shrieked, tried to shove the sludge off me in an unthinking reflex, and only found both my hands covered in thick glue as a result – as if I'd been swishing them around in a bucket full of egg whites.

At the other end of the window seat, Creon sat watching my frantic attempts with shining dark eyes, his grin entirely too satisfied.

'*You*.' I had planned to find something better to say, some impressive and mildly frightening insult – but at that moment, the cold substance slid down between my legs, over the inside of my thighs, and I gasped as all but pure, primal disgust evaporated from my mind at once. 'You horrible, *horrible* ...'

I don't suppose you need any help from amateurs? he signed pleasantly.

I blinked at my hands, covered in sticky, colourless glue, and then at the many-coloured pillows around and under me. No way to suck the colour out of anything without making a horrid mess of Lyn's library. No way to throw a few demonstrative bursts of red at him, just to make my point.

The only other sensible thing to do ...

I launched myself into his lap, hands stretched out for his face.

He dodged just a fraction too late – unprepared, it seemed, for anyone *this* suicidally stupid. I found a black-clad shoulder and a pointed ear under my glue-covered hands and latched onto him like a particularly vengeful leech; he rolled onto his back, shaking with laughter, and I followed without letting go, smearing goo on his shirt, his hair, any inch of skin I could find. My limbs met rock-hard muscle wherever they landed, thighs, stomach, chest, until finally I found the tight velvet of his wing under my fingers and rubbed a long smudge of stickiness on that taut surface, too.

He gasped, his soundless laughter stilling at once.

There. *That* would teach him.

Sprawled out over his sculpted body, my lips mere inches away from his, I ran my palm over the smooth expanse of his wing again and watched his eyes flutter shut in unwilling surrender. So sensitive. So dangerously sensitive ... I let out a triumphant chuckle and trailed my fingertips in small circles over the dark velvet, revelling in his catching breath, his tightening muscles, his uncontrolled twitches at every sensitive spot I passed. His hand came up and clawed into my bare, glue-covered thigh. His cock ...

I shifted, rubbing myself against his crotch, and was met by the familiar jolt of his arousal coming to life.

His breath turned rough, irregular. I prodded the growing bulge of his erection and sweetly muttered, 'Amateur.'

He laughed, lifting his hand a fraction. *Show me how it's done, then.*

I wrapped my sticky fingers around his shoulders and slammed my mouth into his.

He received me with hot, insatiable lips, burying both his hands in my hair to yank me closer, deeper, locking me against him. Our tongues tangled together in a frenzied battle for victory; I moaned, pressed myself even harder into his chest. Damn the magic, then, and damn the risks. I'd been careful enough for the day. If this was what we were now, unable to keep our hands off each other for longer than five unsupervised minutes—

A door opened, half a room away.

Oh.

Oh no.

In a flash, the spell was broken. I tore away from him, shot to the other side of the window seat, and frantically yanked my skirt into place without caring much about my sticky hands. Next to me, Creon moved so fast I didn't follow half of his motions – wings tucking in, lightning-quick sparks of red wiping glue from the most incriminating places – morphing back, somehow, into a fully composed, slightly glue-stained fae prince in less than the time it took to blink an eye.

There was no morphing me back into anything presentable with half of my body and dress covered in slime, my hair a wild mess of curls over my shoulders. "Slightly dishevelled" was the best we were getting.

Footsteps approached between the book cases, light and quick and alarmingly familiar. Creon closed his eyes for a fraction of a moment as I threw him a wide-eyed look of panic, a flash of that reckless grin breaking through the indifferent façade of his face.

I smothered a hysterical giggle and loudly said, 'Lyn?'

'Oh, Emelin!' The footsteps quickened. 'Didn't know you – Inika have mercy, what have you two been *doing*?'

She emerged small and bright-coloured from the nearest aisle, two enormous leather-bound books clenched against her chest. Creon's presence didn't seem to startle her in the slightest. The thick layer of glue that still clung to my hands and thighs and dress, on the other hand, received a good heartbeat of unwelcome and undivided attention.

I cleared my throat and uttered a reasonably composed, 'We're practising yellow magic.'

She blinked at me, then at Creon, who sent her his most apologetic grimace, and then at me again. 'With *glue*?'

'He started it,' I said.

I was provoked, he signed.

'He says he was provoked,' I said to Lyn, who stared at me in growing bewilderment, 'which is a shameless lie, obviously. I'm the embodiment of peaceful timidity. You know I'd never do such a thing.'

Next to me, Creon stifled a soundless snigger.

'See?' I said, pointing an elbow at him – one of the few clean body parts I had left. 'That's his guilty conscience coming through.'

I knew the way he clenched his jaw – the look of a burst of laughter about to break through any arrogant, apathetic mask. Lyn threw another befuddled look at us, the expression on her young face oddly reminiscent of a mother trying to figure out which of her children has run off with the leftover cake this time.

Had she ever seen him like this, all dignity gone, all deadly power gone, just a rumpled, vulnerable fae male fighting silly mock-fights over even sillier insults?

'Do I need to worry about leaving the two of you alone with my books?' she said cautiously.

Creon shrugged and signed, *Tell her not if I'm here to keep an eye on you.*

'He says not as long as I'm here to keep an eye on him,' I said, and he broke – slumped in the pillows of that window seat shaking with laughter, the sight of his amusement so contagious, the entire situation so utterly ridiculous, that I couldn't help myself and followed his example.

Lyn stood staring at us as we sat there, giggling uncontrollably like a pair of children, her small nose wrinkling in what seemed to be suspicion as much as confusion. 'Well.' Too composed. Whatever she had expected at her reunion with Creon, this wasn't it. 'Practise all you want, then, but if I come back to find even the tiniest speck of glue on *any* of my books, I'll personally skin the both of you alive. Hope that's clear?'

On the other side of the window seat, Creon abruptly pulled himself together and sent her the most demonstratively innocent look I'd ever seen on him, looking all the more suspicious for it. I desperately smothered the next unhinged laugh that welled up in me and somehow managed a demure, 'Yes, Lyn.'

She sent us a last bemused glare, turned around on her heels, then faltered halfway through. 'Oh, and Creon ...'

He stiffened as she met his gaze again, and for a single frozen moment, all mindless amusement was gone.

The look they exchanged ... it was a look that contained a hundred and thirty years of unspoken words, decades and decades of buried feelings and sleepless nights. Lyn parted her lips and hesitated, and for just an instant, I was sure she would crack – that every single minute of that thorny, tangled history would come rolling over her tongue with the next word she'd speak.

Then she sighed, nodded, and said, in the most casual, conversational tone imaginable, 'Marika finished another work on planetary ellipses last year. It's pretty ground-breaking, apparently – if you'd like me to get you a copy ...'

An outstretched hand. I could see it in the way the lines and shadows melted off his face – an expression that looked nothing like the superficial boredom he put on display for the rest of the world, that was somehow utterly joyless and utterly relieved at once. An acknowledgement of her peace offering and an apology, too.

I'd never seen him so much as part his lips in the vicinity of anyone else, but now he mouthed, *Thank you.*

'Wonderful.' She sent me a bright grin, added, 'Good luck with that glue,' and vanished without waiting for a reply from either of us.

We were both silent for at least a minute after the door fell shut behind her.

Creon sat staring at the bookcases with quiet, contemplative eyes, adjusting, recalculating. I waited. Whatever was going on behind that wall of blank wistfulness, I wasn't going to disturb it – not if this was the culmination of over a century of brooding, a sudden end to decades and decades of worry.

When he eventually loosened his shoulders against the windowsill, it was with a sigh that could have imploded his bones. *Sorry about that.*

'About what?' I said, pulling a face at him. 'Covering me in glue in a public space?'

There was nothing wistful about the laugh that curled around his lips, all wicked amusement again as he cleaned the glue off my hands with a few careless swings of red magic and unfurled his left wing to gesture at the traces I'd left behind. *You can't claim any high ground here, cactus.*

I snorted. 'I was provoked. Also, planetary ellipses?'

I have a bit of a soft spot for astronomy. He folded his wing against his back and shrugged. *The mathematics behind it is quite fascinating.*

I stared at him. 'Mathematics.'

Yes?

A slightly dazed laugh fell over my lips. 'Gods help me. Might take me a few more questions before I fully understand what's going on in that brain of yours.'

Let's get back to your training first. He chuckled as I opened my mouth to object and added, *You get one question for every successful exercise.*

Hell. He was really getting better at teaching.

Chapter 12

'Morning, Emelin,' Lyn cheerfully greeted me when I wobbled into the living room six days later, my thighs unusually sore due to an unfortunate combination of Tared's newest exercises and a particularly strenuous night in Creon's bed. 'Breakfast?'

I crashed down on the bench opposite her and grumbled, 'I'd kill for breakfast.'

'We're making an excellent alf out of you,' she said, plucking two buns from the impressive pile on the table and shoving them onto my plate.

Ylfreda and Hallthor had already eaten, presumably; they were always up early. Edored would come stumbling out of bed in an hour and a half and devour whatever food the rest had left for him. Tared I wasn't sure about; most days he and Lyn ate breakfast together, but he was nowhere to be seen today.

I cut open my bun, covered the bottom half with an amount of cheese and ham that would have been a full meal on Cathra, and pushed away the usual sting of guilt as I took my first bite. All extra food the fields of the Underground produced was smuggled onto the human islands above, but my growing muscles needed their fuel; there really was no need to feel like a traitor merely for feeding myself properly for the first time in my life.

Lyn returned to her notes as I ate, scribbling comments in the margins of her own writing with annoyed hums at every mistake she found. Only as I started on my second bun did she look up again and say, 'Oh, are you joining us in the Wanderer's Wing? Beyla has returned with some troubling observations.'

I had to rewind that question twice in my mind before I could believe I'd heard her correctly. 'You're ... you're inviting *me*?'

'Yes?' Her smile was too meaningful. Tared must have told her about my listening at the door, then, about my frustration over not even knowing what I wasn't allowed to know. 'We thought you might have some thoughts. So if you'd like to join ...'

'Oh.' It took all I had not to laugh at the sudden lightness cascading down my chest. *Thoughts*. No sending me off as a mindless weapon, after all. Perhaps this wasn't an invitation to the Council itself yet, but I was starting to suspect that the group I'd met in the Wanderer's Wing may be no less influential; somehow, their innocuous discussions appeared to steer most of the decisions made in the official heart of the Underground. 'Thanks. I'll ... I'll try to say sensible things, then.'

Lyn just smiled and went back to work.

I finished my breakfast in nervous silence, packed up some bread and cheese for Creon, and returned to my room to put on something more presentable than the comfortable tunic dress I wore for training. After a moment of consideration, I picked a moss green dress I'd pilfered from Lyn's impressive adult wardrobe, a design that followed the White City fashion of square necklines and slightly puffed sleeves to the letter. The Alliance might need my magic, but if I was about to get involved in discussions of politics and loyalties, I preferred to look as human as possible.

Plans? Creon gestured as I slipped into his room to deliver his breakfast and found him halfway dressed, the shirt I'd stolen from Hallthor and adjusted for his wings unbuttoned. Books lay scattered around the room, some he'd taken from the library, some Lyn had pushed into my hands to pass on. Around the floral chairs, messy sketches of constellations and circular shapes covered the floor, leftovers of his attempts three nights ago to explain the complexities of planetary orbits to me. *Mathematics.*

Not for the first time, I found myself wondering what he might have been if his mother hadn't been so determined to see him grow up as a weapon, if his father hadn't been so determined to see him dead.

'Wanderer's Wing,' I said, examining his seemingly light expression as I put down his breakfast on the nightstand. A morning ritual, by now, to quickly scan the lines around his lips and the tension of his jaw to assess how well he'd slept, how violent his dreams had been, how long he'd safely deal with the Underground on his own. 'Lyn said Beyla found something worrisome. I'll report back.'

He nodded, buttoning his shirt with quick, practised fingers. A shame. *Will see you in the library afterward, then.*

'Yes.' I squashed the usual itch of discomfort. No need to worry, I reminded myself. He looked composed enough on this particular morning, which suggested his demon senses had at least allowed him a decent night of sleep. The library was safe, and Njalar and his company had miraculously kept their word and not attacked again in the past days. But in a way, it was *more* unnerving, this absence of any active violence. At least when they'd been camping openly at our front door, I'd known where to look for them.

Now ... who knew when they'd strike again?

Em. Creon's gaze trailed over my face, studying me with those eyes that had always seen straight through me. *I've faced worse.*

And I had no desire to see him repeat the experience. How could he expect me to merrily leave him alone if one stubborn alf too many might mean this was the last time I even saw him alive?

'Alright,' I muttered, because we'd had that conversation often enough, and the outcome was always the same. 'See you in the library, then. Anything else I can do for you?'

The slight tilt of his head was an unmistakable challenge, an obvious and deliberate attempt to soothe my anxiety. *Kiss me?*

Hell take him, there was no being frightened when confronted with that look. I heaved a dramatic sigh, folded my hands behind my back, and said, 'I don't know what makes you think that any respectable cactus-hugging half fae would even *consider* doing such a thing, Your Highness. Unless you were planning to cruelly abduct me ...'

Have to say you're looking particularly abductable today, he signed as he sauntered leisurely towards me, crossing the ten feet between us ever so slowly, eyes trailing down my modest cleavage with far too much interest. Warmth tingled in my lower body, and that vexingly all-knowing smile twisted around his lips. *Would you be angry if I did?*

'I would call you various unflattering names,' I said primly.

His smile became a suppressed burst of laughter. *Tempting.*

'Or I'll punch you. Or ... or ...'

Words and thoughts abandoned me as his musky fragrance rolled over me. He was close enough now that I had to tilt back my head to hold his gaze, his eyes shining with that gleam of reverent want that made my insides swim. One last unhurried step, and his hands moulded to my waist, warm and strong and feathery gentle.

Or? his lips said.

'Or perhaps,' I whispered, my skin tingling from the touch of those confident fingers even through my dress, 'I'll be as cruel as you are and take my revenge very, *very* slowly tonight. So I'd be careful what you ask for. How long do you think you can stand those kisses before you're begging for mercy?'

His eyes had gone wholly dark between his long lashes, hunger burning just below the surface. His fingers answered not in signs but in their slow trail down over my hips, languid caresses worshipping the new firmness of my muscles, the new softness of my curves.

My knees wobbled. His lips parted a fraction, preparing for the taste of me.

'Still not deterred?' I murmured, rising to my toes. 'At your own risk, then ...'

The breath of a silent chuckle brushed over my lips just before his mouth came down on mine. He met me with surprising gentleness, a slow, single-minded kiss that spread through me like a sip of honey mead and warmed me to the tips of my fingers – a kiss that could have sent me collapsing if not for his calloused hands holding me.

The room blurred around me. My thoughts stilled, focusing only on the unbearable smoothness of his firm lips enticing mine. When he finally pulled away and I emerged back into the world of the living, there was nothing left on my mind but thoughts of the most pleasant, most sinful revenge.

His smile was pure torture as lowered me back to my own feet and signed, *Don't forget your meeting.*

I breathed a dazed laugh. 'Abduction is starting to sound better and better, I must say.'

Later. He pressed a kiss to my forehead, then stepped back, allowing the cold air back between us. *They need you there.*

And I need you with me, I almost retorted, the shape of the words so tangible on my lips, even though I'd never spoken them out loud. *I want you with me, not just these stolen moments, not just these secret nights ...*

It would be so gods-damned easy to say it – such a relief to give up on this gruelling balancing act, this dancing on the thin line between being with him and keeping my heart safely away from him. Why did I still try to resist the magnetic pull between us if these good moments were so utterly glorious, if this thing I felt for him was growing so alarmingly close to ...

Love?

Dangerous thoughts, dangerous words; I swallowed them as I had before, pretending not to notice the tension settling over him in the loaded silence. I should know better. Two days ago, he'd woken up unwilling to even leave his room, and in those hours of arguing with his numb, unresponsive mind, I'd been mortally relieved that at least I wasn't betting my own future on the state of his wellbeing.

He'd been burned once too often already. I wasn't going to blurt out any declarations I'd regret the next day.

'Suppose you're right.' Time to pull myself together. Time to be, at least for a few hours, the Alliance's prudent unbound mage. 'See you later, then.'

See you, Em.

So very sane, so very sensible – but I had to pause for several deep breaths in the winding Underground corridor before I dared to face the company in the living room again.

Tared had shown up in the meantime to eat a second breakfast at Lyn's side, discussing some issue with the house of Svirla over his generous-ly buttered bread. He interrupted himself mid-sentence as I came in, looking content at the sight of my waddling.

'Bastard,' I told him by way of morning greeting. Nothing got my mind off Creon as easily as offended alves.

'Careful, brat,' he said, throwing me a skewed grin, 'or I might just decide to double the work tomorrow. Are you ready to leave?'

I frowned. 'Aren't we training at all today?'

'I'll probably spend the rest of my day chatting with some people.' He looked exasperated at the prospect. 'So unless you're willing to accept Edored as your trainer ...'

'She's not,' Lyn said, throwing her pen at him; he easily avoided the projectile. 'And sorry, Emelin, there will be no reading lessons either this afternoon. You'll miss the Faerie vocabulary dearly, I'm sure.'

'I'll probably cry myself to sleep,' I said. 'But if you two need your time for another round of shameless manipulation, I'll gladly sacrifice my lessons for that purpose.'

Tared snorted. 'I'm an honourable alf, Emelin. I don't manipulate.'

'Ah. You just have chats with friends ...'

'Yes.'

'... who just happen to be members of other houses ...'

'Yes.'

'... who will in turn be making suggestions to their house representatives on the Council, who will then follow those suggestions, even
though you are entirely not a leader?'

He faded to my side for the sole purpose of elbowing me hard in the
ribs; Lyn laughed out loud at the table. A double reward.

I scowled at Tared, rubbing the spot where he'd hit me, and grumbled, 'Time to go, then?'

'Yes, let's go.' He grimaced. 'You're getting far too clever for your own
good.'

Lyn closed her notebook and clambered off the bench, and he
grabbed my shoulder while he held out his other hand to her. The
black and gold and green of the room blurred the moment her fingers
touched his palm, melting away for the wood and parchment and dazzling alf light of the Wanderer's Wing,

Beyla was already there, coat and bag standing in the corner, her
two swords next to them. Anaxia sat basking in the alf light in the
windowsill, chatting with the purple-haired nymph with antlers who
went by the name of Valeska. Nenya walked in a moment after Lyn and
I sat down, her hair braided into a crown-like shape on this particular
morning. She was followed within half a minute by the silver-blond alf
called Thorir who always took snacks to Council meetings. Unsurpris-
ingly, he pulled a bag of pecans and dried oranges from his jacket the
moment he took the chair on Lyn's other side.

'We just had *breakfast*!' she said, then stole a pecan and glared at me
when I chuckled.

'Who else are we expecting?' Beyla said, her fleeting smile at Lyn
already fading. 'Should we wait for Edored?'

Tared fell into the chair to my right with that long, loud groan he
reserved only for his cousin. 'I tried to find him, but he wasn't in any
of the usual spots. May have fallen into a drunken stupor in some dark
corridor, for all I know.'

'Or some bed,' Thorir muttered, loud enough for only Lyn and me to hear.

I laughed, but Lyn threw him a burning glower that looked like a warning I didn't understand. It mellowed only after he sneaked a few more pecans into her hand. In the meantime, the rest of the company had decided that waiting for Edored would be about as useful as watching grass grow, and that he was at least old enough, even if unfortunately not wise enough, to show up when he recovered from wherever he had ended up last night.

'So,' Nenya said, sitting down next to Thorir in her high-collared dress. Anaxia and Valeska took their seats too, their conversation broken off. 'What is all the noise about this time?'

Beyla was the only one left standing, looking frail in just her travelling tunic and trousers, her silvery blonde hair a long braid over her shoulder. She merely sighed as all eyes in the company turned towards her and bent over the table to point out a small island on the map inlaid in the wooden surface.

'I was on Verna ...'

'One of the places with tribute trouble last year, wasn't it?' Thorir said, and Beyla nodded.

'Yes. They were on my list to check this month, just to see if there was anything we could do to help. So I popped by two nights ago. Which was just in time to hear a visiting fae emissary tell those poor souls of the northern town that if they failed to get the tributes in order *again*, he would be sending the Silent Death after them.'

It was quite miraculous how quickly a circle of nodding, chewing magical creatures could stiffen to the very tips of their fingers.

'What?' Nenya said, a moment too late.

'Yes,' Beyla said, her smile thin as usual. 'Exactly.'

Thorir coughed. 'Well. Unless our guest is regularly sneaking out of the Underground and torturing the occasional villager to death in order to stay in shape ...'

'Don't be ridiculous,' Lyn said, throwing him another glare.

'You can expect Valdora to suggest it, though.'

She rolled her eyes. 'He's not getting out of the Underground without alf assistance. Perhaps one of us should remind Valdora in advance of the next Council meeting that she can't throw those suggestions around without implicating that someone is betraying his honour *very* damn badly.'

'I'll ask Ylfreda,' Tared said, amused. 'Valdora aside ... what in hell, Bey?'

'I know.' She sat down as well, tanned fingers on the smooth wood of the table. 'So I checked a few other islands where we have informants, all the places where they've had tribute trouble in the last two years or so. Some of them received the same threat. The Mother seems to be flinging his name all over the archipelago, which is all the more surprising because ...'

'She never used him as a threat,' Lyn said slowly.

'Yes.'

Not as a threat? It took a moment before I figured out the implication of those words. The Silent Death *was* a threat, of course, a constant looming danger living in the back of every sane human mind, the horrors of his crimes told again and again around the fires at night. But he'd been a vague, abstract fear, too, like the plague or the flu that swept over the islands every few years, and when he finally came to Cathra ...

His arrival had not been announced.

And now that Lyn mentioned it, I'd never heard tales of advance notices, of last warnings before he was sent to rebelling islands. He just *appeared*, like a crash of thunder from a bright blue sky, deadly and unexpected as a bolt of lightning. Part of the dramatics, probably, yet another way to keep the lowly humans looking over their shoulders – but now, suddenly, the Mother was wielding his name as a clear and concrete consequence?

'Is she trying to cover up that she's lost him?' I said, my voice too loud in the puzzled silence.

Beyla gave me that eerie, empty smile. 'That's what it looks like to me, yes.'

'But ...' Lyn leaned over with her arms folded on the edge of the table, her freckled face three-quarters frown. 'Good gods. Apart from those armed forces she sent out to hunt him down, has she actually spread the word that people should be looking out for him?'

'Not that I've heard,' Beyla said. 'Which is an answer in itself, I suppose. If she'd made a point of spreading the news of his treason, I would have known.'

'And Emelin ...'

'No word on Emelin either.'

A meagre comfort, but I felt relieved nonetheless. The idea of having every single island, human or otherwise, ready to betray me as soon as they caught sight of me ... Even here, deep below the earth, it sent unpleasant shivers along my spine.

'So she's actively pretending he's still with her,' Lyn said, rubbing her face, 'and actively pretending Emelin doesn't exist – but why? She should know she'll find them a damn lot faster if every child in the archipelago is looking out for them.'

Anaxia giggled. 'I presume she's scared.'

'Yes,' Nenya said, sending her a look of understanding as she tapped a fingertip against her perfectly reddened lips. 'That's what I'm thinking. Seems to me she's not sure how her empire will react to the news she's lost her strongest weapon and gained a dangerous enemy at the same time.'

'I doubt they'll rally on the barricades against her,' Tared said, his voice nonchalant despite the grim darkness in his eyes. 'If they didn't turn on her when the entire magical world was fighting her, one Silent Death and a little human brat aren't going to make the difference.'

'*Half* human brat,' I said indignantly.

He threw me a quick grin. 'Still little.'

'I doubt she's afraid of the entire empire turning against her,' Lyn interrupted before I could retaliate. 'But there have been rumours of rebels over the past decades, so what if those join the revolution as soon as they realise there is one underway? And also ...' A look at Beyla. 'She likely doesn't know who Emelin's father is, either.'

Beyla shook her head.

'So all she knows is that somewhere, some fae had a child with magical powers and didn't tell her. What if that fae parent is still involved?

What if there are others like them? She's just been surprised by the existence of an unbound mage – it sounds likely to me she wants to exclude any other unpleasant surprises before she opens the hunt.'

'Unpleasant surprises sound good to me,' Thorir said next to her.

Lyn grimaced. 'Yes, if they exist.'

'I've been thinking ...' Beyla started but hesitated. An unusual thing, for her to falter; as quiet and insubstantial as her voice sounded, the sense of *purpose* was always there in her words. 'I was wondering ... Emelin, do you have any idea – does Creon have any idea – whether there's any truth to those rumours of fae secretly resisting her?'

I blinked. 'He's never mentioned any fae allies to me, but ...'

This time I was the one to pause, the words I'd planned to speak evaporating on my tongue as my conscious thoughts caught up with them.

But I could ask him, I'd wanted to say. Which I could, of course. And then I could report back to this group, or to the Council, and they would have more questions, which I would dutifully pass on to Creon again ...

As if he was some pox patient, to be kept in safe isolation lest his darkness taint the poor unblemished souls of the rest of this world.

For Zera's bloody sake. If I wanted to know who he was without centuries of hate pressing on his heart, people would have to change their minds about him sooner or later. How would that ever happen if he was content enough to spend his time holed up in a deserted library hall and the rest of the world was glad to tiptoe around him and have me play messenger?

'You could just ask him, of course,' I said, and perhaps those words came out a little too much as a challenge.

Lyn and Tared stiffened simultaneously on either side of me. Thorir abruptly stopped chewing on his pecans, and Valeska flinched. But on the other side of the table, Anaxia beamed her sharp-toothed grin at me.

'Last time I asked him anything,' Beyla said flatly, 'he gave me a stare of death until I gave up and left him alone. I doubt he'd appreciate any curiosity from my side.'

'That was over a century ago, yes?'

She closed her eyes. 'Yes, and he's still locking himself away.'

How very odd, for a demon not to invite himself to dinner with the people who hated him to death. More words I might be better off swallowing.

'We could go see him together, then,' I suggested, sensibly and maturely. 'He might have questions in return that you could answer, and I'm not going to pass endless messages back and forth just because all you immortals refuse to have decent conversations with each other.'

'You do realise,' Thorir muttered, 'that half fae are also ...'

I did realise, and was very much determined not to think about it until I had actually survived this war for long enough to profit from my presumed immortality. 'Yes, and you're ignoring the point. Everything has changed since last time he was here, and if everyone keeps pretending it hasn't, no one is going to get anywhere. Just go ask him. He's happy enough to help. As long as you don't come barging in proclaiming Tared to be the greatest individual to have ever seen the light of day ...'

Tared choked on a laugh. 'Did you try?'

'I'm an honourable little half human,' I said, glaring at him. 'I don't tell lies.'

'Oh, for hell's sake,' Nenya interrupted his retort, folding her arms over the lace and velvet of her corset. 'Is it at all useful for us to know whether those rebellious fae actually exist? They haven't made much of an effort to find us over the past decades.'

'In all fairness,' Lyn said, fidgeting with her curls, 'we've made quite an effort not to be found. If they did the same, it stands to reason we didn't run into them. And if we're to go to war again, we'll need every ally we can get.'

'One way of finding them would be to spread the word about Emelin and Creon, I suppose,' Tared said. 'If she's afraid her people will rise against her – well, let them rise.'

'And then?' Lyn said slowly.

He grinned at her. 'That's not a question I ask until I need it.'

She rolled her eyes, unsuccessfully suppressing her grin. 'If we spread the news now and some hidden pockets of revolutionaries suddenly jump onto the barricades, we lose all control we still have on our timing. The war might start itself before we know it, and I'm not sure if we *want* to speed things up as long as ...' She hesitated.

'As long as I'm not ready,' I finished gloomily.

The silence was painful. Of course they all knew exactly why we hadn't tried to blow the Mother off her throne yet and why we wouldn't be making any desperate attempts for a long while. They'd survived that stark white battlefield. They knew too well I wouldn't have.

'Don't worry about it, Emelin.' Lyn's smile was too forced to be comforting. 'Not getting you killed is more important than speed now.'

They were worried, though. I didn't point it out; they'd politely deny it anyway.

'Letting the rest of the world know could also be a delay tactic, of course,' Nenya said, smoothing over the moment of deadlock with steely resolve. 'If she has to deal with internal issues first, it might take her longer to realise the Alliance is involved.'

'*Might*,' Lyn muttered.

'Can't avoid risks,' Tared said with a shrug. 'And I'd personally rather get things going than wait for her to come at us.'

'That's easy to say when every single member of your people carries a sword,' Valeska said, abruptly breaking her silence. Her voice had that same dreamy, melodious quality as Anaxia's, but there was nothing dreamy about the brisk glance she gave the three alves around the table. 'Starting a war is not nearly so amusing for the communities who can't easily defend themselves.'

'I wouldn't say we're defenceless,' Anaxia said with another pearly-white, razor-sharp smile at the rest of the table. Thorir audibly swallowed his pecans. 'But it shouldn't be—'

Behind me, a familiar voice hollered, '*Lyn!*'

For what had to be the hundredth time in this place, I almost snapped my own neck by jerking around too fast.

Edored had appeared in the middle of the room, looking even more battle-ready than on an average morning – his eyes wild, his lip curled up in a ferocious sneer, as if he might draw the sword on his back any moment and take a swing at the world in general. Before anyone could so much as open their mouths, he aimed that furious steel-grey gaze at Lyn and burst out, 'What in fucking hell is he doing in the *library*?'

It took a moment of stunned silence for that question to register.

He. Library. With that violent, unrestrained fury.

Which meant ...

Next to me, Lyn coldly said, 'I presume you're talking about Creon, Edored?'

Oh, gods help me.

'No, about bloody Orin himself,' the alf sneered, swinging his arm in the direction of the history hall as he stalked to the table. 'Of course I'm damn well talking about Creon. What for Korok's hairy balls are you *thinking*, letting him—'

'I thought he might best spend his time in the least likely place for you to run into him,' Lyn said in a lethally honey-sweet tone that sent Thorir flinching on her other side. 'How is he troubling you? Don't tell me you suddenly became interested in literature on war history.'

'He scared a friend of mine to absolute death, Lyn darling. Did you even think about—'

'Oh, it's about a *friend* of yours,' Nenya interrupted, her voice such an unusually frosty sheet of ice that words abandoned me. 'How fortunate for your *friend* that you're around to heroically save her from every little trouble, Edored. Imagine if you—'

'Nenya,' Tared said, his voice low but sharp enough to stop her mid-sentence.

She snapped her mouth shut and slumped back into her chair, her crimson lips such a thin line that even her scars paled around them, her shallow breathing a clear indication of the effort it took to stay quiet. The glare she aimed at Edored was as sharp as her fangs, but with an edge of helplessness to it – no, an edge of *hurt*.

Oh, gods. Was this more than an impressive history of mutual annoyance?

If it was, Edored himself appeared blissfully unaware of it; he fell into a chair between Tared and Beyla with such genuine shock on his face that I might have felt sorry for him in any other context. 'Fuck's sake, Nen, what did poor Olena ever do to you?'

Tared closed his eyes with that cousin-specific look of exasperation on his slender face. Ah. A history indeed. 'Edored.'

'What? *I* didn't—'

'Could we focus on one thing at a time?' Lyn cut in, audibly willing herself to stay calm. 'Edored, could you be a little more specific in your complaints? Is there anything in particular Creon did to scare poor Olena so terribly?'

'Existing?' Edored suggested sharply. 'How would you feel if some winged fucker was suddenly strolling through your workplace, giving you ... looks?'

Nenya scoffed a shrill laugh. 'Looks? Oh, bless your *friend's* poor little heart.'

'That's all?' Lyn said, throwing her a warning glance. 'You're storming in like a madman because he has ... eyes?'

'Would look a damn lot better without them, wouldn't he?' Edored said defiantly.

I sucked in a breath to tell him where to stick his sword, then caught Tared's look and thought better of it. Lyn was presumably handling the situation more diplomatically than I ever could. On the other side of the table, Anaxia sat looking around the company, blue eyes glistening with satisfied amusement. All these tangled emotions, all these poorly hidden secrets ... if she wasn't drowning in it, this had to be a demon's equivalent of an abundant banquet.

She grinned at me as our gazes met, noting, without doubt, the fury itching in my fingertips. I swallowed and looked away, even more determined to control myself.

'... and where else would you want him to spend his time?' Lyn was saying next to me, in that overly clipped, meticulously articulated tone of an exhausted parent talking to an overwhelmed toddler.

Edored snorted. 'In chains?'

'You're being unreasonable, Edored. He's been sitting here for a week and hasn't caused any trouble, which is honestly more than I've been able to say about *you* at—'

'And I'm not some fucking fae bastard running after you, am I, Lyn sweetling?' he burst out, jolting up as if to lunge at her over the table.

'Are you seriously allowing him to keep ... loitering ... around you ... after all he—'

Oh. So there was the core of the matter? Alf protectiveness again, enough to kill for it on Tared's behalf, if need be?

'I don't think I've given you any reason to be concerned about his loitering,' Lyn snapped, the restraint cracked, the patience gone. 'You can't—'

'And what about *him*? Why does he have to pick this place to—'

'I wouldn't worry too much about that, if I were you,' Anaxia said. I flinched, but through the clamour of Edored's fury, no one paid any attention to her words.

'Must be a very foreign concept to you that he might just like books,' Lyn bit out, and Edored rolled his eyes so violently he must have had an excellent view on the inside of his skullcap.

'I'd also tell the world I liked books if I wanted to—'

'Edored,' Tared interrupted, and although his voice still sounded level as before, the clenched fist in his lap told a different story. 'Let him be. It's all under control.'

'You can't be serious,' Edored sputtered. 'He's as controlled as a damn wildfire – you *know* he is. Sooner or later he's going to cause—'

'And we'll deal with that when the time comes,' Tared cut him off, closing his eyes. 'Anything else? If not, just go punch yourself in the face a couple of times to calm down, will you?'

'You're mad. You're absolutely—'

'*Edored.*'

For a moment, the alf sat still as a statue, his fingers clenched into his long leather coat, his eyes narrowed in furious suspicion. Then, abruptly, he kicked back his chair and rose in a single forceful motion, biting out a last glass-edged chuckle. 'If you think I'll just let you dig yourself into this madness—'

'Go. *Home.*' Even I couldn't suppress a shiver at the unbendable steel in Tared's voice. 'We'll talk. *Later.*'

Edored gave one last scoff, scowled at Lyn, and vanished into thin air, leaving a silence behind that could have cut through stone. Nenya was breathing too fast, Thorir had frozen over his bag of nuts, and Valeska looked like a nervous mouse desperate to crawl back into the nearest safe crack in the wall. Only Anaxia remained utterly unfazed, humming a near-inaudible melody as she threw beaming smiles at every person present.

I bit my tongue so hard it hurt. Not the moment to move, no matter how badly I wanted to take a swing at someone. Not the moment to speak. I could start moving and speaking as soon as I'd figured out how much danger we were in.

'Well,' Lyn finally said, her voice too demonstratively flat to be at all convincing. She exchanged a single quick look with Tared, then slid off her chair, avoiding all other eyes around the table. 'If none of you mind, I think I'm going to have a word with Olena. Unless there's anything urgent we need to discuss first?'

Tared groaned a sigh. 'I don't think we can make any decisions about hypothetical rebellious fae if we don't know whether they exist. So ... Bey?'

Beyla glanced at me, and I shrugged, pretending not to see the hesitation in her pale blue eyes. She wasn't to blame for Edored's mindless rage, of course – but if he was about to embark on a new campaign against Creon's presence in the Underground, I wasn't going to pause my attempts to get everyone on speaking terms.

'Do you want to go see him now?' she said, interpreting that shrug correctly.

'Apparently he's in the library anyway,' I said wryly, and even Tared managed a bleak chuckle at that.

Beyla gave me the faintest of smiles, but got up. 'Let's declare the meeting finished, then. I'll send word when we know more.'

There were nodding heads and mutters of agreement as chairs scraped back and most of the company got to their feet. Valeska announced she was coming to see Olena with Lyn, who mumbled something grateful as they both exited the room. Thorir vanished with a few remarks on a number of people he'd have a word with.

Anaxia dawdled, fidgeting with the pink tips of her hair as she waited for anyone else to speak. When Beyla turned away to pick up her swords, Tared remained silent in his chair, and Nenya continued to stare furiously at the farthest wall of the room, she finally breathed an annoyed sigh and said, 'Tared?'

'Hmm?'

'You know he's just concerned about you, yes?'

He groaned, burying his face in his hands. 'Why do you think I haven't broken his nose yet, Naxi?'

'Next time, feel free to do it anyway,' Nenya muttered as she rose from her chair and marched towards the door without another word. Anaxia pulled a face at me by way of goodbye, then danced after the other female. Their voices slowly died away in the distance, Anaxia's light and melodious, Nenya's curt and cold.

For a moment, Tared and I were silent as Beyla calmly and meticulously buckled her swords over her shoulders. Only as she turned back to the table did he look up and let out a long, weary sigh.

'Apologies for all this nonsense, Emelin. Long stories.'

'More people making life harder for themselves?' I guessed.

'Yes. You're in excellent company.' He grimaced, then got to his feet and nodded at Beyla. 'Let me know if you need any assistance.'

'Let me know if you need any assistance not breaking Edored's nose,' she said with a flicker of pale amusement on her face, and with a last joyless chuckle, he vanished too.

CHAPTER 13

BEYLA SEEMED TENSE AS she gestured for me to leave the Wanderer's Wing first, entering into the public part of the library with its buttery alf light and its smell of ink and parchment and its never-ending whisper of scratching pens and rustling pages.

Should I tell her not to worry? I doubted it would help much; if anything, it would make her doubt my sanity even further. So I bit my tongue as I hurried after her, following her slender back through the familiar maze of books and scrolls and unintelligible inscriptions. The faint shine around her shimmered brighter whenever it collided with the rays of alf light falling in from the fields, as if the glow of her magic recognised itself in the almost-sunlight and reached out to strengthen that bond.

So different, so very different, from the darkness rippling off Creon's every motion, the shadows on his face, the night in his eyes.

We walked past the biology aisles and the dark room devoted to the study of divine magic, past the clay tablets and the birch bark inscriptions, until we reached the main gallery. When I glanced down over the balustrade, nothing about the scribes around the tables suggested that Olena's moment of shock had left much of an impression.

I barely suppressed a curse. Damn Edored and his fuming exaggerations; damn every hot-headed alf still craving revenge. What if Lyn and Tared weren't around when another of these occasions arose?

Beyla was already descending the stairs to the lower gallery, and I shook off those ominous thoughts and followed her as quickly as my aching muscles allowed me. Best to follow Tared's example and not worry about the next emergency until it was actually here. I had better things to lose sleep over.

Fae allies. The Mother's secrets. Decisions that could start a war before I was prepared to fight it.

Beyla's quiet, purposeful strides didn't falter until she halted at that familiar door leading to the history room. Before she could say anything, I muttered, 'I'll just go first and let him know you'd like to have a word with him.'

Her mirthless smile told me she approved of the general strategy, although not necessarily of the phrasing *you'd like to*.

I pushed open the door and slipped two steps inside, realising only then that the sounds welcoming me were not the usual serene quiet and the occasional thump of a heavy book cover hitting a wooden surface. Instead ...

Edored's voice.

He was speaking in Alvish, too fast for me to make sense of the words with my limited grasp of the language – but the tone of his voice was disconcerting enough, that heated, unrestrained sharpness I knew to go with his most scornful of sneers. On the other side of the threshold, Beyla's eyes widened abruptly. Before I could ask what was going on, she shot forward and pushed past me with that alarmed readiness every member of the household shared in Edored's vicinity.

Her voice, soft as it was, effortlessly cut through the other's tirade. 'What in hell is happening here?'

'Oh, hello Bey.' That was not a friendly greeting at all. I stumbled over my own feet in my hurry to follow Beyla to the window-side of the room. Gods help me, was Creon here? Was this Edored's idea of solving the matter on his own?

And as if he'd heard the frantic questions my mind was screaming, the alf chose that moment to add a bored, 'No reason to worry, I'm just having a chat with our old friend here. Bit one-sided, but I never liked the sound of his voice that much anyway.'

Oh, the *bastard*.

I shot out from between the bookcases, almost colliding with Beyla as she came to a halt in the open space around the windows. My eyes needed no more than a single panicking heartbeat to take in the scene before us. Creon, standing at the window with his back towards us, shoulders too tight, wings twitching ever so slightly, the stiffness of his posture betraying just how close to tearing his self-restraint had stretched. Edored, lounging in the same seat where I'd fought a battle with glue and kisses mere days ago, his eyes shining with wild, malicious ferocity.

What in hell was he planning to do? Annoy Creon until he left the library of his own volition and keep doing it until his presumed enemy gave up on returning?

Bastard. *Bastard.*

'Can't imagine you have anything helpful to say to him,' Beyla snapped, her eyes clinging to the menacing shape of Creon's motionless figure fifteen feet away. Ah. She noticed them too, those subtle signs of a nearing outburst. 'Would you please leave us alone so we can deal with more useful matters?'

Edored bit out a cynical laugh. 'Oh, he's finally going to be useful? Doing what – sacrificing himself in battle?'

'Will you shut *up*?' The words burst over my lips like bare-knuckled blows to the head. To hell with the diplomacy; this vicious idiot had never cared about it anyway. 'Nobody asked you—'

Creon snapped around at the sound of my voice, meeting my eyes with that cold, primal focus I knew far too well. A look of survival. A look of crumbling control, of his violent instincts tearing desperately at the chains of rational thought. Whatever venom Edored had been spouting before this interruption, I didn't think I wanted to know. I didn't think Edored wanted me to know, if he liked the current look of his pretty face.

What in hell had the fool hoped to achieve? Even his reckless alf brain had to realise he was no match for Creon's powers on his own, and what would he win by getting himself blasted into the fields outside?

'Of course I'm not shutting up, Emelin,' he said, interrupting my frantic thoughts with another of those stinging laughs. 'I've waited a little too long for a chance to tell our princeling exactly what I—'

Creon broke into motion, long, snappish strides towards the door. His glance at me was a warning and an apology at once – *Please don't make me deal with this*, it said, *because we'll all regret the consequences.*

I swallowed another string of curses and muttered, 'See you in a minute.'

He brushed his fingers over the back of my hand as he passed me by, the faintest touch, but just enough of a reassurance that I managed to stay where I stood. He would be fine for a few more minutes, and if I came running after him now, I might never figure out what in the gods' names Edored had been thinking. Or worse, how I was going to stop him from—

'Running away again, Hytherion?' the alf sneered, the title a vulgar insult from his lips. 'You're making a habit of that when things get hard, aren't you?'

I heard Creon stiffen behind me before I even turned towards him.

The wrong kind of stillness. The *worst* kind of stillness. He had stopped dead in his tracks four strides away from me, a tall, winged statue between the towering bookcases, his back towards us, wings trembling with restraint, scarred hands clenched to bloodless fists. Around him ...

Oh, no.

On either side of him, the dark leather book covers paled.

The breath caught in my throat. Zera help me. I'd seen this happen once before, and I could still hear the shattering glass as I stormed out of the pavilion – the sound of his magic breaking free from every last restraint. His paralysed silence ... this was not a silence of indifference, of wilful blindness and deafness. Far worse, it was the silence of a thread about to snap.

Explosively and catastrophically.

'Creon?' I blurted. I had to get him out of here. Had to calm whatever slumbering monster Edored had awoken with his taunting and worry about anything else only when I was very, very sure the danger was gone. 'Creon, let's—'

'Pathetic, isn't it?' Edored interrupted with a biting snigger. 'One unfriendly word and he loses his mind. No wonder he'd rather go back to dear mommy telling him he's such a pretty little—'

'*Creon.*' Half of my mind was screaming at me to drag him out of this room – by force, if need be. The other half was shouting just as loud for me to turn around and send a few good punches of red magic into Edored's balls. Frozen between instincts, my limbs obeyed neither; I could only stand and stare, in breathless, horrified awe, as the black stone around Creon's feet paled to a sickly grey. 'Creon, ignore him. Please don't—'

Edored laughed out loud behind me. 'No ignoring the truth, Emelin. Isn't it all true, Your Deadly Silence?'

'Edored, what are you *doing*?' Beyla hissed, her voice choked. 'He's going to damage something if you go on like this!'

'Oh, I know.' He sounded content as a purring cat. 'You might want to get out of here before he blows the place to shreds.'

To shreds.

Lyn's library – to shreds.

And only then did it hit my numb, frightened brain, a flash of un-derstanding that sent the gall up my throat – Lyn. Her books. The one transgression she would not forgive, not forget, no matter how desperately she wanted to save the offender – which Edored knew as well as anyone. And so, in his furious resolve to rid the Underground of Creon's presence ...

No. No, no, no.

'Oh, you fucking *idiot*,' Beyla was saying, her voice a blur to my ears. 'What did you think ...'

I stumbled forward without waiting for Edored's answer as a burst of panic broke through the paralysis. 'Creon?'

He didn't move. Nothing but the torturously slow rise and fall of his shoulders, the rhythm of his breath unnaturally controlled – as if a single unrestrained inhalation would be enough to tear through every last shred of self-control, every last hold on his magic. His fists were clenched so tight that even the crude black lines of ink grew paler.

I risked another step forward, bringing me close enough for his trembling wings to lash out and slap me away. Behind me, the two alves abruptly went quiet.

'Oh, fuck,' Beyla said, her voice an octave too high. 'Emelin, get away from him. You don't want to be there when he – *Emelin.*'

I ignored her, focusing only on Creon's winged back as I took another cautious step forward. So close, now, his strained body within reach for me to touch him. What would he do if I did – deflate or explode?

On the edge of my sight, the moss green leached from my dress, leaving only a pallid minty sheen behind.

So much colour. So much power. So, so much destruction. My mouth was dry as ash as I lifted a trembling hand to his shoulder and whispered, 'Creon?'

'No. No, wait.' Edored's shrill voice sounded not nearly so satisfied all of a sudden. 'Emelin, what are you doing? Come back. Don't do that. I wasn't trying to blow *you* up! I ...'

'Emelin?' Beyla repeated, a thousand warnings in those three syllables alone.

'Creon,' I breathed, my fingers hovering half an inch above his shoulder. The soft gold seeped from my skin ever so slowly, leaving my hand and arm unnaturally pale. He didn't move, didn't turn, but his breathing quickened, grew shallow.

Would the bargain allow him to lash out in my face? Or would it, and kill him in retaliation a moment later?

A fool's gamble – but Lyn's books, those books she would kill for ...

'Get out,' I heard Beyla say far, far behind me. 'Get the *hell* out and leave this to me.' And then again, 'Emelin?'

I drew in a shaky breath, prayed to every single god and whoever else might listen that it wouldn't be my last, and grabbed Creon's rock-hard shoulder.

Like a coil releasing, he snapped.

An eruption of movement, of jolting limbs and slapping wings and Beyla's alarmed cry behind me; his powerful hands wrapped around my waist, and my back slammed against the shelves, breath rushing from my lungs at the impact. Feverish breath scalded my cheeks. Wing and muscle closed around me, locking me against the wood. When I blinked the tears from my eyes, his strained face hovered inches above me, every line and curve of his features endlessly familiar and yet entirely unknown – his lips bloodless and pale, contorted into a grimace of restraint. His scars paling against the bronze of his skin. His eyes …

Darkness had swallowed the white around his irises. I stared into a wall of night, a whirlpool of howling power, and found not a trace of the male I knew in that wild, empty abyss.

Not a trace of recognition as he fixed his gaze upon me, a wild animal marking its prey.

'Creon?' I managed, willing myself not to shrink from his towering body even as every fibre of me roared in alarm. Fuck. The colours gathering in his eyes … Tousled locks of my hair were losing their dark brown in the corners of my sight; I didn't dare to look down and see how my skin was faring. 'Creon, it's me. It's Emelin. You …' *You love me.* 'You know me.'

He didn't move, pinning me against the wooden shelves, scanning my face with those wide, haunted eyes. His hands shook feverishly on my waist. His fingertips were glowing embers even through the linen of my dress, the full force of his power burning red-hot and sizzling just below his skin.

Ready to explode. Ready to destroy.

Could he still let it go?

'Please.' My voice trembled. 'I need you to stop this. I need you to release those colours – let them return where they came from. Calmly. Quietly. Can you do that for me?'

His lips twitched, letting nothing but jagged breath escape. The void in his eyes was so very cold, so very deep – like the ocean trench to the east of Cathra, that dangerous spot where the sea floor suddenly fell away and the bright azure of the water became an inky midnight blue so bottomless it made even grown men shiver.

Too much magic for anyone to control. Too much power for any heart to bear.

'Creon.' A quiet, breathless plea. 'Come back to me.'

A spark of recognition flickered in the depths of his eyes.

'You promised,' I whispered, holding his gaze with every shred of persuasion I had in me – summoning every soothing, calming thought I could find through the whirl of my fear, unfolding the barest of me for his demon eyes to see. 'You promised you'd come back to me. And I need you to do it *now*. I – I need you ...'

A violent shudder ran through him as he closed his eyes. Darkness welled between his eyelids, tears of ink rolling down his cheeks – the colour bleeding out of him with nowhere else to go.

'No – stop that.' My hands clung to the bookshelves behind my back, a desperate attempt not to claw into his chest and send him erupting after all. 'Stop torturing yourself. Let it *go*. I don't want to see you like this, I ...'

The words drifted off as I grasped for something to say, *anything* to say. His fingers dug into my waist so tightly I had trouble breathing. *Running away again, Hytherion?* Words punching straight into that lingering core of shame and guilt and self-hate eating at him, straight into that heart that still believed him to be detestable demon brood ...

'Creon.' I barely breathed the words. Damn it all to hell, then. Damn me ten times over – as long as it saved him. 'Please. I love you.'

For one everlasting heartbeat, not even the dust whirling in the alf light moved.

Then, so fast I blinked and missed it, the colour whooshed back into place around us – pale grey turning brown and green and gold again, unused magic blooming vibrantly on the edges of my sight. With a ragged gasp, Creon released me and staggered back. The bleeding ink on his cheeks faded into crystal-clear tears, the black drops that had gathered at the tips of his fingers paled a moment later. As he met my gaze, his eyes wide and bewildered, his irises had shrunk to their own shape again.

In dead silence, we stared at each other, two feet of colourless air between us.

Love you.

Love you.

Had he heard – did he remember?

The expression on his face was the expression of a sleepwalker waking in a strange room with no recollection of how he ended up there. His eyes flashed over the unscathed books and back at me, horrified understanding finally rising on his face.

Em, his lips said, and again, *Em.*

'I'm – I'm alright.' I didn't sound alright. 'Are you—'

A footstep broke through the breathless silence, and he jolted around, left hand jerking to the taut black surface of his wing. Only then did I remember we were not alone – that we hadn't been alone for a moment.

Edored had disappeared. But Beyla still stood in the middle of that open spot by the windows, pale blue eyes moving back and forth between us, her lips parted a fraction in wordless disbelief.

'What for Orin's loving heart,' she whispered, a good two heartbeats too late, 'did you think you were doing, Emelin?'

With a jerky motion so unlike his usual fae grace, Creon snapped around and walked.

I no longer had the mind to stop him. He was at the open window before I opened my mouth, wings flaring wide behind his shoulders. One step up the sill, one last moment of hesitation, and he flung himself into the open air behind, soaring over the fields and out of sight without a single look back.

CHAPTER 14

LYN'S FURY WAS BLOOD-CURDLING even for those who weren't on the receiving end of it.

She raged around the living room of the family home for fifteen minutes of undiluted wrath, delivering a tirade laced with curses in six different languages, flames bursting from her skin and sizzling out in flurries of scarlet and purple sparks wherever she turned. Glasses were broken. Tableware was thrown. The few unwise alves who faded by in a misguided attempt to defend Edored fled the room with scorch marks on their clothes or ended up quiet and demure in a corner with the offender himself, shrinking half an inch every time Lyn stamped by like a fuming little bonfire on legs.

I found myself slinking closer and closer to Tared, who had taken up position on the other side of the room and stood leaning leisurely against the wall, observing the scene like a spectator at a particularly interesting game of kickball. He grinned at me as I approached him within arm's reach and muttered, 'Feeling sorry for him already?'

I scoffed. His grin turned sour.

'... the very last original volume in existence!' Lyn ranted on the other side of the room, swinging her little arm at Edored's face. A burst of fire seared the green tapestry just next to his ear; around him, his unlucky friends flinched in solidarity. 'Gods save us from the clever plans of stupid people! And from yours in particular, Edored!' A glass shattered from a poorly aimed burst of heat, and this time I flinched, too.

'Oh, don't worry,' Tared said, looking amused as he pulled his traveller's flask of honey mead from a pocket and took a quick sip without taking his eyes off the spectacle. 'She rarely kills anyone. Need a drink?'

I might have chugged down the entire bottle if not for Ylfreda, who faded into the room with her eyebrows slinking close to her hairline and her medicine bag over her shoulder. One look at Lyn was all she needed; she vanished and appeared right next to Tared with a stiff 'Ah.'

He raised his eyebrows at her.

'Beyla said you might need a healer here,' Ylfreda clarified and threw a vaguely concerned look at the next fizz of sparks twirling towards the ceiling around Lyn's stomping figure. 'What did he do this time?'

'He tried to blow up the library,' Tared said.

'Did he.' She closed her eyes for a moment. 'I've always thought he might be adopted.'

I sniggered despite the sickening nausea holding my guts hostage. Ylfreda glanced at me, turned back to Tared, and added, 'Isn't it about time we put an end to this?'

'Go ahead,' he said dryly.

'Orin's eye, Thorgedson. I'm not *that* brave.'

He took the flask from my hands and grinned at her, then raised his voice slightly. 'Lyn?'

She whirled around halfway through an aggressive enumeration of influential historians whose works might have been lost if a particular dull-witted fool had gotten his way. 'What?'

'Emelin's in dire need of your advice,' he said, nodding solemnly at me. 'Perhaps you should give the family idiot a few minutes to gather the last shreds of his dignity while we discuss—'

Lyn jerked back to Edored and his friends before I could object to his use of my non-existent questions. Like a tiny general to a bunch of numb and battle-weary warriors, she planted her fists on her hips and snapped, '*Out.*'

It took approximately half a heartbeat for the lot of them to vanish.

She let out a last heartfelt groan and turned back towards us, flames finally settling on her skin but amber eyes still flickering. 'Don't think for a *moment* I'm done with him yet.'

'I wouldn't dare,' Tared said dryly. 'But Emelin—'

'You could have continued a little longer, as far as I'm concerned,' I said and threw him a glare. 'I quite enjoyed the show.'

Lyn gave a joyless chuckle but stalked over to our side of the room, shoulders falling a fraction. 'No, you're right. Time to be sensible.' A snort. 'As opposed to *some*—'

'Could anyone tell me what in hell happened?' Ylfreda interrupted.

It took three sentences from Tared and several muttered strings of curses from Lyn to summarise the past hour. My involvement was mentioned with only a few throwaway words – ' ... and then Emelin stopped him ...' – but Ylfreda's narrow-eyed glance at me betrayed how she saw straight through the disguise of Tared's nonchalance.

'You *stopped* him?'

I shrugged sheepishly. 'Seemed a better idea than letting the library blow up.'

Lyn muttered another unfriendly word under her breath as she flopped onto the nearest bench. Ylfreda blinked at her, at me again, and slowly said, 'Well, that's an improvement.'

'What?' I said.

'I tried to calm him down a couple of times,' Lyn grumbled. 'Never really worked.'

A *couple* of times – oh, hell. No wonder Edored had known exactly what to aim for, and no wonder Beyla had been so righteously incensed as soon as she figured out what he was trying to do.

Next to me, Tared's look of faint amusement had given way to a look of faint grimness. *A couple of times.* A couple of times in which Creon may nearly have killed her, no bargain to keep her safe from his magic – and yet she'd still tried to save him.

What had he said? *So I panicked.*

At times, I couldn't help but feel sorry for that version of him decades ago, demon brood or not.

'So,' Ylfreda said, interrupting my thoughts with her usual firm impatience, 'where is he now, if I may ask?'

Deafening silence was the only answer.

She cursed. 'You don't *know*?'

'He flew out,' I said weakly. 'I thought he might need a moment to calm down.' And then Beyla had grabbed my arm and faded me to the family home, and then hell had broken loose within the mere two minutes it had taken to alert Tared and Lyn to the near-catastrophe Edored had caused.

Ylfreda didn't look like any of that would make her feel milder about the situation. Her glare at Tared was the coldest I'd seen her wield, a glare of acute disappointment that said, *I expected* you *at least to know better.* 'You're letting him roam around the Underground on his own? In this state?'

'He'd settled down enough,' I said sharply, and she let out a breath that was almost a scoff.

'For now, yes. What if anything else ticks him off?'

Even Lyn didn't argue with that point, sitting small and sullen on the edge of her bench. Tared exchanged a quick glance with her, the doubt visible in the thin line of his lips.

'Are we bringing him back here?' he said slowly.

Lyn hunched up her shoulders. 'Where else?'

'The thought of sleeping next to some living volcano doesn't sound exactly pleasant to me,' Ylfreda snapped. 'Can't we at the very least put some alf steel on him from now on?'

'So he's entirely defenceless against the hordes of alves waiting to murder him?' I said with a scoff. 'Could also just stick a sword through his throat immediately if you wish to make things easy for them.'

'He could *kill*—'

'Perhaps,' Lyn interrupted, hands clenched around the bench, 'we should go look for him and see how he's doing, before we decide whether he can or cannot be trusted with his own powers?'

We. The image of Creon having to deal with a handful of vexed alves after the mess of the past hour was enough to push my next words over my lips.

'I'll go.'

Three pairs of eyes shot towards me, their looks ranging from sceptical to concerned.

'At least you know he won't hurt me,' I said defiantly. 'If you're afraid he'll burst anyway, clearly I'm your safest choice.'

'Yes,' Ylfreda admitted, visibly unwilling, 'but ...'

'But what? Are you afraid I'll assist him in cutting Edored to pieces after all?'

The way her mouth snapped shut told me I'd guessed right. Ah, yes. The thorny question of loyalties, again. Because I may have told the Council that the fight against the Mother was all I cared about, I may be able to keep up that pretence to most of the Alliance ... but within this household, even if they didn't know about the nights I spent in his bed, it was clear enough that Creon Hytherion meant *something* to me. Ylfreda was sensible enough not to gossip about it, not to burst into Council meetings and dramatically accuse me of lying, but the obvious doubt in her eyes told me clear as day that it did make her question my sanity.

And at this moment, my peaceful intentions.

'Look,' I said testily, 'I'm still trying to keep him alive and well, and dead alves are bad for everyone's wellbeing. I'm happy to leave Edored to Lyn. Just let me make sure Creon is alright before all of you send him over the edge again.'

Ylfreda looked hardly convinced.

Tared sighed, however, and held out a hand to me before his cousin could protest. 'In that case – Emelin?'

I grabbed his wrist and allowed him to pull me out of the ravaged living room, into the golden alf light and the warm, earthy smells of the fields.

We had appeared a few hundred feet beyond the library, a quick glance over my shoulder told me, the arched windows gaping holes in the dark stone walls from this side. Around us, rows of vibrant green crops stretched into the distance to where the wide cave of the Underground bent out of sight. Barefooted nymphs were tending to plants wherever I looked, whispering and singing softly; I caught a few shreds of those soothing melodies Anaxia was so fond of humming during quiet moments.

Next to me, Tared threw a quick glance around as I released him. 'Oh, Masha?'

A tiny female with green-and-chestnut curls came hurrying towards us, effortlessly avoiding the growing leeks and onions with her muddy feet. 'Looking for Hytherion?' Her voice oddly resembled the peaceful bubbling of a creek.

'Emelin is,' Tared said, nodding at me. 'Do you have any idea where he went?'

'Direction of Etele's quarter,' the nymph said cheerfully, waving at the distance to our left. Her small hands were more like cat's claws, the nails ending in gnarled tips. 'We didn't follow him, if you don't mind.'

Tared grimaced. 'I would have minded if you had. Emelin?'

'I'll be fine,' I said and tried to look convinced as I peered at the farmland stretching out before me. There was more to the fields than I had imagined, and who was to say he hadn't slipped back into the inhabited part of the Underground again to find a quiet spot there? 'I'll find him and report back as soon as possible.'

Which might not be very soon. The shadow drawing over Tared's face suggested he knew it, too, and wasn't happy with the idea of waiting hours to know where the Silent Death had gone. But he just nodded and said, 'Good luck, then.'

I blinked, and he was gone.

Masha patted me reassuringly on the elbow and returned to her gardening, leaving me with little else to do but go on my way.

I found a narrow path between the patches of crops and walked in the direction she had indicated. Between the nimble, light-footed figures of the nymphs, it was hard not to feel like a plodding workhorse struggling through mud as I slowly crossed the fields, scanning the distance for a trace of a winged silhouette or a flicker of magic.

There was nothing. With so many watching eyes around, I shouldn't have been surprised.

It took me a quarter of an hour to leave the bustling acres behind and cross into the wide stretch of grass that marked the fields behind Etele's quarter. The vampires took care of the cattle, Lyn had said, and indeed, a handful of goats stood grazing peacefully on the other side of the field. There were no nymphs to be seen here, and no vampires either. That seemed more promising as a hideaway for fugitive fae.

The heavy, overwhelming Underground silence returned with full force in this part, not broken even by the occasional bleating goat in the distance. My heartbeat was a drum in my ears. I tried to drown it out, tried to focus on the grass under my boots and the windows gaping in the outer walls of the inhabited Underground to my left – but it was hard to wonder where he had gone without worrying, and it was hard to worry without doubting. Had it been a mistake to let him out of sight? Should I have followed him at once after he emerged from wherever his magic had taken him, even though it seemed abundantly clear he wanted to be left alone?

Last time he'd wanted me to leave him alone for weeks on end, obeying his wishes had only worsened the situation.

No sense in thinking about that now. I pressed ahead, throwing suspicious glances down every corridor leading between the houses of Etele's quarter – no traces of panicking vampires, no traces of violence and destruction. Zera be damned. Not that I *wanted* him to leave a trail of ruin behind, of course, but then again ... at least a couple of corpses would have made it easier to find him.

I was so occupied by the city to my left that I barely paid attention to my right, where I presumed to find nothing but the river Lyn had mentioned and behind it the outer wall of this enormous cave. If not for the goat startling me with its unexpected bleating by the waterside, I may have missed the doorway gaping in the black stone.

My feet faltered in the grass as I examined this newest surprise of the world below.

The tunnel wasn't high; I would probably be able to touch its curving ceiling if I jumped. Yet the entrance had an air of significance to it, lit by five small faelights and surrounded by inscriptions I didn't recognise from the distance. As I hurried closer, I could identify the shapes on either side of the low doorway, guarding whatever this place was.

Two wild cats carved out of the dark stone, staring majestically at the grazing goats.

Etele's quarter.

Cats.

I broke into a trot.

As I came closer, I saw the river for the first time, running around the ring of the fields as Lyn had said. The water churned and gurgled around the worn-smooth rocks just below the crystal-clear surface, foam shimmering silvery in the glow of the alf light. Behind it, the outer wall was as inky black as everywhere in this buried world, but the lower few feet were wet from the splashing water and shone iridescently like dark mother of pearl.

A low bridge ran over the underground river, just broad enough for two wingless people to walk side by side. There were no footprints to be seen in the thin layer of dust and earth that covered the stone surface on my side ... but on the other side of the water, just before the ominously dark doorway, two small smudges of dirt had been swept aside.

Traces of landing feet.

I stood still just before the narrow bridge and threw a quick glance over my shoulder. No one to be seen. No one to ask where this corridor was leading, the darkness behind that low doorway deeper than it should have been with the alf light falling in abundant rays around me. Going in might be dangerous or forbidden or just generally unwise.

But Lyn or Tared should have warned me if the Underground hid any dangers, and Creon ...

I was already walking before my conscious mind had finished that thought. Creon might need me, and in any case, generally unwise was a specialty of mine.

The two cats were brilliant pieces of art, so vividly created that I could have sworn their eyes followed my hurried crossing of the bridge. But whatever magic had put them here, whatever magic lingered in those elegant curls and swirls etched into the stone around the doorway, it didn't stop me as I walked on and the shadows of the tunnel swallowed me.

The passageway was so dark I couldn't see the hands I stretched out before me, the bright light of the field strangely dimmed behind my back. I shuffled forward, holding my breath, testing the floor beneath my feet before lowering my weight onto them. No sudden traps emerged from the darkness, no traitorous bends in the tunnel. Whatever this place was, it didn't seem hell-bent on killing me.

Not yet, at least.

The thought of Creon kept me moving, and as I took my fifteenth step forward, the shadows abruptly cleared.

CHAPTER 15

Around me, lit by a multitude of softly glowing orbs, a vast cave materialised, jagged and grotesque and *beautiful*.

It should have been a disorderly mess, this construction of sparkling colours and blue-black stone, of mirror-smooth surfaces and razor-sharp edges. And yet every line and glimmer seemed to be exactly where it should be, the whole of it somehow as familiar as the palm of my hand. Crystal mosaics covered the uneven walls of the cavern, a fierce but perfectly balanced harmony of the most brilliant colours I'd ever seen. Crooked stalactites dripped from the high ceiling, sharp as knives and yet painfully graceful in their cruelty. At the centre of the room, a pentagonal basin was filled with a deep golden liquid that shimmered restlessly in the glow of the faelights, looking like it might be a deadly poison as easily as the elixir of life.

Menace and ferocity, destruction and fear, and such mesmerising perfection that I could have cried with awe.

Beauty and war.

Two extremes of the same scale, two sides of the same coin; it did make sense to me in that moment.

Creon sat slumped against the rough stone wall on the farthest side of the cave, eyes closed and wings half-spread. Like a fallen star trapped in a fae body – a shred of night, the shadows shifting around his silhouette as if even the magic of this place shied away from his power. He blended so seamlessly into the blood-curdling beauty of his surroundings that I expected for a moment to find his eyes dark again, the colour oozing into every fibre of him.

But his eyes were his own when he looked up to meet my gaze across the room – weary yet bright, and all that unbridled power laced with a hint of ... relief?

As if he'd been waiting for me.

'What in hell is this place?' I breathed.

A memorial. He sat up straighter, eyes never straying from my face. *For faekind.*

Built by the goddess who'd given the fae their powers, who'd then seen them take advantage of those powers to throw the world into centuries of war ... I swallowed and tiptoed towards him, pausing to examine the syrupy golden liquid in the central basin a little more closely. It looked *alive*, in the most unpleasant of ways, the shimmering surface pulsing ever so slightly like the rhythm of a heart.

'And this?'

Creon pursed his lips. *Blood, I suspect.*

'Hers?'

A nod.

I swallowed again, the taste in my mouth bitter. It was too much blood, *far* too much blood, for a single body to contain. Etele must have filled the basin slowly, day after day, cut after cut. 'Why would she leave that here?'

Not sure. He waved at the dark tunnel behind me. *Text didn't go into specifics.*

Those inscriptions above the gate? I should have known he'd be able to read them. I glanced at the rippling surface again, suddenly overcome by a near-irresistible urge to dip my fingertips into the molten gold. 'What do you think would happen if we touched it?'

A wry grin slid over his face. *I don't think you want to try.*

'Why?'

She went insane with hatred towards faekind near the end. He let out a soundless groan as he rose to his feet, none of that cramped stiffness left in his motions. *Depending on when she built this room, she may have cursed either my mother's bloodline or all fae in general. Regardless, I should stay away from her magic.*

I blinked at him. 'And yet you're here.'

Had to go somewhere.

The air seemed to grow darker around him as he gestured those words – as if the shadows themselves joined him in his memory of those moments in the library, the disaster that could have been.

I managed a grimace and said, 'I just watched Lyn unleash the full force of her fury upon Edored. Have to admit that a mad goddess sounds like the safer option.'

His chuckle didn't reach his eyes. *I'm so sorry, Em.*

'You didn't cause it.'

Should know better than to lose my mind over gods-damned Edored.

'He was very damn determined to make you lose control,' I said bitterly, and Creon scoffed, sauntering closer to the menacing gold in the basin at my feet.

More reason to know better.

'Same is true for him.' I hesitated. 'Especially because – well, it's happened before around them, hasn't it? You losing control?'

Creon nodded slowly.

'Is it a problem of anger?'

No. Just what you said – losing control. He rubbed his face. *Did we ever talk about mage strength?*

'Not much, I think?'

Typical, he signed wryly, and I couldn't help my chuckle despite the palpable tension hovering around him. *Part of what determines an individual's power is how easily they draw. For you it's barely an effort, is it?*

Less than an effort, really; at times the magic was rather an urge to resist. I glanced at the scarred fingers of his left hand, those fingers I'd seen absorb colour with such bewildering thoughtlessness.

'You're saying you're not drawing at all?'

He closed his eyes. *It's more that I'm holding it back the rest of the time.*

'*All* the time.'

A tired shrug.

'Oh, for the bloody gods' sakes.' I let out a joyless laugh, stepping away from the basin, closer to him. 'You're constantly being badgered by the colours around you? Weren't the intrusive emotions enough?'

Magic is not nearly as disruptive as emotions, he gestured hastily – as if that would make me feel any better about the situation. *I've learned to keep it out instinctively. It's like breathing. It's not an effort to keep doing it even when I'm asleep or otherwise occupied.*

'But when something brings you off balance too violently ...'

I slip. And once it starts flooding me, it's hard to get rid of it in a controlled way. He averted his gaze, shrugged, and added, *Two hours ago, I'd have told you it was impossible.*

Oh. Oh, gods. And then I'd jumped in his way, beloved and bargain-protected, and somehow that had been enough for him to wrestle back control over the colours overwhelming his conscious mind.

Or at least my words had been enough.

I love you.

He didn't move, standing tall and quiet in the warm glow of the faelights, staring at the pool of divine blood before us. Was he thinking of the same thing? Hell, had he even heard me – had he even been present enough to register what I'd said?

An unpleasant feeling stirred – a nervousness, a loss of words I'd rarely felt before in his vicinity. If he'd heard me ...

Love you.

Words I hadn't planned to say, words I hadn't *dared* to say – and although they had tasted true on my lips, I suddenly wasn't sure whether that even mattered. I hadn't spoken them because they were true. They had been a necessity, the confession wielded as a weapon; their sincerity was secondary, a mere happy coincidence amidst what had been strategy as much as love.

Perhaps this was how Creon had felt after that first, desperate kiss in the Labyrinth, unable to feel triumph over a victory that had happened for all the wrong reasons. *Regretting*, he'd said that day, and the unease aching in my guts came very close to regret, indeed.

He stood so very still, the sharp contours of his face cold, his eyes unnervingly hollow. Noticing my worry, without doubt, noticing every painful feeling snaking through me, and yet he didn't look at me, didn't speak.

Did he think I regretted saying it entirely?

'Creon—'

He lifted his hand so abruptly I jolted. *We need to talk.*

That didn't help. That didn't help at all. 'About what?'

This mess. Every single fibre of him seemed at war with itself as he paused, fingers clenching and unclenching two, three times, breath faltering with every hesitation. I waited, petrified, prepared for the most damning of statements – *Just leave me alone* or *I knew you didn't want to love me* or *I figured I don't actually like you that much* or ...

The gestures blurring on his fingers, he signed, *I can't stay here.*

My mind abruptly stilled.

Can't stay.

Here.

It took two full heartbeats for those words to break through, the full, deadly implications of them – he wanted to *leave*? With the Mother out there, hunting him?

I let out a bewildered laugh. 'You ... you're not being serious, are you?'

Something twitched in his face as he turned to meet my eyes. The apology cracking through the hard layers of his mask was enough of an answer – oh, Zera help me, he *was* serious. He *was* planning to leave ...

Me?

Perhaps the most damning of statements hadn't been that bad yet.

'No.' The word tore from my lips like a wild animal escaping. 'Creon, be reasonable. You said it yourself – you won't be safe outside. You can't just—'

I'm not safe here either.

I stared at him, a pit opening in my stomach. 'No, but—'

Edored figured it out – that if he's not powerful enough to harm me, I'm still powerful enough to harm myself. He rushed through the gestures, as if he didn't dare wait for my objections. *They promised not to kill me. They never promised to protect me from myself. If they keep trying, I will end up hurting someone* – he spelled out the *will* – *and that's going to cost me, Em. Dearly.*

'That doesn't make sense!' My voice soared. He couldn't be right – the crumbling heart in my chest wouldn't allow him to be right. 'If Edored or any of his friends are determined to make you blow their heads off, no one can blame you for—'

Don't underestimate protective alves.

'But—'

Doesn't matter who starts it. If I harm Edored, Tared isn't going to rest until he has my head on a silver plate. He looked away, drew in an overly restrained breath. *And I can't even entirely blame him.*

'Edored's an idiot!'

An idiot who's effectively his brother.

I tried to find an argument against that point – but Tared is sensible. He knows Edored is as unmanageable as an unbroken horse; how could he blame you for losing your temper with him? Hell, I just watched Lyn unleash a firestorm at the fool, and he seemed to find that amusing more than anything else.

Lyn didn't truly harm Edored, though.

And she was effectively family, too.

I snapped my mouth shut, fighting my quickening breath. The point was shaping itself in my mind, no matter how much I willed it not to: as much as any member of the house of Skeire wished to beat the living daylight out of their most unruly cousin at times, he was still *theirs* to knock about. No one, not even the most rational of them, would ever pick an outsider's side against him – and certainly not the side of Creon Hytherion, Silent Death, traitor and wrecker of relationships.

Edored and his friends might not be invincible, but the ties of loyalty surrounding them were. My pathetic attempts to make everyone see eye to eye wouldn't be enough to change that, wouldn't be enough to shift centuries of unyielding family honour. Not soon enough, at least. Not if a handful of aggravated alves might decide to spend the next week driving Creon just mad enough to lose control, just mad enough to explode.

Sooner or later, one of the reckless idiots would be hurt ... and the Alliance would know who to blame.

Which meant, if I forced myself to be far more reasonable than I wanted to be ...

We'd run out of options.

Ice cold dread rose in me, numbing me from my toes up, a sensation like standing in frigid water for just a little too long. His defeated posture slumping against the wall as I came in ... He'd known already. Figured it out, made his decisions, and waited here to inform me of what was about to happen.

He winced as my anger flared, the plea in his eyes a knife cut. *Em.*

Oh.

I swallowed. Oh, hell. Perhaps ... Perhaps I was the one making assumptions this time.

Because I'd told him to stop making decisions for me. Had told him to talk next time he felt like fleeing. And he *was* here, talking to me; he hadn't tried to find his way out of the Underground on his own, hadn't tried to avoid this confrontation, hadn't set out a full and finished plan for his future travels yet.

So perhaps he wasn't informing me at all. Perhaps this was the discussion I had asked for.

I pressed my nails into my palms, throat tightening, and managed, 'So if you can't stay here ... what other options do we have?'

There was a flash of gratitude in his look the fraction of a moment before he averted his eyes again. Five feet of distance between us, and all of a sudden it felt like five miles. We couldn't be lovers now. We couldn't be *in love.* This was a matter of strategy, of cold and ruthless calculation, and giving our hearts too much of a say in the discussion might end with death.

What a terrible, terrible moment for heartfelt confessions.

His gestures were too stiff, too jerky, as he gestured, *I'm not sure yet. Why was Beyla with you?*

'Some questions that came up during the discussion. She ...' I sucked in a deep breath. 'It seems the Mother is trying to hide that you betrayed her. She's still using you as a threat to human isles, and she hasn't spread the word that the rest of the empire should be looking out for us, either. So they were wondering why.'

A small line had grown between his brows. *That's ...* A pause. *Interesting.*

'Do you have any explanation?'

Fear.

A faint laugh escaped me. 'That's what Anaxia and Nenya said, too.'

I think they're right. She didn't see any of this coming. And she really, really dislikes being taken by surprise. He slowly turned back towards the wall he'd come from, considering his gestures for a moment as he wandered three thoughtless steps forward. *She might be worried about your fae parent. And about whoever is with them.*

'Yes. That's what the others were wondering, too – if there are any rebellious fae she might be concerned about.'

His lips quirked into a joyless smile. *Oddly, rebellious fae rarely decided to confide in me.*

There was no stopping my laugh, mirthless as it was. 'You may have heard rumours, though.'

There are always rumours. Some of them a little more credible than others. I could ... He sat down in his old spot at the wall and tucked in his wings, his glance at me a cautious apology. *If I were to leave this place, I could go take a look.*

I.

That damning, damning singular.

My stomach rebelled. But I forced my voice into a flat, efficient line, even though he had to feel every tremble of dread, even though we both knew it to be a pointless, pretty lie. 'Don't you mean *we*?'

The way he closed his eyes, even if it was just for the briefest of instants, was enough to send my heart plummeting.

He did not mean *we*.

He had not for a moment meant *we*.

'Creon.' My voice cracked. And there they were again, his bloody demon powers, ramming themselves between us in entirely new ways. 'You're *not* dumping me here. You're *not* flying out into her arms without even a way for me to know if you're safe, if you're ... if you're ...'

Alive. When had those few stupid syllables become so hard to force over my lips? I sucked in a shivering breath and repeated, 'Creon.'

He tensed, but his left wing shifted, unfurled a fraction – like an invitation into its safe embrace. *Come here.*

I shivered, feet glued to the dark stone. 'I – I don't ...'

Em, his lips said as he met my gaze. *Please.*

There was no resisting that gleam in his eyes, that look that suggested the most powerful mage in the history of faekind might well perish on the spot if not for the touch of my skin and the taste of my lips. I should have been thinking of all it might do to my cracking heart, to hold him even if he would flee me before the day was over ... But I stumbled towards him without another thought, self-restraint waning.

He caught my wrist as soon as I got within reach, pulled me into his lap. I curled up against his chest, clutching my arms around his rock-hard torso, breathing in the scent of him. A fragrance like safety. A fragrance like home.

The scent of something I couldn't afford, couldn't *bear* to lose.

'I want to come with you.' There was too much of a plea in my voice. Damn my efforts to keep my heart safe; I found out in that exact moment that I'd failed, utterly and laughably. 'And you don't want to leave me here either – I *know* you don't want to. So don't tell me ...'

He curled his wing around me, a smooth, heavy blanket over my back and legs. A shiver ran through him as he lifted his hand and signed, torturously slowly, *We can go together. If you want to.*

'We ...' I blinked at his inked fingers, at the part of his face I could see, sitting pressed against his sculpted body. 'Are you serious?'

A mirthless chuckle vibrated through him. *I've been informed I should stop telling you what you want. And the gods know I want you with me. So if you decide to come, I'm not stopping you.*

I slipped from under his wing and scrambled up to look him in the eyes, momentarily lost for words. He wasn't stopping me? Wasn't attempting to convince me it would be too dangerous and too lonely out there and that surely he wasn't worth all that bloody trouble?

Then ... then the choice was obvious, wasn't it?

So why was he still looking like a male about to make a kill he truly didn't want to make; why was there still not a shred of joy in that bitter smile on his lips?

'But you expect me to stay.' That was the only explanation, as little sense as it made. My thoughts lagged seconds behind my voice. 'You're assuming I'd rather stay here.'

He closed his eyes and rested the back of his head against the grim mosaics behind him, small tremors breaking through the cold murderer's mask of his face. *I suppose it would be ... more sensible for you to stay.*

'Why?' I said sharply. 'Just because going out would be unsafe? I can't avoid the danger forever anyway.'

No, but ... His chest rose with the deep breath he drew into his lungs, muscles straining against his shirt. *This is going to be messy enough. I won't have time to keep track of the Mother's every movement out there. Won't have time to look for your parents. There's not going to be any Faerie reading or sword training. No Council meetings or ...* A helpless throwaway gesture; he didn't open his eyes. *Or any of that.*

I parted my lips. Closed them again. Tried to figure out what I'd planned to say, and couldn't quite remember.

Any of that.

Leaving the Alliance behind meant giving up on any influence I might still have. It meant giving up on training I needed, allies I needed, if I was to walk into battle and come out of it alive. Creon could help me with my magic, but would that be enough to survive whatever role the world needed me to play?

'No,' I whispered.

Whatever I'd planned to say, that wasn't it. Perhaps I hadn't planned to say anything but *fuck.*

And we could still train your magic. But most of the things I can teach you are useless, and the things you should learn are hardly my greatest talents.

He was so tense, the motions of his fingers such anxious twitches. *You'd come back knowing every damn constellation by name and cooking a very decent eggplant stew, but I'm shit at diplomacy, Em. I'm shit at dealing with armies and making plans involving more than me and my knives, and I'm not sure if the joy of my bubbly company outweighs all those skills you will very much need.*

Because I wasn't ready.

Even he knew I wasn't ready.

'No,' I said again, and then I added, 'fuck,' because it seemed the only reasonable thing left to say. The mosaic walls were spinning around me. *I* was spinning – spiralling deeper and deeper into a pit of inevitable conclusions I wanted so, so desperately to avoid.

His eyes remained closed. Still, I knew by the slight twitches of his eyelids that he was keeping track of my every movement, my every feeling, my every hesitation as I opened and shut my mouth two, three times.

'If I were to let you ...' Merely speaking those words, tentatively and hypothetically, felt far too close to defeat already. If I were to let him go. If I were to throw myself back into those first weeks in the Underground, without his secret smiles to keep me sane, without his arms to keep me warm at night. 'If you were to leave ... what would you do? Just go look for those fae rebels and come back again?'

A stiff shrug. *Or some other helpful mission. They may hate me just a fraction less if it looks like I will actually be useful this time.*

Edored's voice echoed in my ears. *Running away again, Hytherion?* And that single sneer, just a little too close to the truth, had been enough to wrestle all that explosive magic from Creon's fragile control – all that self-hatred, all that regret.

Perhaps it wouldn't just be the Underground hating him any less. Perhaps he would feel just a little better about himself, too.

Could I begrudge him that just because I didn't want to miss him?

'How long?' Forming full sentences was a near impossible effort. 'How long would you be gone?'

Long enough to contribute something useful. I'm not sure ...

I swallowed. 'Three weeks?'

A joyless grin grew around his lips. *I was going to say three months, but—*

'Oh, no.' I clenched my fists in my lap. 'Don't even *think* about it, Creon. If you dump me here for three months I'll ... I'll ...'

Kill me? he suggested wryly, opening his eyes a fraction.

'Hunt you down all over the archipelago, I was going to say, and you know very well *that* isn't going to keep me safe.' I snorted. 'Not a chance. A month, perhaps.'

A month. Somehow I had yielded a *month* – what was I doing?

Two months, he signed.

'You'd miss my birthday,' I said. 'That would be very uncourteous of you, and I would still not kill you, but I might hide some cacti in your bed at your return. Six weeks and not a single day more, and that's my final offer.'

Something like a smile twitched around his lips. *Don't be so gods-damned convincing, Em.*

'It's called being sensible!' My voice cracked. '*You're* the bastard who somehow persuaded me to ... to ...'

To let him go.

To let him *go*.

The air burst from my lungs, my mind finally catching up with what my tongue had already known – that I was going to let him throw himself into this plan, that I was going to give Edored exactly what he wanted. Not for me. Not because sword training and diplomacy sounded like they might for a moment rival eggplant stew and endless conversations under the open starry sky, but because he needed to get out, and this world needed me to prepare for whatever was waiting for me – whatever open war would ask from me.

And if I failed because I'd chosen him over my responsibilities ... that would hurt him far more than his absence would hurt me.

He sat watching me, jaw clenched tight. He, too, felt the panic clenching tight in my chest. And although he didn't move, didn't pull me back into his embrace, I suspected he'd rather have pulled his own teeth out than force this dilemma on me.

And yet he had stayed. Waited. Talked.

'Alright,' I whispered.

A lie. He didn't make a point of it.

It might be better than you think, he signed, a plea in his gestures. *You might like this place more without me and my cursed magic between you and the rest of—*

'That's not why you're running off, is it?' My voice came out taut. 'Because you think you're robbing me of something by merely ... existing?'

He shook his head, lips a thin line.

'But?'

But there's no other place in the world so welcoming to halfbloods. And you need friends – you need a home somewhere. So if this is happening anyway ... His jaw tightened in accordance with his stiffening fingers. *Just try, Em. Don't lock yourself away out of justified fury and decide you hate them all on principle.*

Gods damn me, he knew me far too well. I averted my eyes, rubbing my face, and grumbled, 'I *have* friends. I have you.'

I don't want to be all you have. I ... A tremble of his fingers. *I can't be enough for that.*

Not enough.

Numb dread climbed up my throat, hollowed out my chest until breathing gave me trouble. Fae prince, living legend, mage of incomprehensible power, and yet ... not enough. Because there was still that dark, deadly part of him he couldn't face, couldn't accept – there was still that little voice telling him time and time again that he was a monster and a coward and good for nothing but hurt and destruction. And I could tell him I wanted him a hundred times, could tell him I loved him and mean it too ...

But as long as that core of self-hate lingered, could I ever tell him often enough to truly make him believe it?

Em. He leaned forward, curling the fingers of his left hand around my chin. *Breathe. I'll be back.*

'I know,' I whispered. I knew. He *would* come back for me. He always would. But if not for one stupid alf too many, if not for that gods-damned darkness eating at him, there would be nothing to come back from in the first place. There would be nothing to flee. There would just be me and him and ... us.

Whatever that was.

I love you.

I didn't even cry. None of it seemed real enough to cry over. All I could do was breathe and keep breathing and ignore the treacherous heart crumbling like barren earth in my chest, until finally he got to his feet in the spine-chilling silence and held out a hand to help me up.

Will go have a word with some people.

Any other moment, I would have offered to come with him, to help him survive Tared's cold hate and Edored's fury and whatever else he'd have to face to get himself safely out of the Underground. Right now ... I wasn't sure if I'd be able to bite my tongue like I should.

'Come see me when you're done with them,' I managed.

And with a last nod, he turned and walked, vanishing into the shadows of Etele's doorway with long, inaudible strides.

CHAPTER 16

THE DAY PASSED IN a haze, every hour somehow an eternity and an eye-blink at once.

The family home was deserted when I found my way back to Orin's quarter, the corridor eerily quiet, the living room in a state of utter disarray. I tried to distract myself by collecting the glass shards and the cutlery that had ended up in various corners of the room, but it was hard to clean up without imagining the similar mess that might have been left in the library if not for me, and it was even harder to think of my intervention without thinking of Creon, roaming around somewhere in the Underground, trying to survive a handful of furious alves with every reason to think bad of him.

Should I have gone with him? But the thought alone made me want to crawl into bed and never get up again.

Six weeks.

How in hell was I going to survive forty-two days of this, forty-two days of not even knowing whether he was alive?

After half an hour, Lyn walked by to ask me if I was alright – her questions so circumspect, her amber eyes so concerned, that I knew the details of Creon's plans must already have reached her. I told her I was doing perfectly fine. Keeping myself standing despite the leaden weight of defeat on my shoulders was hard enough without a seven-year-old's commiserative glances.

She left looking no less concerned than when she'd come in. Ylfreda faded by fifteen minutes later and told me to leave the mess to her, be a little happier about all I had achieved today, and find something more entertaining to do. I retreated to Creon's bedroom and spent the next hour and a half lying on his bed, staring at the iridescent flickers of light reflecting in the vaulted ceiling.

His pillow smelled like him, and somehow that made everything worse.

I wondered where he was and who he was talking with. Wondered why I hadn't prevented this, why I hadn't tried harder to mend the chasm between him and the people who called themselves my allies while I still had the time to do so.

Wondered how I would ever be ready to save the world if I couldn't even save a handful of stubborn immortal individuals.

At some point, the smell of herb bread and grilled chicken reached me through the chink below the door. Was it dinnertime already? I didn't get up to check; I wasn't hungry, and if there was food on the table, Edored was likely around too. It seemed wise to avoid him for a little while. More murder was not what anyone needed.

It was a tempting thought, though.

Then again ... I could hardly deny that Edored's stunt would have been utterly futile if not for the easy bait of Creon's thorny past and explosive powers. If he'd ever learned to control his demon senses, none of this would have happened. Even now, if he'd just ask Anaxia ...

I pushed it away, that ominous, uncomfortable almost-thought of the choice he'd made.

He'd be back. That was the one reassurance I could cling to: he'd promised me he'd always come back. But even if nothing killed him before these six weeks were over, what were we going to do when he returned? The memory of his father would not be gone, or the little voice in the back of his mind that wouldn't stop whispering about the lives he'd taken. Who was I to think I could undo centuries of suffering with a few pleasant smiles and a cactus joke or two?

He'd be back ... and then how long would it take for him to run again?

Why had that stupid heart of mine decided to feel so very much at home with a male who couldn't even be home to himself?

It was in that eddy of bleak despair that Creon finally found me when he slipped into the room an everlasting two hours later, his face a battlefield of sharp-edged shadows, his eyes cold with icy focus, but his shoulders sagging in that exhausted signal of a battle won. I knew what he was about to say before he'd lifted a single finger – that they had listened. That they had agreed.

That he was leaving.

'When?' I managed as he shut the door behind him, and a single gesture was all it took.

Tomorrow.

Tomorrow.

Somehow it was a relief. Part of me had expected him to vanish as soon as the Underground allowed him to – a last goodbye, a last kiss or two, and nothing more than that.

Em. He sat down on the edge of the bed, fingers hesitating a few inches from my cheek. *I'm sorry.*

'It's not your fault.' I'd run out of anger. I'd run out of everything but that heavy sense of failure pressing on my chest. It *wasn't* his fault. The only ones to blame were the Mother and perhaps those plague-cursed alves who'd been more than happy to rub salt into every single wound she'd ever carved into her son's heart. 'I just ... I ...'

Creon waited – wings drooping, eyes quiet, face tired.

'I just wish I'd been born a few centuries earlier,' I whispered, curling up in the blankets. The words felt so useless, so maddeningly powerless on my lips. 'I just wish I could have spared you all that hurt.'

His smile was a creation of dreary twilight as he lifted me into his arms and rolled himself back into the mattress, holding me on his chest. With his free hand, he signed, *I'm quite relieved you didn't know me a few centuries ago. I was a mind-bogglingly worthless piece of shit.*

I snorted despite myself. 'And you think I'd have allowed you to stay like that?'

A wry grin flitted across his mouth. *No, but you might have killed me.*

'I never even killed anyone.' I wasn't sure where those words came from – why Gish's voice was echoing through my mind again. *Will the girl be ready?* 'I'm not sure if Silent Deaths are the easiest practice targets.'

I'm a surprisingly defenceless target when it comes to everything you do, he gestured, closing his eyes. *I doubt I would have given you much trouble.*

I breathed a chuckle, lifted my hand, and cautiously brushed a long lock from his forehead. My fingertips barely brushed over his bronze skin, and yet that gossamer caress was enough to send a shiver through him, wings slumping against the mattress as finally his shoulders loosened below me.

Defenceless, indeed.

For the first time, there was nothing pleasant about that familiar flush of power, nothing triumphant. If anything, the sensation felt clammy in my hands. Power, yes – and with it came a responsibility I wasn't sure I could bear. If I asked him to stay, truly, genuinely begged him to ...

He *would* stay.

Whether it killed him in the end or not, he would stay.

Which meant I couldn't beg. Not even if I felt so desperately safe in his arms, not even if every fibre of me revolted at the thought of ever letting go of him. Because he would stay, and the Underground might be the death of him one day, and then I would have killed him after all.

If I could make one demand, though ...

'Creon?'

He blinked open his eyes – feeling, no doubt, the cautious tingle of resolve running through me.

'When you return …' *If you return*, my mind supplied. I pushed away the dread clenching in my gut. 'Could you promise me something?'

The way he quirked up his scarred eyebrow a fraction was sufficient as a request for elaboration.

'If the Underground hasn't magically changed its collective mind about you by that time,' I said, stumbling over my words, 'and if it's still dangerous to go anywhere else – will you reconsider the option of learning to shield yourself against those demon powers? Even if it's just a bit? Just to … to take the sharpest sting out of it?'

A small twitch at the corner of his lips was his only response.

'I'm not asking you to promise you'll *do* it,' I added, my voice shriller now. 'Just that you'll *think* about it. Just that you don't immediately discard the option. Could you—'

His fingers interrupted me, stiff and hurried, as if he couldn't bear to hear a single more word from my lips. *I'll try.*

'You'll …'

I'll try to … A deep breath; lying on his hard chest, I was lifted a few inches. *I'll try to think. I'll try not to panic. That's all I can promise, Em.*

Six weeks.

What were the chances he'd stop panicking in six weeks?

I buried my face against his chest, too tired to keep thinking, too tired to make sense of it, and yet unable to stop. He'd die for me, but not accept his powers for me. Because dying was easier for a male who hated himself. Because dying was a punishment, while alleviating a little of that emotional background noise … it came far, far too close to a reward.

And that he may not be able to give himself. Not even if this was the price to pay.

I curled up tighter against him, further into the deceptive safety of his embrace. How had I ever thought that all of this would work out fine if I just gave it some time, if I just wanted him hard enough?

His hands circled over my back, my shoulders, drawing slow shapes of comfort on my body, every circle another promise, another apology, another reassurance. *I'll always come back for you. I'm sorry. I want you.* Words he'd signed before, and yet those soft, insistent touches were more consolation than any memory of the motions of his fingers, numbing the fear simmering in my guts for a few blissful moments.

I couldn't bring myself to move or speak. I couldn't bring myself to end this.

Hours passed. The alf lights dimmed, and still Creon did not let go, stroking and brushing the mortal dread from my bones as if he'd never stop. In the darkness, my head on his chest and his hands on my skin, it seemed he was the only living thing left in the world, my only beacon, my last log of driftwood on a tempestuous sea.

His caresses brushed over my shoulders and my neck, raked through my hair until every inch of my scalp was tingling, drew down along my spine until the ripples of his touch spread into the very tips of my toes and fingers and that drowsy, familiar pleasure dulled the last memory of that paralysing fear. There was not a spot on my body his fingers didn't pass. Back. Bottom. Down to the sensitive hollow of my knees, and back up again, drawing feathery lines over the new curves of my hips.

By the time he stripped my dress off and settled me in the rough pillows and blankets, my skin was fire wherever he went – a dim, smouldering fire, but burning no less hot for that reason. And still there was no hurry in his touches, no sense of an ending ... He kissed his way down my breasts, my belly, as if he had centuries left to pleasure me, hands roaming over every inch of my thighs as if he was exploring them for the very first time. *Nothing gentle about me*, he'd said, but he *was* gentle now, so heartbreakingly gentle, as he finally lowered his head between my legs and brushed his lips over my yearning flesh.

Even then he went slowly, no matter how much I moaned and writhed and pleaded for more. This was not a night for savage passion, for teeth and nails and roaring desire. He traced his tongue along the lines of my body so infinitely patiently, kissing and nuzzling, teasing and tantalising, until the sheer intensity of that never-ending bliss left me lightheaded and drowsy enough to forget I had been unhappy for a minute in my life.

When my climax finally swept over me, unstoppable as the rising tide, it did not so much burst free as wrap around me, safe and unspeakably comfortable. Like a warm, downy blanket – like a lover's embrace. Like Creon's arms and wings around me as he held me until I fell asleep, his presence filling my dreams with impressions of the softest velvet and the scent of honey and hazelnuts.

Still here.

Still mine.

But when I woke in the morning, the alf lights bright again, the bed was empty, and his weapons and clothes were gone.

I found his letters in my own room, on the pillow of the bed where I hadn't spent the night for ages. There were three of them, the first one very familiar – the note he'd scribbled down for me that first day in the library. *I meant it when I said you were a first.* He must have taken it from the wardrobe shelf where I'd kept it, safely tucked away between the dresses I'd borrowed from Lyn and Ylfreda.

It still filled me with warm, fuzzy gratitude, and that feeling hurt like hell this morning. Should I have said something that day – should I have told him he was a first for me, too, even if I didn't dare to be sure what that meant?

Would he still be here if I'd stopped biting my tongue just a little sooner?

With a muttered curse, I picked up the second letter. It was newer and longer – a list of exercises to continue my magic training and my use of yellow in particular. No loving sentiment to be found in the concise suggestions, hints and explanations; this was a note fit to be seen by the rest of the world.

1. Change a towel into a mirror (more yellow than you think you need)
2. Make a list of properties that influence the required brightness of your yellow (there are some 40 of them; try to come up with 20 at least)

3. Open a closed lock without destroying it (don't use any red)
4. Create a hidden niche in the wall (red for creation, yellow for hiding)

And on it went. Forty-two items. One for every day of his absence.

I tried to ignore how bloody long the list looked and how little idea I had of how I would ever complete every single one of these exercises without his comments and improvements. Others might be able to help – Lyn, the few half fae in the Underground, or even the books on magic if all else failed. I could worry about my training when I had a proper reason to.

The last note was the shortest and hurt the most.

Em,
I'm sorry. I'll be back.
Always yours,
C.

Mine.

And yet he was gone. Leaving me in this place with the people who were supposed to be my best hope for family but felt like the opposite.

The Skeire home seemed nothing like a home when I gathered my courage and made my way to the breakfast table, the winding corridor too dark, the voices coming from the living room far too lively for this cursed morning. Just the thought of having to look any of them in the eyes again – of having to pretend I wasn't heartbroken and frightened for my lover's life – almost sent me straight back to bed for the rest of the day. But I had forty-two days to go, and no one would consider a sulking damsel a valuable ally.

I steeled myself and walked on. To battle, then.

Ylfreda had taken over my cleaning work; the broken glass and scattered tableware were gone, and only a handful of new scorch marks on the green and brown tapestries betrayed the firestorm that had raged through the room the previous day. The healer herself was nowhere to be seen, and neither was Hallthor or Edored. But Lyn was sitting in her usual spot at the table, reading a book about the size of her entire body, and Beyla and Tared were playing a lightning-quick chess game that, judging by the latter's curses, wasn't progressing quite to his advantage.

Only when I shut the door behind me did they look up, their faces too neutral to pretend there was nothing remarkable going on.

'Oh, morning, Emelin!' Lyn said brightly. 'Something to eat?'

I hadn't eaten dinner last night. I should have been ravenous. But I hardly managed to chew down a single buttered bun, and even Tared's blistering defeat at Beyla's hands couldn't lift that nauseating weight off my heart.

Couldn't tear my mind away from Creon, slipping out of the Underground like a thief in the night.

Where was he now? Out there, soaring through the bright blue skies again, in the open for the Mother to find him? Hell, for all I knew, she already had him in her clutches again. Who was to say she hadn't laid a trap somewhere, waiting for him to show up?

I barely registered Tared's voice. 'Time for training, Emelin?'

Oh. Yes. Training.

As if nothing had changed. As if Creon's departure was just another triviality in the stream of alves coming and going, no more remarkable than Beyla's many spontaneous disappearances.

Even Tared's breathing exercises couldn't get me to focus; I stumbled through the morning's session, nearly hit myself with a training stick in the face on several occasions, and found my own defence reflexes so hopelessly slow that only Tared's superior control over his weapons saved me from what could have been a couple of nasty bruises and cuts. He didn't comment on my sudden setback, didn't joke, didn't needle. Just corrected me time and time again, infinitely patient and much too understanding, and somehow that was worse. At least if I'd been angry, I might have felt a little less hopeless.

Lyn was no better, with her subtle questions and her honest concern. I tried to stick around in the Wanderer's Wing after we'd finished our usual session of Faerie reading, tried to distract myself with news and discussions of the Mother's movements of the day – but Anaxia kept glancing at me with those all-knowing demon eyes and Nenya kept scoffing whenever Creon's name was mentioned, and I gave up on my attempts to be composed and sensible before the hour was over.

With nothing better to do, I locked myself in my bedroom and set myself to the exercises Creon had left for me.

Changing a towel into a functional mirror took me about an hour and did indeed require more yellow than I'd thought it would. With every attempt, I found new properties that needed to be changed – cloth to glass. Pliable to rigid. Soft to solid. Rough to smooth. I ruined several towels in the process, producing a small pile of glass-strewn linen and folded cloth so hard I could have broken a skull with it before I finally managed to deliver something in which I could recognise the features of my own face.

I had looked better, I concluded as I studied myself in the reflection of my newly created mirror. Frankly, in the glow of the alf lights, I looked like a worn-out rag.

Gods be damned. I wasn't going to roam around the Underground like a ghost for six full weeks, was I?

It was the sight of my own dreary face that lit that first spark of anger I so desperately needed, searing through the fog of my distress and disappointment. Hell's sake, what was I doing? I ought to know better, ought to be more than some melodramatic damsel moping over her absent lover. I still had a war to fight, still had a world to save. Creon hadn't left me here so I could follow his example and make life harder for myself, and being demonstratively unhappy until he returned was pathetic at best and potentially dangerous at worst.

He would be back. If there was nothing else I could do, I might as well just believe that and do something sensible in the meantime.

So I worked on my assignment for the next day until the smell of melting cheese and roasted pumpkin lured me to the living room for dinner, where I forced myself to chat about Beyla's travelling plans and the new set of daggers Hallthor was forging, as if the mention of travels or weapons didn't make me feel like wincing. Edored, thankfully, was still nowhere to be seen. Lyn's glower at the one mention of his name suggested he might be avoiding her as much as me.

I didn't exactly feel *better* by the time I finally allowed myself to leave for bed an hour earlier than usual. I felt differently miserable, though, and at least this new misery seemed more manageable than the last.

Still, I lay awake for far too long, tossing and turning, unable to figure out where to leave my arms without a fae male to hold. The blankets were too cold without Creon next to me, the room too silent without the soft sound of his breathing. And without the household to distract me, it was far too easy for my thoughts to wander into the world above again, where the Mother was preparing for a war I couldn't win yet, where her warriors were combing the archipelago for me and their former brother in arms ...

I must have spent about an hour and a half in quiet, restless panic when, without warning, the fear abruptly sank away.

In its place rose a feeling strange and familiar at once, a calm that couldn't possibly have arisen from my own fretful mind and yet seemed as essential a part of me as my very own skin. It bloomed through me in the blink of an eye, a sensation of steaming hot tea and baths smelling of lavender and blankets tucked in tight and crackling hearth fires – started in my chest and seeped into every fibre of me until I was drenched with it, until I could almost *taste* the certainty that one day soon, all would be well again.

And as quickly as it had come, it was gone.

I lay frozen in the blankets, hands clenched in the wool and down, and stared into the darkness of my bedroom with wide, unseeing eyes. What in hell? Had I just *imagined* that sudden change of heart, a strange half-sleeping dream? But it had been so vivid, so strong it was almost tangible, and so at odds with everything else I had been feeling today ...

As if it hadn't come from my own mind.

Oh.

Creon.

The air escaped my lungs in a burst of tangled emotions – relief and confusion the foremost of them. Could he do that, miles and miles away from here? It seemed too fantastical to be true, but then again, he *was* a damn powerful mage and he *did* know my mind better than anyone else. If anyone would be able to do it, it was him.

And if he was sending messages, he was alive.

And if he was using magic ...

A sob-like laugh tumbled over my lips. Using *demon* magic, no less. Comfort for me, stirring the opposite feeling in him – still not exactly a peaceful acknowledgement of his powers, but it was a start. A sign that perhaps, one day, he might be able to set that lethal revulsion aside for me, for himself, for his own peace of mind.

And all *would* be well.

Sleep found me within minutes, the frantic jumble of my thoughts finally soothed. I woke to the brightening alf lights what seemed like minutes later, my mind clear as a summer sky.

CHAPTER 17

EDORED AVOIDED BOTH LYN and me for a full eight days; only the amount of food vanishing from the kitchen in the mornings and evenings suggested he was still showing up in the Underground at regular intervals.

But when I walked into the living room on the ninth day, stretching my arms and shoulders in preparation for my daily training session, he sat lounging at the breakfast table as if he'd never been gone, shoving chunks of garlic bread into his mouth at such speed that he had to be swallowing them whole. Lyn sat next to him, munching aggressively, throwing quiet glowers at him from below the mess of her bright red curls, but apparently resigned to his presence. On the other side of the table, Tared and Ylfreda were eating with expressions of sharp vigilance, prepared to intervene at the first spark of fire or weapon drawn.

I stiffened in the doorway, my morning exercises abruptly forgotten.

I had more or less made peace with Creon's absence – an effort made significantly easier by those short reassurances his magic wrapped around my heart every night. As long as I knew he was safe, I could at least manage to focus on reading lessons and training sessions and playing the sociable unbound mage during the rest of the day. But grudging tolerance was not nearly the same as acceptance, and being suddenly confronted with the face that had so maliciously thrown its hate at Creon ...

Should I just turn around and pretend I'd never set foot in the room? But before I could bring my limbs to move, Edored jumped up, interrupting his gorging to beam the most oblivious of grins at me.

'Emelin!' His voice was entirely too loud. 'Good to see you! Was almost starting to think you'd left as well!'

Lyn abruptly stopped chewing.

Oh, Zera help me. I *strongly* considered rectifying my lack of murderous experience right there and then. But Tared snapped 'Edored!' before I could figure out how bad an idea it would be to start throwing flares of red magic around, and the undertone in his voice suggested he was ready to swing a sword at anyone threatening the unravelling peace in his living room any further.

I limited myself to a murderous glare and a quiet 'Fuck off.'

'What?' Edored blinked at me, then at his cousin. 'You told me to be nice. I'm supposed to tell her I'm happy to see her, yes?'

'You're supposed to shut your mouth,' Lyn grumbled, eyes flashing alarmingly. 'And morning, Emelin. Ignore this piece of garbage, will you?'

'*Garbage?*' Edored echoed even more loudly. 'Orin's fucking eye, Lyn. I spared an entire piece of cake for you! If that's not even enough to—'

'Edored,' Tared said through clenched teeth, 'knock it off. And Emelin, take that hand off your dress. No need for magic here.'

I hadn't even realised my left hand had pressed itself against the black cloth of my training dress. With a muttered apology, I yanked it away, slammed the door shut behind me, and stalked to the table, taking the seat next to Ylfreda, as far away from Edored as I could get.

She stoically handed me the bread basket, then turned back to Lyn and said with impressive icy calm, 'A dinner with the Tolya nymphs, you said?'

'That's what Valeska suggested, yes,' Lyn said. Every syllable was laced with resolve not to send a fireball or two into Edored's face; it took her a visible effort to ignore the alf as he indignantly returned to his garlic bread, giving Tared accusing looks in between bites. 'There's some unrest among them now that the Mother is increasing surveillance on the islands above – worry about family, worry about the trees, you name it. Valeska suggested that an informal occasion to chat with some of them may alleviate the worst of their fears.'

'I have a couple of old friends among the Tolyi,' Edored said contently before Ylfreda could reply. 'Could check if they have any reason for a party at hand? Or we just tell them it's to introduce them to Emelin. She has much more time at hand now, after all.'

'Will you shut *up*?' I burst out, slamming down my butter knife. More time, indeed. Time I hadn't asked for, time I spent making desperate attempts to stop missing and worrying, and then the bastard thought he was doing me a *favour*? 'I'm really bloody trying not to knock a fist into your nose here, but you're not making it easier by—'

'I'm inviting you to a *party*,' Edored said, looking mortally offended. 'And either way, it's not as if you could break my nose even if you tried, with two weeks of—'

I huffed a furious laugh. 'Don't challenge me.'

'*Challenge* you? You're what – twelve?' His skewed grin carried exactly the wrong hint of self-satisfied triumph. 'We're not all as easily impressed by your magic as your princeling and his—'

'That's enough,' Lyn snapped, throwing him a glare that probably curdled every bottle of milk in the Underground. 'Go finish your breakfast somewhere else, and Emelin, don't you *dare* listen to—'

Too late. I had already listened, I had already heard; the words hurtled over my lips all by themselves, aimed at that sharp alf face without any regard for Lyn or the blurry shapes of Tared and Ylfreda on the edges of my sight. 'Oh, and I should be more intimidated by *you*? The only thing impressive about you is that you still have any friends or family left, at the rate you're fucking up your—'

'*Emelin*.' Tared jumped up to my left, his interruption louder than my own ranting; something about *him* raising his voice made the rest of my tirade freeze dead on my tongue. I snapped my mouth shut, clenched my hands around the edge of my bench, wrestled down my uneven breathing. A small part of me noticed Edored had gone white as sea foam on the other side of the table, his lip curled up in a sneer that no longer held the slightest shred of reckless amusement. Most of me was too busy not killing him to think about whatever old wound I may have prodded, though.

'I suggest,' Ylfreda said, with the imperturbable calm of a female used to bloody feuds and violent screaming matches, 'that Emelin leaves for training with Tared while Lyn and I have a little chat with Edored about nymph festivities. Yes?'

'The nymphs can go fuck themselves,' Edored snapped, jolting up with a cutting laugh. 'I'm not going to let some little fae brat—'

'You are not touching our little fae brat with a *finger*,' Tared coldly interrupted him, his voice still too loud. 'Emelin, time to leave. *Now.*'

I knew better than to object to that tone. But as I clambered off my bench, Edored scoffed and sneered, 'Another one running from trouble, I see?'

Red flashed before my eyes.

Damn the common sense, then, damn the family peace and the good impressions. I barely heard Lyn's soaring voice repeating my name. My fingers tightened into fists – all I could do not to blow the bastard's eyes from his face the very next moment.

The words were out before I could take a second to think them through. 'Why don't you join us at training, then?'

'Oh, for Orin's bloody sake,' Ylfreda said.

'Edored.' Tared's voice was dripping with acid. 'Do *not* join us at training. Emelin, get—'

'Why not?' Edored cut in, jumping from his seat with a wide swing of his hand at me. 'She wants to break noses, doesn't she? Let her try and break noses. Should teach her a thing or two about the real world.'

How had I ever doubted I was ready for battle and bloodshed? Taking a sword in the guts seemed a reasonable price for the opportunity to knock a few teeth from the bastard's mouth; even the Mother herself had rarely evoked such an acute lust for violence in me.

'Exactly,' I said, jutting up my chin at Tared. 'Just consider it a training exercise.'

'What she says.' Edored threw me a look of hostile agreement. 'Gods know she needs the bloody training – don't you, Emelin?'

'Desperately,' I said, scowling at him. 'Especially when I can train with some fucker who won't be missed if I happen to make a little more progress than expected.'

The jeering grin he gave me was oddly amiable, in the bloodthirstiest of ways – a grin that told me we could be perfectly companionable about our attempts to put each other six feet below the ground. I sent an appreciative snort back. Reckless, of course, and most likely more stupid than I knew ... but hell, the senseless fury searing through my veins gave me far too much life to step back now.

'We're far too outnumbered to start killing each other,' Tared snapped. 'Are you two done?'

'Could have a chat after lunch?' Edored suggested and threw me a meaningful look. 'If he keeps being the boring one?'

'Oh, for fuck's sake.' Tared grabbed my arm, nodding at Ylfreda on the bench beside me. 'Can I borrow your ring? And Edored, leave Fury here.'

Fury? I was about to say it seemed overly optimistic to think Edored would ever go anywhere without at least a good bit of slumbering rage, when the alf pulled a face and unbuckled the sword from his back, throwing it on the bench next to Lyn. The next moment, he was gone, leaving nothing but an air of fuming recklessness behind.

'Inika help us,' Lyn muttered, throwing me a look like a thundercloud. 'I *told* you not to start any duels.'

I snorted. 'You told him to keep his mouth shut, too.'

'Which has never been his greatest talent,' Ylfreda said, pulling a broad, sparingly decorated ring from her left thumb. 'You might want to get used to it.' She dropped the ring in Tared's outstretched hand, gave him a mirthless smile and added, 'I'll just wait here, then.'

'Much appreciated,' he said wryly and faded with his fingers still locked around my upper arm.

Edored sat waiting for us when we emerged in the training hall, lounging on one of the benches along the wall with a training stick in his hands. He was no longer so mortally pale, but he *did* still look absolutely furious, and the grin he gave me was a less than pleasant prelude to violent murder.

I gave myself no time to wonder how senseless I was being, prodding this hornet's nest. Sooner or later I had to get used to these things, didn't I? At least that bloody punchable face of his seemed an excellent place to start.

'So,' Tared curtly said as he released my arm and stalked to the other side of the hall, slipping Ylfreda's ring onto his own thumb. 'If you idiots insist on this madness, a couple of rules – Edored, no teeth. Emelin, no aiming at eyes. As soon as I tell you to stop, everyone stops. If that bothers anyone, I'll gladly remind you I'm currently the only person with a sword in this hall. Any comments?'

Neither of us answered. Edored was too busy glowering at me; I was too busy figuring out the fastest way to his nose. Tared didn't seem to have expected any confirmation. He pulled another stick from the chest at the wall and threw it into my hands from twenty feet away, giving me no more than a single curt nod as I caught it from the air with infinitely more ease than a few weeks ago.

His subsequent glare at his cousin was sharper, though. 'You heard me?'

'Of course I heard you,' Edored said indignantly. 'You don't think I'd fucking kill her, do you? *She's* the one who started shouting about breaking noses.'

Tared groaned. 'Yes, and you're the one who cut off an ear last time I let you duel anyone until first blood, so ...'

'It *was* the first cut!'

Tared glared at me as he stuck his hands in his pockets. Deceptive nonchalance – it would take him less than the blink of an eye to draw his sword. 'Still convinced this is a good idea, Emelin?'

I was convinced of no such thing. Quite the opposite: I strongly suspected duelling with Edored was by far the worst idea I'd had in this place. I didn't care. Creon's absence was a constant ache in my chest, the almost-safety of the Underground a persistent itch just below my skin, and I'd never felt so perfectly at home with the training weapon in my hands as in this moment, looking at this bloody idiot with his bloody grudges, anger pulsing through my veins.

So I scoffed and said, 'Do you really expect me to be deterred by some honourless prick's drivelling?'

Edored vanished in the corner of my sight.

It was my only warning, the only announcement of an attack to come. A month ago, I would have been too slow. But hours and hours of honing new reflexes had left their mark on me, and the burst of acute danger firing through me did the rest; I spun around faster than I'd thought possible, my training stick already on its way up as my brain whirled to pinpoint the threat. Every next observation came through in flashes of instinct and panic. Edored, mere feet behind me. Stick, swinging down at what had been the back of my head. My own hands, moving in a rush of brand new routine ...

Wood hit wood with a loud, violent clatter. Pain shot down my wrist at the impact, stinging up my arm – but Edored's weapon uselessly bounced off, and for the shortest blink of an eye, he seemed as surprised as I was.

I dropped my left hand to my dress before he could regain his composure, stretched two fingers of my right hand at him as I held my stick with the rest, and shot a spark of red at his bare wrist. Too slow. He vanished into thin air before the colour hit its goal, and if the whoosh of air at my right ear hadn't warned me, I wouldn't have ducked in time. Now the stick just missed me, close enough to hit the messy strands of hair standing up from the crown of my head.

I whipped around, but by the time I had completed my turn, he was already gone.

His chuckle came from a little farther behind me, only slightly out of breath. 'Not as proud of yourself now, are you?'

I turned, finding him some ten feet away from me, twirling his stick in a particularly vexing imitation of Tared's usual nonchalance. The grin around his lips was a wolfish warning of bloodshed to come.

'You're the one who keeps running,' I ground out, clutching my stick a little tighter. Madness, reckless madness ... but if he never stayed in one place for longer than the beat of a heart, I would have trouble hitting him with any magic. 'Scared to stay and fight me?'

He snorted. 'Thought you liked cowards?'

I flung a burst of red at his face.

Tared snapped something about avoiding eyes on the other side of the hall – but Edored was already gone, and my magic slammed uselessly into the wall behind him, digging a deep niche into the dark stone. I dodged like I had the previous time, when turning and ducking had been enough to avoid the weapon hurtling at me from behind. Bad idea. Edored's attack hit me mercilessly against the shoulder, a lash in the vulnerable spot between shoulder blade and upper arm, sending a fierce flare through my arm that almost had me dropping my own stick. I scrambled to counter the attack but found the hall empty where he had been a moment before.

Oh, fuck.

This wasn't going to work.

It was barely a thought as I snapped around again and somehow managed to fend off his next swing at my face. I didn't have time for thoughts. Flashes of insight were all my brain was able to produce in between those frenzied reflexes. Danger. Problem. Hopeless. Smarter.

I had to be *smarter*.

He was far too good. Far too experienced. Anger and magic alone weren't enough to break through his impeccable defences, five centuries of understanding between him and his weapon. I dodged and blocked, blocked and dodged, every next turn more desperate, every next clash of our sticks more painful to my poor unprepared wrists and fingers. Hell, he wasn't even trying, was he? The strikes hitting my back and shoulders whenever I was just a tad too slow told me as much; they were just vicious enough to hurt, but not as bad as they could have been. Not bad enough to end the game at once.

He was *toying* with me.

Gods damn him. My next swing came with twice the force of the last, a burst of anger lending unexpected strength to my motions. So he thought that would put me in my place? A slow but inevitable defeat, a helpless struggle for even the smallest bit of wiggle room ...

Smarter.

Something sparked in my brain as I whirled around for the tenth time, finding him just behind me as I had last time ... and the time before last ... and the time before that ... Close enough to hit me, every time. Because even if I tried to attack him in turn, even if I successfully fended him off every now and then, he'd be out of reach fast enough to send me spinning all over again.

Fast enough ...

It was not even a plan. I had no time for plans. Edored's stick swung down at me again, bit me ruthlessly in the right upper arm. I hardly felt the sting, hardly felt my fingers jump open, hardly heard my own stick clatter against the floor. It didn't matter – not if this worked.

The fingers of my left hand were already on my dress, magic trailing up my arm. Fast, now, before he faded again ...

Bright, buttery yellow sparked from my right fingertips the moment Edored vanished, aimed at the smooth stone floor three feet behind my back.

Hard to soft.

Edored appeared in that exact spot as the magic hit, stick halfway up for a next swing ... and wavered.

Because suddenly the floor below his feet was no longer solid rock but a fluffy, pillowy surface that couldn't possibly support his perfectly balanced motions. Suddenly his feet were sinking into five inch of rock-coloured squishiness, suddenly his weight was moving in all the wrong directions ...

A bewildered curse burst from his lips as he flailed to regain his footing.

I turned and shot forward.

My full weight slamming into his faltering body was the last nudge. He grabbed my shoulder to keep standing, and I rolled over in yet another brand new reflex, sending both of us plummeting to the floor. Edored cursed again. I slapped his sword arm aside. And then we both hit smooth rock in a tangle of limbs and fury, all rules and strategy forgotten as he dug his nails into my face and I found a handful of hair in my left fist and all I could hear amidst his furious cries was ...

Running away again, Hytherion?

Creon.

Tears of ink, bottomless eyes, a hundred and thirty years of bitter regret, and I could no longer think. Rage throbbed through me, pulsing at my temples and the tips of my fingers; Tared's voice in the background was nothing to my ears, drowned out by the echo of those venomous sneers. *Thought you liked cowards. Running away again?* And then Creon *had* run, and if not for this gods-damned bastard, if not for all that useless fucking hatred, he might still be here, might still be mine.

My fist came down, an instinctive swing at the face still pinned into place by my left hand full of hair.

Bone cracked.

Edored howled a curse, kicking me off him. I no longer felt the pain. I barely felt the warm blood gushing from his broken nose as I hit again, barely saw the face under my punches. It wasn't *him* I was breaking anymore. It was decades and decades of violent grudges. It was the justified hatred of an Alliance that had fought too long and lost too much. It was a locked bedroom door and my empty bed and that darkness in Creon's eyes that not even I could lift, and I lashed out again and again, every blow cracking through another layer of grief and anger ...

Hands locked around my upper arms, pulling me back.

I snarled a curse, kicking back at whoever dared to pull me from the pits of my mindless rage. The hands didn't let go. I clawed my fingers into my dress by pure instinct and drew – tried to draw – to free myself.

No tingle of magic followed.

It was the confusion that cleared my mind more than anything, the unexpected sensation of *something* amiss. My magic. Why couldn't I use my magic? And only then did I become aware of the cold metal pressing into my bare left arm, just where that hand was still holding me so tightly it hurt.

Alf steel.

A ring.

Ylfreda's ring. *Tared.*

As if the mere thought of his name was enough to bring my senses back to life, his voice finally reached my ears. '... think you made your point, Emelin. No need to damage the bit of brain he has left, and don't forget to keep breathing ...'

Breathing.

Breathing I could do.

I slumped in his hold and stumbled back as I sucked cool air deep into my lungs. The red mist cleared before my eyes. Around us, the hall took on its own dusky shape, familiar smooth walls and vaulted ceilings.

And before me, the much more unfamiliar mess of Edored sitting on the floor, gaping at me without noticing the blood that gushed from his crooked nose.

The sight of him had my breath hitching again.

A bruise was beginning to form around his left eye. A knuckle-shaped red blot covered most of his cheek. Smudges of blood still showed where my hands had been, the long, dark brown hairs sticking to his fingers clear evidence I hadn't been the only one aiming for the head. He looked like he'd crawled straight from a battlefield or two – a battle he hadn't been even close to winning.

'Oh,' I heard myself say.

Edored blinked, cautiously tapped a finger against his nose, and started, 'What in hell ...'

'Go see Ylfreda,' Tared cut in from behind me, in that tone that didn't allow for objection. 'You need to stop the bleeding.'

'She ...' Edored blinked at me again. 'She broke ...'

'You quite literally asked for it.' Cold, knife-edged words; the hands on my upper arm tensed painfully tightly. 'Ylfreda. *Now.*'

A last stunned instant and Edored was gone, leaving only a few bright red drops of blood and the pillowy patch of floor behind. Tared's fingers relaxed their hold on me a fraction, but not enough to release me from that ring still stinging my skin. I didn't even try to wrestle free without my magic. Weeks of training had taught me how useless the attempt would be.

'Well,' he said.

I breathed. I didn't dare to do anything else, rage still ringing in my ears.

Tared sighed and added, 'On the bright side, it seems you've been paying attention to my lessons.'

A weak, joyless laugh escaped me.

'Very decent defence work.' He didn't move behind me, holding me on my feet as if I'd collapse without his hands to keep me in place. 'Attacks weren't bad at all, but pay attention to your backhanded swings next time. You were giving him too much room for rebound. Bonus points for magic use – very inventive. Quite effective too.'

I swallowed. Something about the undertone below his words suggested he wasn't done yet.

'On the more unpleasant side ...' He whirled me around so fast I had no time to pull away, both hands gripping my shoulder again before I regained my balance. His grey eyes were calm, but in a disconcerting way – that unmovable composure, the most civilised of warning signs. 'How many times have I told you that a clear mind is everything in the thick of a fight?'

'Good couple of times,' I grumbled, averting my gaze to the floor between us. Only now, the rush ebbing from my limbs, did the full realisation of what I'd done hit me. 'I ... Well. I suppose I got a little carried away.'

He clucked his tongue. 'Very observant.'

'He *was* being an arse,' I muttered.

'Yes.'

'And he *did* ask for it.'

'What he asked for,' Tared corrected me, voice cool, 'was a good punch on the nose. Not seven blows to the face, and before you ask, yes, I did keep count.'

'But ...' I forced myself to look up and meet his eyes again, his eyebrows raised a displeased fraction. 'But he ... he ...'

Tared waited, unmoving.

'But he started this mess!' My voice cracked. 'You didn't hear him in that bloody library, the things he was saying – and then he shows up *gloating* about it, as if he did me some grand favour by ... by ...'

Tared closed his eyes, finally releasing my arms. 'Emelin.'

'I'm so sick of it!' I burst out, and something frighteningly close to a sob escaped me with those words. 'So gods-damned *sick* of every single one of you acting like he's some filthy stain on the face of this world – acting like he asked for any of this, acting like I should be glad to turn my back on him as soon as he's gone. How many times do I have to tell you—'

'Emelin ...'

'—that I actually *care* about him? That you're doing me the opposite of a favour with—'

'*Emelin*.' Louder now, and sharp enough to shut me up. I swallowed the rest of my tirade, the hall suddenly misty around me, the taste of bitter gall in the back of my throat. Before me, his face clear as day even through the blur of my almost-tears, Tared took a step back, let out a long, overly restrained sigh, and said, 'You made your point.'

I scoffed. 'And you'll ignore it.'

'I'm not ignoring it at all. I just ...' He hesitated, rubbing his face. 'Oh, fuck's sake, Emelin. I'm sorry, alright? I'm trying to empathise, but it's a challenge if all I see in him is ...'

'Demon brood?' I suggested sharply.

'Nightmares,' he said, his voice almost inaudible.

I stared at him. This time he was the one to look away for three, four, deep breaths, each one slower than the last.

'Go have a word with Lyn,' he eventually said as he dropped his hand and met my eyes again, his jaw too tight. 'If what you need is a sensible conversation about Creon, I'm not going to be helpful. She can probably' – a vague gesture in the general direction of the library – 'clear things up.'

I had no desire to clear things up; I just wanted him and his bloody kind to behave. But I *had* made that point, indeed, and seeing as I'd almost punched Edored's nose to the back of his skull, perhaps I shouldn't test anyone's patience too much for a while.

'Alright,' I mumbled.

'Good.' He pressed his lips into a thin line. 'And Emelin ...'

He didn't finish that sentence until I said, 'Yes?'

'Don't try to kill my family members again.' He brusquely turned away, slipping Ylfreda's ring from his finger and into his pocket. 'I'll allow you the excuse of inexperience this once, but expect me to be unpleasant about it next time.' A mirthless smile. 'I don't have that many of them left, you see.'

And before I could reply to that warning – or perhaps to that threat – he was gone.

CHAPTER 18

I FOUND LYN IN her workroom above the Wanderer's Wing, pacing between the window and the back wall, muttering curses at every pile of books in her way. When I slipped into the room and shut the door behind me, she snapped around with what seemed an unreasonable amount of alarm for a phoenix used to a household full of alves.

'Oh, Emelin! You're early.'

'I know,' I said, collapsing onto our usual couch at the window and resolving not to get up for the next three hours. Every spot where Edored had hit me was screaming for attention, and it turned out there were more of them than I'd kept count of. I'd be a patchwork of bruises tomorrow. 'Thought I'd broken enough noses for today.'

'I'm sure Ylfreda agrees.' She gave a bleak chuckle, settling herself on the nearest pile of sturdy leather encyclopaedias. 'He didn't look his best, I have to say. How many times did you break his nose, exactly?'

'Seven, apparently.'

Lyn pursed her lips. 'Rather thorough.'

'I'd say he deserved it,' I said weakly, hoping *she* at least would agree with me after his near-destruction of the library. She nodded, but the gesture came too slowly to be a heartfelt sign of agreement, and she didn't speak.

Oh, Zera help me. 'No?'

'Oh, it's doubtlessly been an educational experience for him.' She sent me a wry smile. 'And the gods know he could use it.'

'But?'

Again she was silent for a few heartbeats, worrying her bottom lip as she examined the book-covered wall behind my head with unseeing eyes. Outside, in the fields below, nymphs were laughing, their voices as bright and sparkling as the alf light that fell through the study's high windows.

Finally, Lyn cautiously said, 'You do realise that Edored isn't to blame for all of it, don't you?'

All of it.

I should have known I wouldn't have to bring up the subject. She may have painstakingly avoided any mention of Creon since his departure, wary as always of hurting my feelings ... but now that the point was staring us right in the face, or rather punching us in the face, of course she knew exactly what had made me lose control in that training hall.

Knew, understood, and politely disagreed.

Even the alf light no longer seemed so bright. I closed my eyes, unable to bear the endless compassion in her gaze – that sympathy that gave me no choice but to admit she was right, that she wasn't trying to clear Edored's name just for the sake of old grudges and an overabundance of family honour.

'I know,' I muttered.

She waited a few heartbeats, then sighed and added, 'I fully understand that Edored is much easier to blame, of course.'

As opposed to Creon, who'd found himself torn between leaving me and learning to deal with his powers and had chosen to run.

I knew.

I just didn't want to know.

My life was much, much more manageable if Edored was the sole problem to blame. Whereas if the issue was not so much the rest of the world but rather Creon himself ...

I'll be back.

For how long?

'I know,' I whispered again. It hurt, that thought, a dull, physical ache chafing away at my heart, heavy enough to make breathing an effort. 'It's just that I don't want him to be miserable like this. I just want him to ... to ...'

I stopped myself just in time. *To choose me instead* – too close to the truth. Far too close to the truth. When I braced myself and looked up, Lyn sat studying me with earnest amber eyes, and somehow she didn't look any less interested as I weakly finished, 'I just want him to be fine.'

She cocked her head. '*Fine.*' There was far too much scepticism in her voice.

'Why are you looking at me like that?'

'That's why you're sulking around the Underground since he's done what's best for him and left to save his own sanity? Because you want him to be fine?'

I blinked. 'What are you trying to imply with—'

'Oh, for Inika's bloody sake.' She jumped from the pile of books, flinging up her hands. 'I'm not *blind*, Emelin.'

'You ... what?'

She threw a glance at the door – still closed – and turned back to me with the most exasperated of sighs. 'Did you really think I could walk in on the two of you in the library and not realise what was going on?'

I stared at her.

'Apparently you did,' she concluded, falling into the couch pillows next to me with a groan at the ceiling. 'Good gods.'

'What? But—'

'I *do* know him pretty well, remember?' she cut in, as if these words had been itching to escape for weeks. 'I've never seen him like that with anyone – nor have I seen *you* like that with anyone, for that matter. What else was I supposed to think?'

'But ...' A baffled laugh fell over my lips. My brain was rapidly turning itself inside out. 'If you suspected ... Why in hell didn't you tell me?'

She shrugged. 'I wasn't fully sure if you realised the extent of it.'

'Of ... of what?'

'Oh, don't be obtuse – of him being madly in love with you.' She shot me a glare. 'Stop playing stupid, Em. You're bad at it.'

Em. I was confused enough to barely register that sudden familiarity – too many steps at once, too many changes at once. 'But ...'

'I caused the both of you enough trouble blathering about the wrong secrets,' she interrupted sourly, waving my objection away. 'I thought I could better follow Naxi's example and keep my mouth shut until I was very sure who was aware of what.'

Oh.

Well. I could see the sense in that, admittedly.

'Naxi ...' I cleared my throat, not sure what to say. 'Naxi knows, too.'

'Of course she does,' Lyn said. 'Her repeated insistence that Tared shouldn't worry about Creon is not exactly *subtle*.'

I stiffened. 'Are you saying ... Does Tared know?'

'Oh, no.' A chuckle. 'You'd have heard.'

'But you just said—'

'Yes, of course she's being obvious,' Lyn said, rolling her eyes as if to say, *men*, 'but do you really expect Tared to consider for a moment that the little half fae he just pretty much adopted would even *think* about murderous demons in any such way?' She hopped off the couch, grabbed the kettle from the floor, and made for the small marble sink on the other side of the room. As she turned on the tap, she added over her shoulder, 'I don't expect any of the alves to figure it out until they find you with your tongue down Creon's throat, really.'

I choked on my own hysterical laughter. '*Lyn.*'

'What?' The grin she gave me looked disconcertingly suggestive on her young face. 'Don't tell me you spent weeks holding hands at that cursed court.'

'No, but ...' I dropped into the couch cushions, wrapping my arms around my face. Was I blushing? Oh, hell, I was blushing. 'Look, I didn't talk about this with anyone, and I *certainly* didn't expect to talk about it with a bloody seven-year-old, alright?'

She snorted a laugh. 'You're closer to seven than I am. Tea?'

'Might need something stronger,' I said, lowering my arms with a grimace at her, 'but I can start with tea, yes.'

Chuckling, she lit a small ball of fire in the palm of her left hand and held it under the full kettle until the water started simmering. 'Glad we've sorted that out, then. And now that I'm prodding anyway, do I need to badger Ylfreda for some contraceptive tonic?'

'Uh.' Good gods. I had expected her to be at least a *little* less businesslike about this madness. Why was I more shocked about my nights in Creon's bed than she was? 'If she has any of it? I didn't think ... you know, with those bindings ...'

Lyn's smile dulled a little at the mention of that – the Mother taking the fertility of every magical female she'd bound. 'Oh, we don't produce it for ourselves. But it's helpful for human women above at times – especially those bound to the court. A lot of them would rather not have children in that situation.'

The situation in which my mother must have found herself. I pushed that thought away. 'In that case, if you could get your hands on some of it ...'

'Will do.' She whisked out the fire in her palm, carrying the steaming kettle to the table beside our couch. As she trotted to the window to pluck a handful of mint leaves from the plant growing on the sill, she added, 'And let me know if you need help with anything else. I'll be silent as the grave.'

'Even to Tared?'

She let out a small groan. 'There are few things I won't discuss with Tared, but Creon is an exception. We've gotten rather good at tiptoeing around the topic.'

'Ah,' I said, and perhaps I said it too curtly, because she sent me another one of those uncomfortably investigative glances as she turned back to me and dropped the mint into the steaming water.

'Hm?'

'Just ...' I hesitated. Tared had shut me up at the first request for details – but then again, she'd just made herself privy to the salacious particulars of my love life. I could probably get away with a couple of nosy questions. 'Don't take this the wrong way, but if you're angry enough at his idiocies to keep tiptoeing for a century, why is there even anything left to tiptoe around at this point?'

She turned away slowly, placing the lid back onto the kettle with exaggerated care. Only as she hauled herself back onto the couch and folded her legs to her chest did she say, 'Valid question.' It sounded tired.

I felt guilty for a moment, then reminded myself this entire bloody mess was half of the reason I had trouble falling asleep at night and that ignorance wasn't going to help me fix anything. 'Thanks.'

'You should keep in mind ...' She groaned. 'Look, first of all, Tared wasn't the only one to blame for that situation.'

'Do you mean Creon ...'

'No. I mean I was being an idiot, too.'

I frowned. 'For trying too hard to save him?'

'No,' she said slowly. 'I never regretted trying to save him. But ...' She rubbed her small hands over her face. 'But I did realise soon enough that he was pulling himself out of that hole for me and me alone and that I was never going to return any of his feelings. Which I should have told him far, far earlier. I was stringing him along like some cruel flirt, Em. It was entirely unfair to both of them.'

'But *why*?'

'He was a mess,' she said weakly, her look at me a silent plea for understanding. 'The Mother absolutely destroyed him, leaving him there to die. He was starting to realise exactly how much suffering he'd caused in the first few centuries of his life, he was desperate for *anything* to live for, and I was afraid ...' She sucked in a breath. 'Hell, I *knew* he'd crumble if I told him. So I didn't – hoped there would be a better moment. At least, a moment where the truth wouldn't kill him.'

Wallowed in self-pity ... I swallowed something sour in the back of my throat. 'And then Tared told him?'

Lyn sighed. 'Yes. In the cruellest possible way.'

'And Creon crumbled anyway.'

'Yes.'

'And yet ... you and Tared ...'

She closed her eyes. 'Tared means everything to me, Em. Always has, always will. But I'm angry about a couple of things, and he's angry about a couple of things, and ...' Another tired sigh. 'And we're too frightened to figure out exactly how much of a problem that is as long as we have a war to fight. The two of us are essentially holding the Alliance together, and we can't afford to get caught up in our personal dramatics when so much depends on our cooperation. So' – she grimaced – 'we tiptoe around. As we have been doing for a while.'

A hundred and thirty years. I tried to find something more sensible to say, something vaguely wise or sympathetic, but the only thing that made it over my lips was yet another numb 'Oh.'

'I know,' she said wryly. 'It isn't pretty.'

'No.' I bent over to pour the both of us a cup of tea, because she'd have to climb off the couch to reach the kettle, and then added, 'I suppose the family knows this version of the story, too?'

'Oh, yes.' She waited until I was done and accepted her cup with a quick smile. 'But it's clearly easier for them to blame Creon than to blame me. Let alone they'd ever blame Tared. Especially because they understand ... well.'

'Understand what?'

She blew the steam off her tea, hesitating for a moment too long. 'Long story. Alf romance is a bit of a heavy topic.'

I hesitated. 'Because of the lifelong bonding? But what would that—'

'Oh,' she said, and something about the undertone of those words sounded entirely wrong, 'he told you about that part?'

'The ... wait.' I jolted upright from the pillows, feeling my eyes widen. 'Wait. Lyn, did he get himself bonded to *you*? Is that a thing that happens with ...'

I didn't need to finish my sentence. The joyless excuse for a smile that tensed around her lips told me all I wanted to know – all I hadn't wanted to know.

'Oh, *gods*.'

She gave me a pained shrug.

'But ... but you're not an alf.'

'No.' A grimace. 'Trust me, we're both extraordinarily aware of that fact.'

'And phoenixes ...'

'Don't bond,' she finished flatly. 'No.'

'But ...' Once again my head was spinning, yet another piece of the puzzle falling into place, answering questions I hadn't even thought to ask yet. *Alves bond for life,* Tared had said that morning, with that empty gaze into the distance. *After my father died, she was a shell ... an empty husk of herself.*

Until she'd eventually thrown herself on her sword, his mother – and he'd been glad for it. And then he ended up bonded to a phoenix who didn't, *couldn't* commit to him in that same all-consuming way, and then ...

Creon.

So I panicked.

Because he'd known – known far too well – how he, too, would end if Lyn ran off with the pretty fae prince that had landed in their midst.

I stared at the steam whirling over my teacup without seeing a thing. So that *was* mortal fear I'd seen in his eyes, that morning I'd shown up in Faewood with Creon's body in my arms. Not a fear of mere heartbreak, but of a grief that could kill, a grief that *had* killed. And Edored, who kept insisting Tared was mad for allowing the Silent Death around, who exploded at Lyn time and time again for not taking the threat seriously enough ...

Oh, hell. He'd seen his aunt wither away, too, after losing most of his family already. He knew the danger Tared was in. Could I really blame him for trying to keep the last members of his house safe, even if his strategies were hardly helpful?

'That ...' I shivered. 'That puts the protectiveness into perspective, I suppose.'

'Yes,' Lyn said quietly, 'it does.'

And her readiness to stay away from Creon, to go out of her way to reassure Tared even if she knew there was no chance she'd end up falling for anyone else ... Because she, too, knew what was at stake. Because she knew that asking him just to trust her and stop worrying might be about as useful as asking him to stop breathing.

How in hell did she survive it, knowing she was all that stood between him and torturous decay?

I pushed that thought away, and the tingle of nervousness that came with it. She'd manage somehow. They'd managed for over a century, balancing on that line between everything and nothing at all; they'd just have to handle it a little longer. Until I was ready. Until this war was over. Until the fate of the world no longer rested on their shoulders.

All I could do ... make sure some alf didn't kill Creon in the meantime.

'Perhaps I should go have a word with Edored,' I muttered.

She raised her eyebrows at me, a spark of wry amusement back in her bright eyes. 'The kind of word that ends with bruises on your knuckles?'

'No. No, not like that.' I took a small sip of tea, more to allow myself time to think than because the tea was anywhere near drinkable. The scorching hot water burned all the way down my throat, offering unexpected focus to the tangle of my thoughts. If all Edored cared about in the end was his family's safety ... if all Tared cared about was Lyn ...

'I suppose we're skipping the Faerie lessons for today?' Lyn said, eyeing me closely.

'I'll do twice the vocabulary tomorrow,' I muttered. I was going to regret that promise. Didn't matter. I could suffer through a few dozen more verbal forms if it offered Creon a safer home in the end. 'Do you think Ylfreda would kill me if I showed up in the family home now?'

Lyn chuckled. 'She won't *kill* you. Worst case she makes you wash the bedpans in the hospital ward for the next two years, but I could probably talk her out of that.'

I pulled a face. 'I'll take the risk, then.'

'As you wish.' The smile had already sagged off her freckled face. 'Be easy on yourself, Em. This is not something you need to solve for us.'

'I know,' I said, staring at the floor, 'but Creon ...'

There was no need to finish that sentence. Her sigh told me she understood – understood and perhaps even agreed.

'Yes.'

We were both silent as we finished our tea, surrounded by the endless piles of parchment and the dazzling rays of alf light and the chatter and laughter of the nymphs outside. My mind was still reeling, my limbs still hurting, and yet I felt ... calm.

Comfortable, perhaps.

Having one less secret to keep made a difference, it turned out.

Which didn't mean I intended to *spread* the information. Lyn I could handle. Revealing to Edored where I'd spent my nights when Creon was still in the Underground ...

Best give that a little more time. In the meantime, I'd just have to be clever and tell the world exactly what it wanted to hear.

I found Ylfreda and Edored in the comfortable armchairs in the corner of the living room, the first busy with ice water and herbal compresses, the latter still in his bloodied shirt, his face spotlessly clean and the dark swelling around his nose and eye all the more visible for it. Tared was nowhere to be seen, although Ylfreda was wearing her ring again.

Both of them looked up at my entrance. Edored scowled, then winced as his facial muscles objected to the contortion.

Ylfreda clucked her tongue at him, sent me a disapproving glare, and flatly said, 'Morning, Emelin. Anything I need to stitch up for you?'

No bedpans, yet. A pleasant surprise. I managed a chuckle and said, 'No, thank you. I made some lucky escapes.'

'*Lucky,*' Edored grumbled with a scoff that sent him wincing again. 'I could have broken twenty of your ribs in those few minutes, if I—'

'Yes, yes,' Ylfreda interrupted impatiently. 'You're very fearsome, no need to remind us. Emelin, unless you have anything of sense to say, I suggest you—'

'I was wondering if you could let me have a word with Edored,' I said.

'A *word*?' Edored sputtered, jerking up straighter in his chair. 'With *you*? You should thank your lucky bones I don't—'

'Oh, shush,' Ylfreda snapped, swatting a hand at him as she turned and flicked her gaze over me. 'Are you mad, intent on self-harm, or just very dense, girl?'

'Fifty percent mad, fifty percent optimistic.' I shrugged at Edored. 'I'd like to make you an offer.'

He narrowed his good eye. 'Of death?'

'The opposite,' I said wryly. 'If you let me live for long enough to make my point, that is.'

He stared at me for a few heartbeats, thoughts spinning behind his eyes, before he fell back in his chair, folded his arms over his blood-stained shirt, and grumbled, 'Fine.'

I smiled, a little more relieved than I'd have liked for him to know. Ylfreda rolled her eyes but got up, muttering curt warnings under her breath – something about not wishing to return to any severed limbs and, indeed, bedpans. Edored didn't seem particularly impressed. I couldn't help but wonder how many years of bedpan service he'd already completed in his life.

With a last warning glance at me, she vanished, leaving us alone. On the other side of the room, Edored produced yet another ill-advised scoff.

'I'd stop doing that,' I said, slipping around the table to make my way to his corner. 'Don't want to hurt that pretty nose of yours any further. Or your pride.'

He grumbled a curse. 'Fuck off, Emelin.'

'That didn't stop you either, so I'll try not to let it discourage me.' I fell into the chair Ylfreda had just vacated and examined the swellings on his face. If I ignored that this hadn't quite been the plan, it was really rather impressive work. 'I figured I should apologise. For punches two to seven, at least.'

He looked sceptical. 'Tared told you to, didn't he?'

'Tared just told me he'd kill me if I did any such thing again,' I said. 'Or something to that effect.'

Edored huffed a laugh. 'So he has *some* good sense left? Good to know.'

No need for subtlety in this company. I should have known. 'Edored ...'

'Don't think you're going to change my mind about the fucker,' he interrupted, leaning forward so abruptly I thought he'd bite. 'Lyn tried enough of that with her sob stories, and I still don't give a damn about his poor misunderstood fae heart, so if that's what you're here for, best not tempt me to—'

'I'm not,' I said, and he fell silent.

'No?'

'No.' I rubbed my eyes. 'I just ... Hell. Could you forgive me for being blunt about this?'

Edored snorted. 'I'm the bloody epitome of forgivingness. Make your point.'

'As you wish.' I settled myself a little more securely in the padded seat, then blurted out, 'You want him gone because you're worried about Tared, yes? Because of the bonded stuff and—'

'Oh, you finally figured that out?' he said sharply, calloused fingers tensing on the armrests of his chair. 'About damn time. Why else did you think I wanted him out of this place, Emelin? Just for the fun of hunting fae princes? I'm not *that* fucking unhinged.'

Not the moment to tell him I had indeed thought him that fucking unhinged. 'I assumed it was because of the Last Battle and all that.'

'If it was just the Last Battle, I'd be happy enough to drag him into the next big fight and see if he's grown a little less worthless over the years.' A brusque shrug. 'But unless one of his fae friends slits his throat for me, I doubt that would stop him from running after Lyn, and *that* ...'

I pushed that image aside – Creon in the world above, at the mercy of whatever old fae friends might find him there. No need to worry about that now. He'd sent me another message last night. He had to be safe. 'He's not running after her.'

Edored bit out a joyless laugh. 'You mean he's decent enough to wait until she's no longer a child? Pleasant surprise.'

'No, no, Edored, that's not ...' Oh, hell. How much could I say without drawing attention to the sensitive secrets? I sucked in a deep breath and soldiered on. 'It's not just that he *says* he isn't. I know him a bit, alright? I'd have noticed if he was making plans to—'

'Aren't you overestimating yourself a *little* there, Emelin?'

I shrugged. 'Did you expect me to stop him in the library?'

'No, but—'

'I do hold some sway with him, you know. And ... and Lyn and Tared are my friends too, in case you'd forgotten that. It's not as if I want him to harm them.'

He blinked. 'Fine, but—'

'And Naxi said the same thing,' I interrupted, faster now. 'Have you even been listening to her? She's told you time and time again that there's no reason to worry about—'

'Naxi always means the opposite of what I think she means,' he said, rolling his eyes.

'Then go ask her, for the bloody gods' sake! Tell her to answer you with yes and no and ask away until you're satisfied! Or ... or ...' I flung a wide gesture at the door. 'Or do you want me to make a bargain? Want me to promise you I'm sure he's—'

'A *bargain*?' If I'd announced we'd serve only salad for dinner tonight, he couldn't have looked any more revolted. 'Orin's fucking beard, Emelin, I don't need any of your fae crap on my skin. Bargains are for dishonourable bastards who can't keep their word. Don't offend me with—'

'Would you trust me on my word, then?' I said.

He fell silent, the eye I hadn't punched purple and swollen widening as he stared at me. His fingers lay clenched around the armrests, gripping the padded wood so tightly that the blood drew from his tanned knuckles.

That look in his eyes ...

For the very first time, it was not just anger and recklessness and violent bewilderment. For the very first time, I found something in his steel grey gaze that came painfully close to fear, a powerless, almost *boyish* despair – a glimpse of that young alf who'd lost almost everyone he knew and then nearly lost his almost-brother to his most hated enemy, too.

'Edored.' I held his gaze. Locked my eyes on that lost little boy within him, lashing out at whatever and whoever threatened the last remainders of the home he'd known. 'Edored, I'm really very serious. I *know* Creon doesn't want anything from Lyn. Whatever promises you want me to make – whatever guarantees you need me to give – tell me. Please.'

His throat bobbed. No attacks, now. No sneers or sharp mockery. 'There are no promises you can make. Not if ... if ...'

I waited. Waited for him to regain control of his words, to wrestle down whatever nightmares I was raking up inside him.

'Do you understand,' he said hoarsely, slumping in his chair, 'do you see that if you're *wrong* ...'

'I know I'm not wrong.' My voice had become a lullaby I didn't recognise, singing the worst of those lethal fears to sleep. This was no longer about telling him what he wanted to hear, no longer about giving the right answers to the right questions. This was sincerity, not diplomacy – and perhaps it was that honesty that hit its target with ten times the force of even my most violent punches. 'But in the unlikely case I ever find out I am, I promise I'll set my pride aside and tell you immediately. As soon as I have the slightest suspicion, as soon as he reveals any hidden interest or intentions, you'll know. And I'll help you to solve the problem. On ... on my honour.'

He blinked at me. 'You'll *help* me.'

'I *do* want them to be fine, Edored. I honestly do.'

Every whirl of his thoughts lay mapped out on his face as he ran his eyes over me, studying me, assessing me – trying to figure out the catches behind my promises. A game that didn't come to him naturally, I realised. There were no masks between him and the world, no filters; he was not a male for trickery, for pretences and politeness and political scheming. If he gave me his word, I would *have* his word, and he'd probably die defending it.

At a fae court, he would be dead before the week was over. And somehow that thought felt like a compliment.

'If I ever find out you're lying to me now,' he said, his voiced too dazed to make it a threat, 'I'll kill you.'

I couldn't help my chuckle. 'I know.'

'So you're not lying.'

'I'm not lying.'

He contemplated that for another few heartbeats, battered face contorted into the most focused frown I'd seen on him. Then he loosened his fingers from the armrests and cautiously prodded his face, releasing an unwilling groan.

'It *was* a pretty good punch, you know.'

That took me a moment too long. 'What?'

A wolfish grin grew around his lips, and at once he looked entirely like himself again - wild, explosive, and ready for war. 'What, what?'

'You ...' Again, I had no choice but to laugh. 'You're *complimenting* me on that nose of yours?'

'Yes?' he said, grin broadening. 'Why not? You did better than I thought you would. Can't hurt to admit that.'

'I was definitely losing, though,' I said sourly.

He shrugged so energetically he almost bounced off his seat. 'So what? I got arrogant. You didn't lose. Speaking of which ...' He ran a hand through his long hair. 'How's your experience with bells?'

'The ... the game?' It was almost unnerving, this switch in him; had he been anyone else, I would have suspected some trap behind his sudden amicable questions. 'I'm not too bad at it, I think? It's been a while, but—'

'Good enough. Coming to Njalar's with me tonight?'

I stared at him.

'I always lose,' he said brightly. 'Some fresh blood at the card table could help. And they'll want to see the little hellion responsible for my face, of course.'

'Edored ...' I blinked. 'Njalar hates my guts. I'm not going to help you win any game if he—'

'Of course he doesn't,' he interrupted, waving my words away with a violent scoff. 'He hates that winged fucker of yours. Like a sensible alf.

But no one's going to mess with you if I tell them not to, and they'll like knowing the unbound mage way too much to make a fuss. So, coming?'

'I ... if you're sure ... but ...'

'Great!' He winked. 'Don't tell Tared, though. Party's probably breaking some rules.'

What in hell was happening? Were we sharing *secrets* now – was this how you won an alf's trust, by breaking his nose and saving his family? And why for Zera's loving heart was he *winking* at me?

Scraping myself together, I managed, 'Wait, Edored—'

He sniggered. 'Don't say you suddenly started caring about the rules.'

'Oh, no, damn the rules, but ...' I sucked in a breath. 'Edored, just so we're clear, I'm really only coming with you as a ... as a ...'

As a friend, I'd have said to any other person, but considering Edored and the many pretty nymphs who bore that title ... it seemed a straight road to misunderstandings.

'Oh, don't worry.' He threw me a crooked grin as he got up from his chair, flinched at the twisting of his face, and patted me reassuringly on the head. 'You're still twelve or so. And Tared would skin me alive. So just ...' He shrugged. 'Just as family.'

As family.

As *family*?

Perhaps I gaped at him a little too mindlessly, because he chuckled as he stepped back and added, 'Anything wrong?'

'I ... no. Not at all.' I forced a smile. 'See you tonight, then. As ... family?'

'See you, Nosebreaker,' he said, and with a last affectionate grin over his shoulder, he faded.

CHAPTER 19

'IT'S THE DAMN FAE blood,' Orlyga of the house of Hroskel confidently stated as she gathered her and her partner's losing cards and threw me that look of amused displeasure she'd honed to perfection in the four weeks since I'd joined their table. 'You arseholes just can't stop playing tricks, can you? I could have *sworn* you had the ten of bells, Emelin.'

'Very odd,' I said, smugly tipping back my chair. Around our table, the noise of the Midsummer celebration in the central hall was a steady blur – clinking glasses, singing nymphs, roaring fires. 'I'm pretty sure it's been sitting in Edored's hand all this time.'

'Edored never waits to play the ten of bells!'

'No,' Edored said, frowning at the remainders of our victory on the table, 'but I really thought Em was taking the round for us with leaves, so ...'

Orlyga let out an exasperated laugh. 'She didn't even have leaves!'

I sniggered and swiped the rest of the cards into a messy pile. Alves, I had learned during the first evening Edored had dragged me into a somewhat clandestine meeting with friends, were utterly incapable of bluffing. As a consequence, my usual strategy consisted of subtly convincing Edored I didn't have the hand I actually had, so he could with loud and utter confidence miss the game I was *actually* playing, and fool the rest of the table with him.

His chances of winning had roughly tripled since he'd partnered with me, he admitted after our third or fourth successful evening of cooperating.

'Definitely the fae blood,' Orlyga repeated firmly.

'A bold claim, if Em is your only example,' Thorir said on the other side of the table, sending me a quick grin. He'd been an architect's apprentice in a previous life, I had learned a while ago, and tended to be more analytically inclined than the average alf. 'Or did you ever play cards with any other fae?'

'Of course I didn't, Ylvirson,' she said, looking deeply offended as she tapped the hilt of the sword on her back. 'If fae are near enough to join me at a card table, they're near enough to take a sword in the guts, too, you see.'

'Well,' I said with as straight a face as I could manage, 'then for reasons of science, we have no choice but to invite Creon to a few rounds as soon as he returns, don't you think?'

Several alves choked on the cinnamon apple bites Thorir had brought to the table, Edored the first of them. And yet the glances were no longer as hostile as the first time I'd taken the risk of dropping his name four weeks ago. Wary, yes, and deeply sceptical ... but my repeated casual mentions of him seemed to slowly bring the point across that perhaps there was a *person* to be found below the layers of power and pain.

'I feel the demon part would be cheating, though,' Njalar slurred as the others were still coughing pieces of dried apple from their lungs. He was drunk enough to take even an idea this mad into consideration, it seemed. 'Wouldn't want him to know what I was feeling during the entire damn game.'

'Because you'd be scared to lose?' I said with a grin.

'Shut it, Nosebreaker.' He sent me a rather impolite gesture. 'At times I almost think you're trying to screw the bastard, with your fawning and—'

'Oy!' Edored said heatedly before I could make the point I was certainly not *trying* to screw any fae princes. 'First of all, that's my sister whose honour you're doubting there, Runarson! And second of all, I happen to know you fucked a Yule pudding once, so who are you to have opinions about where people are sticking it?'

'A *Yule pudding*?' I repeated as half the table once again died a painful death by apple chunk.

'In my defence,' Njalar garbled indignantly, 'I was a little drunk.'

'What kind of drunk barbarian fucks a Yule pudding?' I said, snorting. 'For the gods' sake, Runarson. Everyone knows Midsummer pie is the far more alluring option.'

Edored howled with laughter as Njalar gaped at me with unfocused eyes, trying to figure out what in hell my relation was to the sweet almond-and-raspberry pies that were served in the middle of the hall.

'Anyone in for another game?' Orlyga hastily suggested.

All participants were in for another game. As the cards were dealt, Thorir pulled a large flask with a suspiciously bright pink liquor from a bag and let it go around the table, with stealthy glances at the rest of the hall to make sure no one noticed the drink. Not that it was illegal, he'd insisted on a previous occasion, but he kindly wanted to spare any weaker-willed passers-by the temptation of its divine taste.

I politely refused. Divine taste or not, the one time I'd tried the stuff, it had cost Tared several buckets of ice water to keep me on my feet during training the next day.

My hand was pretty worthless this time. I swatted Njalar away as he made an unsubtle attempt to glance at my cards and tried to estimate how Edored had been dealt – not too badly, judging by the way he beamed at me. Which meant I had to pretend I was worth a few rounds so he would not blow all his winning cards at the first opportunity and leave us with empty hands when the big numbers were played towards the end of the game.

I returned a confident smile, settled back in my chair, opened my mouth to make a breezy remark about fae blood and good fortune ...

My throat tightened.

My chest tightened.

And out of nowhere, a sickening chill spread from my stomach, clenching like an iron fist around my heart.

I gasped for breath, for sense, as that layer of ice slithered up my spine, leaving numb, crawling skin behind. It took me a single shrieking inhalation to name the feeling, that sensation of something deadly creeping up on me from every corner of the room – *fear*, thick and suffocating, tugging at my limbs to dive beneath the table and hide, hide, *hide* ...

Hide from what?

What was *happening*?

'Emelin?' Njalar slurred as I snapped around in my chair, breath quickening. Something was wrong. Something was *wrong*. And I had not the faintest idea what it was, what mysterious sixth sense of mine had so abruptly picked up the signal we were all going to *die* ...

Pain flared through my right upper arm, sharp and clean like a knife cut.

The cards fell from my hand. A brittle cry escaped me. And before I had a moment to think, before I could get out a word to the heads snapping my way, a throbbing, excruciating burn spread over my chest, the skin below my dress suddenly raw and aching as if someone had set me on fire.

From far away, I heard myself scream.

But the hands I clawed to my chest ... they found nothing. No flames. No wounds. At my collar, my skin felt soft and smooth, no scars or open flesh despite that blazing pain that flared hotter and hotter across my ribs. I bent over, struggling for cool air, struggling for understanding. Was I hurt? Was I *dying*?

Around me, frantic hands were shaking me, panicking voices shouting in my ear – 'Em!' That was Edored, loud and terrified. '*Emelin*! What is the matter? Do you need a healer? Do you ...'

'Is she having a heart attack?' Orlyga was shrieking, and then Edored again – 'She's twelve, for Orin's sake! Twelve-year-olds don't get heart attacks!'

Lyn's voice. 'Let me *through*, you idiots ...'

'That isn't hers!' Naxi. 'That isn't *her* pain!'

What?

Not *my* pain?

Through the fierce flares scalding my chest, my thoughts wouldn't come through quick enough to understand. Not my pain. But then ...

Then ...

And at once, as if that agonising ache had been nothing but a figment of my imagination, it was gone.

I found myself panting and shrieking in my chair, my forehead pressed against the cool wood of the card table, my hands digging into the tender skin of my unharmed chest. The fear was gone, too. Voices were repeating my name, the group around me growing larger and larger as I stared at the dark floor with unseeing eyes. It couldn't have lasted more than three, four heartbeats, this phantom pain flooding me out of nowhere.

The pain isn't real.

I stiffened, eyes widening as the memory hit me. *It has no source you can make worse.* Words signed to me by scarred fingers on that night weeks and weeks ago, after Creon returned from Rhudak a sweaty, shivery mess.

Creon.

Not her pain.

'Em?' Lyn's small hands wrapped around my forearm, her fingers soft and commanding at once. 'Em, do you hear me? Can you tell me—'

'Creon,' I rasped.

The circle around me stilled.

I hauled myself upright, away from the solid safety of that cool table – instinctively bracing myself for some lingering pain, *some* trace of that blistering attack on my body, and finding nothing but the last tears pooling in my eyes. I blinked them away. Faces took clear shape around me again, Edored's wide eyes and Orlyga's pale cheeks and Lyn's gaze focused on my face.

'What did you say?' Her young voice trembled.

'Creon,' I repeated, lips unable to form a single other word as my brain sluggishly caught up. *Not her pain.* Not my fear. Sensations planted into my body like those feathery reassurances he sent me at night, except that this ... This was not a reassurance. It was the opposite of a reassurance.

'Danger.' And again the panic flared, entirely my own this time. 'He's in danger. He ... Lyn ... I need to ... to ...'

To run. To save him. To figure out what in hell he was trying to tell me with these few seconds of lightning-quick torment – but before I could persuade my tongue to put any of that into more than breathless shreds of words, she'd stepped back, staring at me with narrowed amber eyes.

The hall around us had gone very, very quiet.

'Lyn ...' I breathed. 'Please ... he—'

'Wanderer's Wing.' Her voice had never sounded less childlike, cutting through the baffled silence like a red-hot knife. '*Now.*'

It took less than a minute for the usual group to show up after Thorir faded me into that familiar room with its maps and wood and sparkling alf light.

It felt like half a century.

My trembling knees wouldn't hold me. I collapsed into a chair at the map table and watched Tared and Edored fade the others into the room, too agitated to register more than flashes of impressions – Lyn, anxious and flaming in her bright yellow festival dress. Naxi, trembling with such violent excitement that petals shook from the Midsummer flower crown on her head and dripped like pink and purple snowflakes over her hair and shoulders. Nenya, her scarred lips even redder from the glass of spiced red wine in one hand and a small raspberry pie in her other.

Beyla appeared last, mere moments after Lyn, Tared, and Edored had fallen into their usual chairs. She was the only one who didn't show a trace of festiveness; I briefly wondered if she'd even been in the hall for the celebration at all. 'What for Orin's loving heart is *happening*?'

'Good question,' Tared said grimly, glancing at me, then turning to Naxi. 'You said ...'

'Demon influence. No doubt about it.' She eyed me with those clever blue eyes, although what she hoped to see beyond roaring confusion and violent panic, I didn't know. 'You think it was Creon?'

I swallowed. 'Who else?'

She exchanged a quick look with Lyn, who grimaced and said, 'I don't see why any other demon would target Em. But why would he—'

'He's in *danger*.' How often had I spoken those words already? Two, three times, perhaps; it felt like dozens, the only certainty standing rock-solid in the storm. 'It was some kind of warning, some kind of ... of ... alarm? I felt fear, alright? Coming out of nowhere, for no reason at all, and then ... then ...'

Even Edored sat motionless as I struggled to find any sense or order in the memory of those bewildering moments. Run. I had to *run*. But I had no idea where to even start looking, and these people must at least know some of his travelling plans, might understand the significance of the sensations he'd sent me.

'It felt like a cut,' I forced myself to say, more slowly now. 'Here, on my upper arm.' I drew the line with my left finger, a clean slash around my bicep. 'And then ... then there was the pain in my chest, and that felt more like a burn wound ... like someone had set my dress on fire ... and then—'

Tared cursed.

I jolted up. He had grown pale on the other side of the table, eyes shooting to Lyn's small figure next to him.

'Inika help us,' she whispered.

'Does this make any sense to you?' My voice cracked. 'Because—'

'Golden Court,' Tared said.

The table fell silent.

'The ... what?'

'The Golden Court,' Lyn repeated, her voice hollow. 'The pain you describe – he was wounded like that at the Golden Court. Blade to the arm. Fire to the chest. If he's trying to pinpoint his location for us ...'

'But how would he know that you know ... Oh.' My brain arrived at its own conclusions seconds too late. 'Fire?'

She sent me a small, joyless smile.

'Gods be damned, Lyn,' I managed. 'That's a *very* unpleasant feeling.'

'I know. In my defence, he was trying to kill me.' She groaned a sigh. 'Beyla, he *was* planning to take a look at the Golden Court, wasn't he?'

Rumours of rebellious fae at that exact court, somewhere in the months before I was born – he'd told me that much. Another wave of panic clenched cold around my chest. And then something had gone ... wrong? Wrong enough that he couldn't solve it himself, wrong enough that he'd seen no other choice but to use his demon powers, that magic he'd rather forget altogether?

Danger. Danger. The word throbbed through my thoughts like a violent headache.

'He was,' Beyla said, pale eyes trailing over the map inlaid in the wooden table surface, 'but do you really think ... the *distance* ...'

Distance. Between us and the Golden Court – which had to mean we were not on the east side of the archipelago, then. Conclusions to store, carefully, for a later moment.

Lyn let out a groan and glanced at Naxi, who sat studying the map as well, a thick line drawn between her blonde brows. 'Would it be possible? For him to reach that far with his magic?'

'Oh, no,' she said, breezily and thoughtfully at once. 'Utterly impossible. But then again, *impossible* is a very flexible concept where Creon is concerned. So he might just do it anyway.'

A shiver ran through me. 'He ... he's done it before.'

'Beg your pardon?' Tared said sharply.

'Sending me ... messages. Just signs of life, really.' *Signs of love.* I wasn't going to tell him that much, or that it had been a daily occurrence, a ritual that kept me up until half an hour past the dimming of the lights. 'A couple of times. The last one was last night.'

He cursed. 'Naxi?'

'I suppose it helps he knows you well,' she said, a flicker of amusement in her voice. I stiffened, but as usual, no one except Lyn seemed willing to notice the suggestion below the words. 'That does make it easier to reach people across a distance. Apart from that ...' She shrugged, sending flower petals fluttering down from her shoulders. 'It isn't news that he has far too much power on his hands. If he really wanted to, he could probably cross the distance, yes.'

The looks Lyn and Tared exchanged didn't escape me. Troubled couldn't begin to describe them.

'So then you're saying ...' Edored started, wavering between incredulous laughter and habitual fury. 'You're saying he's *at* the Golden Court? And that for some reason he decided to start some ... some demonic scavenger hunt? Just when I was dealt the best hand I've been playing all night? Why would the bastard ...'

Danger. Danger.

'Emelin?' Nenya said.

'I need to go,' I blurted. Needed to go *now*. Because he needed my help. Because he wouldn't shake me up like this, wouldn't hurt me like this, for anything less than the most urgent threat to his life, and I'd already wasted far too much time talking and debating while the gods knew whether he might be *dying* ...

'Go?' Edored said shrilly.

I ignored him. 'How do I get to the Golden Court?'

'Emelin.' The last layer of restraint on Tared's voice was flimsier than silk organza. 'You are *not* going to the Golden Court on your own, let alone before we know—'

'We don't have time to figure out what's going on first!' I burst out, jumping from my chair. The dark walls were a prison, suddenly, the weight of all that stone pressing heavily on my shoulders. 'He's not sending out warnings for the pleasure of it – you can't just let him ...'

Tared briefly closed his eyes. 'Thorir?'

Before I could make sense of the request shimmering below that single word, Thorir had nodded and vanished, hand halfway to the sword on his back.

Tared sank back in his chair and looked up at me, eyes cold and yet not unfriendly at all. 'Sit down, Em.'

I didn't sit down – I *couldn't* sit down. My body was liquid fire, aching for movement. 'Where did he—'

'Taking a look at the Golden Court. If the entire island is in a state of acute war, we'll know it in a minute.' A nod at the chair behind me. '*Sit.* I'm the first to approve of reckless undertakings, but if you run off and get yourself stuck on the wrong end of a fae blade, that isn't going to save anyone's life.'

'And less reckless undertakings?'

'Em—'

'You said you weren't letting me go.' My voice soared. 'So what are you going to do – keep me prisoner in this bloody place?'

Tared didn't even flinch. 'I said I wasn't letting you go *alone*.'

My mouth snapped shut.

'So' – he sent me a tired smile – 'are you going to sit down?'

I fell into my chair, all lust for fight drained from my limbs at once. *Not alone.* Was I going mad, or was he suggesting he would be willing to embark on some mission to save Creon's life?

Before I could ask, Lyn turned to Beyla and cautiously said, 'Do you know who's overseeing the Golden Court these days? Is it still—'

'Still Agenor, yes.'

Tared muttered a curse next to me. On the other side of the table, Edored's lip was curling into that most murderous of sneers, and next to him, even Naxi had abruptly stiffened.

I swallowed a sting of bitter fear. 'Is it that bad?'

'Depends,' Tared said grimly. 'Best I can say about the bastard is that he's not really the "let's burn your children at the stake" kind. But he's very much the "let's shove a couple of protocols up your arse and politely bleed you dry" kind, which is terrifying enough with the powers he wields.'

'The protocol ...' Lyn hesitated. 'The protocol for anyone stumbling upon Creon would presumably be to deliver him to the Crimson Court without delay, wouldn't it?'

My heart stilled.

'Yes,' Tared muttered. 'Suppose so.'

'Concerns for his poor soul aside,' Nenya said, toying with her long nails as she examined me, 'it would be unhelpful if he ends up facing the Mother with all he knows about us and this place. I wouldn't gladly let her—'

In a flicker of light, Thorir appeared – unharmed, unflustered, sword still in its sheath.

'All's quiet at the Golden Court.' He stalked towards us and grabbed Nenya's half-eaten pie from the table, muttering a half-hearted apology as he shoved it into his mouth. Crashing into his chair, he added, 'Faded around the island a bit. No trace of trouble anywhere. Didn't get into the castle, though – I'm not that suicidal.'

'Want me to go?' Edored said eagerly.

'No,' Nenya and Tared snapped simultaneously, and he threw them a look like a sulky youth forced to clean his room for the *second* time in a year.

'Do you need me to send out some folks to keep an eye on the place?' Thorir said around his mouthful of dough and raspberry. 'If anything's wrong inside the castle, at some point they'll have to come out again. We could report back if anything happens.'

Tared sighed. 'Thanks, but don't bother.'

'Oh, for Orin's fucking sake.' Edored jolted up again, gaze flying back and forth between his cousin and Thorir. 'Don't say you're planning to go?'

I didn't dare to breathe in the silence that fell. Lyn and Tared exchanged a single glance, so many questions and answers in that short look that they might as well have excluded us from an hour of conversation.

'Well,' Lyn said, sounding cautious.

'*Someone* has to go,' Tared said reasonably.

They both grinned. Oddly similar grins, part recklessness and part nostalgia and part grim resolve, expressions that said *let's go risk our lives, like in the good old days.*

Edored's curse sent even Thorir flinching.

I locked my fingers around the edge of my chair and cut in before he could elaborate on his objections. 'And me?'

'And you?' Tared threw me a look of tired amusement. 'You seemed to have trepidations about real fights at some point, if I recall correctly.'

Had I? Somewhere in the back of my mind, Gish was still making his point – *Will the girl be ready?* The words no longer lingered. The question no longer stung. Creon was in danger, some powerful bastard of a fae lord might be doing the gods knew what with him as we were sitting here in this buried room, and who in hell cared if I wasn't ready? I'd get ready if I had to. I'd handled the Mother with no more than a night to prepare; how much trouble could some stupid fae court give me?

'I'll be fine,' I muttered. 'When are we going?'

'It *will* be dangerous,' Lyn said, smile tipping downward as she brushed a rogue curl from her eyes. 'Are you sure ...'

I shrugged. 'I think it would be more dangerous if I had to bribe some other alf into taking me there. And I doubt that would take me longer than a couple of hours.'

She let out a desperate laugh. 'For the bloody gods' sake. In that case ...'

'Twenty minutes?' Tared said.

'I'm not out of shape *that* badly, Tared. Ten will do.'

He sent her a grin, holding out a hand to me. 'Fine. You've got ten minutes to pack, Em.'

I glanced at the other faces around the table – Edored on the brink of cursing, Nenya cold and stoic, Naxi staring pensively at the map in an apparent attempt to figure out how far Creon's power reached. Thorir had finished chewing, and there was none of the usual light-hearted-ness left in his gaze as he studied me.

He knew where I was headed. By the look in his eyes, it wasn't pretty.

But I recalled that all-consuming fear, that pain Creon would never have inflicted upon me if not for the direst of reasons, and any last flickers of doubt sank to the very bottom of the ocean outside.

I grabbed Tared's hand.

Ten minutes to prepare for war. I'd make do with it.

Chapter 20

At least I didn't have much to pack.

A handful of black dresses. Clean underwear. An alf steel dagger Tared pushed into my hands a minute after we returned to the family home, its hilt covered in leather to shield my skin from the white metal. I stuffed all of it into the leather backpack Lyn flung into my room, then stared at the rest of my earthly possessions for a few heartbeats – books and a pack of cards and an impressive pile of failed magical experiments.

Nothing I needed. Who cared about books and cards? Creon was out there – had been out there for far too long already.

With a brusque turn, I hurried into the corridor, leaving behind that bedroom that still wouldn't feel entirely like my own.

Lyn and Tared were one mind packing two bags, the questions and confirmations exchanged between their rooms a routine of centuries. Yes, Lyn had the maps. No, Tared wasn't forgetting the food. Of course the ink was already sitting in their luggage. As if they hadn't been eating cake at a Midsummer celebration mere minutes ago, as if the threat of war had been at the front of their minds even through the wine and the flower dances.

Perhaps it had been.

As for the past hundred and thirty years and gods knew how many centuries before.

Tared emerged from his room before my thoughts could spiral from that point, bag over one shoulder, sword over the other, coat pockets bulging with emergency snacks. Lyn appeared a moment later, wearing a tunic and loose linen trousers instead of one of her usual bright-coloured dresses. Two alf steel rings sat on the fingers of her left hand, a small alf steel dagger on her belt, a third and sharp-pointed ring on a thin chain around her neck. Her bag was surprisingly small for the amount of noise her packing efforts had produced.

'Ready?' she said.

I was miles beyond ready. I didn't say it out loud; they were ridiculously fast already.

'Always,' Tared said dryly, holding out a hand to her.

She grabbed his fingers and my wrists, squeezing her eyes shut so tightly her nose wrinkled. I remembered to cover my own face with my free hand just before the maelstrom of sounds sucked me in.

Out of the Underground.

Into the Golden Court.

Fading had never taken so long before. Even the journey to Sevrith couldn't have taken more than two or three heartbeats; this time I counted at least six of them before the ground turned solid beneath my feet again. A long distance indeed – hell, how much power had it taken Creon to warn me? To send me those daily reassurances all these weeks?

Sunlight seared through my hand and eyelids as the world took shape around us, although not as painfully as that afternoon on Sevrith.

Evening. It had to be *evening*. I cautiously blinked open my eyes, trying to align the rhythm of the Underground with the world above. The light that flooded me, bright but not bright enough to hurt, filtering delicately through the foliage around us ...

It was *gold*.

A moment too late did the understanding reach me – sunset. I hadn't realised I'd wasted that much time playing cards and nettling alves.

We were standing in a small clearing, surrounded by eucalyptus and lemon trees, at the foot of a slightly sloping hill. Above the tips of the trees, the sky shone in a dazzling blend of pale daffodil yellow and fiery tangerine and every shade in between; the light of the sinking sun gilded the rusting leaves around us and turned the mossy earth into a soft, welcoming carpet. The scenery looked so different from the murderous fae court I expected, so different from the murderous fae court I *knew*, that I found myself blinking at Tared, all but expecting him to admit to navigation problems.

He smiled – a brief, strained smile, not nearly enough to take the sharpness of his watchful expression – and said, 'That's the Golden Court for you.'

'Been a while,' Lyn muttered next to me, tiptoeing a first few steps up the hill. Flames played between her fingers, ready for attack. 'It *does* sound calm, doesn't it?'

There was little to be heard at all except the reassuring whisper of the surf in the distance and the buzzing of nearby bees, chirping birds, gusts of wind rushing through the leaves. No agonised battle cries. No crumbling walls or splitting earth. Just another quiet sunset at the far east of the archipelago.

Doubt stirred in me for the first time, mingling with the fear itching below my skin. What if I was mistaken?

What if I had understood his message incorrectly?

What if there was nothing wrong at all? What if there *was* something wrong, but I was luring us into some fae trap, set up by the Mother and this Agenor fellow to get rid of their opponents in the Alliance? What if—

'Emelin?'

Both Lyn and Tared were already several strides up the hill. I bit my worries away and hurried after them. Time to trust them. They'd played this game for longer than I had, in more dangerous circumstances than I had; if they believed it was safe to walk around this island, then who was I to doubt them?

No one spoke as we slowly progressed through the lush woods, Lyn and Tared on either side of me. Wherever the court proper was to be found, it wasn't like the palace of the Crimson Court, towering above most of the island with its cruel marble peaks. Between the trees, I could distinguish nothing but the bright red and gold of the skies and the occasional bird. There didn't seem to be any village nearby, or even any isolated inhabitation. Just a small army base, Creon had said; most fae would be found at the centre of the island, then.

Wherever that was.

Something rustled behind us, and I snapped around in alarm, dropping my hand to my black skirt. Next to me Lyn had turned as well, fire flaring up to her elbows.

Nothing moved in the sun-streaked foliage.

Lyn muttered a curse and took two steps forward. When I glanced over my shoulder, Tared stood with his back towards us, hand on his sword hilt, his body motionless as he scanned the hills. He didn't even seem to have hesitated or glanced over his shoulder. If this had been a trap, a ruse to distract us from an approaching attack, he'd have covered our backs.

Centuries and centuries of routine, indeed.

I turned back to Lyn, the magic aching under my fingertips. She muttered something in a cold, low voice, a language I didn't know.

High-pitched giggles answered her from the shrubbery.

She flung a blast of fire at the leaves, and the giggles soared into an indignant shriek, followed by rapidly vanishing chatter that sounded like a bird may have acquired a human language. Lyn scoffed and snapped something back at whatever lived in those bushes, turning towards us with an eyeroll that could rival Edored's creations. 'Hadn't missed *those*.'

'What ... what was that?' I said, because Tared's grim chuckle wasn't terribly informative or reassuring.

'Pixies.' She wiped her hands on her trousers as she caught up with us. 'They stalk these parts. If you stumble upon any small creatures that look like they shouldn't be here, they're probably fake.'

'They're shapeshifters,' Tared added before I could begin to look confused.

'Well,' Lyn said, biting her lip, 'they don't really *shift*, you see. They just glamour themselves to—'

'They're little shits of the magical variety, is what we're trying to say,' Tared said dryly. 'Not malicious, usually. Just exasperating. And they bite pretty viciously if you step on them, so watch your feet.'

I swallowed. 'I was planning on doing that anyway.'

He patted me on the shoulder without taking his eyes off our surroundings. 'You get bonus points for common sense.'

Generous, after I'd pulled them into this undertaking with not the faintest idea of what was waiting for us. I didn't make that point. 'So where are we going?'

'The castle,' Lyn said and grimaced. 'Or as close as we like to get. And then ...'

She looked at Tared, who nodded. That, it seemed, was enough discussion for the both of them; they walked on without wasting another word on the matter.

'Then *what*?' I said.

'Oh, sorry.' She jolted from her watchful musing. 'Then the Blood Gate. See if we can find any traces of Creon. *If* he went inside, I'm pretty sure he used that route.'

'The *Blood Gate*?'

She grimaced. 'It's not as unpleasant as it sounds.'

'Still unpleasant, though,' Tared helpfully added.

I resolved to stop asking questions. I *was* ready, no matter what my trembling hands were trying to tell me, but perhaps I shouldn't test my own composure too much.

We hadn't been walking for more than five minutes when the foliage thinned, light breaking through between the gnarled stems of the trees. Lyn and Tared slowed simultaneously, not even an exchanged glance to discuss the option.

I tightened my fingers on my dress. I was ready. I was *ready*. I was ...
I wasn't ready.

Not for the sight that opened up before us, vivid and majestic in the
glow of the setting sun.

A wide plain stretched out across the island, emerald grass and scattered patches of wild flowers, bordered by trees to either side of us. At
the centre, over half a mile away, a lake lay sparkling in the light of the
setting sun. A small settlement formed a crescent around the banks
farthest away from us, no more than a few dozen wood-and-plaster
buildings, and behind those surprisingly humble houses ...

The castle rose towards the darkening sky like a solitary mountain,
massive and yet oddly elegant in its brutal immensity, towering over
the plain as a quiet, watchful eye. It looked nothing like the Crimson
Court. The rough sandstone blocks, glowing ethereally in the sunlight,
did in no shape or form resemble the polished marble I still saw in
my nightmares; the tall, sturdy towers were far too solid to allow any
comparison to the razor-sharp peaks of the Mother's home. But I saw
the winged silhouettes of fae between the battlements, and my mouth
went dry without warning.

Different or not, I shouldn't expect a warm welcome in this place.

'It looks about as peaceful as it ever does,' Lyn muttered, squinting
at the moving figures. 'Although that's an awful lot of people keeping
watch for an average summer evening, don't you think?'

'I think Beyla said something about Agenor fortifying the defences of
the place years ago,' Tared said slowly.

She scoffed. 'Probably some protocol.'

'Probably.' He gave a sour chuckle. 'It does seem excessive, though.'

Excessive. I didn't manage to tear my eyes away from the building,
hidden behind the last row of trees. Excessive enough to guard, for
example, a captured fae prince until he was ready to be transported to
the Crimson Court?

Was he there, behind those golden walls? I could see him in my
mind's eye in that moment, dangling from what I imagined as a more
gold-plated version of the Mother's bone ceiling, wings torn and bones
broken ... Nausea flared. If that bloody Agenor with his bloody protocols

insisted on keeping obsessive watch every minute of the day, then how in hell were we ever supposed to get into the place?

'If he's in there ...' My voice betrayed how my throat squeezed shut. 'Do you have any idea how we could reach him?'

'A few, ranging from bad to worse.' Tared glanced at me. 'Let's take a look at the gate first. I'm not going to risk my head unless we're very sure he's actually inside.'

'Hasn't he given any other signs, Em?' Lyn said slowly.

'No. I ...' My voice cracked. 'I'd have told you.'

She squeezed my hand with her small fingers as Tared started walking, staying just behind those first rows of trees. Following him and watching where I put my feet wasn't nearly enough to keep my thoughts away from that painfully meaningful fact – Creon hadn't given me any other signs, indeed.

Even though I was so much closer now. Even though he must know he'd alarmed me to no end.

Was he no longer conscious? Or worse ... far worse ...

'I doubt he's dead,' Tared said without turning around, his feet finding their way between the dead branches and thickets. 'Agenor is far too much of a stickler for the rules to make a decision like that on his own. As long as we don't see any messengers returning from the Crimson Court, all is safe.'

'But if Creon isn't using his magic ...'

'Might be alf steel,' Lyn said behind me.

'Does that stop his demon magic, too?'

'It does. He's fae enough to have all magical powers blocked by it.' A mirthless chuckle. 'The one half fae, half alf I've known couldn't fade with alf steel on him. You should have seen the smiths when they were told to create an alf sword with common steel.'

'Pretty sure most of them would rather have drowned themselves,' Tared said dryly.

Lyn laughed. 'Shame you didn't allow them to.'

Tared's scoff at the word *allow* was enough to elicit the smallest of smiles from me. Alf steel, then. As long as I could cling to that option, tell myself he'd ended up in some fae prison rather than six feet below the earth, I could bring myself to keep moving.

The dazzling sunset paled as we walked, the fire dancing on the clouds nothing but a faint shine of pink when we finally reached the spot where the forest met the coastline.

There was no beach. Grass and trees grew to the very edge of the island, where a steep cliff led straight down into the endless sea beyond – the outer edge of the archipelago. Before us, the eastern horizon had already turned a deep indigo, the first constellations emerging from the dark. I thought of Creon and his sketches of the night sky, the quick motions of his scarred fingers as he set out planetary trajectories to me, and had to pause for a heartbeat to get my shaking limbs back under control.

Alf steel. I repeated the words to myself as I hurried after Lyn and Tared, following the ragged edge of the cliff through the dusk. It *had* to be the reason.

'The tide is already on the rise again,' Lyn was saying, her voice hushed. 'Gate will be hard to reach like this.'

Tared's answer was a grumbled remark about divine magic in the depth of night.

Divine magic? Oh. *Blood Gate.* Korok had been the patron god of vampires – blood magic, then. None of that made me feel particularly optimistic about our destination.

But Lyn and Tared didn't falter, and neither did I; I was ready, after all. So when a small path loomed up from the near-darkness, slippery stone stairs leading down along the side of the cliff, I didn't give myself time to worry about the ink-black sea to my right, frothing fifteen feet below us. Didn't allow myself to consider banal mortal matters like falling and drowning. Just tiptoed after Lyn, the fire burning in her palm all that illuminated our winding path, and told myself it didn't matter how many ribs I broke on the way down. Ribs would heal. Creon's neck might not.

The narrow staircase made a sharp turn to the left, around a protruding edge of rock. Behind it, spookily lit by the flickering light in Lyn's palm, lay a small, sheltered bay.

Tared cursed behind me. 'Rising water, indeed.'

Only then did I see why that might be a problem.

There was still a small shred of beach left at the foot of the staircase – enough beach, at least, to walk on. But in the middle of the bay, the water sloshed against the cliff, and it was at that spot that a dark hole gaped in the stone wall, the highest waves splashing into the space behind.

If the tide rose any higher, whatever waited for us there would be flooded soon.

Which meant we would be mad, perhaps close to suicidal, to go in now.

'Is that the gate?' I didn't dare to raise my voice in the face of that ominous darkness; the rush of the sea almost drowned out my words.

'The antechamber,' Lyn said, equally quiet. 'The actual gate lies a little deeper into the earth and gives access to a tunnel that runs all the way to the castle itself. An escape route of sorts.'

I glanced at the dark sea, the opposite of a welcoming refuge. 'For whenever the castle is under siege?'

'Yes. And the other way around, too.' She exchanged a glance with Tared behind me, then quietly added, 'This was the spot where the Mother left him to die. She fled into the tunnel with whoever made it through, and he ... well.'

Stayed behind. Blade to the arm, fire to the chest – left for his enemies to kill him.

Except they hadn't killed him.

A shiver ran up my spine, as cold as the spray of the ocean hitting my lower legs at every wave. I slipped past Lyn, keeping my left hand on the smooth grey stone of the cliff, tiptoeing over the dark strip of sand towards that tunnel opening. And now he'd come back? Or at least, I suspected he'd come back, but even that was based on nothing but a few bursts of pain ...

What traces could he have left?

'Em,' Tared said behind me, his voice tense. 'Be careful.'

I didn't reply as I peered into the antechamber, lit by nothing but Lyn's handful of fire and the rapidly fading sunrays. The room lay at a lower level than the beach; from what I could make out in the darkness, at least one feet of water had already gathered on the floor. In the farthest wall, I distinguished the outlines of a high gate. Soon it would be flooded too.

'Odd place to build an escape exit,' I said, and heard the words echo back at me from the darkness.

'There used to be more of them,' Lyn said.

'Used to be?'

Tared chuckled joylessly. 'Two reckless idiots destroyed them, it seems.'

'Oh. Fine work.' I worried my bottom lip, tasting the salt on the air. Tried to imagine how Creon might arrive here, flying into this small, god-made cave to open the gate he probably knew how to operate. And then ... then what would he do?

Not take all his luggage into the castle, presumably.

So where would he hide his bags? Not on the rest of the island, where anyone might stumble upon them.

Wait.

Wait.

Create a hidden niche in the wall, his list of exercises had said.

'Emelin,' Tared said sharply as I sucked in a breath and stepped into the darkness, finding a slippery floor under my soles. 'Don't think drowning will get you out of training duty tomorrow.'

I managed a laugh, shuffling farther into the room. The water reached to my knees already and was cold enough to numb my toes; all I could do was hope I wouldn't step into some trap and disappear below the surface. *Create a hidden niche.* Not in the outer wall, which was too thin, but perhaps ...

I splashed to the left wall, forcing myself to keep my breathing level, even though every wave splattering against my thighs made me want to shriek and heave. The place smelled like rotten fish and old seaweed, a stench so strong I could almost taste it.

It took too long to run my fingers over the rough wall, meticulously testing every inch. All I found as the water rose halfway up my thighs was a surface slippery with algae – slippery and disappointingly solid.

Fuck. The niche I'd created for that assignment had *looked* solid, but I'd still been able to stick my hand into it. Had Creon had a different idea in mind when he wrote down those words, or was I chasing ghosts here?

Biting away the sting of the cold, I turned and struggled against the current to the other side of the room.

Lyn had appeared in the doorway, her hair even redder than usual in the glow of the fire. 'Em, what in hell are you doing?'

'Searching.' The water had reached my hips now. If I didn't find the damn niche soon, the cold might become dangerous. But at least in the firelight, it was easier to make sense of the room around me, low ceiling and walls covered in seaweed and that broad gate embedded so seamlessly into the wall that it would be a challenge to wedge a blade between the two doors.

Blood Gate. It didn't look macabre enough to deserve that title.

'What for?' Lyn was visibly trying to retain her patience. 'If he left anything here, the tide probably washed it out.'

The tide.

'You,' I said, ducking to cup the frigid water in my hands, 'are a genius.'

'And you're not making sense.' Her voice rose. 'What are you—'

I straightened and flung the water at the wall before me.

It hit the rough stone with a loud splat, drops soaking the wall and the algae sticking to it. Nothing looking out of the ordinary. I muttered a curse and repeated my attack, targeting a different part of the wall.

This time, in the right upper corner, the drops bounced back at me.

And while the water coloured most of the rock and algae a darker green and brown ... an oddly square corner of the surface didn't seem to have been touched at all.

'Oh,' Lyn said breathlessly. 'Oh, gods.'

'Please don't say you've found five corpses in there,' Tared said outside, and his tone suggested he hoped the corpses would at least be fae.

I let out a laugh, splashed into the corner, and came up on my toes, feeling for that suspiciously dry part of the wall. My hand sank straight through what looked like stone, straight through that water-repellent layer he'd created, into the niche behind.

Finding warm cloth and smooth leather under my fingers.

I pulled out the bag first and nearly lost my balance at the weight of it. Stumbling to stay on my feet, I flung it out and onto the dry sand with my own stuff and reached up again, taking out his coat this time. The smell of his body ... It took all I had not to bury my face into the dark fabric and drown myself in it.

But the seawater reached to the small of my back now, and if I wasn't careful, I might end up drowning in far more literal ways.

Coat in my arms, I shuffled back and climbed the steps to the doorway, where Lyn wordlessly backed away to let me through. Tared merely raised an eyebrow as I emerged into the night, but it was an eloquent one.

'Do I get bonus points for that, too?' I said.

'You get bonus points for not freezing to death.' He held out a hand, nodding for me to come closer. 'Let's get the hell out of here.'

Leaving the gate behind – leaving Creon behind. I faltered as Lyn slipped past me, throwing concerned glances at the edge of the cliff towering over us.

'Em,' Tared said and briefly closed his eyes. 'That room will be full of water in minutes. I'm not going to mess with divine magic under threat of drowning while I can barely see my own hands in the dark.'

So gods-damned sensible – drowning wouldn't save Creon's life. Still ... dying in an attempt to save him felt oddly more attractive than turning away without even making an effort.

'Fine,' I muttered, forcing myself to step forward. I'd come back tomorrow, I told myself. If he was still alive now, he would probably still be alive by sunrise. Whatever might happen to him in the meantime ...

My arms tensed around his coat. Best not to think about that.

Tared caught my shoulder in his one hand and Lyn's wrist in the other. Her fire sizzled out, and darkness turned to nothingness as Tared faded us out of that bay.

It took merely an eyeblink this time. When the world brightened, we stood in a clearing in the woods again; around us, all was dark except a few handfuls of glowing mushrooms scattered around the foliage, casting the trees and moss in a buttery light. Just enough to make out the silhouettes of the other two. Just enough to see the seaweed sticking to my legs below the wet mess of my skirt, and my ruined boots.

'We could have been fading the whole time?' I managed, realising only then what odd distances we'd been walking.

'Yes.' Tared pulled a leaf-wrapped package from a pocket and broke off a chunk of date cake, his movements brusque and unmeasured. 'Didn't want to starve myself to the point where I couldn't fade us all out in an emergency. But breaking my neck on that staircase sounded unattractive, too.' He nodded at my dress. 'Go change into something dry before you catch a cold.'

I somehow convinced myself to lower Creon's coat and bag into the grass, tore open my own bag, and pulled out the first dress I found. As I snuck behind the nearest row of bushes, wary of any fae jumping from the foliage, I heard Lyn say, 'Want me to take the first watch?'

Tared's answer sounded appreciative, although I couldn't make out the words themselves.

Hidden behind the shrubbery, I quickly stripped off my wet dress and flung it into the grass. Even though the summer breeze was still mild at night, the drafts that brushed my naked body sent shivers through me; I scrambled to pull my clean dress over my head as swiftly as possible, the linen a soft, warm relief.

The shivers didn't stop.

I knelt in the grass before my knees could buckle in earnest, clenching my teeth to keep them from chattering. With the rush of cold and danger gone, my thoughts caved in, the world of my mind reduced to a little cycle of undiluted panic – *Creon. Here. Danger.* So close, closer than he'd been in weeks, and yet whatever was happening inside those towering castle walls ... I couldn't stop it.

Not yet.

If there was even anything left to stop.

I pressed my nails into my palms, willing myself to calm down, to be *ready* – hell, for all I knew, Lyn and Tared would send me back home if they found me falling apart. I could be more composed than this. I could get a few hours of sleep, gather my wits, and make a *plan*, anything that could get us through that gate and into the castle as soon as the tide sank again ...

Something rustled in the foliage.

I shot up and stiffened, peering at the spot where I'd heard that unmistakable whisper of twigs and leaves. Only a few mushrooms twinkled back at me, releasing puffs of gold dust and a soft glow of light.

A mouse? A pixie? Or something more unpleasant?

My limbs had abruptly stopped trembling. Behind me, Lyn and Tared's voices sounded from a few dozen feet away – investigating our surroundings, leaving me to fend for myself. I could call out for them, but what if it was a false alarm?

I slowly slipped my hand to my dress and whispered, 'Anyone there?'

The world remained quiet for three thunderous heartbeats. Then, slithering out gracefully from below the shrubbery ...

A snake.

A *giant* snake.

It had to be longer than I was tall, at least seven feet of leathery scales gleaming crimson in the glow of the mushrooms. *Crimson.* My heart skipped another beat. But if the Labyrinth had taught me anything, it was to be polite to natural phenomena at all times; I wasn't going to attack as long as this creature wasn't making obvious attempts to sink its fangs into my throat.

And it didn't look on the verge of attacking.

Quite the opposite – it seemed to be *studying* me. As if I was not prey but rather some diverting curiosity showing up in its territory.

Pressing my left hand tight to my dress, I swallowed and muttered, 'Evening?'

The snake cocked its head at me, thin tongue flicking out between its lips. Was I going mad or was that a question blinking in its beady eyes?

'I hope you don't mind we're camping here for a bit?' I added cautiously, not sure if I was seeing ghosts from exhaustion, talking to a gods-damned *snake*. 'We weren't planning to cause you any trouble, in case you were worried. Think we could get along pretty well if you'd return the favour by not biting us.'

Again that flick of its tongue, fiercer now – as if to taste the air around me. It was followed by a nod at the hand still holding on to my black dress for dear life.

'Oh.' I warily loosened my fingers from the dark linen, hovering an inch over my dress. The snake didn't lash out at my face. 'Sorry. Force of habit. Are you—'

'Em?' Tared's voice said, mere strides behind me.

With a jerk, the snake slid back into the foliage, slithering out of view in the blink of an eye. I stifled a shout – hell, was I shouting at snakes now? Or had it been a pixie after all, messing with my tired mind?

'I'm here,' I ground out.

'Everything alright?'

Was *anything* alright? I tore my eyes away from the spot where the snake – or whatever it was – had disappeared, hauling myself back to my feet. Tared stood waiting for me in the middle of the clearing, sheath and sword taken off, but eyes still dancing back and forth between me and the line of trees.

I forced a smile upon my face. I was fine, I told myself. Fine and entirely ready. 'Just a pixie sneaking around, I think.'

'Ah.' He looked about a quarter convinced. 'Time to get some sleep, then. Lyn is keeping an eye on the castle for the next few hours.'

Sleep.

While Creon was still in there. Going through gods knew what.

But I fell onto the mossy ground because I already knew what Tared would say about any suggestion to stay awake and save captive fae princes, and muttered, 'Fine.'

He grabbed his own bag. 'Need a blanket?'

'I ...' I faltered. *Yes*, I should say for the sake of secrecy, and then I should stay far away from Creon's coat for the rest of the night, because *every* sensible person would be asking questions if I were to wrap my-self in a murderer's clothes.

But Tared was hardly sensible where Creon was concerned.

'I think I'll manage,' I blurted, making the decision without allowing myself a second thought. 'I'll just use this one.'

Tared raised an eyebrow as I pulled the dark coat closer. 'If you don't mind, that's more practical, yes.'

'Definitely more practical.' Creon's scent closed around me as I flung the coat over my shoulders, and my breath hitched. I settled myself in the moss, averting my eyes. 'Night, Tared.'

He sighed. 'Sleep well.'

I didn't expect to sleep well. I barely expected to sleep at all. But wrapped in Creon's warmth, in the fragrance of his body, my mind found its way back to his bed in the Underground and the weight of his arms around me, and I dozed off in that deceptive safety moments after I closed my eyes.

CHAPTER 21

I WOKE TO A hand over my mouth.

A small hand. Palm pressed against my lips, fingers squeezing my jaw so tightly I almost cried out in pain. But before I could so much as suck in a breath, Lyn hissed, 'Not a sound, Em.'

That woke me well enough.

I nodded, and she released my face and rose to her feet. Her right hand lay around the dagger at her belt, her left hand rained sparks over the moss. Ready to burst into flame.

I slowly sat up and threw a quick look through the darkness, careful not to move so much as a leaf. A bundle of rumpled blankets lay three feet away from me, a child-sized makeshift bed. Tared was nowhere to be seen – keeping watch at the edge of the forest, presumably.

And on the other side of the clearing, deeper between the trees, twigs were snapping rhythmically.

Footsteps.

Footsteps were approaching us.

My mind cleared so abruptly I almost choked on it. The steps sounded too heavy to be a pixie's; they were human at best, but more likely fae. How many of them? One? Two, perhaps? Which we *might* be able to handle if we had the element of surprise on our side, but we'd have a dead fae on our hands, and then how long would we remain unnoticed on this island?

'Em,' Lyn breathed, her gaze fixed on the dark line of trees as she gestured at some spot behind us. 'Take our stuff and find Tared. *Quietly.* He's at the forest edge, some hundred feet that way.'

Too far away to cry out for him. I swallowed and whispered, 'What are you going to do?'

'Distract them. Now *move.*'

Five hundred years of experience; I wasn't going to object. With Creon's coat still around my shoulders, I hauled his bag onto my back, grabbed my own off the ground, and tucked Lyn's blankets under my arm. The footsteps were coming closer, but slowly, as if whoever was approaching wasn't sure where they were going themselves.

They'd picked a terrible place and time to get lost, in that case.

I hesitated one last moment. Lyn sent me a blistering glare, then turned back to our unwanted visitor with a sharp, crystal-clear gesture in Tared's direction.

I didn't quite run, but I'd certainly never tiptoed so fast in my life.

There were too many trees in this place, too many branches, too much dead wood just *waiting* for some little half fae to step on it and creak through the silence of the night. With two bags and a blanket I didn't want to drop, I was heavy and unwieldy and far too slow. Little step by little step. There I could see the open air between the trees, the silhouette of the castle against the starry night sky ... Nearly there. If Tared—

A flash of fire lit up the trees to my right, nowhere close to Lyn's last location.

Distract them.

I took the risk, fell into a trot, and collided with Tared as he strode out from between the trees with his sword drawn. His left hand locked around my shoulder. I stifled a cry, nearly dropping my bag as he squeezed tight. '*Tared.*'

Another blinding flare broke through the darkness. He abruptly let me go, cursed, and said in an urgent whisper, 'Who in hell is she trying to distract?'

'Don't know,' I breathed. 'Someone was approaching through the forest.'

'From *that* side?' He cursed again. 'No one ever – oh, damn it. That's for later. Stay close.'

I stumbled after him as he slid between the trees, light-footed and inaudible. 'Where are we—'

'Lyn.' One word; even whispered, it fell over his lips like the truth of all truths. 'And then it depends on—'

She came hurtling from the foliage in the same moment.

Tiny and flaming and inconceivably fast, the white of her eyes visible in the near-complete darkness, she slammed into Tared so violently he lost his balance. Grabbed his sword arm with both hands and hissed, voice shrill, 'We need to get *out*!'

Tared snapped around and held out a hand to me before she'd finished, not wasting a second asking questions or demanding explanations. An example I ought to have followed. A panicking phoenix should have been the only answer I needed. But Lyn said *out*, and my mind heard *away from Creon*, and like a deer between hunters, I froze.

Twigs broke, far too close.

'Em!' Lyn breathed, her gaze begging me to move.

'Lyn?' a male voice said loudly, his accent far too fae. 'Lyn, is that you?'

Tared's eyes grew wide.

But just as he lunged for me, just as his hand came down to lock around my wrist and *drag* me out if need be, that same voice burst out, 'Lyn, I've changed my mind!'

Had the Mother herself jumped from the shrubbery to press us to her bosom as her beloved long-lost children, Tared couldn't have stiffened more abruptly.

His hand missed my wrist as he staggered to a halt, dragging Lyn along. Leaves crackled, a pebble shot away and smacked against the nearest tree trunk – enough sound to alert any half-witted bystander to our presence, and yet the forest didn't light up in a sea of lethal red.

'*Please.*' The unknown fae male didn't sound like a male used to the sound of that word. Only then did I realise he was speaking in Faerie – that he'd been speaking in Faerie all along, and that I had understood him fluently enough not to notice. 'I've been looking for you for decades. I need your help. I ... Hell, are you even still there?'

Lyn and Tared exchanged a single glance, the mutual bewilderment on their faces louder than any gasps or curses. Their slow, hesitant nods came simultaneously – the result of a debate taking place in whatever shared plane of existence their thoughts occupied.

Lyn released Tared's arm and reached for the dagger at her belt. A last breath, then she hurled it into the forest, in the direction of that deep fae voice, where it landed in the moss and foliage with a flutter and a dull thud.

Tared stepped back and nodded for me to follow him back where we'd come from. I hesitated, then caught the look in his eyes, and hurried after him *very* obediently.

'There's an alf steel dagger lying somewhere around your feet,' Lyn said, standing unmoving in the same spot. She was speaking in Alvish now. A political statement, perhaps, but I was quite sure it was partly for my benefit, too. 'Be so kind as to pick it up and hold it tight before you come anywhere near me, will you? Sticking it into your face is optional.'

Tared breathed a chuckle, pulling me and my armful of bags and blankets behind a man-high hawthorn bush.

In the distance, the fae male effortlessly switched to Alvish as he said, 'Thank you. I found it.'

'Good,' Lyn said, her young voice eerily cold. 'Let go of it for even an eyeblink and you might get a sword in the back of your head. Just so we're clear about that.'

'Reasonable.' He sounded like he meant it. 'And a good morning to you too, Thorgedson.'

Tared scoffed quietly.

The other didn't seem to have expected a more elaborate response. 'Mind if I come a little closer?'

Fire flared up in the palm of Lyn's hand, bright enough for Tared and me to observe her from behind our hawthorn hideaway. 'As you wish.'

Footsteps moved through the night, no longer as hesitant as before. Lyn didn't waver, pale and tight-lipped; next to me, Tared watched the scene with narrowed eyes and fingers tightening bloodlessly around the hilt of his sword. He didn't appear particularly in the mood to explain anything. A shame, since I was most certainly in the mood to receive explanations.

I lowered my bag and Lyn's blankets onto the forest floor and whispered, 'Who is he?'

'His lordship himself,' Tared muttered grimly, not turning away from Lyn for even the shortest of glances. 'Agenor.'

'*Agenor*?' I whirled back to watch the clearing. 'But ... Wait, what? Changed his mind? Isn't he supposed—'

'Yes,' Tared said quietly. 'That's exactly what we're wondering.'

I swallowed and squinted at the fire-lit spot between the trees, at the shadows moving there. His lordship himself. *One of her oldest and most loyal allies*, Creon had written down months ago, some fae male who'd been around since before the wars, and yet ...

I need your help.

What in hell was going on with those rebellious fae at the Golden Court?

Tared hissed a breath as our visitor finally emerged from the woodline – tall and dark-haired, moving with that immortal fae grace in the shifting shadows of Lyn's fire. I was prepared for danger, was prepared for mortal fear ... and yet that first glimpse of him had me freezing in my spot for the blink of an eye.

Because the Lord of the Golden Court ... he didn't look like danger at all.

Not in the sense Creon did, at least, power rolling off him wherever he went; not in the sense the Mother did either, radiating ancient malevolence in every honey-sweet smile and tinkering laugh. He didn't show a trace of Ophion's vicious ways or Thysandra's proud deadliness. Really, the way he came ambling from the foliage in his perfectly tailored green shirt, an expression of polite curiosity on his bronzed face, he looked ... mild?

Neither Lyn nor Tared loosened their shoulders even a fraction, though.

I shivered, following him with my eyes as he easily stepped over the last low bushes and held still, Lyn's alf steel dagger held clearly in front of his chest. Hell, there was no way anyone with even a shred of mildness in his veins would survive a year at the Crimson Court, let alone a millennium. Something about him, or perhaps *everything* about him, had to be smoke and mirrors ... and even if his shirt didn't contain a drop of red, he still had those black wings to draw the colour from.

Enough magic, presumably, to raze this entire forest to the ground.

I lowered my own hand to my dress and forced myself to keep breathing slowly and deeply.

'Well,' Lyn said, cocking her head and not bothering to brush aside the red locks that fell over her forehead, 'it's been a while.'

'Quite, yes.' Now that he was no longer pleading with his enemies from the dark of night, his voice had lowered to a deep, polished bass, the bland pleasantness of it as meaningless as that ghost of a smile on his lips. 'You don't look a day older, though.'

Unease or no, I couldn't suppress a chuckle.

Lyn merely sent him a withering glare. 'Please keep your pleasantries to yourself, Agenor. What in hell are you doing here?'

'I suppose I could ask you the same,' he said gently.

'Yes,' Lyn said, her voice level even as the fire in her hand flickered blue and scarlet, 'and you could turn this conversation into an interrogation within the first two sentences, but that would hardly make you convincing as the male who claimed to need my help three minutes ago. Why are you here?'

He quirked up an eyebrow, granting her that point without wasting a word on it. 'I was alerted to ... something.'

'Something,' Lyn repeated, her scepticism so thick a grown man could drown in it.

'The snakes were being unusually restless. I figured I should go take a look.'

Snakes. My gut turned cold. Oh, hell, the animal sneaking up on me from the foliage – should I have said something? Warned the other two? But Tared's eyes remained glued to Lyn and Agenor; whatever the matter with the animal had been, this was likely not the moment to bring it up.

Lyn just snorted. 'Well.'

'Well,' Agenor admitted, sounding tired. No trace of wrinkles around his eyes, no fleck of grey in his hair, and yet for a sliver of a moment, something about him looked ... old? Or not old but rather *ancient*, a flash of weariness over his features I hadn't seen in any fae before. 'Anything else you'd like to know before we get to the point?'

'The point of you changing your mind?' Lyn said sharply.

He nodded with the most nondescript of sighs. 'Yes.'

'About *what*, exactly?'

'Everything.' He spoke the word with such flatness, as if it was a self-evident observation. 'They shouldn't have won that damn war. I shouldn't have been fighting for them. I ...' He paused, made a throw-away gesture with the hand clenched around her dagger. Tared jolted, but Agenor's fingers remained firmly around the alf steel as he shrugged and added, 'Frankly, I've been a bloody fool. Do you need me to elaborate on that?'

She'd narrowed her eyes so tightly they seemed closed from the distance. 'Much as I'd love to hear you elaborate on your own lack of sense and decency, may I ask where this sudden insight is coming from? You went a good thousand years without it.'

He pursed his lips. 'A series of surprises.'

'Surprising enough to shove centuries of loyalty aside.'

'As it turns out.'

She remained silent, studying him intently, her suspicion nowhere near soothed. Gods' sake, I had never seen the bastard before, and even *my* suspicions were nowhere near soothed. He was too calm, too calculated, hiding whatever his motivations were behind that unwavering mask of courtly manners and genteel reserve. Then again ...

If he was lying, wouldn't this be the stupidest of approaches? Shouldn't he dramatically declare his devotion to his newfound perspective and bury us in justifications?

Perhaps Lyn had the same thought, because she didn't probe as she finally continued. 'You said you've been looking for us.'

'For some two decades now,' Agenor said, the faintest spark of amusement lighting up his features. 'You'll be glad to hear you're quite hard to find.'

'I'd be lying if I said I was sorry, yes.' Another snort. 'Why make the effort? What do you need our help for, exactly?'

'I'd like to get Achlys and Melinoë off that throne. And find a couple of people."

Tared slowly moved back, the distrust and tension on his face now mingling with a trace of confusion.

As if she'd heard the questions he was thinking, Lyn briskly said, 'People?'

'Yes.' Agenor ran his free hand through his short hair, holding her gaze with the most pleasant blankness I'd ever seen. 'That's a story for later, if you don't mind.'

Lyn let out a joyless laugh. 'For a male who has nothing to hide, you're leaving a lot of stories for later, Agenor. But fine. Tell us more about the past few decades, then. If you're as serious as you're claiming to be, at the very least I hope you've been doing more than sitting on your arse and ruminating on your past failures?'

'The Golden Court is under my control,' Agenor said, all businesslike confidence suddenly. Ah. So this was the bastard's safe ground, indeed – protocols and strategies. 'A good three quarters of its current inhabitants are fae who share my sentiments on the state of the empire, if I'm allowed to put it like that. The other twenty-five percent are the Mother's puppets, and I've let them roam about until now because I'd cause suspicions if I removed all of them. A plan is in place to take care of them as soon as the necessity arises, though.'

Tared breathed a curse next to me. I barely heard it. I was too busy staring at the tall fae male some twenty feet away, so very polished and civilised and yet capable of uttering those words with such bland disregard – *remove them.* I had almost forgotten about that casual fae cruelty, so very different from the heated bloodlust alves tended to put on display ... but this particular male seemed to be the very embodiment of it.

How easily would he *remove* us for the sake of his own interests as soon as the tide turned?

'What kind of occasion,' Lyn was saying, her words clipped and precise, 'would constitute such a necessity for you, if I may ask?'

Agenor was silent for a moment, considering her with those calculating eyes. Then, careful like a male who knows he's opening a door that can never be closed again, he said, 'That depends, for example, on what you'd like me to do with Creon.'

I gasped.

Had Lyn's fire not flared up in emerald twizzles at the same moment, I would have given my presence away. But her flicker of lost control gave Tared enough time to kick me in the shins, and by the time the fire sizzled down to its old palm-sized proportions, I was biting my lips hard enough to leave myself incapable of speaking for three days to come.

Creon.

So something *had* gone wrong. But if Agenor was speaking the truth, if he had turned his winged back on the Mother for whatever reason, then why in hell did anything have to happen with ...

Wait.

Didn't he *know*?

'I understand,' Agenor said, a faint smile brushing over those uncannily symmetric fae features, 'that that's not a matter of complete indifference to you.'

Lyn stared at him, the expression on her face mirroring my own thoughts and Tared's hitching breath. 'You got your hands on Creon.'

'Yes.'

'You ...' She sucked in a breath, releasing another mirthless laugh. 'Oh, Inika help us. You didn't hear?'

I clenched my jaw so tightly it hurt, the pieces of the puzzle clicking together through the whirl of my thoughts. The Mother *hadn't* spread the word, that much Beyla had made clear – but had she kept her defeat so very silent that not even one of her most trusted allies would have heard the story?

A most trusted ally – who'd been working for decades to betray her?

'Heard what?' For the very first time, a hint of annoyance sparked in Agenor's voice, not enough to truly tarnish that layer of smooth civility, but enough to show Lyn's reaction had thrown him off balance. 'I doubt—'

'That he betrayed her,' Lyn said.

Agenor stared at her.

'You hadn't heard,' she blankly concluded.

'That he …' A baffled laugh tumbled over his lips. 'Lyn, forgive me for doubting your otherwise highly respectable good sense, but that's quite impossible. Why in hell's name would the boy suddenly *betray* her?'

'I said nothing about *suddenly*,' she countered, and he blinked with even more reserved bewilderment.

'You're not talking about the War, are you?'

She merely raised an eyebrow.

'Lyn …' He rubbed his forehead with his free hand, uttering another laugh that sounded almost apologetic. 'Lyn, I'm not saying he was not at all attached to anyone on your side during the War, but I think he's made it clear enough over the past thirteen decades that he's as firmly on their side as he's ever been. You're deluding yourself if you—'

'For the bloody gods' sake,' she muttered.

'What in hell should I have heard?'

'That he tried to kill her?' She closed her eyes for half a second – the first, miniscule display of trust, and Tared stiffened accordingly. Agenor didn't attack, studying her with narrowed eyes. 'That she all but killed *him*. He fled the Crimson Court a little over a month and a half ago. Did you really not—'

'I have no idea what you're talking about.' It wasn't loss of composure in his voice, not quite, but for the first time, his gaze wandered in the general direction of our hideaway – quietly hoping for Tared to jump from the bushes and quickly put an end to this inane series of jokes. 'I should have *heard* if any such thing had happened.'

'No,' Lyn said bleakly. 'She's been keeping it quiet. We knew that much.'

'Why would they—'

'She was *blinded*, Agenor.'

The forest turned so eerily quiet I could hear the fire crackle in her hands for one, two heartbeats.

'What?' he said.

'She ... Oh, fuck's sake.' A frustrated gesture almost set her tunic aflame. 'I have no idea what game you're playing, but if this is all new to you ... perhaps we shouldn't have that conversation with swords hanging over our heads.'

He gave a faint chuckle. 'You're the one dangling swords over heads, if I need to remind you.'

'As if I'm to believe you don't have any snakes nearby,' she said, offering him her free hand with an impatient snort. 'So if you don't mind?'

Was she going to *bargain* with him? I couldn't imagine in what world that would be a wise idea, with a male who must know every single trick after all those centuries – but Tared didn't object, although his lips had thinned into a particularly displeased line.

'I certainly wouldn't mind,' Agenor said, infuriatingly courteous. 'I'd like to be sure that alf of yours isn't going to sink a sword between my shoulder blades the moment I move, though.'

'Tempting suggestion,' Tared said next to me, his voice loud enough to make me jump, 'but I'd like to get some answers from you before we cross that bridge. Go ahead.'

Agenor let out another polite chuckle and stepped forward, grabbing Lyn's hand between his much larger fingers. 'In that case ...' He sighed, sounding almost bored. 'I promise not to contain, wound, or endanger you or any of those with you, not to give commands or make suggestions to bring about any such attack on you or those with you, and not to lure or provoke you into breaking the terms of this bargain, under the condition that you and those with you will be observing the same

rules towards me and those you consider my allies, for a duration of ...'
He'd rattled off the words like a routine contract so far but hesitated
now, his eyebrow raised in question.

'Could start with a week?' Lyn said.

'For the duration of a week, after which alternation or continuation
of the same terms is possible. Agreed?'

She shrugged. A routine contract, indeed. 'Agreed.'

Tared finally relaxed his sword arm as blinding light lit up between
their hands, a dazzling yellow glow as warm as the fire Lyn was still
holding in her other palm. Shoving his blade back into the sheath on
his back, he muttered, 'You can leave those bags here, Em. He doesn't
need to know we found Creon's stuff already.'

'We're going to—'

'Have a word with him. Yes.' He groaned. 'What is it with all these
damn fae changing sides these days?'

A laugh escaped me. 'Scared you'll have to start liking them?'

'Careful,' he said, sending me a sour grin.

I chuckled despite the pang of regret as I stripped Creon's coat off my
shoulders, feeling like I was letting go of him all over again. He'd be
fine, I told myself, settling the piece of clothing next to the bags and the
blankets. If I'd convinced the Alliance that the Silent Death was really
not who he'd appeared to be, how much trouble could one uncannily
civilised fae male give me?

One uncannily civilised fae male with the kind of powers that had
allowed him to survive over a millennium of warfare – but I forced
myself to let go of that thought as I tiptoed after Tared, into Lyn's circle
of light.

'Yellow,' I heard her say, sounding somewhat amused as she studied
the bargain mark on the inside of her wrist. 'Change? How very apt.'

Agenor's smile was a fleeting lie, sliding off his face the moment
Tared emerged into view. His glance at me was so quick I doubted at
first if he'd even noticed me. But a thin line drew between his brows as
he turned back to Lyn and said, 'You'll excuse me for wondering what
the aim of your presence is, if it requires you to drag children around
fae territory?'

'I'd be a little more careful whom you choose to offend, Lord Protector,' Tared said coolly, the title an insult as much as Edored's *Hytherion*. 'Don't recall you managing to burn your High Lady's eyes from her face in twenty years of presumed rebellion.'

'Excuse me?' Those fae eyes snapped back to me with significantly more interest. I wasn't sure if I considered it an improvement. There was an unpleasant weight to Lord Agenor's gaze – the sense that he was estimating, in that one fraction of a second, what he might be able to use me for. His mirthless laugh had all the wrong edges to it, too. 'Burn their eyes from ... A *human*?'

Caution be damned. Lyn's bargain protected me, didn't it? I scowled back at him before my common sense could prevail and sharply said, '*Half* human, thank you very much.'

He stiffened to the tips of his dark wings. 'What?'

'She's half fae,' Lyn said curtly. 'I suppose you know the concept?'

Agenor didn't seem to have heard her. He stood staring at me with rapidly widening eyes, that unwavering mask of bland diplomacy gone at once – as if I'd just announced I was the monster under his bed he'd thought a mirage since childhood.

'You're ...' His voice had gone rough. 'You're an unbound half fae?'

'Yes?' I forced a laugh and wrapped my arms around myself, all the more unnerved by Tared's look of utter puzzlement in the corner of my eye. What in hell? Was the bastard so desperate for a weapon against the Mother that even the *suggestion* of an unbound mage sent him straight into a panic? 'Is that—'

'How old are you?' he cut in.

I stared at him.

My age?

He wanted to know my *age*?

But that ... My thoughts turned too slowly, as unprepared for these questions as I'd been for the confrontation with the Lord of the Golden Court in the first place. Why would my age ever be relevant, except if ...

'Twenty summers,' I heard myself say. 'Why would you—'

'Second of hay month?' he interrupted.

I froze.

In the far and utterly irrelevant distance, Tared was saying something. Lyn's fire was moving on the edge of my sight – coming closer, her voice growing louder. My mind registered none of it. I stared at the face before me, the lines of those ancient fae features as thoroughly unfamiliar to me as every single inch of this gods-damned island, the words echoing in my ears in that hurried voice.

Second of hay month.

He couldn't know that.

He couldn't ...

'What?' I whispered.

He burst into motion, striding towards me too fast for me to back away.

Tared snapped a warning. The flickering firelight flared white and bright as Lyn cried out in alarm. But Agenor's hand clenched around my chin before either of them could stop him, his fingers jerking up my head with the ruthless strength of a male used to full and utter obedience.

Bringing my face a mere foot away from his.

Gaping at me with bewildered ditchwater-coloured eyes, the shape of them so infinitely familiar I might as well have been looking into a mirror.

CHAPTER 22

Two thoughts remained even as the world fell away beneath my feet, most of my mind reduced to the sight of my own eyes in that stranger's face.

First of all, this couldn't be true.

Second of all, was patricide a more heinous crime than general murder?

This ... *this* was him, the bastard who'd shoved my mother aside as soon as matters became complicated? This heartless, emotionless creature? A lord far too powerful to toy with human slaves who didn't have anywhere else to go, far too powerful to pretend he hadn't had a choice in abandoning ...

Me?

And as if to make that point more convincingly than even the utter newness of his face could, Agenor said hoarsely, 'What is your name?'

My name.

I was a stranger to *him*, too.

And suddenly I was laughing, hysterical shrieks that welled in me like sobs, the last of my sanity caving in under the implications of that question. He didn't know my *name*. Had not even been around for long enough to know what my mother might call me, had never asked her even after I was born and gone? I staggered back, out of his grip, and couldn't bring myself to utter a single sensible word – could barely bring myself to *think* a sensible word.

His gaze followed me like I might go up in smoke if he blinked, but something stiffened about him, like shutters slamming closed behind his eyes.

'Your *name*.'

It wasn't quite an order, the sound of it too gracious, too *considerate*, to make the words sound truly demanding. But there was an authority below the surface, and I stopped laughing at once, my mind too much awhirl to resist.

'Emelin.' As if I was making some deadly confession. 'I'm ... I'm Emelin.'

A small twitch at his jaw was his only reaction.

But next to me, his muffled voice a thunderclap through the silence of the night, Tared muttered, 'Oh, fuck.'

I snapped around. He'd gone dead pale, looking back and forth between Agenor and me with widening eyes. On my other side, Lyn started, 'Agenor, is she—'

'*Emeia*?' Tared burst out; he didn't seem to have heard her. 'You named her after *Emeia*?'

Silence descended over the clearing again.

The trees spun around me, shreds of thoughts and questions slamming into me from too many sides at once. Who was Emeia? And why would Tared give a rat's arse about any fae female, namesake or not? And why was Lyn looking like she was prepared to physically pull the two of them apart, and how in hell could I be even *distantly* related to this cold-blooded fae male before me, and what did that say about my powers, and ...

'There are many things I'll be glad to apologise for,' Agenor said, cooler now even though still impeccably polite, 'but remembering my sister fondly is not one of those things, Thorgedson.'

His *sister*?

Oh, fuck.

'You know that's not the issue,' Tared snapped. 'Do you slaughter entire houses every time you *fondly* remember someone?'

Oh, *fuck*.

'That was not a mission I planned or commanded,' Agenor retorted, in the exasperated tone of a male forced to repeat the same point once or twice or ten times too often, 'and even if I had, considering that your beloved uncle had just killed my last living family member in cold blood—'

'I doubt anything constructive can be said about this now,' Lyn said, her voice milder than the venomous glare she sent at Agenor. 'And I doubt Em wants to hear any of it, so how about we first focus on whatever in *hell* is going on here before we spiral back into things that have been said a hundred times before?'

Tared closed his eyes, breathing heavily. 'Right. Sorry, Em. Go ahead.'

Ahead with *what*?

I felt like fainting, looking back and forth between the three of them, unsure of what the world expected from me. Hell, my *name*? Even my name was a memento of war now, of some fae martyr and the lives lost in revenge?

And if it was ...

I stared at Agenor, who didn't quite seem to know how to look at me, eyes darting over me as if examining some potentially explosive novelty. He hadn't known. He hadn't even *known*.

'Why ... why was I named after your family members in the first place?'

His emphatic blink was the only evidence of his surprise; he answered without hesitation. 'It was going to be either a fae equivalent of one of your mother's family names or the human equivalent of one of mine. Clearly she picked—'

'After you *abandoned* her?'

He stared at me, brown-green eyes narrowing. Something in that look – something about his fingers clenching tight around Lyn's dagger – abruptly reminded me he had no reason to trust or like me for my blood alone. None at all, and at this moment, he might well be doing neither.

'I ...' He faltered, gaze flicking to Tared, to Lyn, and back to me. His mirthless laugh sounded like the laugh of a male graciously accepting an unwanted gift. 'Good gods. Whoever told you this story seems to have missed some essential parts of it. May I suggest we stop flinging accusations around and sit down to actually answer some questions?'

I didn't sit down. 'Who was she?'

'*Is.*' That single word, for the first time, was almost a snap.

'Oh, apologies for not knowing the details no one ever bothered to tell me,' I bit out, unable to help myself. So I was already failing. Two minutes into meeting my father, and already I was saying the wrong things, making the wrong assumptions. 'Who *is* she, then?'

The way he closed his eyes didn't soothe my knotting stomach at all. There was a weariness about that gesture, a wordless suggestion that he'd have preferred the luxury of his doubtlessly comfortable bed over dealing with this messy, inelegant situation. 'Her name is Allie. She used to be a slave at the Crimson Court, before she ...' He turned the alf steel dagger around between his fingers as he searched for the right word. 'Disappeared.'

Lyn's fire flickered ominously on the edge of my sight. I repeated, '*Disappeared?*'

'Yes.'

'Where to?'

'The issue with disappearances,' Agenor said, a faint and utterly joyless smile on his lips, 'is that the destination is generally unknown. I don't know.'

Zera help me, did he have to be so gods-damned ... *fae?* 'Then how do you even know she's alive?'

He sighed, raised his hand, and turned it – revealing, on the inside of his bronzed wrist, two small gems embedded in his skin. One was a dark yellow, shimmering with fire: the bargain he'd just made with

Lyn. The other was a gemstone as black as the night sky above us, swallowing every spark of light that fell on the surface.

'Lifelong bargain.' Again there was that flicker of exhaustion in his voice. 'If she'd died, the mark would have vanished.'

Oh.

Very damn fae, indeed.

What had they even bargained for? Before I could ask, Tared rather noisily lowered himself into the moss beside me, crossed his legs, and sent the other male a glare like a fist to the throat. 'Didn't know you were the kind to trick slaves into bargains.'

'You think entirely too highly of me,' Agenor said coldly. 'She tricked me five times over before I even realised what was happening.'

I blinked at him. There was no shame in his eyes as he met my gaze again, plucking absently at the sleeve of his green shirt – a ridiculously expensive green shirt, my seamstress eyes couldn't help but notice. Whatever his current opinions on the Mother, his rebellion certainly hadn't harmed his situation in life.

'Tricked ... you,' Lyn said.

'Quite, yes.' His smile had the air of an argument won. 'Shall we sit down?'

I dropped down into the grass and moss next to Tared, unwillingly glad to relieve my knees of the chore of standing. Lyn threw Agenor a last glance, then slid her fire onto the forest floor, where it continued to crackle and burn as she stepped back and settled herself on my other side. He sat down last, the fire between him and me, the alf steel dagger still loosely between his fingers.

Tricked him.

What had Creon said? *She must have been somewhat of a genius ...*

I didn't manage to tear my eyes away from him, to cease the search for *anything* familiar in the lines of his bronze face. That nose wasn't mine, was it? I was pretty sure my own nose wasn't so ... *straight*. My jaw was certainly not as angular either, and clearly I hadn't inherited his dark hair or the shape of his ears ...

Just my eyes. Those, and his magic – that magic that had sent Lyn into a panicked flight the moment she realised who he was.

I suppressed a shiver. Did I look like my mother, then? Did he recognise anything of her in me every time his eyes slid over my face and quickly shot away again?

'If you say a series of surprises made you change your mind,' Lyn was saying, her words curt and clipped, 'should we assume a human slave tricking you into a bargain was one of those surprises?'

He sighed. 'Yes.'

She raised her eyebrows.

'The short version of the story is that she used me to kill another fae,' Agenor said, absently scratching his jaw with her dagger. For all his power and age-old fae grace, he appeared perfectly at home between the leaves and grass; really, he looked like you could offer him a bed of thorny vines and he'd courteously accept it without a blink. 'Then told me I was an idiot when I finally figured it out and confronted her. Proving her wrong turned out to be … somewhat of a challenge.'

A chuckle escaped me. His eyes shot to mine, just a blink before he looked away again – but I knew he'd noted that reaction, noted what had made me react.

Deceptive comfort or not … he was feeling me out as much as I was trying to get a measure of him.

I should start watching my words. I should have started long before this moment.

'And then you miraculously realised you'd been living off the blood and sweat of the rest of the world for decades?' Tared muttered, interrupting my thoughts.

Agenor didn't react to the sharp taunt below the surface. 'Yes.'

Lyn and Tared waited, their faces eerily similar masks of cold fury.

'The wars took a toll on me,' he added slowly, lips pursed as if nothing but good manners pushed him to make that confession. On any other male, it may have been a moment of vulnerability. On him, it was a matter of mild annoyance, a deficiency that he'd noticed and solved to his own satisfaction, and that he mentioned only for completeness' sake. 'I was quite happy to tell myself the world had finally been fixed. And when one spends most of his time in meeting rooms and court halls, there aren't a great many people around to offer a different perspective.'

'How very inattentive of us,' I blurted out – the memory of the empty grain sheds on Cathra briefly trumping my resolve to watch my words. 'Should have remembered to send our notice of objection along with the ships full of grain you were pulling from our hands, I suppose?'

Tared stifled a snigger. Agenor merely cocked his head at me, eyes narrowing slightly – a look that said, *interesting*, and not in the complimentary way.

'I don't blame anyone but myself.' Calm, matter-of-fact, a statement without judgement. As if we shouldn't be judging him either. 'I should have seen what was going on long before Allie slapped me in the face with it. But I'm grateful she did, if that makes you feel any peace regarding the matter.'

Nothing about him made me feel peaceful. He was like a wall – a bland, blank wall, and one that made my knuckles itch with the desire to punch through it.

'And then?' I said through gritted teeth. 'You got her pregnant and ran?'

'No.' The wall didn't budge. 'Then I underestimated the kind of vicious bitches Achlys and Melinoë are when they aren't getting what they want. Which is easy to forget when you've been following their wishes for the past millennium or so.'

Oh, gods help me. *The past millennium* – words spoken so nonchalantly, as if the male before me hadn't been around to drive the humans from their continent, to witness the death of gods, to know the two sisters before they became that single, blood-curdling High Lady I'd met at the Crimson Court.

'Did the Mother know?' Lyn said, her voice ominously low. 'About Em?'

'No.' Agenor raked a hand through his short, dark hair. 'But I was working to improve the circumstances for the humans on that bloody island, and they certainly knew about *that*, because I made the mistake of informing them about it – of assuming they'd do something about it as soon as they realised how bad the situation was.'

'Cute,' Tared muttered with a quiet scoff.

Agenor ignored him. 'Then one day, about a month before ... before Emelin was born, they asked me to go and investigate rumours of rebellion at the Golden Court. I considered telling them I didn't have time, but Al reminded me someone else would take my place and be more unpleasant, and since we still had a month left and it was supposed to be two nights at most, I did go.'

I swallowed, dark premonitions pressing heavily on my chest. 'Were there even any rebellious fae at the Golden Court?'

'No,' he said flatly. 'It was an embarrassingly simple ruse to get me out of the way. As soon as my heels left the island, they arrested Al and a handful of other humans who'd been key players in our efforts over those last few months.'

Lyn muttered a curse. 'She knew you'd object?'

'Yes.'

Human slaves conspiring against her a few weeks before you were born. I didn't dare to breathe as Creon's words returned to me. 'But then how did she survive, if ... if ...'

She had them all executed. Cruel, merciless words.

'The one mistake Achlys and Melinoë consistently make,' Agenor said, rubbing a slender hand over his face, 'is to underestimate human ingenuity.'

Ah, yes. I'd noticed that.

'From what I pieced together after I returned, Al offered them a bargain. Her life, the life of her unborn child, and a guarantee that she could stay at the court until she'd given birth, in exchange for ...' He closed his eyes, as if to recall the exact wording of the pact. 'An end to all rebellious activity on the island and the names of human traitors who'd cause trouble in the villages.'

Oh, fuck. 'Did she betray—'

'Did she specify who exactly those human traitors betrayed and who'd suffer from the trouble in those villages?' Lyn cut in, her eyes narrowed to slits.

Agenor sent her a brief smile. 'And that's the question the Mother didn't ask.'

'Orin's eye,' Tared said, biting out a mirthless laugh. 'She gave the names of humans who betrayed their own kind?'

'Yes. Rallied her underground contacts, told them to cease all illegal activity for at least a month after everything went down, then listed names of traitors who were collaborating with fae and causing troubles for the other humans at the court. Those were the ones executed in the end.'

Zera help me. *She must have been somewhat of a genius* ... A tingling sensation rose along my spine, a feeling like loss but only the echo of it – and that was my mother. No longer some nameless servant of the Crimson Court but a woman who tricked the High Ladies of the empire and *won* the game – won it, at least, for long enough to bring me to safety.

Only to disappear without a trace before she could reap the fruits of her victory.

'And where were you while all of this was happening?' Tared said sharply. 'Taking your sweet time investigating the non-existent rebellion on this island?'

'Trying to escape my chains,' Agenor said, his smile a thinly veiled warning.

'Your *what*?'

'My chains.' He gestured at the west, the direction of the Crimson Court. 'They had planned for everything to be over before I could come back and intervene. But it was another full month until Al gave birth, and Achlys and Melinoë ... even if they had no idea the child was *mine*, they figured out she had an influence on me. Apparently they decided a month of punishment would be more effective to bring me back in line than another month of exposure to her opinions on human rights. So they kept me here at the Golden Court.'

'In chains,' Lyn said, tasting the words.

'Yes.'

'Who?'

'Ophion.' He glanced at me when I stiffened. 'You've met him?'

'I ... I did.' *And he almost killed me, too.* 'Didn't particularly like him.'

'Very few people like him,' Agenor said, a sour smile playing around his lips. 'He likes himself enough to compensate, though. Which wouldn't be a problem if he were a little less powerful, but as it stands ...' Another flick of Lyn's dagger; he still hadn't let go of it. 'He showed up here and caught me by surprise. Not much I could do by the time he had me in alf steel and began lecturing me about giving humans priority over my own kind.'

Lyn glanced at his wrists. 'A month.'

'Yes. Not my best month, I might say.'

Not his best. Still, there was no trace of emotion on his face but a faint, stoic annoyance. Was it a matter of habit to keep up that mask after centuries and centuries in the treacherous halls of the Crimson Court, or did he simply not care *that* much?

Lyn exchanged a quick look with Tared – a spark of sympathy in her eyes, a hard line of scepticism in his.

I hunched up my shoulders, shoving the unwelcome question of Agenor's thoughts and feelings aside, and said, 'And then I was born?'

'Yes.' Again he sent me that estimating glance – as if to assess whether I would get the vapours at the continuation of the story. 'The original plan was for me to take you elsewhere before you could be bound to the island. When I didn't return, Al told the world you were a stillbirth and smuggled you out through the network – which ...' He turned to Lyn, eyebrow raised a fraction. 'Which I'm guessing is tied to the Alliance, then?'

'Not in the way you think,' she said, resting her chin in her hands. 'Finish the story first.'

He sighed. 'I don't know much about the rest. By the time I got back to the Crimson Court, she was no longer there. Her family told me to go fuck myself, in summary. Achlys and Melinoë told me that she was dead and that surely I knew better than to make a fuss about some useless little mortal. I didn't dare call them out on the lie – didn't want them to realise how far that bargain between us went, just in case they were still keeping her prisoner somewhere.'

Lyn worried her bottom lip. 'And the Mother just expected you to fall back in line?'

'It would hardly be his first time prioritising duty over ethics,' Tared said with a scoff. 'Seem to recall a little something about her murdering a god he was sworn to, for example.'

A sharp hiss erupted from the foliage.

I whipped around, but neither Tared nor Lyn seemed at all concerned. Lyn's small, triumphant huff was her only reaction, as if to say, *I knew it.*

'Coral,' Agenor said, his deep voice weary. 'Calm down, girl.'

In a flash of crimson movement, the snake I'd seen before emerged from the bushes, sending Tared another hiss in passing – slithering in one straight line towards Agenor, who lifted her long body onto his shoulders with bewildering carelessness. She curled around his torso without further encouragement and rested her head against his chest, looking as contented as I'd ever known any snake to look.

Oh, hell be damned. I should have been far, *far* more concerned about the creature.

'Is she ...' I cleared my throat, unable to look away from those beady black eyes. 'Yours?'

Again Coral hissed.

'She usually objects to that wording,' Agenor said, a flicker of a smile around his lips as he stroked his thumb over her neck. The snake stilled under his touch. 'She graciously tolerates my existence, though. I'm assuming you ran into her?'

I nodded as Lyn and Tared threw me a simultaneous frown.

'Well. That explains why she was so hell-bent on getting me out of bed.' He ripped up his left sleeve, revealing the marks of a snakebite on the inside of his muscular forearm. The wounds themselves had healed, but the veins around them were blackened with poison. He looked faintly amused at the observation. 'It's been ages since she's last bitten me.'

'Are you saying she *recognised* me?'

Coral raised her head to throw me a sideways glare.

'They're not entirely average snakes – she and the others.' Agenor said, briefly closing his eyes as he nudged her back to his shoulder. 'Divine magic. Long story.'

'It's in fact a rather short story,' Tared said. 'He's godsworn, Em. Snakes were Korok's familiars.' His smile at the other male was about as amiable as a drawn sword. 'You know, that god he helped blow to pieces a few decades later.'

'Yes, thank you,' Agenor said coldly. 'Not my proudest moment. I thought we'd agreed not to dwell on past events for now.'

Tared scoffed. 'That's what I would say if my past was a chain of broken oaths. But by all means, continue the story. You returned to the Crimson Court, and then?'

'Then I found myself thoroughly cured of any illusions about the Mother's good intentions. So I decided the empire had to go.' He shrugged, running his fingertips over Coral's scaly neck – so rational, so *businesslike*, about that earth-shattering decision to resort to treason. 'The first thing I knew was that I didn't stand a chance of changing anything right under their nose. So I dropped rumours of trouble in the east, made a few more visits to this court, until I was by far her most logical candidate to take care of those non-existent troubles. I've been here since, gathering allies, preparing for war. Looking for Al. Looking for ...' He met my gaze, his eyes pensive. 'You.'

For me? I couldn't help but wonder if he'd been looking for me or rather for the proper fae daughter he'd imagined – some well-mannered, courtly-bred girl who wouldn't shout at his face, wouldn't question his motives, wouldn't show up fraternising with his old enemies in the depth of night. Perhaps he'd imagined a child like I'd imagined a parent in my wildest dreams – someone who'd make sense to me.

'The Alliance didn't know I was fae when they smuggled me out,' I said, forcing myself to hold his gaze. 'I spent most of my life hiding my magic on a human island. Suppose that made me harder to find, yes.'

His brows drew together. 'Where did you grow up, if I may ask?'

'Cathra.'

'*Cathra.*' His sharp inhalation told me I'd said enough. 'Gods and demons. Creon, I presume?'

I didn't like his tone at all, but nodded.

'Who then claimed' – the disbelief in his voice grew more and more unpleasant – 'that he wanted them dead? The Mother?'

'Bargained on it,' I said, and his eyebrows shot up another half inch. 'Impossible.'

'I'm not *lying*.' For the bloody gods' sakes, did every single person who called himself my father have to be convinced I didn't carry a shred of truth in me? 'Do you think I'd have blown up a single stone for him if I hadn't been very sure he—'

'I wouldn't blame you for overlooking the caveats,' Agenor said, still infuriatingly unruffled as he rubbed his temple. 'He's capable enough of twisting his words to create a skewed impression of the truth.'

'She tried to *kill* him!'

He breathed a joyless chuckle. 'If they'd truly tried to kill him, he would be dead now.'

'Incorrect,' I said sharply, 'because I got him out before she could finish the job. Not all of us sit on our arses at some distant court for decades while she happily continues her murderous ways, you see.'

'Em ...' Lyn said, attempting to sound chastising despite the laughter bubbling beneath.

I didn't look at her. Agenor hadn't moved to defend himself; dagger in one hand, fingers of his other on Coral's neck, he sat watching me with that unflustered look of mild curiosity, like I was some unbroken horse he hadn't fully figured out yet.

'I'm very curious what game you think he might be playing and what he'd hope to achieve with it,' I added coolly, reining in the outburst itching on my tongue. Damn him, I could play that game too – hide my truths behind a smokescreen of polite wording and reserved smiles. 'I fail to see what he could have gained when he handed himself over to her to keep me alive. Or when she hung him by his gods-damned wings to torture him.'

Agenor's eyes narrowed, thoughts spinning furiously behind his eyes. 'What was the thing about blinding them?'

'I did.'

'You did.' His voice was too calm.

'Had to get him out of there somehow,' I said, making a good effort to sound just as maddeningly unaffected. 'I'm not sure how permanent the damage is, but considering that she's still keeping it quiet, I suppose *something* happened.'

Agenor considered that, then admitted, 'Eyes are complex to heal. So if you did indeed hit the right spot ...'

For hell's sake. 'Which I did.'

' ... I doubt they'll fully recover,' he finished, unimpressed.

'There are precedents for replacements, though,' Lyn said – of course she'd looked that up. 'Like Orin and his moonstone eye.'

'Not a perfect replacement,' Agenor said, shaking his head. 'I heard him complain a few times that he couldn't see colour with that eye.'

I forgot about my resolution to mirror his impossible composure. 'You *heard* him ...'

'Yes.' My shock seemed to amuse him, if anything. 'I've lived for a while.'

And not just lived since the age of the gods, but *met* those same gods – actually saw them walk around on the surface of the earth, heard them speak, spoke with them. I forced myself to snap my mouth shut and muttered, 'I see.'

'In that case, I suppose you understand my concerns as well?' It wasn't a question. It was a thinly veiled command, wrapped in a shiny layer of polite enquiry. 'I've known Creon for a while, and if I understand everything correctly, you've had roughly ... a month or two to get to the bottom of his motivations? I'm not quite inclined to give him a free pass on that basis.'

'So much for the mutual trust,' Lyn said curtly. She was looking far more displeased than Tared, who seemed torn between understanding of Agenor's point of view and irritation at having the law laid down for us by some damn fae lord. 'How were you planning to clarify the situation to your satisfaction, if you seem incapable of taking us at our word?'

'You've spent too much time with alves,' he said dryly. 'I haven't lived to this day and age by taking people at their word. I'll see what my sources at the Crimson Court have to say on the matter and—'

'That's going to take a while,' Lyn cut in. 'She's not allowing word to travel anywhere from the island.'

He shrugged. 'We have time. What is a few months in a fae life?'

'A few *months*?' The implications of that throwaway question rolled through me like slow, iron-clad punches to the gut. 'You want him to sit in a cell for *months* while you—'

'Once he's out, he's not going back in,' Agenor said, looking faintly surprised at my outburst. 'I'd rather take a few years to ensure we understand his motivations than have him go on one of his usual rampages as soon as he's free.' A dismissive flick of his hand. 'Obviously he'll be treated decently. I'm not a monster.'

Decently – for *years*? I gaped at him, scrambling for sense, for any way to explain to the bastard that not all of us had lived long enough to shrug off several years ... but Lyn interrupted before I found the words.

'Unpleasantness aside' – she sounded rather displeased, indeed – 'there are practical issues attached to that plan, Agenor. If you keep him in a cell for weeks, the rumours of his presence here will spread. And even if you don't wish to believe us, *please* take into account that you'll wake up with half an army on your doorstep as soon as the Mother hears about it.'

Agenor pursed his lips, nodding slowly. 'The crucial point, then, seems to be to keep rumours from spreading as soon as possible.'

There was too much meaning in that sentence, too much of that thoughtless bloodthirst that would end a life as easily as blow out a candle. *A plan is in place to remove them.*

Just like that, he'd taken his decision?

I suppressed a shiver, but Lyn merely raised an eyebrow, exchanging nothing but the quickest look with Tared. When he nodded, she added, 'Are you in need of assistance?'

The silence was a silence of mutual aversion – of distrust covered by only the thinnest veneer of mutual goals. But Agenor had made that bargain. He'd told his story. And as much as I doubted how deep his devotion to my mysteriously vanished mother went, as much as I wondered whether he even *had* a heart to lose behind that mask of unwavering politeness ... his allegiance seemed crystal clear.

Which meant it mattered very little how decent a father he was. That in the great scheme of things, it may not even matter how long he'd lock Creon in that bloody castle.

Did he need help? Because we most certainly did.

He glanced at Lyn, then at Tared, then ran his gaze over me for what had to be the fiftieth time – estimating, calculating, assessing my worth. I wondered if he ever did anything else. If his whole life was a matter of balancing the odds and playing his chances, if my mother had merely been a new and diverting game to him. Wondered if I'd have grown up to be merely a puppet of his strategies if I'd spent my childhood under his protection, rather than mixing paints and paying tributes on Cathra.

He rose to his feet without warning, wings flaring to keep his balance as the snake around his shoulders stirred. Whatever the results of his considerations, he sighed, nodded, and gestured for us to get up as well.

'In that case ...' For the first time, there was a flicker of soul to his smile, just a fraction more than the male who'd never show the world whatever his true face might be. 'In that case, it's my pleasure to welcome you to the Golden Court.'

CHAPTER 23

WE WALKED THE FULL distance to the court itself, Agenor unwilling to have Tared fade him, the others unwilling to let him out of their sight. Our path led out of the forest and onto the open field, where we could see the sky paling at the eastern horizon. The surface of the lake was eerily still, stars and sandstone reflecting in its indigo surface. Not even the faintest breeze ruffled the leaves of trees and bushes we passed – as if the island itself was holding its breath for what was to come.

Treason and death.

Or at least, I supposed that was the summary of it.

Lyn hurried along next to me on her short legs, peppering me with concerned glances. Tared and Agenor walked a few strides before us, the first speaking stubbornly in Alvish, the latter replying equally stubbornly in Faerie as they discussed whatever grim fate awaited the Mother's last loyal servants between the castle walls. I tried to follow the discussion, but there were too many names and Faerie words I didn't know, and my head was spinning. Within minutes, I gave up on Agenor's businesslike summaries of strategies and focused on my breathing exercises instead.

A clear mind was everything in the thick of a fight, after all.

And if Agenor truly intended to leave Creon in chains for months or years, that fight was far from over. Not even if he was an ally – not even if he was my father.

My *father*.

My thoughts faltered every single time they brushed past that word, the full realisation of it still too large, too heavy, for my reeling mind.

I didn't force it. Not yet – not as long as there were other problems left to solve. By the time Creon was free again, I could start thinking about the mystery of my mother's disappearance and whatever Agenor thought about it – whatever he thought about *me*.

I groaned inadvertently. If I was honest, that last question wasn't so much of a mystery but rather a question I very much didn't want to think about.

'Em?' Lyn said beside me, sounding cautious. 'Want to talk about anything?'

Anything. I threw a glower at Agenor's winged back before me, the red snake still wrapped around his shoulders like an exceptionally lethal scarf, and muttered, 'Do you think he's going to budge on that?'

'On Creon?'

'Yes.'

She pulled a face. 'I'm not sure.'

'That's a no,' I muttered, swallowing a string of curses.

'That ...' She rubbed her face. 'Oh, hell. I don't know. I do think we can trust his word that he'll treat Creon decently, if that reassures you at all. He's one of those who always seemed honestly convinced they were doing the decent thing.'

I scoffed, half taking note of Tared's sharp questions about escape routes. He didn't sound particularly trustful.

'Em ...' Lyn was rubbing her face when I turned back to her, her bag bouncing on her back with every hurried step. 'Some time to check our conclusions isn't an unreasonable demand. Try to see it from his point of view. You didn't know Creon before the War, or the façade he must have kept up at the court in these past decades. Trust me when I say it's a big leap.'

A mind-bogglingly worthless piece of shit. I almost groaned again. Hell, of course they'd left their traces, those centuries in which he truly hadn't given a damn about the lives he ended, had truly believed himself the finest individual faekind ever brought forth. The problem, though ...

'I wouldn't be so offended if he just doubted my conclusions,' I muttered, glaring at Agenor and his unreasonably straight posture. 'But he doesn't even believe my *observations*, and that ... Either he thinks I'm a liar, or he just assumes I'm an idiot.'

'Well,' Lyn said, even more slowly, 'clearly you're not an idiot, but don't forget, twenty-year-old fae are still very much children. I don't think he expected to run into a daughter with a mind of her own for a few more decades.'

I threw her a sideways glance. She was fidgeting with her curls, examining Agenor with a look of what seemed closest to ... *concern?*

Oh.

Gods help me. She had already started saving him, hadn't she?

I almost let out a bitter laugh. I should have seen that coming. Bad conscience, problematic love life, far too many troubles she could solve for him – of course she was jumping at the chance, even if he was an enemy of centuries, even if he'd murdered Tared's house for the sister in whose honour he'd named me. Ever the defender, ever the diplomat. Seeing things from his point of view – like hell I would.

'Yes,' I said absently. 'That's probably true.'

She sighed. 'Em ...'

The tone of her voice betrayed the many well-meant suggestions she was biting down. Don't judge too fast. Don't take stupid risks, don't say things you'll regret. You only get one father; why not see if you could get along with him once you get through these awkward first days?

Which was all wonderful advice, of course. Had the situation been slightly different, I might even have listened.

But as it stood ...

Creon was still sitting in that cell. And between a father I didn't know and a lover I missed like summer rains, choices were easily made.

'Don't worry,' I said and forced a quick smile at her. 'I'll be sensible.'

Close enough to the truth by fae standards. I had my own game to play, after all, no matter how hard she'd try to keep the peace – and it was about time I got rational about it.

The castle grew no less impressive as we approached along the shores of the lake, its walls so high I had to tilt back my head to make out the winged figures keeping watch. Increased security, indeed – not to protect the court from Creon, but rather to sound the alarm at the first sight of any outsider trying to make their way in.

There was no sign of alarm as we walked up the paved road to the gate itself, though. Not with Agenor in our midst, the snake on his shoulders enough proof of his identity, even in the sparse illumination of the faelights on the sandstone walls.

The dark wooden doors creaked open at the merest swing of his hand. Behind them ...

As determined as I'd been not to freeze, I froze.

The hall behind the entrance bore not the faintest resemblance to the stark exterior of the castle – as if by stepping through that gate, I'd stepped into a whole new reality, one miles removed from the rough blocks of sandstone and the mild morning air outside. The room was all clay walls and polished wood. It was carved arches and slender pillars. It was mirrors and stained-glass lanterns, bright colours and twinkling lights, and *plants*, their vines climbing over the walls and dangling from the ceilings in such abundant amounts I could have believed I'd walked into some lush southern forest instead.

A place so full of light, so full of *life*, that it was hard to imagine its creator was the same god who had dreamed up the cruel nightmare of the Crimson Court.

Agenor handed out commands behind me as I wandered ten steps deeper into the hall, eyes drinking in the dazzling colours. Geometric murals surrounded the windows and doorways, gem-like patterns in lemon and tangerine and the brightest azure. Behind the arches, I caught glimpses of a wide open courtyard and other castle buildings, the shapes of them hard to distinguish in the night. Most of the court seemed deserted, but here and there, winged figures moved past, carrying baskets of food or piles of linen.

Fae handling their own damn chores? Hard to believe, but no matter where I looked, there were no human servants to be seen.

'Emelin?'

I whipped around.

Agenor had finally finished his instructions; the handful of fae around him scattered, a feverish excitement filling the hall as they rushed off to take care of their respective tasks. No one seemed to consider me worth more than half a glance, and I was too glad for it to correct the oversight.

'Yes?' I said.

For a heartbeat, I was afraid he'd ask what I thought of his court or make some other attempt at small talk. But quite to my relief, he just nodded at a doorway to his left and said, 'This way. Stay close to me.'

Thank the gods. As long as he didn't try to be much of a father, I didn't have to decide how much of a father I needed.

'So where are we going, exactly?' I said as I hurried after him, Lyn and Tared following us in a few strides.

Agenor threw me a mildly puzzled glance, apparently unable to see why I'd ask such nosy questions. 'Seeing a few people I prefer to deal with personally. My second will handle the rest.' He waved at a corridor to our right to indicate our destination, then added, 'Don't worry about the details. It's all quite under control.'

That was exactly what I was worried about – little chance I'd manage to sneak into some fae prince's prison during the chaos that might have ensued under anyone else's command. But the tone of his voice pissed me off enough to mutter, 'Very reassuring, thank you.'

'Beg your pardon?' he said.

I bit my tongue. 'Never mind.'

Unfazed, he turned away to hand out a few more commands to a passing fae, something about keeping an eye on possible escape routes. He didn't resume the sorry excuse for a conversation as we hurried on.

The castle may be more compact than the Crimson Court, but it was a maze all the same. Within the pentagonal outline of those massive sandstone walls, about two dozen smaller buildings had been erected around at least three courtyards, from towers to low barracks; we crossed hall after hall in search of some elusive collection of people Agenor needed to set his plans in motion, some of those rooms grand and imposing, others cosier and more like the living rooms of some of the larger Underground alf houses. There were kitchens and bakeries, gardens and laundry rooms, smithies and stables ...

Truly, the only thing the castle didn't seem to have was a prison.

I tried to map out the place in my mind as we walked, keeping an eye out for any structure in which one might conceivably lock a dangerous murderer. None of the buildings we encountered seemed to qualify. Everything was too elegant, too open; the only thick-walled, windowless wing smelled strongly of citrus and rosemary and turned out to be a bathhouse.

Around us, the court woke in the five, ten minutes that we wandered from hall to hall. Fae rushed past with bright red shirts and weapons in their hands. In the distance, a piercing scream rose from one of the barracks. The whooshing of wings through the darkness outside betrayed even more movement, dozens of individuals following some plan that had been made and perfected years ago.

It was after some ten minutes of walking and searching that a dark-skinned fae male burst around the corner, skidded to a halt at the sight of Lyn and Tared, and turned to Agenor with a wide swing of his bejewelled hand. 'What in the name of the gods is the meaning of *this*?'

'Ah, Theron,' Agenor said gently, 'if you don't mind?' After which he blew two lightning-quick bolts of the brightest red into the other's throat without even slowing his pace. The unlucky fae male stumbled back against the wall and fell gurgling to his knees, then slumped onto the floor and stayed there in an ever-widening pool of blood.

'Efficient,' Tared said, in a tone that could either be a compliment or a scathing insult.

Lyn didn't say anything, but she grabbed my sleeve and dragged me along before I could make the mistake of taking in too many details. Still, a faint nausea lingered as we walked on through the next gallery. All those windows on the first and second floor, curtains closed against the slowly brightening morning light ... How many of the people sleeping in those rooms would no longer be alive in an hour?

Hell. If I wasn't careful, I'd end up whining in a corner when things went down, and that really wouldn't do my credibility any good. But where would I go if—

Wait.

An idea sparked.

I didn't give myself too much time to consider the wisest strategy. This was not a night for thinking and waffling. So as we rounded another corner, somehow striding back into a garden I was *sure* should be at the other side of the castle now, I forced myself to hesitate and muttered, 'Lyn?'

As expected, she was alarmed at the first hint of helplessness. 'What is it?'

'I'm thinking perhaps I shouldn't stay here when the fighting starts,' I mumbled, deliberately timid, but with a dash of annoyance to not stretch believability too far. 'Since ... Well. You know. I'm not entirely used to those things.'

Something flickered in her eyes, a determination far fiercer than anything I could believably have brought forward. Good. I'd counted on her protective instincts to make my case; I doubted my dear father would take my personal wishes seriously enough to change his plans.

'Agenor?' she said sharply.

He whirled around mid-step in the twilight of early morning, his fingertips resting on Coral's blood-red scales. 'Hmm?'

'Don't you think it might be better if Em finds a slightly calmer place to spend the next few hours?'

If the thought had occurred to him, he hadn't paid much attention to it. 'She's arguably safest with me near.'

'Yes,' Lyn said briskly, 'but there'll also be corpses with you near.'

Tared stood studying me and my demure silence with slowly rising eyebrows – waiting, without doubt, for the objections I was forcing myself to hold back. When those didn't come, he tilted his head at me with a glimmer of amusement and said, 'Perhaps you have a preference, Em?'

Not bad. Thank the gods Edored's sense of strategy didn't run in the family.

'Well,' I said, biting down several snarkier alternatives, 'I do suppose there are *some* safe places where I don't have to worry about anyone blowing my head off? Some ... some library? Or—'

Agenor sighed before I could come up with another innocuous suggestion in the right direction, glancing at a tower rising behind the garden walls. 'I suppose my study should be safe enough. If you prefer to spend the morning there ...'

'Oh.' *Good.* It took an effort not to grin. 'That does sound more peaceful, yes.'

He nodded, lifted Coral off his shoulders, and gestured for me to follow him. I hesitated a last moment, unsure if the looming battle required me to say goodbye to the other two in slightly more elaborate ways.

'Don't expect me to come with you,' Tared said, sending me a grin. 'I doubt his lordship is going to let any alves into his private rooms.'

'Nothing personal,' Agenor said, sounding like it was, as a matter of fact, quite personal. 'To the left here, Emelin.'

The notion that I might want to say goodbye to the only people I knew in this place didn't seem to occur to him. Fine. I scraped myself together, reminded myself Lyn and Tared had survived worse than a struggle with an outnumbered group of Crimson Court sympathisers, and moulded my face into a smile I didn't feel. 'See you later.'

'Later, Em.' Lyn didn't look entirely reassured; next to her, Tared looked positively distrustful. I ducked through the doorway Agenor had indicated before either of them could speak up and raise suspicions.

We navigated the labyrinth of the castle in high-strung silence, the both of us equally unsure of what to say and equally happy to solve the conundrum by not saying anything at all. What would we even talk about? I could hardly ask him how work had been; he could hardly tell me to go clean my room and remind me of my homework.

Hell, we'd survived twenty years without exchanging a single word. We could go a few more hours without meaningful conversation.

Our destination, it turned out, was a tall tower at the north side of the castle, the outer walls covered in ivy and bright trumpet flowers. Inside, four floors of stairs ran up to a heavy wooden door, which Agenor opened with one of the three keys he kept on a thin chain around his neck.

'Come in.' He held the door for me. 'Ignore the mess.'

Such an ordinary thing to say – such a *human* thing to say – that I accidentally chuckled as I tiptoed inside and he shut the door behind me.

His personal study was a comfortable square room, covering the entire tower floor. Most of the clay walls were covered in bookshelves, and more piles of books had gathered on the two desks and the small table by the couch. Notes, maps, and all kinds of small trinkets lay scattered on every other available surface; broad windows on all four sides allowed a spectacular view over most of the island. In the glow of the faelights, it was messy indeed – but cosily messy, with an air of diligence and deep thought rather than hopeless chaos.

As if I'd walked straight into the mind of the Lord of the Golden Court himself.

My feet faltered as that thought hit. Perhaps there was more to find in this place than just the information I was hoping for.

'Emelin?' Agenor said.

He pronounced my name with uneasy care, as if it was some foreign concept, an exotic spice he wasn't yet sure what to think about. I turned and found him by the southern window, next to a narrow ladder that led to the floor above our heads. Two keys were back around his neck, but the one he'd used to let me into the room lay on the edge of the nearest desk.

Whether he was uneasy or not, his expression was still entirely efficient as he nodded at the key and said, 'I'll leave this one here. There's alf steel in the door, so as long as you don't unlock it, no one should get through.'

Unless they broke down the entire tower – but he'd notice that from the outside and might even do something about it.

'Alright,' I said, drawing in a deep breath to calm my sudden nerves at that thought. 'Anything else I should know?'

'There might be ...' He sighed and raised his voice a fraction. 'Oleander?'

Something stirred under a pile of parchment to my right. I squeaked.

'Don't worry,' he said, looking amused. 'She doesn't have much of a temper, and you're here with permission. She won't bite. Apart from that ... feel free to take a look at the books, but stay out of everything else. There's a bathroom on the next floor. Snacks are in the cabinet over there. I suppose ...' His sentence drifted off as he threw a quick look around the room, then returned his gaze to me, lips set in a tight line.

'Thanks,' I said quickly, before he could accidentally say something about fatherly duties or proper daughterly expectations.

His shoulders didn't loosen under that silk shirt. Green – it seemed almost overconfident to fly into battle wearing *green*. But he wouldn't have survived for centuries by being overconfident, and the gods knew his orders had sounded resolute enough. He must know what he was doing.

'I suppose we'll talk ... later,' he said.

Was that a demand, too? I couldn't make sense of the tone of his voice – no longer so resolute at all, but nowhere near a question, either. Perhaps, after a thousand-and-something years of giving orders, one eventually lost the ability to do anything else.

'Yes,' I said. 'Suppose so.'

This was not the moment to start being clever – not if I wanted him to leave me alone with his personal documents in a minute.

'Alright.' He sighed. 'See you in an hour or so.'

'See you. Good luck with the murdering.'

He let out a laugh as he turned away. 'It's a routine operation. But thank you.'

And before I could object that surely cutting his ties to the court he'd served for a millennium wasn't such a routine at all – before I could remind myself I shouldn't be saying such sensible things under the circumstances – he'd swung open the window, stepped onto the windowsill, and launched himself into the night outside, wings carrying him out of sight in the blink of an eye.

I dropped my backpack beside the nearest desk, locked the door, and closed the window behind him. I had no need for the sounds reaching me from below, shouts and shrieks and slamming doors – the noise of a court turning violently and lethally against itself.

An hour or so. No time to lose.

I gave myself five minutes to explore my new surroundings – the bookcases, the cabinet with snacks, the bathroom above the study. There was a sparsely furnished bedroom on that floor as well, which contained no more than a bed, a painfully well-organised wardrobe, and another small pile of books. I climbed the ladder to the next floor, too, but the hatchway was locked, and the study key didn't fit.

One of the other two keys, probably. He wasn't reckless enough to leave me alone with *all* his secrets.

I returned to the study, where Oleander had slithered out from below the parchment. She was a slender, ink-black snake of about half Coral's size, and although she eyed me sharply as I tiptoed in a wide circle around her, she seemed uninclined to set her teeth into me.

'There's no need to watch me so suspiciously,' I said, even though there was admittedly plenty of need to. 'I'll just look for something to read and relax for a bit while things are ... happening outside.'

Oleander hissed softly.

'I assume that means we're in agreement.' I stood still before a bookcase and slid my gaze over the long rows of leatherbound spines. Lawbooks. Of *course* the bastard owned a small library of lawbooks. Moving on to the next row of shelves, I added, 'I'm Emelin, by the way. His daughter, apparently. But perhaps Coral already told you that much?'

She hissed again.

'Well. Lovely to meet you, then.'

No answer, this time. I focused on the next two sections of books – a number of treatises on warfare, governance, and philosophy. All very interesting for any other day, but none of these tomes was going to tell me where this court hid its dangerous prisoners.

And I didn't have *that* much time.

'Oleander?'

When I turned around, the snake hadn't moved, watching me with those beady green eyes from one of Agenor's desks.

'I'm looking for a map,' I said.

She tilted her narrow head.

'We just walked around the castle for ten minutes or so, and I was utterly unable to make sense of it.' I gave her a slightly awkward grimace. 'I'm thinking ... if I'll stay here for a while, it would probably be helpful if I didn't get lost every time I try to find the kitchens. So if you know of any maps he's keeping in this room, I—'

Oleander slithered into motion, from the desk onto a bookshelf, and from there over the windowsill, another shelf, the back of the couch. One straight line to the messy pile of documents on the floor by the side table, a good five inches of parchment upon parchment.

She nudged her nose against the pile, then threw me a piercing glare, as if to ask what in hell I was waiting for.

'Are you saying ...' Good gods. That was easier than expected. 'You don't mind if I come closer, do you?'

Oleander shook her head.

I'd have to take her at her word, then. I tiptoed closer, and she shrunk away as I picked up the pile and settled myself into the couch pillows. Notes, letters, military reports ... and then finally, so old the parchment was showing small tears around the fold lines, a map.

Pentagonal outlines, a mess of halls and gardens – the Golden Court indeed.

A laugh fell over my lips as I unfolded it over the couch, the full document large enough to cover most of the seats. 'You're a damn clever snake, do you know that?'

Oleander sent me a glare as she slipped back onto the couch as well, wrapping herself around the armrest on the other side. Something in her look oddly reminded me of Lyn whenever I called her a seven-year-old.

'You know that,' I concluded. 'You ... you're probably older than me, now that I think of it.'

A nod.

'A lot older than me?'

Two nods. Zera help me. Divine magic, Tared had said – how old could these animals get when the god they'd been bound to was long dead?

But the question I heard slide off my tongue was, 'Did you know my mother?'

Oleander tilted her head, then nodded again.

'Did you ... did you like her?'

This time the snake's nod came immediately. Liked her a lot, then? I swallowed and barely kept my next question inside – did *Agenor* even like her that much, with that minimum of feelings he'd shown so far?

Questions this snake might not be able or willing to answer, and either way, I wasn't here to dig into the history of my parents' affair. I had my own lover to find, first. So I forced myself to focus on my new-found map, the tangle of rooms and corridors no less intimidating on parchment than in reality, and systematically combed the floor plans for anything that could be a prison.

Barracks and training fields. Kitchens and dining halls. A bathhouse, an infirmary, bedrooms and studies and meeting rooms ... but unless they'd chained him down in the wine cellar, there was no sensible prison location to be found.

That didn't make sense. Hadn't Creon said this was a military outpost? That did suggest the occasional fight, and even fae would take captives every now and then, rather than slaughter everyone who annoyed them.

337

I muttered a curse and went over the map of the ground floor again. So many lines and drawings and names and ...

Wait.

My eye paused on a small, scribbled dot just to the left of the wine cellar. No exceptional shape or location, but it was the only dot on the entire map drawn in blue ink rather than in black.

It had been added later, then.

Only then did I find the corresponding label between a tangle of other descriptions, two letters in blue ink, scribbled down in a hand so messy I had to squint to decipher them. *BG.*

BG?

I rubbed my eyes, leaning back a fraction. An abbreviation of some kind, but what kind of marking point would one add later to a map as thorough as this one? Unless it was some dangerous secret ...

Oh.

Blood Gate.

I stared at the dot with unseeing eyes.

A tunnel that runs all the way to the castle itself. Of course there had to be an entrance on this side, too – an entrance protected with the same divine magic, if I could trust my interpretation of that abbreviation. But if there was a tunnel just below the castle – if there had once been multiple tunnels, according to Lyn and Tared – then who was to say there wasn't more to be found down there?

Like cells?

Hell, what would be a *more* sensible place to keep prisoners?

Which meant I'd have to make it past a god's magical defences. The short spark of triumph sizzled down in my chest, making me suddenly aware of the muffled noise outside the tower, the flickers of red that flashed through the night below my windows. How much time did I have left? Enough to find whatever books on divine magic Agenor may have in his possession, decipher the Faerie texts, and extract the information I needed?

That didn't sound too likely.

I could ask Lyn and Tared for details about the gate when all of this was over. Lyn would have opinions on honouring our new alliance and practicing patience, though, and even if Tared wouldn't care much about Agenor's approval, I doubted he'd be much inclined to disagree with her just for Creon's benefit. So they might not tell me how to open the damned thing. Worse, they might try to stop me, and I didn't need my friends working against me while circumventing a god's security measures.

So perhaps—

A tremble ran through the tower.

I shrieked and shot up in the couch cushions, grabbing the nearest armrest – as if that would help me if the whole building came plummeting down. But the floor stilled below my feet, and no next tremor followed.

What in hell?

I jumped up, map forgotten, and hurried to the nearest window. The sun had to be hovering just below the horizon; the sky was a pale blue everywhere except to the west, where the last stars were still visible. Below me, the whole court seemed awake now, small groups of fae making rounds of the castle, some of them dragging bodies along.

The worst of the fight must already have ended, at least on the courtyards I could observe from above. No one seemed to be using magic at the foot of my building, either.

Another of those violent rumbles rolled through the floor below my feet.

I snapped around and hurried to the next window. Nothing to be seen on that side either. Were Agenor's people fighting on the stairs below me, then? But if that were the case, I should *hear* something, and even when I pressed my ear tight against the keyhole of the door ...

No sounds of battle.

But I *did* hear a muffled bang at the next shake of the tower, and when the last creaking died away, the ragged, shrieking sound of panting breath reached me. Not a sound of battle; there was not enough noise for that. Rather ... someone trying to flee?

Were they breaking out through the walls?

I stood up straight and threw Oleander a helpless look – as if a bloody snake would have advice on what to do next. She'd curled up in my seat on the couch already, enjoying my body warmth lingering in the velvet, and didn't look up.

Again the tower shivered. Whatever the fae below me were doing, I doubted I had much time to stop them. Should I sound the alarm? But how was I even supposed to reach Lyn or Tared or Agenor if the stairs were blocked?

I could just ... let them go. At least I would be safe where I was, unless whoever was down there tried to break through the floor of the study. But if they escaped – if they made it back to the Crimson Court and reported back to the Mother – we'd have bigger problems on our hands than a broken tower and some bodies.

Another fit of creaking tore through the walls, and I moved without further thought. Grabbed the key from my dress pocket. Pulled Tared's dagger from my bag, the weight of it strange and yet reassuring in my hands. Opened the door as quietly as I could and peeked around the corner.

Muffled sobs reached me, and a female voice cursing under her breath. A single voice – I could handle a single fae, couldn't I?

And if not ... well, at least the fight would likely alarm someone.

I shut the door behind me and tiptoed the first steps down, giving myself no time to reconsider how reckless I was being. I wasn't a help-less child, damn it. Creon and Tared had trained me for this work. I *was* ready, and I *could* solve whatever in hell this problem was. Clenching my dagger with tight fingers, cautious not to touch the alf steel blade itself, I sneaked down the winding stairs. There, just around the corner ...

A crumbling hole of roughly a square foot gaped in the thick wall, rays of dusky light falling in through the dust.

Just a square foot?

I paused, blinking at the gap. All those shocks I'd felt, at least five of them – and this was the result of all that work? An opening not even large enough to let a grown person through?

A flash of red filled the tower. I flinched, expecting half the wall to vanish under an attack that bright – but the portion of sandstone that shattered under all that force was no bigger than a fist.

340

Oh.

Your magic is rather strong.

Right. We weren't all children of bloody Lord Agenor himself – and it was that thought which gave me the courage to jump down those last steps, my limbs falling into the routine drilled into me by hours and hours of exercises. I barely registered the details of the scene before me. Wings. Body. Wide eyes; shrill cry. I dove forward, and we slammed against the wall together, her wings against the rough stones, my left hand pinning her in place.

My knife hand flung up so easily. Pressed against the pale skin of her throat so naturally, as if I'd done the same and worse a thousand times before – flat side against her vulnerable artery, a flash of white metal in the morning twilight.

The fae female stiffened at that lethal touch, her ragged cry stilling in the back of her throat. For one everlasting heartbeat, we stood frozen, bodies pressed into each other, her limbs tense and trembling.

She smelled of sweat. Sweat and blood and fear.

Her hair must once have been auburn, a little lighter than my own. It danced around her dark face in pale green strands now, all but the last trace of red sucked out in her attempts to find a way out of the castle. Her dress was a pale green too, her cloak still black – dark enough to hide her from the view of the watchers outside. Her hands ... they were covered in a strange, white-greyish fluid. It took me a moment too long – blood, the red drawn out to the very last drop.

Had she wounded herself just to gain access to that magic?

My stomach turned as I looked back at the face above my knife, traces of tears on her dusty cheeks. Bright violet eyes gaped back at me, pleading.

Desperate.

My hand started trembling.

I was being nonsensical. I knew what I had to do – force her back downstairs, hand her over to any of Agenor's people, and let them decide her fate. So what if the answer was death? She must be one of the Mother's puppets, they'd have no reason to hunt her down otherwise.

That plea in her eyes didn't mean a damn to me, not if she'd easily shrug off the pleas of any human caught up in—

'Please,' she rasped, hands clawing into my arms. 'My children – they're still at the Crimson Court.'

Her *children*?

Oh, Zera help me.

'Please.' She had to see my hesitation; her breathless appeals grew stronger. 'Please, my twins – they're only seven – Lyssi is just starting to fly ...' Fresh tears rolled over her cheeks. 'I shouldn't even have *been* here. It was just a few days, I have nothing to do with whatever ... whatever ...'

She must have seen enough, though.

I clenched my jaw. A few days or not, she knew what had happened to the court. So I should still drag her back down. The word *couldn't* spread, whether she was an innocent messenger or not; wrong time, wrong place, the unfortunate accidents we couldn't avoid ... Weren't those the sacrifices we should make for the greater good of the archipelago?

But her children – her children would grow up wondering who their mother had been.

I wasn't ready for this.

The Underground had been right. Gish had been right. I was nowhere near ready for this. I was a weak-willed, sentimental idiot, and hours upon hours of training hadn't prepared me for *this* part of the game, for teary eyes and hands covered in snow white blood.

'Don't tell anyone anything,' I heard myself whisper.

Her breath caught, violet eyes widening.

'Not a word about anything you've seen here. About anything that's happened.' I should make a bargain with her, mutual secrecy or something like that – but someone would see my mark, would figure out what I'd done, and how would I explain any of this to Lyn and Tared? To Agenor? She'd have to keep her word – hell, wouldn't she do that for her children? 'Promise you'll keep it quiet and I'll let you go.'

'Anything.' Her voice cracked. 'Please – I promise.'

So stupid.

So very, very stupid.

But I stepped back, lifting the alf steel off her skin. Turned around and finished the hole she'd created, a single muted blow of red that opened an exit the size of a small door in the wall.

'Get out.'

She all but threw herself outside, wings flaring out, dark coat billowing around her as she fell into the depths. When I glanced down, she just landed at the feet of the castle wall, curling up into the shadows for an opportunity to move again.

One last time our gazes met, and I realised I didn't even know her name.

Then a shrill cry of pain rose from somewhere else in the castle, shaking me awake. I jumped back and flung a flash of blue magic at the wall, melting the hole shut. She wisely hadn't used any colour from the tower, and only the blood drops on the stairs proved someone had been here; I wiped them away as well as I could, until at least the red no longer stood out so starkly against the dark wood.

I should never have come here.

I should never have tried to stop her.

My heart was beating in my throat when I sprinted back up to Agenor's study, stormed into the room and flung the door shut as if it would make the world behind it vanish. *Stupid.* But her children …

Damn the map. Damn the fight out there. I cowered in the couch for the remainder of the hour, arms over my head and face pressed into the pillows, until finally the sounds of battle stilled and the first sunrays filtered through the windows and Agenor knocked on the door to announce breakfast would be served soon.

CHAPTER 24

'DIDN'T THINK WE'D EVER spend Battle Eve in bloody Agenor's home,' Tared grumbled, pacing back and forth between bed and balcony door of our guest room, his sword still on his back even though it had been hours since Agenor declared the castle fully in the hands of the resistance. 'Wait until Edored hears about this madness.'

Lyn chuckled. 'Were you planning to tell him?'

'It probably wouldn't be beneficial to our alliance if he showed up to challenge a few dozen fae to a personal duel, would it?'

She grimaced, lying back in the abundance of pillows at the headboard of her bed. 'Best stay away until he's too drunk to wonder where we are, then.'

Tared huffed in confirmation and continued his pacing, mulling over the situation. It was the first time since the fight that we'd been left to ourselves, no fae or snakes around; Agenor had vanished after showing us the way, with some quick apologies about things to do that no one had asked him to elaborate on.

I didn't mind; quite the opposite. At least if I didn't have his opinions to worry about, I could focus on the more important matter of freeing captive princes.

'You're quiet, Em,' Lyn said, as if she'd heard that thought and was determined to stop me.

'Very odd,' I said. Damn it. Perhaps I should make a better effort to pretend my limbs weren't buzzing with the thought of Creon. 'It's not as if anything noteworthy has happened in the past twenty-four hours. What's Battle Eve?'

Tared turned at the window. 'Anniversary of the Last Battle. Four days after midsummer.'

The name could have told me that much. 'Are we missing anything in the Underground?'

'Not really. Most of the Alliance spends the day with family in the world above.' He rubbed his face as he sat down onto the windowsill. 'And those who don't have family in the world above usually just drink themselves into a stupor to get through it. They won't need us, in any case.'

They both sat in heavy, gloomy silence for a moment.

'Well,' I said, sitting up straight from the bed where I'd crashed on our arrival. Would they be suspicious? Perhaps they would, but I doubted I'd find a better moment. 'If we're staying for a while anyway, I think I'll go for a walk.'

Lyn groaned and sat up, red curls cascading over her shoulders. 'On your own?'

'Do I look like the person in need of a nursemaid here?'

Tared sniggered; she stuck out her tongue at him before turning back to me. 'You may have liked company.'

'I think I'd rather go alone. Need to think about some things.' Like divine opening mechanisms and underground tunnels. Her lawful intentions would hardly be helpful. 'Don't worry, I'll be careful as always.'

'That sounds like a reason to worry,' she said sourly, but she didn't stop me when I bounced off the bed, swung my bag over my shoulder, and took my leave with a quick goodbye. I heard them continue their conversation as soon as I closed the door behind me, but through the thick wood, I couldn't make sense of their words except for the regular repetition of Agenor's name and an occasional mention of me.

Worries for later. Creon came first.

I hurried down the nearest stairs, heart pounding in my throat. Now that I'd seen the floor plan of the castle, finding my way was easier: the trick was to realise that most of the corners weren't actually square corners, even if they looked like it. Keeping that in mind, I managed to navigate closer to the kitchens, slipping from shadow to shadow to avoid as many fae as I could. Even if I knew they *likely* weren't here to kill me, something about the sight of so many wings in one place made me feel uncomfortable to the core.

Thankfully, most of Agenor's people were still too busy cleaning blood off the walls and untangling weapons and limbs from the abundant greenery to notice a little half fae sneaking around the place. I found the kitchens without incident and slipped past them, past the wine cellar, towards ...

Oh, fuck.

I ground to a halt around the corner, heart skipping a beat. The gate *was* there, that was the good news – the outline of the doors drawn sharply in the wall of smooth, dark rock, so different from the sandstone, wood, and clay that made up most of the castle. But six fae warriors stood idly around it, dressed in black, armed to the teeth, looking like the chaos of the morning had missed them entirely.

I considered jumping back. Too late; they'd already noticed me.

'Oh, hello.' The crooked-nosed male closest to me didn't look unfriendly as he whipped around and loosened his fingers around the sword hilt at his hip. No sign of hostility, but I flinched nonetheless. 'You're the human the Alliance brought along, aren't you?'

Human. The Alliance. I nodded, not sure what to make of that – Agenor hadn't spread the truth of my identity, then? To protect me, or because he wasn't entirely sure he even wished to claim paternity of the unexpected almost-human that had come bursting into his life?

'Are you looking for something?' the guard said.

The gate the six of you are protecting with your lives. Hell, that wouldn't do. I could ask some questions, of course, tell them I was just exploring the castle and hope they'd let slip how one could get past Korok's magic – but if they were trained with Agenor's love for discipline and diligence, the chances were too great they'd tell him about the encounter as soon as I left. He might realise what I was trying to do.

'Oh, I was on my way to the kitchens,' I said, making my decision in a heartbeat. 'Someone said they were around here, but I think I took a wrong turn somewhere?'

'Just around the corner – wait.' The crooked-nosed male nodded at his brothers and sisters in arms as he strode up to me. 'I'll show you the way.'

There were no suggestive glances and sniggers between the others. None of the leering jokes the fae at the Crimson Court had been so fond of making as soon as I turned my back. Perhaps there were indeed some decent individuals to be found among their kind – a small, hopeful sign.

It was damned impractical at this particular moment, though.

I'd just eaten breakfast. My stomach was still close to bursting with sesame bread and honey pudding. I had no reason to be anywhere near a kitchen, and with my guardian striding alongside me, there was no way of sneaking away quietly.

Then again, if I couldn't get to the Blood Gate from inside the castle ...

By the time we walked into the steaming, bustling chaos of the castle kitchens two minutes later, my plan was made. And when a short female with a giant auburn bun and flour-dusted emerald wings came hurrying towards us and asked what she could do for the court's human guest, I sent her my most determined smile and told her I'd like to take something to eat along on my walk around the island.

'Of course, lovely, of course – anything you had in mind? Spinach pie, perhaps ? Oh, or I have some of yesterday's lemon cakes left, if you'd like that?'

The gate guard gave me a last pat on the shoulder and left as the auburn-haired cook rapidly gathered a pile of food that could feed an orphanage for a week. 'And some strawberries with cream as a snack, perhaps? But be careful, sweetie, the pixies *love* those ...'

'Yes,' I tried, 'I think that should be enough to—'

'Oh, how about some of the pumpkin casserole, too?'

When I eventually fled the kitchen, it was with five pounds of food on my back and a sturdy leather bottle of water to make sure I wouldn't perish from thirst. I contemplated leaving some of it my bedroom, but decided against it. If I got myself locked into an underground tunnel, an extra meal might just come in handy.

The guards at the castle gate fussed for a few minutes about the possibilities of me getting lost, injured, or attacked by pixies. When they finally thought of asking for my age, I told them I was thirty-six years old and used to islands full of alves, and they begrudgingly allowed me through.

I hurried in a straight line to the forest, as far away as possible from anyone who could change his mind and stop me. By the time I reached the first rows of holm oaks and lemon trees, no one had come flying after me yet, and I finally dared to slow down as I slipped into the shadows of the rustling foliage.

Time to make a plan.

I had presumably gotten lucky today, with Agenor unusually occupied by the organisational trouble of his rebellion. Tomorrow he would have more time for me – more time to ask questions and look politely disappointed at every word I spoke – and then it would be a challenge to reach the little bay with the Blood Gate unnoticed. So I had to make the most of this opportunity ... which would be less daunting if I had the faintest idea how to use it.

First things first. I'd have to get to the damn gate.

It was still early in the morning, no later than nine. It must have been around twelve hours ago that we'd stood in the dark antechamber of the Blood Gate; if the tides at this island were similar to those on Cathra and Ildhelm, it should be ebb now. The water may already be rising, though, so I shouldn't—

Something shrieked below my feet, and I jumped higher than I'd have thought my seven pounds of food and water would allow me to.

On the forest floor, in the shadow-flecked grass, sat a spider about the size of my head.

What in hell? My thoughts tumbled across each other as I staggered back, fingers on my black bag even though the creature didn't move any of its eight long legs. Could spiders even get this large? And why had it *shrieked*? Did it even have a mouth to shriek with, or …

With a high-pitched, magpie-like titter, the spider morphed into an equally oversized rabbit and shot away between the bushes.

'Oh, for fuck's sake,' I said out loud.

Hysterical giggling answered me from four sides at once.

I rolled my eyes and stomped forward, watching my feet more carefully just in case another pixie came up with the suicidal idea to throw itself in my path. Nothing appeared before me, but an acorn hit the back of my head two minutes later, hard enough that I was sure it hadn't dropped from the nearest tree.

When I snapped around, I just saw the maroon flash of a squirrel rushing up a tree. Halfway through, the brown turned black, and a small jackdaw shot out into the sky above me, cackling loudly.

'Little shit,' I muttered.

Another acorn hit me just below my left ear.

'Hey!' Gods *damn* them. I hadn't dealt with mysterious demon messages, divine magic, absent fathers, and decisions of life and death only to find myself the target of a bunch of fake squirrels for the sake of some easy fun. 'How about the lot of you stop this nonsense?'

More giggling from the foliage; it sounded louder this time. Oh, so they were all joining the fun now?

I briefly closed my eyes, scraped together the last of my patience, and snapped, 'What do you want?'

No answer.

'Then just stay away, will you?'

Again they remained silent. But as soon as I lifted my foot to take another step, no less than seven acorns flew from various branches and bushes, hitting my ribs and shoulders with unfortunate accuracy.

Hell be damned.

It suddenly seemed an attractive possibility to blow up half the forest and take these damned pixies with it – I couldn't deal with this now. Not *now*. Not with Creon closer than he'd been in weeks and yet so far, arcane magic and unwilling fae lords between us. I needed my sanity intact in this place, and these little arseholes weren't helping in the slightest.

Something told me Agenor might be unhappy if I blew up half of his forest, though. If he wanted to be rid of the pixies, he'd probably have handled it himself already.

So instead …

I groaned. Always be polite to nature, the Labyrinth had taught me.

'I've been told you like strawberries,' I said out loud.

They stayed silent.

'You'll have to speak a little louder for me to hear you,' I added, sticking my hands into the pockets of my dress. 'Or not, if you don't like strawberries after all. I might as well just eat them myself. They're pretty good ones – with cream and a bit of honey. But—'

'I like strawberries-strawberries!' a squeaky voice interrupted from the foliage.

I huffed. So now we were conversing, weren't we? 'You do?'

'I do-do!'

'Well.' I demonstratively hoisted my bag a little higher on my shoulders. 'So far you haven't really given me a reason to share them with you. Is that how you treat all your new friends in this place?'

'It was just a joke-joke,' the voice indignantly declared, and some muffled murmuring around me confirmed that. 'You humans-humans are always so *serious*.'

I decided not to tell them I'd love to jokingly smash their heads into a tree. 'Look, I've got some things to do on this particular morning, and I don't have time for jokes. But if we can come to an agreement on the strawberries, I hope that'll make up for the lost fun to you.'

Some more feverish murmuring. 'How many strawberries-strawberries?'

'Fifteen.'

That elicited some delighted cries. The first speaker hushed the others, then said, 'What is your name-name, human?'

'Emelin. Yours?'

'Irie-Irie.'

'Wonderful,' I said, which was a lie. 'Lovely to meet you, Irie-Irie.'

'No need to repeat it,' the pixie said, sounding annoyed. 'I heard you the first-first time. What do you want for your strawberries-strawberries?'

The subtleties of pixie linguistics were clearly escaping me entirely. Lyn would probably know more about them. Suppressing a groan of impatience, I said, 'I'll leave the strawberries here for you to eat, on the condition that you won't be harassing me again today. And if you keep that promise, I'll leave all my leftover food here for you when I return from my mission, too. I've got too much of it anyway.'

Irie – I assumed that was his name, then – contemplated that briefly. 'What other food-food do you have?'

'Do you like lemon cakes?'

Judging by the squeals, they did like lemon cakes. Irie, apparently a better negotiator than most of his company, prudently said, 'Lemon cakes-cakes are acceptable. What else?'

'Spinach pie?'

'Spinach-*spinach*?' He sounded mortally offended. 'What do you think we are-are, rabbits?'

I snorted. 'Amongst other things, yes.'

'What-what?'

'Never mind.' All of this nonsense was taking far too long. 'I'll give you the strawberries with cream now and lemon cakes when I come back, and in return you won't annoy me with your jokes for today. Is that a deal?'

A last flurry of frantic discussion around me, then Irie said, 'Deal-deal.'

So I untangled the lacing of my bag, cautiously extracted the bag of cream strawberries the fae cook had piled onto my generous provisions, and settled it on the mossy forest ground. 'Enjoy your meal.'

Nothing moved around me as I walked on, but as soon as I'd stepped between the next row of trees, the high-pitched snarling and screeching behind me suggested there were more than fifteen pixies to divide the treats amongst each other.

Good. Perhaps they'd be a little too busy to set traps for nearly innocent passers-by for a while.

The delay had only worsened the impatient itch in my feet. I walked faster now, following the outer line of the forest, staying just far enough between the trees not to be seen from the castle. Around me, the world dazzled in gold and green, drenched in the scent of pine resin and grass ... but I couldn't bring myself to stand still and admire the scenery, could barely bring myself to *notice* it.

How far could that damn gate be?

Finally I reached the cliffs at the south-east side of the island, where the last trees balanced dangerously on the protruding edges. Here I had no choice but to walk out in the open until I found the rocky stairs leading down to the gate bay ... but what were the chances someone would look this way, paying enough attention to notice one young woman from such a distance?

I decided to risk it. Once again, there wouldn't be a better moment.

Half-walking, half-running, I made my way along the jagged edge of the island, hair fluttering around my face in the salty sea breeze. Now, by daylight, I could see the waves breaking on the rocks beneath me, a steep fall of two dozen feet in some places. Perhaps it was for the best that it had been darker last night; I may not have dared to descend those slippery steps by just the light of Lyn's small fire, had I known what awaited me if I fell.

I'd survived it once before, though. So when the stairs finally loomed up before me, I sent Zera a quick prayer, pulled my bag more tightly against my back, and began to tiptoe down for the second time.

The water was indeed rising.

It was not yet as high as it had been last night, but the first waves were already brushing over the antechamber threshold, and the beach was hardly two feet broader than last time I'd seen it. No time to lose, then.

My boots were still a little soppy from my antechamber visit of last night. I didn't mind much; at least I didn't have to worry about ruining them even more as I hurried towards the gaping door in the cliff wall and stepped into the seaweed-and-algae stench of the room behind.

There was barely any water on the floor. Small drainage canals had been built in at the lowest points, valves preventing any sea water from seeping back. But even in a drier state, the room carried an air of weathered, faded glory, too shabby for the majestic gate of which the outlines were just visible in the dark rock.

Eight feet high and five feet broad. A weight that even strong men wouldn't easily push aside. I nudged the palm of my hand against the two doors nonetheless. Quite as expected, they didn't shift even a fraction.

I'd have to be cleverer, then.

I stepped back, folded my arms, and considered the structure. I could just let loose my magic and hope that would do. But I might permanently ruin something, leaving the castle with a wide open entrance just after it had declared war on the Mother herself. Or Korok may have anticipated such attempts … What if the wall sent all that red straight back into my face?

I probably shouldn't try. And then again … there *had* to be a way to open the thing. Little use having an escape route if no one could actually escape through it.

The Blood Gate.

I wouldn't have to sacrifice anyone to be allowed through, would I?

It's not as unpleasant as it sounds, Lyn had said. That *probably* excluded any sacrifices – good news for those damn pixies. What else might a god of life and death come up with to keep a castle safe? Something similar to the blood magic he'd given to the vampires?

What if that was all the gate needed – blood?

But no, that didn't make sense. I let out an annoyed huff. If it were as easy as pressing a bleeding hand against the stone, any idiot could walk into the castle whenever he wanted; in that case, Korok might as well not have closed the tunnel at all.

Unless, of course …

I narrowed my eyes as a new thought welled up. Unless *not* any idiot could walk in.

It would make sense if only a select company of trusted supporters would be able to sneak into those underground tunnels, wouldn't it? The castle would become far too vulnerable if everyone with the right magic trick or the right password could come in unchecked. So what if that was what Korok's blood magic did – identify people at the gate and allow only those with permission into the tunnel behind?

If that were the case, I had a problem. I doubted the magic had been designed to let little half fae with murderous intentions towards the Mother through.

Perhaps I needed to turn back and ask Lyn for help before I took any risks with divine magic. Not that Lyn would be able to do much if Creon and Agenor were the only ones at the Golden Court able to open—

Wait.

Agenor.

I stared at the gate, eyes widening as new thoughts rolled into my mind with avalanche force.

Agenor *could* open the gate, presumably. It would be odd for the Mother to deny one of her most trusted people access to this under-ground place. But if he could ... and if, as the name of the gate and the nature of Korok's magic suggested, it was his blood that enabled him to do so ...

Then wasn't that *my* blood, too?

Or was I going mad now?

He was my *father*. It didn't matter that he'd been absent for the first twenty years of my life. Didn't matter that I knew him about as well as I'd known the average passer-by on the streets of Ildhelm, or that I may not even like him that much. Blood was blood, and his should still be running through my veins.

Was it too much of a risk to take?

I was already opening my bag, digging under the layers of spinach pie and pumpkin casserole to find the dagger I'd put back in after my encounter with the green-haired fae female on the tower stairs. My heart cramped; I forced myself to let go of that memory. No undoing what I had done. All I could do now ...

I unsheathed the dagger, staring for a moment at the whetted white metal. Behind me, the first waves sloshed lazily over the threshold, splattering cold and wet over my calves.

Oh, damn it, then.

With a single resolved gesture, I slashed the blade across my left palm.

The knife edge was so sharp I didn't feel the pain for the first two, three moments, even as the blood pulsed from the cut in the rhythm of my heartbeat. Only as I stepped forward did the sting hit me, like piercing, ice-cold fire. I lowered the dagger with a muffled curse and pressed my bloody palm against the dark stone of the gate, wincing as the cold rock met the wound.

Heart pounding, hand throbbing, I waited.

Blood trickled over my wrist, my lower arm. The gate didn't budge. I pressed a little harder, and still nothing happened; I waited ten more heartbeats, my fingers growing cold against the icy layer of granite.

Well, fuck. That had been too optimistic.

I pulled back my hand, wincing again at the sight of my blood sticking to the stone. Time to heal myself and think a little harder, before the water rose so high I could no longer—

Before my eyes, my blood dissolved.

I stiffened.

Were my eyes deceiving me? No, that palm-shaped print I'd left on the gate was truly *shrinking*. As if the impenetrable stone was drinking in my sacrifice, absorbing the blood like a sponge. And as the last drop vanished ...

The gate creaked.

The stones shivered.

I stood frozen in my place, clenching my bleeding hand into a fist, as ever so slowly, the walls receded and the Blood Gate swung open, revealing a low and dimly lit tunnel cutting straight through the massive rock behind.

CHAPTER 25

I FORGOT ABOUT TIDES and time.

So what if the gate would be blocked in half an hour? So what if I had to spend the rest of the afternoon in this world below? I was *in*, and if Creon was here ...

Well. I could think of worse people to be locked in with.

I dashed inside without thinking, and the gate closed itself behind me with a thud like a coffin falling shut. Didn't matter – I'd probably manage to open it again, and if not, at least I had enough food to last a week. Someone would find me in that time.

So where should I start?

My aching hand stung for attention – ah, yes. Healing myself. I rested my left fingertips against the dark wall and quickly sparked some blue magic at the cut, then flexed my hand a few times to make sure the wound wouldn't start bleeding again. There was some pink scar tissue left behind, but I suspected that would fade soon enough.

With the dagger in my bag and my bag on my shoulders again, I started walking.

This dusky tunnel looked nothing like the Labyrinth, with its abundance of colour and irregular shapes. It was all vaulted ceilings and sharp corners, lit by nothing but the glowing glass orbs of the fae-lights every twenty feet. The walls were dark, but with an odd, almost scale-like texture to them – reminiscent, I realised, of Oleander's ink-black skin.

I shivered. A snake god, indeed.

Nothing else moved down here; at every bend, I heard my own footsteps echo back at me. Still, I paused when I finally reached the first door in that scaled black wall and threw five looks down either side of the corridor before I dared to pull it open a chink.

The room beyond contained piles and piles of blankets. Judging by the layer of dust on the finely woven wool, no one had used them for a while.

An emergency cellar. How many people could take shelter here with the castle under attack?

The next room contained candles and small burners and kettles; the third was filled to the ceiling with wooden barrels, probably storing beer or water. All very sensible, and I'd be grateful if I ever found myself in need of a safe hideaway ... but for now, every single one of these rooms mostly contained an annoying lack of fae princes.

The rest of the corridor was empty. I walked on, ignored a collapsed side passage, and found a new row of doors around the next bend. Most of them looked similar to those I'd left behind, but one ...

One had a lock on it.

A *lock*.

I fell into a trot, heart suddenly racing. It was a simple lock, no alf steel, only iron. Which meant I could get past it. It had been one of Creon's first assignments – *Open a lock without destroying it.*

Had he written that list with the potential for rescue missions in mind, or had these tricks simply been at the forefront of his thoughts as he was making his own travel plans?

Didn't matter. I laid my fingers against the dark brown wood, drawing out the yellow as I held my right hand against the iron lock. The metal turned pliable and elastic under my magic, and when I yanked at the handle, the door slid open without so much as a creak.

Before me – a prison.

Oh, gods help me.

The largest detention house I'd ever seen was the one in Miss Matilda's town on Ildhelm, which boasted a grand total of two cells; on the rare occasion of a tavern fight, the drunks were simply piled atop each other until they sobered up. But *this* place ... Iron bars and chains and so many thick wooden doors that the farthest ones weren't even visible by the light of the single glowing orb above the entrance.

Enough room to lock half an army. But in times of peace ... how many of these cells could be occupied?

I sucked in a breath and loudly said, 'Anyone here?'

Dusty silence whirled back at me.

And then – sharp and unmistakable – a knock.

Just that single sound, like the blow of a knuckle against wood, yet it was enough to send my heart thumping in my chest. Sound. And not a *voice*. Which meant ...

'Creon?' I was going to faint. Already the light was flickering before my eyes, dark spots storming me on the edges of my sight. 'Is that you? One for no, two for yes.'

A knock. And then another.

Gods save my poor rattling heart.

'If you're anyone else trying to mess with me, I might just kill you,' I announced, dashing in the direction of that sound. Hell, there were multiple aisles, too – had Korok planned to lock half the populace of the archipelago below the earth? 'Where are you? Keep making sounds.'

Four knocks, then silence. Four? I hurried towards the fourth door to my left, stumbling over my own soggy boots, and pressed my right hand against the heavy iron lock. The surge of yellow magic I sent into the metal was far too strong; the iron didn't only turn elastic, but grew fuzzy and velvety soft too.

Someone breathed an audible chuckle behind that door.

'Oh, for fuck's sake,' I said, swinging it open so violently it banged into the wall with enough force to break a skull.

He was laughing as I stumbled to a halt in his cell – full, honest laughter, shaking his shoulders and revealing the creases around the corners of his eyes even in the muted light of the gleaming ceiling orbs. And at once, it no longer mattered how dark this cell was. How narrow that bed, how thick those alf steel chains around his wrists. He could have been sitting in the middle of a battlefield and I would have seen nothing but him – nothing but his undamaged face and his unbloodied limbs and the unexpected brightness of the twinkle in his eyes.

Air rushed from my lungs, and it felt like releasing a breath I'd held for four straight weeks. 'For the bloody gods' sakes – *Creon.*'

His grin broadened as he raised an ink-scarred hand, his gestures just a little slower than usual with the chains impeding his movements. *Less than twenty-four hours? I'm impressed.*

'Oh, you idiot!' I staggered half a step forward, then faltered, limbs unable to reach a decision – should I throw myself into his arms or punch him in the face? 'You weren't going to get in trouble, you said! You weren't going to be reckless! And now I have to come pull you out of some fucking fae cell straight below the bloody Golden Court itself? As if I didn't save your life often enough yet?'

He still hadn't stopped laughing. *Thought you were interested in the rewards for that sort of thing?*

'Piss off! You might have been dead!' And instead he was here, looking far more alluring, far more *alive* than any male in captivity had a right to – even those stark chains around his wrists merely emphasising the powerful lines of the muscles below, the sober grimness of this cell an echo of the magic shimmering off him. 'And wipe that grin off your face!'

Can't. Too good to hear your voice again. He shoved to the edge of the bed – barely more than an upgraded wooden bench – and stretched out his left hand as far as the chain allowed, muscular forearm bulging under the alf steel cuff. *Especially if your first sentence is a murder threat. Come here.*

I snorted. 'Say please?'

Five more heartbeats without you and I'll tragically succumb to my desperate longing, Em.

'That's not please,' I said, jumping out of reach as he gave a yank at his chain. Power flushed through me, a familiar thrill of excitement that had left the Underground in his wake. 'And don't you agree you're still suspiciously eloquent for a male on the brink of succumbing?'

He fell back against the wall, lips twitching, free hand dropping back to the bed in a sign of surrender. *Need you. Please.*

Gods help me. I flung myself into his arms.

The chains clunked and rattled as he pulled me into his lap and squashed me against his chest, fingers digging so tightly into my shoulders that I yelped, lips brushing against the crown of my head. And at once I was home. As if he'd never left. As if I'd never been furious and heartbroken. Four weeks of absence were instantly reduced to the faintest of bad memories – safe in his arms, wrapped in his scent, I could have gone through the same thing ten times over for just the unimaginable reassurance of his presence.

'Creon …'

He buried his face in the hollow of my neck, kissed my shoulder just above my collar, and held me tighter.

'Please say you're alright,' I whispered into his shirt. He *felt* alright – oddly alright, for a male who may have survived a violent confrontation mere hours ago – but I didn't dare to be sure until I had his word for it. In threefold. In writing, confirmed by two witnesses. 'Are you hurt? Injured? Anything?'

His finger found my chin and tipped up my head so I could watch his gestures. *I'm fine, Em. Better than I've been in a while, frankly.*

'Better? You're sitting in a dungeon!'

A blissfully deserted dungeon with no one to hate me. A new grin grew on his face. It was too bright once again – the shadows in his eyes gone, the hard lines of his jaw mellowed a fraction, the hard, tormented edge to his power no longer so rough and razor-sharp. *I'd consider it a short vacation, really.*

'Gods have mercy.' I sagged sideways against his chest, unable to suppress my laughter. That *smile* – I might have given up my firstborn child to see that smile again. 'Did I tell you what an utterly dramatic person you are, Creon? "I'm not feeling too well, best go sit in an actual bloody dungeon to calm down a little!" Suppose I should be grateful you didn't—'

Am I allowed to conclude you're alright, too? he dryly interrupted.

I huffed. 'I'm first of all furious.'

You aren't.

'I'm absolutely enraged, and it's bad form to accuse a lady of lying, Your Highness. Where are the courtly manners?'

Ah. He ran his gaze over me in a manner that made me feel quite un-ladylike and quite incapable of objecting. *It's Emelin Thenessa, daughter of Agenor's house, then?*

I stiffened. 'Wait, you ... what?'

Creon just raised a scarred eyebrow, that expression that never failed to make me feel both acutely ready for violence and painfully aroused.

'When ... when in hell did you figure that out?'

Roughly the moment the bastard walked in on me admiring his highly illegal alf steel hoard. He gestured at the world behind me – another room down here, hiding more dangerous secrets? *His eyes are the spitting image of yours.*

I blinked. 'And you never realised that before?'

It may surprise you, he gestured, a flicker of a smile on his lips, *but I never spent that much time gazing lovingly into his eyes.*

'Well,' I said blankly, 'I suppose that's good news.'

He let out a silent laugh. *And then the other pieces fell into place. Your name. Some odd behaviour he was displaying twenty-one years ago. His presence near a pile of alf steel that the Crimson Court most definitely doesn't know about or approve of.*

'And that's when he captured you? When he found you down here?'

Creon shrugged. *I allowed him to capture me.*

'Why would you ... Oh, hell.' Some pieces fell into place. 'Because you figured out he was my father?'

Had to do some quick thinking. He rested his head against the wall, fingers not faltering. *I could have fought, would have won. But with the magic he wields ... Damage control is a challenge at that level. The chances were great it would escalate to deadly violence, and he might be the only person who could answer your questions.*

Answer my questions. Not the only person who could claim the Golden Court for the resistance, not a powerful ally in our fight against the Mother – just the male I would very much like to have a few words with before someone put him below the ground.

I swallowed hard. 'He could have killed you on the spot.'

He's not that kind, Creon signed with a shrug. *Haven't seen him made a reckless decision in my lifetime. If he was going to kill me, he would think about it first. And since he knew about that alf steel, I could only conclude I had been oddly wrong in my assumption he was one of her most loyal supporters, which suggested he wouldn't hand me over to the Crimson Court either. So it was a pretty safe bet.*

'A safe ...' My voice cracked. 'That's not a safe bet, you fool! He could have thought about it and killed you two days later!'

He couldn't, Creon pleasantly corrected me, *because by that time you'd be here to stop him.*

I stared at him. 'You've gone mad.'

He flashed me a grin.

'Why would you possibly assume that I would actually manage to—'

A shrug. *You're here.*

'You couldn't know that!'

Of course I could. You're brilliant like that.

'I ... Oh, you *prick*.' Somehow, missing him and worrying about him, I'd forgotten just how impressively infuriating he could be. 'You can't just start using compliments as arguments! How am I supposed to refute those?'

He chuckled. *You're not supposed to. You're supposed to tell me I'm right and a genius and also coincidentally the single most beautiful specimen you've ever seen walk around on the surface of the earth, and I'll humbly refrain from further arguing my point.*

If his chains and the sheer weight of all that bloody muscle hadn't stopped me, I would have shoved him off the bed. 'You're really feeling better, aren't you?'

Infinitely better. He grimaced. *Not that the Underground set the bar very high. But I'm doing ... surprisingly fine.*

'No more pits of self-hate?'

He shook his head.

'Nightmares?'

A shrug. *Nothing worse than usual.*

My heart was speeding up, pounding with something that was both hope and fear. 'Does that mean ...' Please. *Please* let that be what it meant. 'Does that mean you'd feel better about Naxi's help, too? If you got all the hate out of your system and ... and ...'

For one infinite moment, my unfinished question hung fragile and lethal in the air between us. His smile froze, then dwindled – a clearer answer than any motions of his fingers could ever provide.

The bubble of hope deflated, with what felt like a physical tug at my midriff.

Em. He tightened beneath me, as if to brace himself against the assault of my feelings. The alf steel didn't stop his demon senses, then? Just his active magic? *Let's talk about that later. I need to get out of this cell first.*

Out of his cell ... and then where would he go? Not back to the Underground. Not back to any place with enemies or dubious allies around, for that matter. Which meant I had the choice to either join him in this unsafe world above or spend a great many nights more in his absence, neither of which—

His hand tensed on my waist, tearing me from my frantic thoughts. *I said later, cactus. I'm not out yet.*

The sight of that nickname made me feel like crying and kissing him at once, dragging my memory straight back to the Underground library, straight back to our many illicit meetings in his bedroom. It took two deep breaths to get myself back under control.

'Fine, all-knowing genius.' I shifted off his lap and pulled my knees to my chest, throwing a quick glance at the deserted prison aisle outside. 'Tell me how we're going to get you out of this place, then. There's a lot of colour here, at least – can't destroy alf steel with magic, but I could probably dig a hole in the wall and smuggle you out that way?'

I strongly suggest you don't, he signed, grimacing.

'Why not?'

Divine magic. He nodded at the wall with its uneven, scaly texture. *I'm a little fuzzy on the details, but I know for sure the walls of the castle are drenched with protective powers. Very likely that these tunnels are also somehow fortified. Lyn and Tared had enough trouble breaking them down during the War.*

I considered that. 'But they did manage in the end.'

They weren't sitting on the inside to enjoy the consequences.

'Alright, alright.' I suppressed a curse. That was an annoyingly convincing argument. 'I could steal Agenor's key? I suspect it's one of the three he wears around his neck, so perhaps if I play the loving daughter very convincingly ...'

He pursed his lips, looking unhappier than I'd expected at the prospect of freedom. *He'll be very damn displeased if you start stealing from him on your first day in his company. You'd be better off just talking sense into him than making an enemy out of him.*

'I tried talking sense into him,' I said bitterly, 'and so far it's done exactly nothing useful. You could be sitting here for years if we let your freedom depend on his plans.'

Creon shrugged. *He likes to exaggerate. It would be a couple of months at most, probably.*

'Do you even hear yourself? You could be sitting here for *months!*'

There was not nearly enough alarm in the way the corners of his eyes wrinkled as he sent me that unburdened smile again – as if it was a hilarious prospect, spending ages in some cell an eternity away from the civilised world. *I'll be fine, Em. Honestly, this place is a lot easier to handle than the court itself.*

'You ...'

Words escaped me for a few dazed heartbeats. He would be fine. *He would be fine.* And so he wouldn't even try to arrange an escape out of this hole? He'd just send me after Agenor to save his life yet again, and then he'd ... wait?

His smile stiffened as the unexpected deluge of emotions washed over me – a messy tangle of disbelief, disappointment, and most disconcerting of all, an unmistakable spark of fury. *Em—*

'You're going to sit here for months to avoid everyone's feelings again?' My voice cracked. I was sitting in that dark Underground corridor, talking to an unmoving door, carrying the weight of his life on my shoulders – such an impossible weight – and the words blurred together as they tumbled over my lips. 'Is that what you're saying? Because we did that before, Creon. *I* did that before, and if I have to solve this all on my own again – if you—'

His left hand locked around my chin.

The raw strength of his fingers was so familiar, the pressure of his grasp so demanding, that my rising voice caught in the back of my throat. My tongue froze. My mouth snapped shut. I clenched my jaw, breathing heavily, and glared at him with as much dignity as I could muster – not much, with my thoughts in a tangle and my tirade reduced to directionless mumbles.

Still, glaring at him was the only way not to feel the tears stinging behind my eyes.

Everything was supposed to have been better after this damn trip. He was supposed to have come back. He was supposed to have been *mine.* And instead ... instead, we were right back where we'd started, those unchecked demon powers still holding him captive in entirely new ways.

I drew in an unsteady, shivering breath. His fingers on my jaw loosened.

Emelin, his lips said.

And there were the tears after all, burning down my cheeks despite my best attempts to hold them back, doing away with my last illusions of composure. 'I ... I just hoped ...'

Damn it, Em. He released my chin and hooked his arm around my waist, dragging me against his rock-hard body. The cold weight of his chain lay heavy against the small of my back; his breath brushed over the crown of my head, too fast and agitated. *I'm terrible at this entire concept of being cared about.*

I produced a sound that was half-sob, half-chuckle. 'I really am happy you're doing better! It's not ...'

I know. A joyless chuckle into my hair. *Don't worry. Your feelings speak for themselves. It's just that your thoughts are still a mystery to me at times.*

'There's nothing mysterious about me,' I mumbled, sniffing. 'I just miss you, you idiot.'

Very mysterious to me.

'Oh, hell.' I slouched against his shoulder, keeping my eyes on his fingers. 'You really assumed I'd be perfectly fine going another year without you?'

His breath faltered for a moment, and I could hear the retort even though his fingers remained motionless. What else was he supposed to think, when I'd made such a point of keeping my heart out of whatever went on between us?

This may not be the moment to tell him I'd hopelessly lost that fight.

I assumed ... His signs came more slowly now, a cautiousness that suggested he was holding back words as much as I was. *I assumed some of the others would be around to help you with all of this. Are they not?*

'Yes, yes, they are.' I pulled away from him with a mirthless laugh. 'But Lyn is trying to keep the peace and save Agenor from the consequences of his own stupid actions, because of course she's jumping on the chance to save another tormented bastard from himself ...'

He grimaced. *Of course.*

'... and Tared is pissed about everything Agenor does, but I doubt he loathes him enough to start caring about you only to make a point. So it's just me. And since Agenor is convinced you're some dastardly villain and I'm a witless five-year-old who's fallen prey to your lies ...'

One out of two correct, Creon dryly signed. *He's had worse days.*

It would have been funnier if not for the violet-eyed female still staring at me in my mind's eye, if not for the lingering fear that perhaps Agenor wasn't all wrong to distrust my judgement. 'I ... I don't think I can do any of this alone, honestly.'

There's very little you couldn't do on your own. He sagged against the wall, fingers absently clenching into a fist and unclenching again. Something about my outburst seemed to have brought him further off balance than the chains around his wrist or the prospect of months of captivity. *But I didn't realise ...*

That I'd still miss him, even after weeks of less volatile company? That I'd still want him?

He didn't finish the sentence.

'I need you to escape this place,' I said, my voice wobbling. 'I need you to help me.' *And then I need you to stay and stop running.* A premature request, presumably, if I didn't even know how long it would take for him to manage those first two steps – if he even *could* manage those first two steps. What if he stepped out of this cell and promptly collapsed under the emotions of Agenor's people, who likely weren't too fond of him either?

It's not that I don't want you to break me out of this cell, Em. He sat straighter, drawing in a deep breath. *If that's what you prefer, please go ahead. You'll do a glorious job of it. But ...*

'I'll make enemies if I resort to stealing and violence,' I finished, forcing the words out.

Yes.

Which wouldn't make matters easier for either of us, and Agenor and Tared would probably hold a fierce contest to see who could blame Creon most of all.

I muttered a curse.

I can help you figure out how to get through to Agenor, he added, signing the words faster now, more desperately. *It might be more doable than you think. Even if he doesn't value your opinions of the world as much as he should, he'll probably worry about your opinion of him personally. He'd handle it very poorly if his own daughter loathed the sight of him.*

I scoffed. 'He's not off to a great start, in that case.'

There was a touch of wry amusement to his grin. *Talk to him, Em. See how far you get. Just make sure he doesn't figure out this ... thing between us.* His wings sagged a fraction at the hesitation, a sign so small I was sure it was unintentional. *He's not going to be pleased about it.*

'As a good rebellious daughter,' I muttered, 'that sounds like an excellent reason to be found half-naked and covered in seed in your cell.'

He burst out laughing, that tremble of wistfulness gone at once. *More than happy to assist when the time comes. Think you could pick a more scandalous setting, though.*

Oh, gods. Four weeks of separation had done exactly nothing to soften the sting of arousal that burned through me at the slightest provocation, the abrupt awareness of his arm wrapped securely around my waist. I nestled myself tighter against his solid body, glancing up at him with more innocence than the sensation of his nearness evoked in me, and muttered, 'Hmm. His study?'

Creon snorted. *There are some body parts I'd rather keep away from those damn snakes.*

The vision of Coral confronting a naked fae prince on Agenor's study couch had me giggling like an idiot, no matter how hard I tried to hold back. 'Castle wall? Gardens? His dinner table?'

More promising, he signed, lips taut with suppressed laughter. *Could also just throw some feathers and candlewax around, of course. That would give him something to think about.*

I really shouldn't entertain this game for a moment longer. Not while he was a prisoner and I a trespasser, not while he might still leave me as soon as he was free again. But my body flared hot at the images his fingers were painting, Creon's eyes went dark in response, and whatever self-control I'd thought I possessed went hurtling out of the figurative window.

'From that perspective,' I said, smiling sweetly at him, 'these chains are quite promising, aren't they?'

He cocked his head at me, a siren's call in the depths of his eyes. *Do I hear any pleasant plans there?*

Not the right moment. Not a wise idea. And yet … 'What if I was planning to be unpleasant instead?'

He chuckled. *Sounds tempting.*

Oh, damn him – so this was a challenge now, wasn't it? There was a game to be won now? My common sense followed my self-restraint out of the window as I climbed back into his lap, all aching uncertainty forgotten, and straddled him. 'I don't think you'll be smirking like that when I make a true effort at cruelty, Your Highness.'

Would love to see you try. Every twitch of his fingers was a provocation. His lips parted, and my eyes abruptly decided there was nothing in the world worth focusing on but that sensual mouth of his, the tip of his tongue sliding along his bottom lip in a wordless invitation. *Shall we see who's begging for mercy first?*

Zera help me. I shouldn't be defeated this easily, not after this loaded conversation full of unspoken words, not in a bloody fae cell of all places ... but I'd missed this far too much, equal against equal, the sizzling rivalry quickening the blood in my veins. And he was just *asking* for it now, wasn't he?

'What do I get when I win?' My voice had gone rough.

If, he corrected me smugly.

'When.' I drew my finger down over his chest, crossing the hard ridges of his muscles, holding his gaze. Hell below, the dark fire burning in his eyes ... I hadn't been the only one suffering in his absence. 'What do I get?'

Me, he signed with exaggerated slowness, *kneeling.*

There was no need to respond; my body spoke in my place, warmth flushing through every fibre of me at the vision of his winged form before me, hands worshipping me, tongue ... oh, gods. I drew a laugh over my lips, too husky and breathless, and managed, 'Kneeling? You? The most beautiful specimen to ever have walked the earth?'

His eyes flashed, but he didn't react to the taunting. *However, if you lose ...*

'I can kneel,' I said, perhaps a little too quickly.

I know. The shameless suggestion in his gaze sent my breath hitching. *But since you started this war, I feel you deserve some higher stakes. If you lose, you're the one in chains next time.*

Fuck. The soft, molten warmth at my core became a vicious sting of heat, arousal sharp enough that, for a moment, I considered handing over my pride and the coveted victory before we could even start this game. But damn him, that was just what he wanted, and I hadn't moved heaven and earth to find him just so I could melt at his feet at the first battle of wills.

'Deal,' I muttered. 'Prepare to suffer a blistering defeat, then.'

He breathed a laugh. *You seem to forget I've been trained to endure worse than your touches.*

'Ah, yes.' I scrambled back into his lap, making my unwise decision in a heartbeat. 'I suppose that is true. But ...'

Creon didn't move or react as I slid off his thighs, back onto my own feet, only his predator gaze following my every motion as I leaned over to kiss the pointed tip of his ear. His body was hard as a statue below me, every sharp edge and taut muscle honed for survival. His hands lay on either side of him, fingers tense against the hard wooden surface of the bed.

'The question is,' I whispered, brushing my lips over his silky skin, 'how well you'll survive the *absence* of my touch.'

He stiffened.

Then grabbed for me.

But I'd prepared, anticipated the inhuman speed of his motions, and jumping out of reach was infinitely easier with the alf steel chains constricting his reach. I danced back, holding his gaze, unable to help the dangerous grin that settled around my lips. 'Can't run away from me this time, can you?'

He closed his eyes for the briefest of moments as he leaned forward, elbows on his knees, muscles bulging at his wrists and shoulders. *Getting farther away from you is hardly what I need right now, viper.*

Warmth spiralled down my core at that single dangerous word, *need*, and he sucked in an audible breath.

'You should be a little more careful,' I muttered, 'saying such terribly enticing things. You'll only make it worse for yourself.'

His lips parted a fraction. *I doubt you need my help imagining all kinds of terrible things.*

'I had four weeks to imagine the most terrible of things,' I reminded him, sinking down against the wall beside the door. Even through my skirt, the stone floor was viciously cold against my burning thighs. 'Which, believe me, I did. The nights were long and lonely, and a girl needs her dreams. Want to hear more about them?'

He tensed, dark and menacing in the dim glow of the faelights. An *excellent* tension. I smiled sweetly, nudging my thighs apart a few inches, and his wings shuddered behind his shoulders.

Em. The movement of his lips didn't look particularly hopeful.

'I thought of you so much in that bloody library.' I trailed my fingertips over my bare left arm and watched him shiver as the tingling sensation hit both of us simultaneously. 'It's so damn quiet there, you see. I've wondered once or twice if anyone would hear if you were to fuck me against the bookcases while they were working downstairs.'

His eyes were pools of ink between his long lashes, narrowed so that his sharp cheekbones became knife slashes across his face. I leisurely ran my fingers across my chest, my belly, hunger trembling through my skin in their wake; his gaze followed the motions of my hand with primal focus, like a predator about to strike.

A *caged* predator about to strike.

'And then there's the alf homes.' Parting my thighs another few inches, I brushed a caress over the soft skin on the inside, making no effort to hide my own shallow breathing. I could *see* it now, with him close and gorgeous before me – those vengeful visions that had carried me through the longest of evenings, past the worst of their insults. 'Every single time they mentioned you, every single time they scoffed at you, I imagined how you'd take me over their dinner tables as soon as they were gone.' Imagined how I'd scramble for grip on the weathered wood as he pounded into me, imagined how his hand would clutch over my mouth, smothering my desperate moans in the silence of the night ... Intoxicating lust washed over me, and Creon gritted his teeth on the other side of the cell, wrists straining against the merciless steel of his chains.

'It really is a shame,' I muttered, hitching up my skirt to my hips, 'that I had to make do with my fingers all this time. Such a setback when one is used to pretty fae princes.'

Creon let out a rough laugh. *This pretty fae prince wouldn't mind helping you out.*

'Say please?'

He demonstratively clenched his fists.

'Shame.' I tugged my underwear aside with a single probing finger, finding my flesh slick below the linen. 'Hope you enjoy the view, in that case.'

His fingers locked around the edge of the bed as he watched me, lips a tight line, eyes half-lidded – watched my fingertip swirl through my pooling wetness, flick over the delicate bundle of nerves where my lips met. A moan escaped me, and he tensed against his chains, wings spreading wide as the last of his restraint evaporated.

'I *would* kneel for you, you know.' Slow, lazy circles around that most sensitive spot, driving up the heat pulsing through my veins until it pounded like a heartbeat in my ears. 'I missed the taste of you.' Musky, earthy, an undertone of sweetness; I could taste it at the thought alone. 'Missed the weight of your cock on my tongue.'

He let out a slow breath. *Come and get it, then.*

I brushed a fingertip over my drenched entrance and chuckled at his hiss. 'No.'

Very sure? His free hand lifted to his crotch, started loosening the tight buttons with snappish yanks. *We can both play that game.*

Zera help me. His cock jutted thick and greedy from his dark trousers, a reminder of all I was missing. He palmed himself, hard flesh quivering at the first pump of his scarred fingers – such a gods-damned tantalising quiver, and for the first time, my resolve wavered.

A wicked grin slid across his face as he looked up to meet my eyes.

'Don't you dare,' I breathed, my mouth dry with want. 'I'll take cruel and bloody revenge.'

He chuckled, stroking himself to the rhythm of my own circling fingers. *Good luck with that when I chain you up.*

Oh, damn the smug arrogance on his face. Never mind about the doubt, then. Never mind about that glorious cock of his luring me closer, a first drop of moisture pearling at the tip. He could stick his illusions of invincibility up somewhere else – I was aggravated enough to be cruel even to myself if it would secure the victory.

'You're not chaining me up before you get out of this place.' I held his gaze as I raised my hand and slowly, leisurely, licked my fingers clean.

'And if you don't let go of that pretty murder weapon you're holding right *now*, I'll be out of this cell without touching you again today.'

His eyes flashed. His left hand faltered around his shaft. *And who'd suffer most from that?*

I sent him a wolfish grin. 'Oh, we'll see.'

He knew I was serious. He could *sense* I was serious. And as much as he wanted to win this bet ...

Slowly, with obvious reluctance, his fingers folded open, baring all of that bronzed erection to my gaze. A throaty laugh escaped me, and he gripped the edge of the bed again without bothering to cover up.

I returned my attention to the slick flesh between my thighs, stroking and brushing. His cock jolted as pleasure coiled through me; his knuckles drew pale as his hands tensed up.

'This could be so much more satisfying for both of us,' I reminded him, every caress twice as enjoyable for the sight of his unravelling restraint. 'All you have to do is ask me nicely, Creon. I promise I'll take very good care of you to soften the sting of the defeat.'

A muscle twitched in his sharp jaw. *We could declare it a draw.*

'Or,' I suggested sweetly, 'we couldn't.'

He wetted his lips, his grin closer to a grimace. *Em ...*

'And don't wait too long.' The last word trailed off in half a moan. 'I might be done soon, you see.'

Don't you dare, he signed with cramped fingers, lips curling up in a sneer of restraint, *or I—*

I slipped my finger in half an inch, yelping as my muscles contracted around that first digit. And perhaps it was that sound. Perhaps it was the pleasure his demon senses felt blaze through me or the sight of me on that prison floor, rumpled and on the verge of breaking. With one last yank at his chains, he gave in, sagged back against the wall with a shivering sigh and signed, *Please.*

I stilled, body twitching under my fingertip. 'What was it you said there?'

You little monster. The corners of his lips were straining, equal parts pained grimace and suppressed laughter. *Please. You win. Just ...*

My knees were unsteady when I scrambled to my feet. His cock stood straight from his dark trousers, a beacon luring me closer. 'Just?'

Take what you want. His hand fell down on the bed beside him, but his lips added, *Please.*

'Well,' I muttered, stepping out of my underwear so quickly it was a miracle I didn't stumble and break my neck, 'if you're asking so politely ...'

He didn't move as I came within his reach, his eyes following my every motion with feral hunger. Didn't move as I straddled him, my slender thighs over his muscular ones. Waited, still motionless, as I brushed a loose lock from his forehead, tucking it carefully behind his pointed ear.

But a soundless curse escaped him as I curled my fingers around the base of his shaft, and his eyes fluttered shut at the first slow stroke upwards.

I should take longer – savouring the silky hardness of him against my palm, eliciting more of those quiet moans from his lips. But every jolt sent twangs of painful arousal searing through me, and the gods knew it had been a long four weeks ...

I lowered myself onto him.

The first touch was enough to make me gasp, his thick head pressing against the tightness of my slit with a weight not even the liveliest of daydreams had remembered. My body twitched and throbbed around him as I sank farther down, his girth stretching me open all over again, filling me so much better than my fingers ever could ... Deeper. *Deeper.* I clawed my nails into his shoulders and took him in, watching his eyes go glazed, watching his wings draw taut, until every gorgeous inch of him was inside me and it took all I had not to whimper at the delightful sensation of fullness, of *rightness.*

'Creon.' His name was a moan. 'Touch me.'

His hands were on me before I could blink, slipping below my dress, grasping my bottom with a ferocity that made me whimper. He grinned and clawed his way up my body, claiming my hips, my waist as if to commit every dip and curve to memory – as if to make sure not an inch of me would ever forget his touch. I came up on my knees again, and he yanked me back down hard enough that all thought rushed from my mind for a single blissful moment.

I was fire under his hands, fire and madness, and not a soul in the world would ever dare to hurt me.

Strong hands on my hips, he lifted me effortlessly, then pulled me down as he thrust up and filled me so brusquely that an irrepressible cry tore from my lips. And again. And again. The world blurred to shreds of sensations around me. Hard wood under my knees. Cold air on my skin. Calloused fingers digging into my body, ruthless cock taking possession of me, and his inhumanly beautiful face before me, lips curled back in a sneer of insatiable need.

'I ...' Another rough thrust. Another surge of bone-shattering pleasure. My brain no longer managed to string words into sentences. 'Creon ... going to ... *break* ...'

With a devilish gleam in his eyes, he slipped one hand over my bottom, parted the cheeks, and brushed a finger over the tight hole between as he plunged into me again.

It was too much.

I snapped like a string drawn tight. Release barrelled through me and took the last of my sanity with it, hurtled me into a void in which nothing existed but his name on my lips – nothing but his long, deep strokes as he fucked me, driving me over the edge again and again and again.

When I became aware of my own limbs again, they were shaking, drained of all strength and life in that glorious eruption of madness. 'Creon ...'

He lifted me, cock slipping out of me, and wrapped his arms around me. The sting of cold alf steel on my skin brought me back to life – enough, at least, for my mind to become aware of its own existence again.

'Creon.' I may not be saying anything else for the next hour or two. 'Creon ... you ... oh, gods.'

A silent chuckle shook his chest as he turned me with his left hand, positioning me where I could see the motions of his right. *Don't think the gods would have done it better.*

I snorted, haze gone at once. 'Arrogant bastard.'

Complaints?

'No,' I grumbled. 'Don't forget I won.'

You certainly won. The twinkle in his eyes suggested he didn't mind too much. *I think I recall some promise to take good care of me. Do you want me to plead for that, too?*

His cock was prodding my thigh, still hard as steel and glistening with the evidence of my pleasure. How he'd managed not to come five times over in that moment of excruciating bliss, I'd probably never know.

'Hmm.' I rubbed my thumb over the rim until he winced. 'Perhaps I'll be merciful and set the right example. After all ...' I slipped off his lap, between his knees, and flicked my tongue over the tip. 'At least this won't leave too much of a mess. Can hardly return to dinner with Agenor with seed stains on my dress *before* you're free.'

He released a rough laugh. *I'm trying very damn hard not to make that part of the allure, Em.*

'What – that you're fucking his daughter while he has you chained up here?' I pressed two slow kisses to his shaft, the satin skin taut under my lips, and looked up to watch him squirm. 'Please make it part of the allure. May help me to not do something reckless and try to free you anyway.'

Don't bother. A grin. *If these are the terms of my captivity ...*

I kissed his tip, then parted my lips to allow him in. Muffled around his hard flesh, I muttered, 'Not sick of your chains yet, then?'

A sharp hiss was my only answer.

I took him deeper, flicking my tongue over his scorching flesh, revelling in the taste of him – so close to the scent of his body, but heavier, headier, and somehow ten times as masculine. Pulling back, I wrapped both my hands around his base, following the rhythm of my lips as I sucked and licked and kissed.

He raked his fingers through my hair as I worked him, gathering my locks in a messy bun on the back of my head. His hands steered me without words, moving me faster, harder. The taste and scent of him filled my nose, my mouth, my throat as he thrust into me, and I gave in to the demands of his cock and fingers, gave in to the twisted delight of that thought ... The Silent Death himself, fucking Agenor's newfound daughter's throat.

The dangerous thrill of it almost sent me shattering again.

He came within moments, his tightening hands my only warning – thrust forward one last time and filled my mouth with musky flesh and warm seed, drowning me in the taste of pleasure. I swallowed that first surge and kept going until the last drop was spent and he finally softened between my lips.

Still holding my hair, he pulled me back up, into a kiss that tasted of devotion and power and endless midsummer nights.

I wrapped my arms around him. Curled against his chest without breaking our kiss and waited for him to settle back against the wall, where he could fold his wings over his chains and close them carefully around me.

I wanted to tell him I was home.

Wanted to tell him I loved him so madly, so deeply, that it felt like the force of my feelings alone could break this prison to pieces.

But the last time I'd told him, he'd run – had left me behind rather than face those damned powers he still couldn't control. What reason did I have to believe he'd choose differently next time?

So I buried my face against his chest, unable to stop feeling, unable to stop this stupid heart of mine from wishing for something he might never be able to do, and merely whispered, 'I'm glad I found you.'

CHAPTER 26

IT TOOK SEVERAL HOURS before I dared to trust that high tide had passed; we ate spinach pie and pumpkin casserole in the meantime and discussed all Creon knew about Agenor's time in the Mother's service as her negotiator, strategist, and altogether unpleasantly devoted servant. By the time we'd covered three centuries of courtly gossip, I was quite sure the Blood Gate should be accessible again.

'I'll be back tomorrow,' I said as I hoisted my bag onto my shoulders, the weight far easier to bear with only the lemon cakes for the pixies left. 'Unless I don't manage to sneak out unnoticed, but I'll try. Don't panic, in any case.'

He raised an amused eyebrow. *I have more faith in you than that, Em.*

An unwise amount of faith, really, but I decided not to tell him that much. It would likely start another round of pleasant discussion, and who knew when Agenor's people would return to check on him?

So I repaired the iron lock, kissed him a last time and then a *very* last time, and closed the cell door behind me as I left.

As if I was locking him up all over again.

The water stood inches below the gate when I stepped out. I took off my boots, waded out and into the bay, and only put them back on when I'd safely reached the narrow stairs back up the cliff. No fae stood waiting for me. It seemed I had indeed escaped the Golden Court's notice, at least for this single excursion.

Irie and his company found me within minutes after I entered the forest and promised they'd let me through another time if I brought them more strawberries with cream. I reached the castle gates unharmed and triumphant, mind already spinning to figure out how I'd escape the watching eyes tomorrow.

Agenor sat waiting for me.

It took me a moment too long to notice him between the dazzling colours and the twisting vines and the guards swarming around the antechamber. For a powerful mage with a snake in his lap, he was uncannily inconspicuous, watching the routine movements of his people without comment or interruption. But he moved the moment the gate fell shut behind me, lowering Coral to the floor with an apologetic gesture, and then I could hardly pretend I hadn't seen him and run off to hide below my bed for the rest of the day.

Where did that unreasonable sting of panic even come from? I'd faced worse. And I *had* to face him, if I wanted to get Creon from his cell without causing half a war between me and my allies. But a weight settled over my stomach as I tripped to a standstill in the middle of the hall, and when I tried to find words, they lay clumsy and inadequate on my tongue.

'Oh.' What did I mean, *oh*? How was I going to talk sense into the bastard with monosyllabic stammering? 'Hello. Were you, um, looking for me?'

He threw a quick glance at the gate as he approached, his handsome face an assemblage of vagueness – vague amusement, vague annoyance, vague politeness. There was unnervingly little emotion in his deep voice as he said, 'Thirty-six years old?'

Oh, hell. I hadn't planned for that lie to end up with *him*. Then again ... there would have been no need for lies if the guards hadn't been convinced I was a helpless, magicless little creature.

'Human?' I said, mirroring his tone of voice.

He blinked, briefly brought off balance. 'That seems an entirely different point to me.'

Of course it was a different point; it was *his* lie, after all, and therefore justified, whereas the matter of my age was *mine*, and therefore morally reprehensible. I bit my tongue to hold that retort back and settled for a slightly more polite, 'Well, they wouldn't let me leave.'

'Wisely.'

Because I might stumble and scrape my knee and need my father to pick me up? I considered telling him I'd walked around on islands unsupervised for most of my life and survived several weeks at the Crimson Court, too – but the lines of his proud face suggested he might barely hear that point. He'd already decided I couldn't be trusted on my own.

And considering that I'd helped an apparent enemy escape the Golden Court last time he *had* trusted me on my own, perhaps he wasn't even entirely wrong.

'I didn't have any trouble,' I said, swallowing a bitter sting of regret. No need to think about that, now. I was here to get Creon his freedom back. Once he was out of that cell, at least he could prevent me from committing any other stupidities. 'Just took a walk around the forest. Tried to think a bit. It's quite beautiful.'

His face softened. 'It is.'

There didn't seem to be a sensible reply to that. Fae walked past, circumventing us so deliberately Agenor must have told them not to distract him. Which was a shame. If no one interrupted this tense mess of a conversation, I'd have to keep it going myself.

As I should want, but ...

Hell. What could I say to this stranger whose blood ran through my veins? Something that didn't make me sound like an idiot but not like I was clever enough to break into prisons, either. Something that didn't come across too hostile while not letting him in on anything more vulnerable than the bland, polished wall of nothingness he was showing me. Something—

'I thought we should have a word,' he said, interrupting my thoughts. I was too relieved to pay attention to the near-command that once again laced his voice. 'Would you like to see the gardens? Or one of the sitting rooms, if you prefer something calmer?'

Oh, Zera help me. My guts clenched again. It felt like a test, all of this – would I make the right choices? Would I react correctly to whatever he had to say? With Valter and Editta, at least I'd *known* what they wanted from me … but how in the world should I appease a parent I'd met mere hours ago?

'Of course,' I forced myself to say, the stomach cramp growing into a faint nausea. 'Gardens sound good.'

A quick nod at the nearest exit was his only answer. Of course. Why have conversations if you could just settle for orders?

I couldn't make sense of my own thoughts as I hurried after him. He was being a cold bastard, wasn't he? So why did I even care? Why was the mere presence of him enough to reduce my tongue to dead meat when even the Mother herself had never left me lost for words that way? I didn't need him to like me, didn't even expect to like him. I could just settle for hating him. Civilly disliking him, if necessary. From what I'd seen of fae families, that wasn't too bad – at least we weren't killing each other.

My stomach didn't calm down.

If I hadn't known about the fight of that morning, I wouldn't have known it from the court around us; somehow Agenor's people had managed to clean out all traces of the struggle in the few hours I'd been gone. Part of the plan, probably, a rigorous maintenance schedule to follow up on the equally rigorous decisions of life and death.

My children …

I pushed the thought of those violet eyes away. She'd keep her word – wouldn't she?

Agenor led the way in silence, through a low, light gallery into a wide garden I hadn't seen before. It was surrounded on all four sides by walls as brightly coloured as the flowers that grew between the meandering paths; although it was smaller than the gardens we'd flown over at the Crimson Court, the clever outlay of paths and ponds and flowerbeds made it sizeable enough for a generous interlude of mindless wandering.

We sauntered along the paths in silence. I glanced at Agenor to make some polite remark about the place, then noticed something squirming in his chest pocket and blurted out a far less polite curse instead.

He glanced down. 'Oh. Basilisk. Don't worry about him.'

At the mention of his name, a tiny green snake stuck his head out, beaming at me with even tinier black eyes. Agenor offered him a finger, and the animal curled around it like a living piece of jewellery.

'Good gods,' I said, kicking myself for my overreaction. I'd gotten used to alves. I should be able to deal with a couple of animals in unexpected places, too. 'How many of those snakes are graciously tolerating your presence in this castle?'

'Three, at the moment. You've met them all.' He sounded amused, but when I glanced aside, his face didn't show a trace of it.

'At the moment?'

'Their number has varied over the years,' he said slowly. 'I don't control when and where they come to me – they appear whenever they like and then stay for decades or centuries. Coral and Oleander have been with me since before the Last Battle.'

A lot older than I was, indeed. 'Because you're ... godsworn.'

He sighed. 'Yes.'

'What does that even mean?'

'It's a magical arrangement of sorts between gods and ... well, any other race.' He absently raised his hand to his shoulder, allowing Basilisk to slither onto the collar of his shirt. 'A gift of divine magic in return for some service or duty. Before the plague, most of the human priests and priestesses were godsworn, giving them some magic to wield.'

I worried my lip, considering that. 'So what did you do for Korok?'

'Save his life,' Agenor said flatly. 'A good number of times.'

'Until you didn't.'

He didn't reply to that, but Basilisk threw me a deadly glare from his seat on Agenor's shoulder. A sore spot, then.

Good to know he had those, even if he tried very hard to give the opposite impression.

We walked on in silence, past a pleasantly unkempt rockery and a fountain the shape of a sea dragon. I wanted to ask whether dragons were real, too, if so much of what I'd believed to be the stuff of legends turned out to have been tangible history – but he probably hadn't come here to chat about gods and dragons, and if I wanted to free Creon, it may be better not to test his patience too much.

'May I ask,' I said – a sprinkle of manners to soothe the bluntness of the question that was about to follow – 'how old you are, exactly?'

'A respectable twelve hundred and fifty-four years,' he said dryly.

Gods help me. Our history lessons on Ildhelm didn't even go back that far; they discussed everything up to the plague that had sent humans fleeing the continent, and regarded all that had come before as little more than myth.

'So you were born just before the Mother's Conquest, then?' I said, trying to add up the timelines from Lyn's Faerie texts.

'A few centuries before, yes.' I wasn't sure if he was agreeing with me or correcting me. 'I spent my first years on Hedylia, which is an island just to the south of this court. My family was ...' He hesitated as we followed a sharp bend in the path, passing a circle of gnarled olive trees. 'You may not be very familiar with the fae dynasties of old.'

My gut clenched. That *was* disappointment in his voice, wasn't it? Or at the very least, some mild annoyance that no one on my human backwater island had bothered to inform me of the details of my glorious ancestry?

'I ... no.'

'No.' He sighed and raked a hand through his short hair without meeting my gaze, staring instead at the sandstone walls he must have seen a thousand times before. 'I was born into the lineage of Erion Thenes, who earned his title during the War of Thorns a few millennia before – not a terribly illustrious house, but it goes back a long while. I inherited it at the death of my father when I was twenty-five.'

Emelin Thenessa, Creon had said. Of course he knew.

'Your father's death ...' I started hesitantly.

'He was killed over a feud between islands,' he said, his deep voice still so unnaturally calm. 'As was most of my family that day. Achlys and Melinoë were the ones who showed up after the fight to save what was left. Dug Emeia and me from the rubble, healed the town's injured, then suggested we may want to stay with them while they looked for a way to stop that kind of violence once and for all. Which we did.'

Oh, gods. Twenty-five years old – a child in fae years, and abruptly orphaned. Could I blame him for following them, for not seeing what they would one day become?

'If you knew her – them – as separate people,' I said, momentarily distracted from the thought of Creon, 'do you know who is who?'

Agenor let out a chuckle. 'Blue eyes is Achlys, dark eyes is Melinoë. They're inhabiting what was originally Achlys's body.'

That was a part of their history I'd never spent much thought on. 'Where did they leave the other body, then?'

'I never asked. Melinoë is a little touchy about the subject.' Another small smile trembled around his lips when I glanced at him. 'They made Korok pick between their bodies. First time I had to save his life.'

A laugh broke from my lips. He met my gaze, amusement sparkling in his familiar brown-and-green eyes, and for a moment, I forgot to civilly dislike him.

'Didn't she – they – mind?' I said after a moment of slightly more comfortable silence, our feet rhythmically landing on the gravel path. 'That you bound yourself to Korok when you should have been loyal to her? She doesn't come across as someone who shares well.'

'They absolutely don't share well,' he said wryly, tapping Basilisk aside as the little snake tried to climb up his neck. 'But my magic was bound, so I couldn't have harmed them anyway. And I don't think they were ever concerned about my loyalty.'

Rightly so, I wanted to say – but then again, I already knew Korok's death was somewhat of a sensitive topic, and perhaps rubbing more salt into the wound wasn't the most beneficial way of getting through his defences.

'What did she take to bind you?' I said instead.

He shrugged as he picked Basilisk up from his shoulder and tucked the snake back into his chest pocket. 'A memory.'

'A ... what?'

'Their preferred method for people they don't want to damage in any other way. Binding unnecessary memories.' He gestured at the southwest. 'I ... well, I clearly don't know which one they took, but they told me back then it was an unpleasant one. Which I have enough of even without whatever they bound.'

Twelve hundred and something years of war. A cold shiver ran down my spine. Little as I liked the way he'd spent his time, perhaps I could understand his hunger for peace in these last few decades.

Hell, what did one even do in twelve centuries of life? I knew humans who'd squeezed three marriages and half an orphanage of offspring into mere decades. With such infinite time on one's hands ...

'Did you ever have other children?' I blurted out.

'No.' He didn't look my way, staring at a burbling fountain instead. 'I've been a little too busy fighting wars to think about families.'

Which meant I was the firstborn heir to that ancient dynasty of his? Despite not even being fully fae? His face didn't betray what he thought about that – an heir who didn't even speak his native language, didn't even know his history, didn't even have wings.

'If you don't mind me asking ...' he started as I stayed silent. 'Did Creon ever suggest he might know more about your ancestry?'

'Creon?' I blinked. 'No. I mean – he didn't know.'

Agenor glanced at me, his steps not faltering. 'All we can say in that case is that he didn't *openly* know, of course.'

Oh, damn him – damn that layer of patronising smugness in his voice. My ill-advised sparkle of sympathy died a quick and merciless death.

'I doubt he could have kept it silent if he'd known,' I said coldly. 'He made a bargain to find my parents.'

He raised an eyebrow, not at all brought off balance. 'Did he bargain on *finding* them or on *telling* you when he'd found them?'

'He ...' Oh, fuck. 'On helping me find them, if I recall the wording correctly.'

His sigh crossed into the territory of groans. 'Then it's perfectly possible he did as a matter of fact know about your origins in some way or another and fulfilled the requirement of helping you by luring you to this court rather than by directly telling you. I don't suppose the bargain contained any deadline or demand of immediate action, either?'

If I had any way to deny that, I'd have done it solely for the purpose of getting that self-satisfied confidence off his face. But lies might be brought to light sooner or later, and that wouldn't make anything better.

I shook my head.

'Well.' He rubbed his temple, looking both vaguely triumphant and vaguely puzzled. 'Then we can't be sure. I'll have to send some people after the matter.'

What did he think – that Creon may have taken me hostage with the pre-existing intention of using me as negotiation material against him? It took an effort not to grab those infuriatingly muscular shoulders of his and physically shake sense into him, to remind him that he'd be a damn lot less confused if he stopped looking for some dastardly game that did not exist ...

But he'd probably take me for a small child throwing a tantrum and stop listening to anything I might have to say on the topic.

'You truly can't imagine it might all be much simpler than this?' I said instead, willing my voice into a cool, flat line. 'That he just might want her dead, and nothing more than that?'

'Why would he?' Agenor shook his head with a joyless chuckle. 'He's always been perfectly at home at the Crimson Court. Except perhaps for that mess after the Last Battle, but even without his voice—'

'She took his *voice*. That doesn't bother you at all?'

'The question is whether it bothers *him*,' he corrected me, still far too certain of himself. 'Considering that he never even attempted to find another way of communicating, I think we can safely say he's not lying awake at night over it.'

Zera help me. Blowing up a few walls probably wouldn't help to make my point, would it? I sucked in a useless breath and sharply said, 'Did it occur to you he might not have been showing you his true feelings and opinions on any of this, considering that you were still fully supporting the Mother most of this time?'

'Emelin ...' His boots ground the gravel as he halted and turned towards me, his face full of a well-intended condescension that made my knuckles itch. His voice was too calm – like a parent soothing their toddler back to sleep after a nightmare. 'You need to understand that Creon has many more faces than I suppose he's shown you. He can be pleasant enough when it suits his goals, and you're not at all to blame for taking his words for the truth, but ...'

He didn't finish his sentence. There was no need to. That gods-damned undertone in his voice spoke loud and clear: *what is more likely*, it said, *for him to deceive me, the ancient strategist who's known him for centuries, or you, some witless child of not even two dozen summers?*

'But?' I got out through clenched teeth, a vexing nervousness stirring in my guts.

He pursed his lips. 'But speaking as someone who once counted several gods among his acquaintances, I'm not exaggerating when I say he's the single most dangerous individual I've known in my life. I would sleep much more peacefully if that particular combination of power, intelligence, and ruthlessness had simply never seen the light.' He sounded tired. 'There's no taming a male like Creon Hytherion, Emelin. There's just not getting in his way. And you'd be wise to keep in mind that whatever game he's playing ... it's not benefitting anyone but him in the end.'

I swallowed the smallest, most treacherous sting of doubt. No. Damn his twelve hundred and something years of experience; he truly had not the faintest idea what he was talking about. The tears in Creon's wings, the shadows in his eyes, the colour burning under his skin in Lyn's library – benefitting *him*?

'I got in his way,' I said, voice unintentionally soaring against the backdrop of sparkling water and rustling leaves. 'Quite dramatically so, at times. If he was in this for his own gain, he should already have killed me five times over.'

'And since you're still alive,' he retorted, far too patiently, 'you should ask yourself whether perhaps you were exactly where he needed you after all.'

'You ...' Oh, gods *damn* him. Had he been anyone else, I'd have shouted. To hell with his pride; he had more than enough of it anyway. But something in his look, something about that shield of distant reserve that shimmered so tangibly in the air around him, smothered all my impertinent remarks before they could be uttered, leaving me lost for words at even the thought of his reaction.

It wasn't fear. Powerful as he was, that glimmer of annoyance in his eyes was nothing like Creon's dangerous menace, the kind that made sensible people feel like hiding and hoping they'd be alive at their next breath. It was rather a very polite sort of distance, deflecting all prospective questions with a faint implication that I was truly making matters unnecessarily difficult and wouldn't it be far more convenient for all parties involved if I could just swallow the words on my tongue?

Don't be difficult. Don't be a burden.

'Perhaps Creon's history is a topic better left for later,' he said before I could shake myself from that wordless paralysis, resuming his walk so I had no choice but to hurry after him. 'There are some very unpleasant stories there, and for someone your age—'

I broke.

'My *age*?' The words slammed out of me. 'For hell's sake – I survived three winters of famine before I even turned fifteen, Agenor. Watched children starve to death during the worst of them. Attended twenty years of tribute innings, lived through twenty years of fae threats, and that was *before* I set foot in the Crimson Court and fought my way out of it alive.' I let out a breathless laugh, clenching my fists so tightly it hurt. 'Don't worry about tainting my innocent young mind with your unpleasant stories – I've lived in them for long enough. Now what was your point?'

He blinked a fraction too emphatically – *surprise*, finally. Good gods, how many fae had my mother made him kill before he finally reached the point of opening his eyes?

'Please tell me more about your childhood,' he said.

That *please* was a lie. A transparent and utterly unconvincing attempt to make his deflecting command sound a fraction less like a command and a little more like a father taking some interest in his newfound daughter's history. And yet it pulled the anger out from below my feet just as easily – his voice so calm and composed and so much more reasonable than me with my unmannered ranting ...

You embarrass me, Emelin.

No, those hadn't been his words – had they?

Stifling memories closed around me. Editta's tight lips, Valter's agitated pacing. *What do you want, Emelin?* And Agenor with his questioning demands, not a clue on his face as to what the right answer would be ... What did *he* want to hear from me? That I'd hated my childhood surrounded by humans? That I was overjoyed to finally have found a home among fae? But I was at home in this place as much as I'd ever been at home at the Crimson Court, and that was surely not what he wanted me to say ...

I settled for a safe, bland, 'What do you want to know?'

'What was your home like?'

Was. Because he knew it had been burned – knew there was no home left for me to claim in the human world. I stared at my hands, my fingers clawing into my dress even though I couldn't remember tensing them, and hated how vulnerable I must look. How easily he'd punched into the worst of my memories while I couldn't even elicit the slightest emotion from him.

'I didn't know I was fae.' Simple facts, then. I could hardly blunder with those. 'My parents – adoptive parents – they never told me I wasn't theirs. Told me it was some loose streak of magic that ran in my mother's – Editta's – family and just ... hid me.'

He stood studying me when I looked up, thoughts spinning behind his eyes.

'It was an accident Creon found me there. He had to explain all of it. Valter and Editta – they didn't bother to tell me anything before ...'

I faltered, not sure how to finish. *Before they cut me off. Before they kicked me out and washed their hands clean of me.*

Agenor's frown turned puzzled. 'They died on Cathra, didn't they?'

'Oh. No.' Gods be damned, I should have realised he didn't know that part of the story. 'Creon let them all go, sent them to the White City instead. The Alliance confirmed they arrived there a while ago.'

There. *That* should be an argument in favour of his good intentions, shouldn't it?

But Agenor barely reacted, save for his eyebrows quirking up a miserable fraction. 'Interesting.'

My voice creaked. '*Interesting?*'

He cocked his head, as if that reaction, too, was a fascinating novelty more than anything else. 'Well, yes. Also ... fortunate, I suppose?'

He *supposed?*

That was as far as his empathic capacities went? He could reasonably imagine I'd prefer not to have my alleged parents burn to death? Had it been interesting for my mother to disappear, too? Did he think it interesting that Creon had spent that entire night swaying from the Mother's bone ceiling, bones broken, wings torn?

'I *did* love them, you know.' I wasn't even sure where the words came from, flung into his face with such desperate sharpness. 'I know they didn't understand my magic, and they shouldn't have kept all their bloody secrets, but at least they were *there*. Do you really think I'd consider them any less my parents just because they weren't family by blood?'

My voice had grown too loud, the words too breathless. But surrounded by the backdrop of rustling leaves and towering walls, Agenor didn't flinch – didn't even blink.

'I see.'

And that was all.

Lashing out at Creon had *helped* – had cracked through his defences, put some of the power back into my hands. Nothing about this outburst made me feel powerful. Staring at Agenor's unruffled composure, my hands clenched into pathetic fists, I only felt small and violently ashamed of myself.

Whatever might have been the right thing to say ... this wasn't it.

'Alright,' I said weakly.

He didn't scoff at that. Didn't reprimand me, didn't tell me to watch my words. Judging by the unaffected manner in which he continued his walk, I might have thought he hadn't heard my thinly veiled rejection at all.

But he deflected every question I asked about Creon for the rest of our conversation, and when we parted ways not much later, I couldn't shake the feeling that my stupid outburst had only lengthened his prison stay below the Golden Court.

CHAPTER 27

'LORD AGENOR HAS SUGGESTED you no longer leave the castle alone,' the wiry fae female guarding the gate told me.

I'd been inclined to like her up to that point; she had the first lines of the Ballad of the White City inked on the inside of her left wrist, a recklessly unsubtle sign of her political sympathies. But then she'd opened her mouth and mentioned bloody Lord Agenor, and my initial sympathy scurried off grumbling and cursing.

'Well, you can tell Lord Agenor I politely reject the suggestion,' I said, hoping my determined yet innocent smile would do the trick.

It didn't.

'That's not entirely how Lord Agenor's suggestions work, little one.' She seemed amused. 'If there's no one you'd like to take along in particular, we can find someone to accompany you on your walk, of course.'

Gods damn them. I had returned from my trips alive and well for the past three days, albeit more and more frustrated; having to leave Creon behind in that bloody cell got worse with each click of the lock behind me. Meanwhile, Agenor seemed determined to spend every waking minute buried in meetings and training, where I could hardly storm in and plead my case again.

And now I was no longer allowed to even leave the castle?

Perhaps Agenor hadn't heard of the last two excursions until now; I certainly hadn't mentioned them during the tense dinners at his table. Perhaps he'd decided to take measures as soon as he realised my forest walks were becoming a regular habit.

Measures he'd communicated to his guards, and not to me. Typical.

'Well,' I said, unable to hide my annoyance. If Agenor insisted on playing the game this way, I might start blowing up prisons soon, despite all excellent reasons not to resort to such drastic measures so quickly. 'I'll see if Lyn and Tared have time.'

'As you wish.' She still sounded far too sympathetic.

I turned and made my way back through the maze of the castle, cursing under my breath but forcing myself to smile at every fae I encountered. They really weren't too bad in this part of the world, annoying loyalty to their commander aside. Presumably those who volunteered to spend their days at the Crimson Court were the most treacherous individuals, not a very representative sample of faekind as a whole.

Which still didn't mean I wanted any of them on my heels outside.

Lyn wouldn't do either; she'd been far too concerned with keeping the peace so far. Tared, on the other hand ... I might stand a chance.

I found him at the courtyard where Agenor's warriors trained – flashes of wings and limbs and weapons everywhere I looked, faces stern, eyes cold with concentration. They all knew they'd need their skill soon enough. Tared stood talking with the tall fae female called Doralis, who'd been one of the first to join Agenor at the Golden Court with her half fae lover and was generally considered his second in command.

As far as I knew, even she had no idea of my identity. Her quick smile as I appeared didn't reveal a trace of special interest. 'Morning, Emelin.'

'Morning,' I said and turned to Tared. 'Could I pull you away from slicing up fae for a few minutes?'

He snorted a laugh. 'I've been very restrained today.'

'You started out very restrained yesterday,' Doralis pointed out, thumb brushing over the hilt of the short sword at her hip. 'And we all know how that ended.'

'Nothing a bit of blue magic couldn't fix,' he said, his smile too strained. 'But I could take a break, yes. What's the matter, Em?'

Doralis got the hint, muttering something about those bloody alves as she walked off. I waited until she was out of earshot, then said, 'And they haven't even met Edored yet.'

'Oh, I know,' Tared said, sheathing his sword and leaning back against the ivy-covered clay wall. 'They kept asking why we wouldn't just inform the rest of the Alliance of the situation. I told them after that little row yesterday that I'm quite a mild-mannered alf when it comes to fae, and so far no one has asked again.' A chuckle. 'Anyway, what is it?'

I glanced over my shoulder. No ears anywhere near. 'Agenor isn't letting me out of the castle on my own.'

'Ah.' He raised an unimpressed eyebrow. 'Of course. Imagine if you got lost or attacked by wicked fae. You'd be defenceless as a little fledgling.'

'Oh, fuck off.'

He laughed. 'Annoyed about something?'

'I was just ...'

'Very much looking forward to your *forest walk*,' he finished, throwing me a look as he stuck his hands in his pockets. 'We all know the forest is prettiest around this time of the day, after all. Charming morning sunlight. Moderate temperatures. Low tide. Not that that has anything to do with the matter, of course.'

Oh, hell. So much for my skill at secrecy. 'The tide seems entirely unrelated, indeed.'

'As I thought.' He shook his head, looking no less amused. 'Well. I should probably suggest you stay inside the castle if that's what his lordship prefers. You know, don't rock the boat, think of the future, everyone's acting with the best of intentions ...'

'*Do* you think he's acting with the best of intentions?'

Tared glanced up at the broad tower on the far side of the courtyard, where Agenor was having his daily briefing with his advisors. Lyn was probably there, soaking up every bit of intelligence she could get her hands on, working out how exactly we were going to introduce a hundred-and-something fae to the Alliance without causing any fatalities.

'I suppose so,' Tared said after a brief pause. 'Then again, a few centuries in Edored's company taught me that even the best of intentions can lead to the greatest of folly. And the bastard has no business telling a grown adult where she is and isn't allowed to go.'

I could have hugged him for that alone. 'Thanks.'

'You're always welcome to enjoy my occasional bouts of wisdom,' he said dryly. 'Which is probably not what you came here for, though.'

'Of course not,' I said, sticking out my tongue at him. 'If I needed wisdom, I'd have been looking for Lyn. I was hoping for the opposite, honestly.'

He groaned a laugh. 'I'm not going to save your hide if Agenor is unhappy about this, Em.'

'Oh, no.' I pulled my most innocent face. 'You didn't know about his instructions to the guards, obviously. I just told you my ankle was hurting and I didn't feel like walking all the way to the forest.'

'How very helpful of me,' he said, holding out his hand to me. 'Just this once, then. You'll have to figure this out with him yourself tomorrow.'

Fine. I'd have an entire evening to make my point before low tide tomorrow – time I didn't have today, with the water already rising again.

'Did I tell you you're my favourite alf?' I said and grabbed his wrist.

He snorted. 'Brat.'

The castle blurred around us before I could retaliate. In its place, the green and gold of the forest emerged, a small clearing just behind the first line of trees. Judging by the position of the lake and castle on the open field, we were close to the Blood Gate already.

Sparing me not just another confrontation with the guards at the gate, but half an hour of walking, too.

'Thanks,' I said. 'I could swear the flattery is working.'

He chuckled, ruffled my hair, then stepped back. 'Be careful, Em.'

'Always,' I said.

'Liar,' he said and vanished.

I laughed and pulled my backpack a little tighter against my back. No pixies to be seen. Should I leave my daily dose of strawberries here for them to find, or was it better to wait until they'd noticed me?

Likely the latter. I shrugged and began to walk, keeping a careful eye on my feet just in case one of Irie's reckless friends threw themselves into my path again.

But there were no suspicious animals, no projectiles flung at me from the branches. The forest as a whole was oddly silent this morning, not a rustle or twitter to be heard from the foliage – as if Agenor had decided to lock the wildlife away in the castle with me.

Which was unlikely, wasn't it?

But the silence *was* unnatural, a heavy, stifling quiet, smothering the woods like a pillow over the face. The longer I walked, the stronger the sense of unease grew. Even if I told myself that it didn't matter, that I would be safe behind the Blood Gate in a few minutes …

Didn't it matter?

Oh, hell. I was a secret weapon at a rebelling fae court, and something appeared to be off on the island. Of course it damn well mattered.

'Anyone there?' I said without raising my voice.

No reply. That, too, was unusual. They always found me within minutes after my arrival in the forest, and so far they'd been faster every subsequent day.

'I know you're there,' I added, trying to sound reasonable. 'Why aren't you coming out? You know me. And I've brought you strawberries.'

A branch snapped behind me. I whipped around, but only a few swaying leaves betrayed there had been any motion at all – as if whoever was hiding in the foliage had momentarily lost control of themselves at the mention of the strawberries, then recalled they weren't supposed to show their face.

This was … concerning.

'Hey,' I said, as reassuringly as possible. 'I figure something unusual is going on, but there's no need to be scared of *me*. Can I help you with something? More food? Any other problems you need me to solve?'

Four, five counts of silence.

Then Irie's familiar voice piped up, 'It's the ship-ship, Emelin.'

I almost breathed a sigh of relief, then registered his words and stiffened all over again. 'What ship?'

'The one with the glamour-glamour.'

Glamour? A *shapeshifting* ship? I threw a bewildered look in the direction of his voice and said, 'What's the matter with it?'

'There'll be blood-blood in the woods!' His shrill voice creaked higher. 'When fae-fae come and fight-fight, it's always us-us suffering the—'

'Wait. Wait.' I snapped around, eyes scouring the foliage for signs of danger, some trap or ambush. 'You need to start at the beginning for me – what fae? Fighting who?'

'The one-one with the cat eyes!'

'The ...' My stomach turned. Fuck. *Fuck.* 'Ophion?'

Irie let out a whimper.

'He's ... he's *here*?' But that couldn't be. What on earth would Ophion be doing at the Golden Court, unless he knew ...

Unless he knew.

The ground spun below my feet. Three full days since Agenor had gained control of the castle. Three full days for a desperate violet-eyed fae female to make her way to the Crimson Court and alarm the Mother, tell the world about my presence in the east, and send an army of warriors to retrieve me.

'Irie.' It took all I had not to run, to scream, to curl up on the forest floor crying. My moment of weak-heartedness might be far worse than just that, and I *couldn't* afford to crumble now. 'Irie, I'm going to need your help. How many of them are there?'

He wailed again. 'Too-too many.'

'Is there anyone who could count them? Even if just roughly?'

'Count-count?' he moaned. 'Do you think we want to die-die?'

'But ...' I sucked in a deep breath. My hammering heart didn't take notice. 'Listen, you can disguise yourself, yes? If you become an ant or something, they can't see you and kill you.'

'He likes-likes killing us!'

Oh, the *bastard*. 'Well, he likes killing me too, but I doubt I'll be able to run away from him. So I'll have to face him. I really, really need your help, Irie.'

He was silent for a moment. 'Killing-killing *you*?'

'I suspect that's what he's here for.' Hell, how long did we even have? What if a full-fledged army of vengeful fae was going to burst from the trees any moment and surprise the court in the middle of a calm training morning? 'I won't be able to bring you any more strawberries if I'm dead, you know. Just so it's clear what dire consequences we're talking about.'

There came no reply this time.

'I'm not asking you to fight.' Although I'd damn well like to see Ophion caving under the force of three dozen pinecones to the face. 'Just let us know what to expect. How many of them there are, where they're moving. We can't defeat him if we have no idea what he's doing, and then he might just move into the Golden Court himself for all we know.'

Several small gasps around me proved Irie was not the only one listening.

I folded my arms and grimly said, 'That's what I thought, yes.'

'The snake lord doesn't like-like us either,' a little voice from behind me ventured.

'I'll tell him to stop being an idiot,' I said. That had been the plan anyway. 'I'll convince him to send you some food every now and then. Strawberries and lemon cakes, all of that. But he can't do that if Ophion removes him from the castle in an hour.'

How was it possible for my voice to sound so incomprehensibly soothing, as if I'd never been calmer in my life? *Remove him.* Was that what they were here for? Did they know about Lyn and Tared – did they know about Creon? What if I'd killed them all with my stupidity, what if—

'You promise-promise?' Irie said shrilly.

'I promise. Keep an eye on them, report back to the castle, and I'll take care of it.' I pulled my bag from my shoulders. 'And I have strawberries now for anyone who volunteers to help.'

They were silent as I laid the package in the moss. But when I stood up, Irie whispered, 'We'll look-look for you and tell-tell you, Emelin.'

'You are the bravest little pixies I know,' I told him, 'and I'll try my very best to protect you. Is it alright if I leave to warn them?'

'Yes-yes!'

I ran.

I could only pray that whoever was hiding in those woods wouldn't see me as I sprinted the endless distance over the open field, past the lake, past the village. The fear spurred me on, kept my feet moving even with my heart rattling in my throat and my breath a ragged, shrieking mess. Ophion, of all people – *Ophion*, who'd torn Creon's wings, who'd kept Agenor at this court while my mother was giving birth to me ...

He likes killing us.

How long did we have?

Either no one noticed me, or they knew they'd draw more attention by showing their face to stop me. I reached the gate unharmed and found myself pulled inside by the female with the ballad tattoo, who looked bewildered rather than furious to find me on her doorstep.

'How in the world—'

'No time,' I interrupted, gasping for breath. 'Need to find Agenor – warn him – we—'

'Lord Agenor is in a *meeting*, Emelin. You can't just—'

'We're under *attack*,' I snapped.

She stared at me, fingers loosening on my wrist. 'What?'

I yanked myself from her grip. 'A meeting, you said? Thanks.'

'What? But Emelin—'

I was already running again.

Damn my lack of wings, forcing me to climb all these bloody stairs and sprint through all these bloody corridors rather than fly in a straight line for the balcony of the meeting room. The castle was a haze of pillars and colours and amused faces around me. I wanted to shout at them to arm themselves, defend the walls, whatever one did in the face of looming battle – but Agenor would know what to do. What was the sense in causing a panic before he could let loose his beloved protocols on the situation?

The door to the meeting room wasn't locked. I burst through it like a hurricane, less of a proper daughter than ever before, and unable to care.

'Agenor!'

Conversations stilled; heads snapped around. I stumbled to a halt at the long table, most of the seats occupied – about a dozen fae and Lyn, who was sitting on a bunch of pillows to match the height of the others.

At the head of the table, Agenor had already shot up, Oleander hissing around his shoulders. 'Gods and demons, Emelin – what in the world—'

'Ophion.' The name burst from my lips, and at once my mind was clear, the panic somehow sharpening my thoughts into a focus that could cut steel. 'He's here. In the forest. I don't know how many others he's brought with him – the pixies will let me know as soon as they've counted – but they're absolutely terrified, so I—'

'The *pixies*?' Even now he barely raised his voice. 'I thought I'd given clear instructions that you weren't to go out into—'

'Yes, and I ignored them,' I interrupted sharply. 'Is that really the point you want to focus on?'

He glanced at a fae male to his left, who'd gone pale as chalk. 'Any chance that the unusual sounds you heard last night may have been a little more problematic than estimated?'

Unusual sounds. So that was why he'd tried to keep me inside? Without explanation or apology – just a cold order, and he hadn't even done me the honour of aiming it at me?

'I ...' the fae male stammered. 'I – I suppose – if they've been exceptionally quiet ... Philia went out to take a look a while ago and should ...'

'Yes,' Agenor said grimly. 'I'm not necessarily expecting her back, if Ophion has caught wind of us. What exactly do you mean about the pixies counting anything, Emelin?'

'Just what I said. They promised they'll count and report back. They'll let us know when there are any problematic movements, too.'

He raised a slow, annoyingly stoic eyebrow. 'They never involve themselves in fights.'

'Not for *you*, you mean.' I snorted. 'Perhaps you should have tried offering them strawberries.'

'Strawberries,' he repeated, the word laced with disbelief.

'Lemon cakes work pretty well, too,' I said tartly. 'I still feel like we're focusing on the wrong things here. You're under *attack*. There might be a bloody army camping just out of sight, and—'

He closed his eyes, cutting me off with a single raised hand. 'Theora, check the bays for signs of trouble. Hali, send out scouts – keep someone in view of the court at all times. Lychas, tell the gate ...' A deep breath. 'Tell the gate any pixies are to be allowed access. And ask Doralis to call for arms, just in case.'

Just in case. Because I might still be lying. I might still be an idiot.

The fae who'd received orders left quietly and efficiently, throwing me unsettled glances as they passed me in the doorway. Agenor sat down again, gesturing for me to take a seat with a look that told me he hadn't yet forgotten about my ignoring his rules.

Good, because I hadn't forgotten about his bloody rules either.

I sat down, evading Lyn's obvious attempts to catch my gaze. Agenor pressed his fingertips to his temples as if I was a headache he could press away and slowly said, 'How did you get out of the castle?'

'I lied to Tared,' I said with a shrug. 'Told him I didn't feel like walking.'

Lyn looked highly suspicious but didn't speak. Agenor merely raised an eyebrow.

'Obviously,' I added, raising mine back at him, 'if I'd known you'd noticed suspicious activity around the island, I wouldn't have taken that risk. But without that information ...'

He muttered a curse. 'I didn't want to frighten you.'

'Ah. That worked out splendidly.'

'She's not *twelve*, Agenor,' Lyn said, sliding from her pile of pillows with an unusually annoyed glare at him. 'I'll be looking for Tared. Back in a—'

The door swung open again, and the gatekeeper with the ballad lyrics on her wrist appeared with a particularly noisy magpie on her shoulder. 'Lord Agenor?'

Lyn slipped out onto the stairs as the magpie burst into a tirade that didn't sound very birdlike at all – a pixie, then, speaking in whatever their native language was. Agenor needed no more than a minute before he interrupted, just about the moment Lyn and Tared faded back into the room. One quick command was enough to send the pixie and the fae carrying them back into the castle; the door fell shut behind them with a heavy, echoing bang.

A short and deeply uncomfortable silence descended over the room. 'And?' I said.

'Ophion, indeed,' Agenor said curtly, wings flaring out a dangerous fraction. 'With what sounds like a full battalion. So that's about five hundred of them, against ...' He glanced at Tared. 'What are the chances we can get any alves to support us here?'

'On Battle Eve?' Tared said, and only then did I realise he must have been at the training field mostly to distract himself from the memories of that stark white battlefield. 'You're not going to find a single sober alf in the Underground today. Or anyone else with a brain left in their skulls, for that matter.'

'I see.' If he was at all discouraged by the news, Agenor didn't show it. 'Five hundred against our hundred and seven, then.'

That summary was met with an even more deafening silence.

'Well,' Tared said, taking a chair uninvited. 'Do your protocols have anything to say about this situation, Lord Protector?'

'In protocol terminology,' Agenor said stiffly, 'this would be called a problem.'

An involuntary chuckle escaped me.

Lyn threw me a concerned glance, then climbed into the seat next to Tared and said, 'How did the Mother even figure out that something was wrong so fast? You said no one escaped, didn't you?'

All lust for chuckling left me at once, but Agenor didn't even glance at me. 'I have no idea. We must have overlooked something.' He sounded annoyed to admit it, and I almost winced. 'It doesn't quite matter now. We have plans to make.'

Lyn briefly closed her eyes. 'Fleeing is not an option, I take it?'

'Only if you're fine with moving ten dozen fae into the Underground on Battle Eve and leaving all our documents and alf steel behind,' Agenor said, somehow managing to make it sound like a rather sensible option. Her shoulders sagged half an inch nonetheless.

'Never mind.'

He turned to the fae around us without a reply, rattling off some quick commands referencing strategies and plans I'd never heard of. Most of them hurried out at once, glad for something to do; the ones who were left behind without a clear task at hand looked thoroughly unhappy about that fact. Only then did it get through to me, as the training noise outside swelled into a far sharper bustle of loud commands and hurried preparations ...

We were going into battle.

This was really, truly happening, our small group at the Golden Court against the far superior force of the Crimson Court, and it was entirely my fault.

People were going to die, and it would be *my fault*.

I wanted to throw up. Wanted, more than anything, to break through the damn Blood Gate and find Creon and cry in his arms until there was no denying the truth anymore. But I'd let my pathetic lack of readiness get the better of me once too often already, and with Ophion preparing to attack in minutes or hours ...

'Em?' Lyn said, and only when I jolted up and saw their expectant faces did I realise she had asked me a question.

'I'm sorry?'

'Where you prefer to go. If you'd rather not stay for—'

'What? No.' I let out a joyless laugh, ignoring my cramping guts as my decisions made themselves. 'I'm staying here. I'm not going to let you deal with—'

'You're *not* staying here,' Agenor interrupted, his voice sharper than I'd ever heard it. For once, he didn't look so awfully polite, his narrowed eyes a suggestion he might well get unpleasant about this matter if I forced his hand.

'Beg your pardon?' I said.

'You're not staying here.' It would have been an indisputable command if not for the clear tension in his voice. 'I'm not going to let you walk straight into a battle against gods-damned Ophion.'

Like he wouldn't let me pick my own walks around the island, like he wouldn't inform me of my own damn risks. I bit out a cutting laugh. 'Did I ask for your permission?'

'Emelin.' Something twitched in his jaw; the female next to me swallowed audibly. 'I'm the commander of this court. If I'm telling you you're not allowed to join the fight, you—'

'Oh, my apologies,' I said sharply. 'I'd momentarily forgotten I swore fealty to this court. How silly of me.'

Tared stifled a grim chuckle.

'For the gods' sakes,' Agenor snapped, glaring at him. 'Is it a crime for me to be concerned about your safety? Hell, you don't even have *wings* – what are you going to—'

'I don't have *wings*?' I repeated, spitting out a laugh. 'That's what it's all about? I'm not a proper fae warrior, so I must be a weak, useless liability?'

He tightened. 'That's not at all what I'm saying.'

'Are you very damn sure?' I said coldly. 'Because if I understand everything correctly, you're currently trying to lock away the second most powerful mage at this court. Even if I'm not as perfectly trained as some of you, I'm *damn* well capable of blowing a few wings off backs.'

The handful of fae around the table looked more and more bewildered by the entire exchange. Lyn was nervously chewing on a lock of her hair; Tared leaned back in his chair, following the discussion like a card game with some unexpected twists.

'I'm trying to keep you safe,' Agenor said between clenched teeth. 'As should probably be expected from me, considering ...'

All self-possession left me.

He was going to play the father card *now*? After days of concealing that crucial little fact from even his most trusted people? As soon as he needed it to make me fall back in line … I was suddenly no longer such a secret?

'Considering that's what a decent father does?' I finished, voice soaring.

He stiffened.

There were gasps. There were cries of confusion. There was Lyn's piercing glance telling me to be careful. I ignored all of it. Secrets were the least of my concerns through the white-hot fury bubbling up in me, days of walking on eggshells, days of painful nervousness and desperate self-restraint welling to the surface.

'Do you know what I missed about having a decent father, *Lord Agenor*?' My voice cracked as the words broke out of me. 'Someone who actually considers me worth a damn. Someone who doesn't try to limit me in even more ways, doesn't tell me I'm deficient in even more ways. I was never a proper human, if you want to know. I'm never going to be one of your proper fae warriors, either. If that bothers you …' I breathed a sharp-edged laugh. 'Perhaps you shouldn't have stuck it into a human in the first place.'

He'd gone wide-eyed. Under any other circumstances, I might have felt triumphant about that – Lord Agenor himself, panicking.

Right now, it only fanned my fury.

'I'm not hiding from this fight,' I added, swallowing the unforgivable words I couldn't speak. *I caused this fight.* 'So tell me what needs to be done and I'll do it. I'll find my own part to play if you don't.'

The room had turned into a blur of gaping eyes and paling faces, bewildered glances shooting back and forth between me and the tall fae male at the end of the table. Agenor looked like he'd accidentally set his teeth into a rotten piece of shellfish. So much for his secrets. So much for his embarrassing offspring.

But at the very least, they couldn't call me a coward.

'You have no idea what we're up against.' His voice was bucking against the reins of his self-control. 'There's a good chance we'll lose. I can't—'

'Yes,' I said tersely, ignoring how very true that first sentence was. 'I'm well aware we're hardly in the best position, and it seems to me there are better solutions to that problem than moving your strongest mages out of the way.'

His eyes narrowed. 'I fail to see where you're going.'

'Oh, good gods. You've got the most dangerous bloody mage in history sitting in your dungeons, waiting to fight the good fight for you.' I fell against the low backrest of my chair, crossing my arms. 'Get him out. He might just win you this battle.'

'He might turn against us before the battle has even started,' Agenor said coldly.

I shrugged. 'Well, the day when we'll all die without him sounds like a good moment for some risky experiments. What are your alternatives?'

Agitated murmurs raced around the table, murmurs I could read far more easily than the stone-faced male on the other side. They didn't trust Creon. They might never fully trust him. But they knew, too, what fate was waiting for them in Ophion's hands, and any way out of the trap the Mother had created – no, the trap *I* had created – was better than waiting for death.

'He won't turn against us,' I said, swallowing the bitter taste of guilt. 'I *know* he won't, Agenor. In my very damn bones. So either you get him out of that cell or I'll do it. I'm not going to watch you throw yourself into a desperate fight if—'

'Don't make empty threats,' he snapped, waving my words away like annoying flies. 'You can't reach his cell. I—'

I scoffed. 'Are you sure about that? The Blood Gate hasn't been giving me much trouble so far.'

He stared at me – finally out of words.

'Surprised?' I said sweetly.

'For hell's sake.' He averted his gaze, wings straining as if it took all he had not to lunge over the table and shake the obedience into me. Next to him, Lyn had buried her face in her arms – realising just now what she could have realised days ago, if not for her unfortunate faith in my good intentions. 'Emelin, what in the world have you—'

'Played my own game.' I shrugged. 'Since you didn't allow me to join yours. Don't treat me like a child just because I don't have those bloody *wings*.'

He blinked, then sent Lyn and Tared a desperate glance. 'Did you tell her about—'

'No!' Lyn burst out, jolting up from the refuge of her arms, red curls jumping everywhere. 'Of course we didn't! She can think, Agenor! And you *should* be releasing Creon instead of waffling until Ophion is sitting on our doorstep, because—'

'The risks—' he started.

'Don't think there are that many risks, truly,' Tared said sourly. 'If he didn't kill me when he had the chance, I doubt he'll kill anyone else.'

A frown brushed over Agenor's face, and for a moment, I wondered if he knew the details of that entangled backstory. Hard to imagine Creon had ever confided in him, but then again, the Mother had at least suspected something was going on with Lyn.

Before anyone could ask, however, the door swung open, and yet another fae male came barging in, armed and out of breath. 'Lord Agenor! The pixies report the battalion is preparing, my lord – no movements yet, but it can't be long ...'

I demonstratively raised my eyebrows.

Agenor met my gaze for a heartbeat – just long enough for me to know the last hadn't been said on my deliberate insubordination. But he rose to his feet as he looked away, jaw clenched, eyes narrowed in an expression of headache-inducing dilemmas.

'Want me to go?' I offered helpfully.

That snapped him into motion. With five long strides, he was around the table, shooing the baffled messenger aside as he reached the doorway. His glare at the gathered company was no less than a murder warning.

'Stay here.'

And with a last slam of his dark wings, he was gone.

CHAPTER 28

THE WAITING WAS THE worst part.

I stood at the arched window looking out over the training field, pretending not to notice the hushed whispers repeating my name. Lord Agenor's daughter, his firstborn heir – I wondered how fast that news would spread.

Although the fae hurrying around the castle below, bellowing commands and dragging buckets of black paint around, didn't look like matters of genealogy were the first concern on their minds.

A hundred and seven warriors. Against a force five times that size.

I had no idea what was waiting for me, but I knew it wasn't good.

Lyn perched on her chair, absently polishing the pointed alf steel ring around her finger as she watched the fae running in and out. Tared paced the room, all patient nonchalance except for his narrowing eyes at every loud noise from below our tower. There hadn't even been talk of them fleeing and leaving Agenor to fend for himself, I realised. A minute of preparation and they were ready for battle – as they'd been for centuries.

As opposed to …

I swallowed, refusing to finish that thought.

Doralis barrelled in with a floor plan of the castle and began moving wooden figures around in frantic discussion with two other fae around the table. Someone yelled a few words about the doors to the alf steel hoard that had been opened, and Tared abruptly dropped all pretence of nonchalance, demanding to see what exactly these bloody fae had been hoarding, just in case there were any items he knew.

Then it was just Lyn, Doralis, me, and two fae males whose names I didn't know, one of them dark-skinned and wiry, the other so sturdily built it was a miracle to me his wings were able to get him off the ground. The four of them quietly discussed formations and archer placement and the position of the sun while I sat on the windowsill and stared outside, watching the dark line of the forest beyond the castle wall.

Ophion was there.

For me.

Because of me.

And where the hell was Agenor? How long could it take to loosen a couple of chains and walk out of that damn prison again?

It was the silence that eventually told me the wait was over – the sudden quiet of cries stilling and warriors stiffening, ripples of terror flooding the courtyards and corridors. Most of them, I realised in that moment, hadn't even known he was here. They were in no way prepared for the sudden sight of Creon Hytherion strolling through their safe refuge, all ruthless power and menacing darkness.

I thought *I* would be prepared. But when he finally came sauntering in, Agenor in his wake …

Gods help me. My breath hitched.

I should no longer have been surprised by the way he could claim a space by merely walking into it. Should be wiser than to let it get to my head, the way his presence alone turned this room of wood and gold into a monster's lair, some dark and forbidden sanctuary. But it had been too long since I'd seen him like this, all chains gone, all Underground agony gone ... Knives in his belt and boots. Hair bound back, emphasising the sculpted line of his jaw. A predator freed of his cage, his eyes burning with the promise of bloodshed – the Mother's assassin prince again, born for nothing but these moments, alive for nothing but death.

This was not a male who hated the power he yielded.

Rather, the opposite – this was a male who revelled in it. And perhaps ... perhaps the court had been right to fall silent around him.

His gaze found me first, as if Lyn and the fae around the table were mere decoration to whatever game he was playing. As convincing as it was, that mask of the proud, reckless creature he wore, the starless flicker in his eyes was an infinity removed from it.

A shield, again. Of course it was. Anything to hide the brilliant mind behind, the lengths he'd go to win this battle, the sacrifices he'd make. He must have worn that mask around Agenor for a long, long time – after all, an indifferent prince who cared only about himself couldn't be suspected of playing entirely different games in the shadows.

Every inch of me ached to jump up and throw myself into his arms, but that look in his eyes was a clear enough warning. *Not here. Not now. There's a play to perform first.*

If only I knew exactly what play it was.

'Well,' I said, resting my back against the cold glass of the window, 'looking significantly better without the chains, I must say. Did you manage not to slit any throats on your way up?'

He chuckled – that silent chuckle that made me expect to see blood gleaming on his teeth. On the edge of my sight, Doralis shoved a few inches back in her chair.

For a last moment, Creon hesitated, his hand halfway to raised before his chest; then, quickly, almost indifferently, he signed, *Sorry about this, Em. Not going to give him that power over me.*

Agenor had frozen in the doorway, gaping at Creon's signs with eyes that could have fallen from his face any moment.

Right.

An alliance of a few days, still too fickle after more than a century spent on different sides of this conflict. It would be unwise – worse than unwise, really – to show any vulnerability to a male like the Lord of the Golden Court.

Like I'd just done, losing my calm with him.

Best not to think about the consequences of that outburst. Best not to think about my stupidity four days ago and the unfathomable mess *that* had caused.

'Very understandable,' I said, and somehow my voice came out light for the ears of our audience. 'I don't suppose the rest of this place gave you any trouble?' The closest I could come to the question I wanted to ask – *Are you alright?*

The corners of his lips quirked up, from languid boredom into a far more sinful smile. *Do I look like I've been in any trouble, Em?*

I snorted a laugh – I couldn't help it. 'Arrogant prick.'

'What …' Agenor started, and if I'd spontaneously grown wings, his gaping eyes couldn't have been wider.

Creon ignored him as he let out another quiet chuckle, fell into the nearest chair, and folded one arm over the backrest. That carefully crafted air of effortless superiority didn't falter even as he looked back at me and signed, *If there's one thing I can do, it's killing. Don't worry about me. Are you—*

'What in hell' Agenor interrupted, staring at the both of us and sounding impressively more likely to commit bloody murder than the winged predator who'd just come prowling into the room, 'is going on here?'

Only then did I notice the new bargain mark he wore – a deep, flaming orange. Its mirror image was sitting on the inside of Creon's wrist, next to the crimson bargain mark he shared with me.

Ah. So my dear father still hadn't trusted me on my word.

'Just greeting a friend,' I said as I jumped from the windowsill, and the painful tangle of shame and fear and blistering annoyance spurred me to smile a little more sharply than I'd otherwise have done. 'I told you he isn't as bad as you think.'

I'm rather confident I've been treating you far worse than he thinks, Creon signed dryly. *You can tell him that.*

Warmth coiled through me. How did he do this every time again, soothing even the worst of my doubts with just an outrageous remark or two?

'I'm not telling him any such thing,' I said briskly, ignoring the twinkle of amusement flaring in his eyes. 'He has better people to kill today.'

'For the bloody gods' sakes,' Agenor snapped as he stalked to the table. His glance at me was a new one, almost ... apprehensive? 'Could the two of you stop this ... whatever this is and focus on the matters at hand? We don't have much time.'

Creon's raised eyebrow at him was a lazy challenge, as if to say, *Make me.*

Agenor gave the impression only the presence of other fae witnesses kept him from lashing out. Had this always been the interplay between them? Creon taunting and challenging the other's polished exterior, as if even the Mother's most trusted people were merely tools for his personal amusement, and Agenor annoyed and occasionally revolted, but all too happy to make use of his powers whenever the need arose?

I exchanged a look with Lyn. She sat small and tense on the edge of her chair, watching the scene with gleaming amber eyes – working on her own analysis, no doubt. As she caught my gaze, she dryly said, 'Shall we get to work, then?'

'Yes.' Agenor's voice was tight with annoyance. 'Lychas and Tyndarion, start getting our forces into position. Emphasis on the east wall, as in the Dawn plan. And tell Tared to get back here, wherever he is.' A sigh. 'And Emelin—'

'I'm still not going anywhere,' I said, my stomach rolling again.

Creon's eyes narrowed at my distress, but he didn't move as the two fae males tiptoed out of the room. Only when they closed the door behind them did Agenor settle back into his chair, wings still on the brink of flaring even as he folded them in over his back.

'The danger ...' he started.

'... is still there,' I finished, chest tightening. 'I *know*, Agenor. How many times do you want to have this discussion when we do indeed have better things to do?'

He glanced at Doralis, who appeared too paralysed by Creon's presence to have much of an opinion, and then at Lyn, who glared back with the exasperated air of a teacher who really expected her pupil to do better. When he finally met Creon's gaze, it was with a look of resolved displeasure, an expression that said, *What has it come to that I'm begging for his help?*

'Can't you explain to her that she has no business in this fight?

'Explain?' I said, voice rising. 'You think I need an *explanation*?'

Creon let out a soundless laugh, turning towards me. *What did the bastard do to you?*

'What ... what do you mean?'

You're having all sorts of feelings you shouldn't. What are you ashamed of?

'I ... nothing.' Oh, damn his demon eyes. Damn those treacherous guts of mine, cramping and churning no matter how hard I clung to the fearless mask I'd moulded onto my face. Even while he sat sprawled out in his chair like a male with not an enemy in the world, I should have known he'd notice every oddity in the whirl of my emotions. 'I'm just a tad frustrated.'

He had to know that was not all of it, but he didn't dig deeper – not in this company. With a deceptively careless shrug, he snatched Doralis's pencil from the table and scribbled down a single sentence on the edge of the floorplan. Written in Faerie, aimed at Agenor – *I've never known you to be foolish over sentimentality.*

Agenor levelled a cold glare at him, jaw twitching. 'Your point?'

You should be thanking your lucky bones she's willing to fight in your name. Things tend to end poorly for people pitting themselves against her. A lazy chuckle. *And you shouldn't need me to tell you that, either. Where has your eye for talent gone?*

I didn't need demon senses to read the slide of emotions that rushed over Agenor's face – anger, worry, and most unwelcome of all, a flash of humiliation. 'Ah, yes.' His voice had gone from cold to frigid. 'I don't suppose the concept of personal concern would mean that much to you.'

'Hey!' I snapped.

Creon looked faintly amused. *Not sure what you'd be concerned about. She'll have Ophion's balls nailed to the wall before you can blink.*

Lyn snorted a laugh. Agenor looked about to throw up.

'I would prefer any other body part, though,' I hurried to clarify.

Creon threw me a grin, then returned to his writing. *She's one of the best you have.* Short, snappish, and written down with such mind-boggling certainty. *Behave.*

I stared at those words as he flung his pencil down and shrugged, that confident shrug of a male who's said all there is to be said on a topic. *One of the best.*

My stomach knotted even tighter. I wasn't sure what would be worse – for Agenor to laugh that statement off or for him to believe it. For all of them to think there was anything commendable about my stance, about my reckless courage, while in truth I was doing nothing but paying off a debt I had so stupidly created myself.

'I see,' Agenor said, sounding tired. 'In that case, thank you, Emelin.'

Oh, fuck. This was far, far worse than his doubt, indeed.

I muttered something like *you're welcome*, not managing to convey a shred of triumph in the words. Creon turned towards me again, worry in his eyes, and for a moment, I thought he might throw off the princely façade just to ask me what on earth I was so upset about.

Then Tared's cold voice sounded behind me. 'My presence was requested, I understand?'

In the blink of an eye, all traces of vulnerability were gone.

'I thought I suggested you not leave here in the first place,' Agenor said, equally coldly.

'Lofty suggestion,' Tared said with a scoff. 'If I may make one in return, try to collect alf steel *without* resorting to grave robbing next time. There's a good number of swords down there that should have stayed below the ground, if anyone had an ounce of decency in their bones.'

Agenor muttered a curse. 'I simply bought every piece emerging on the black market in the past few decades. We can return whatever you want returned, but would you mind discussing that *later*?'

Tared fell into a chair by Lyn's side without an answer, gaze lingering on Creon for a moment too long. I hadn't seen them in one place together since the evening Creon had emerged into the living room of the Skeire household weeks ago. Judging by the double-edged daggers in their mutual glares, not much had improved since then.

'So you're planning to stay this time?' Tared said finally, crossing his legs as he leaned back. 'What a novel idea.'

'Tared,' Lyn snapped.

I didn't dare to breathe, all but expecting the table and floor to draw pale again around Creon's dark shape. Somehow, the colours retained their brightness. But the flicker in Creon's eyes was an unpleasant one – far more unpleasant than anything he should have shown under the guise of the arrogant murderer he'd taken such care to assume.

A novel idea.

On Battle Eve, of all days. If my heart hadn't given another twinge in my chest, I might have laughed at the bitter irony of it.

Don't worry about me, Creon had signed, but how could I not worry when even the sharpness of his shrug told me exactly how much he hated every damn minute of this? How much he hadn't wanted to be this person ever again, death and cruelty personified, the nightmare that terrorised children and adults alike?

And if not for me, none of this would have been necessary.

I had trouble focusing on the conversation. The Blood Gate would be blocked, Agenor said. Ophion would likely attack from the east, where we'd have the sun in our faces and they'd have the wind at their backs. Knowing the bastard, he'd first send a smaller force to exhaust us, then come swaggering in himself to claim the victory.

A victory that was almost guaranteed, with the force he'd brought.

My fault.

Creon scribbled questions, drew arrows on the floorplan, thoughts whirring behind his eyes with that lethal focus I knew so well. Doralis said things about snake poison and archers and alf steel arrows. Messengers walked in with jackdaws and seagulls and even one giant bat on their shoulders, pixies in all shapes and forms who brought detailed news of Ophion's preparations and left for a portion of strawberries in the kitchens.

Outside, blades clattered and bowstrings twanged as the court prepared for war. The pungent smell of paint wafted in through the open balcony doors, and for the first time in my life, there was no nostalgia for it.

My fault.

There was discussion of the distribution of manpower, the number of fae who'd have to fall on any side of the castle for them to be replaced by another unit. *Fall* – that meant death. That meant some people would never see the sun set over this court ever again, and I'd caused all of it.

And then Tared was saying my name, and I shook from the haze of guilt and shame just in time to register the rest of his sentence. Where would I take my position to help defend the castle?

Agenor looked like he wanted to suggest a safe little room in the dungeons. Doralis chewed her nails and muttered something about not enough people on the south side of the castle. Creon turned towards me before he wrote down anything, and by the look in his eyes, he was well aware I'd absorbed close to nothing of what had been said so far.

Stay close to me. That might just be the most reassuring command in the history of faekind. *I'll get you through.*

I swallowed and nodded and tried not to remember there'd have been nothing to get through if not for my own foolishness. 'And what are your plans, exactly?'

He turned to the map, eyes shooting over the abstract tangle of arrows and numbers and colours. The smile that flickered on his lips was a shared secret hidden below a challenge.

We could probably hold the south together.

I blinked. 'Are you mad?'

His smile broke into a grin.

'Oh, gods.' A laugh escaped me, the fear miraculously waning. 'You're being serious? There's only *two* of us, Creon.'

Equivalent to roughly thirty others, he signed dryly, *which is less than most of the walls get. Have some faith in yourself.*

That sentence did the opposite of what it was supposed to do. My guts churned – faith. In my own ability to murder and maim. Even though last time I'd held a knife to an unprotected throat ...

I'd caved.

But I couldn't tell him that, not when he so honestly believed me capable of more, of better, not when he'd just made an enemy of bloody Agenor himself just to make that point. So I forced a smile I knew he wouldn't believe and said, 'South sounds excellent.'

'The south side is undermanned,' Agenor said sharply. 'Surely that's—'

'Well, not anymore,' I said.

Creon grinned, stretching out with catlike laziness. Drawing, I realised, the force of Agenor's ire away from me and straight back to his own exaggerated insufferability.

Hell. I *deserved* that ire. Even if this was not the crime I'd committed, couldn't anyone just be furious with me for a moment?

'If anything happens to her ...' Tared was saying.

Nothing would happen to me. Not with Creon beside me – not with him defending me until his very last breath, if need be. But the others might die around me, so many others, and there was so damn little I could do about it. No brilliant escapes. No secret magic powers. No ...

No hidden weapons.

A thought sparked.

A thought that made me jolt even before it fully took shape, no more than a glimmer of pulsing gold in my memory. *Blood. Don't touch it.* A stretch, of course it was, but what if ...

Creon had already turned towards me, noticing my hammering heart. *Em?*

I looked at Agenor instead. 'Imagine ...' I hesitated. This might just be yet another stupidity in his eyes. Childish naivety, wishful thinking. But if it wasn't ... 'Imagine we found a pool of Etele's blood somewhere. Would that be helpful?'

A heartbeat of silence pulsed through the room.

'A *what?*' Lyn said.

'A pool of blood.' I glanced at Creon, who'd narrowed his eyes in a most appreciative way, and then at Agenor again. 'What would you do with it?'

'Hell's sake.' He let out a joyless laugh. 'Run for my life, probably?'

Promising, Creon signed dryly.

Agenor blinked at him. 'Are we speaking in hypotheticals now? Where in hell would anyone stumble upon—'

'Oh,' Lyn said, brightening. 'In the memorial?'

'The what?' Agenor snapped.

'The ... Creon, it *is* a memorial, isn't it?' Lyn glanced aside, swiping curls out of her eyes. 'Or at least, that's what I assumed, based on the inscription. What was it, something about traitors and—'

'Can someone tell me what for the bloody gods' sakes we're talking about?' Agenor interrupted, throwing a haunted glance between the two of them. The thought of Etele frightened him? Promising, indeed. 'What inscription?'

With a shrug, Creon grabbed the pencil and began to replicate the elaborate curls and whirls I'd seen inscribed around that pitch-dark doorway in the Underground. Even upside down, Agenor read along effortlessly – at least if the abrupt widening of his eyes was any indication.

'You went *into* that place?'

'Would anyone mind translating?' Tared said, frowning at the text. 'My Divine Tongue is a little rusty. Doesn't help that someone blew up all five native speakers a little while ago.'

Agenor muttered a deeply unflattering curse as he fell back in his chair. 'It's a warning. *In memory of the traitor folk. Only they may enter, but no fae will leave this room.*'

I blinked. 'Cosy.'

'Quite,' Tared said wryly. 'Did you say you've been inside too, Em? You seem to have come out about as sane as you've ever been.'

Creon shrugged and circled a single word on the parchment before him, then dropped his pencil again.

'*Elazar?*' Agenor said slowly. 'You mean she could have used *viti* instead?'

'Wait, what?' I said.

He ignored me. 'And that's all? That's the only clue on the basis of which you decided—'

'*Elazar* is the word for full-blood fae,' Lyn said quietly, leaning over to me with a nod at the inscription. '*Viti* is the more general term for anyone wielding colour magic. Which are both generally translated as fae, but ...'

The flash of understanding came a moment too late. Etele had emphatically only warned fullblood fae, and ... 'And we're both half-bloods?'

Creon sent me a smile, turning away from Agenor mid-sentence with that princely indifference that seemed designed to get on the other male's nerves as efficiently as possible. Tared cursed – unsure, apparently, whether he should be amused at the utter lack of thoughtful planning or be habitually furious at whatever Creon did.

'Were you always that damn reckless?' Agenor said tartly.

Could you tell him not everyone has time to consider their strategies for ten years and then fail anyway? Creon signed, rolling his eyes.

'He's praising your commendable thoughtfulness,' I told Agenor.

'I doubt it,' he said and threw Creon an icy look. Creon returned a pleasant smile. 'How certain are you it was the blood that was supposed to enact the curse?'

Creon picked up his pencil. *It felt rather malicious.*

'It had a *feeling?*' Lyn said, sounding deeply unnerved.

Of sorts.

'Well.' Agenor rubbed the bridge of his nose, glancing at Doralis, who appeared determined to stay as quiet as possible with Creon anywhere near – as if a single wing twitch might remind him of her presence and send his knives flying. 'What do you say?'

She glanced at Tared, hesitating for a moment. Outside, the clamour of running footsteps and yelling voices didn't waver.

'How long would it take for you to go get the stuff?'

'I'm not setting foot into that place,' Tared said with a joyless grin. 'But I can fade Em into the Underground, in which case – mere minutes, I suppose.'

My heart jumped painfully. Thank the gods. Even if his proposal was mostly based on an unwillingness to take Creon anywhere, at least I wasn't shoved aside this time. At least I could *do* something. Handling a pool of murderous blood may not be enough to atone for my carelessness, but at least it was a start – at least it was better than sitting in a quiet room and waiting for the rest of the court to die.

For me. Because of me.

My heart twinged painfully, and it was at the same moment that Creon easily rose to his feet and signed, *I'm coming with you.*

Nonchalant gestures, nondescript smile. But the look in his eyes left no room for the illusion he was merely bored enough to join me on this short mission – that piercing demon gaze again, pinning me in place with the weight of his knowledge.

He'd felt every little twinge of guilt. Every little twinge of shame. And like a predator who'd smelled his prey, he wasn't going to let those dangerous observations go.

'No need for that,' I tried against my better judgement. 'All I need to do is scoop some blood, isn't it? You're probably needed here. You're—'

Em. The definitiveness of that gesture was a sharp contrast to the demonstrative looseness of his shoulders. *I don't give a damn who else might need me. Not if you do.*

Oh, fuck.

How dare he be so gods-damned devoted to me if I couldn't even slit a single throat for him?

But Agenor was watching, looking for more reasons to distrust him; Tared stood mere feet away, hoping for any excuse not to fade him anywhere ever again. I swallowed my objections. Swallowed the menacing sense of secrets floating to the surface no matter how hard I tried to keep them chained to the ocean floor forever, threatening to bare all my failures to the merciless sunlight.

'Fine.' It came out choked. 'Let's go, then.'

CHAPTER 29

THE AIR SIZZLED WITH unspoken words as we faded into a deserted Underground, where even the cattle behind Etele's quarter seemed quieter than usual.

Tared was tense in Creon's presence, every look between them a prelude to murder. Creon dropped his air of cocky fae royalty the moment we left the court behind, and resorted instead to that primal focus that left no eyeblink unnoticed.

Which would have been a good thing, if not all of it had been aimed at me.

I tried to avoid his gaze. Tried to chat to Tared, who was not at all in the mood for chatting, tried to busy myself with preparations for battle, while I had absolutely nothing to prepare. Even the flimsiest lie was better than the truth, my failure to live up to even the humblest of their expectations.

If I'd just warned someone – if I'd just called for someone ...

No one would be dying. And Creon wouldn't be forced into the merciless killer's skin all over again.

But Tared vanished to see if he could accidentally find anyone sober, with a last warning to me not to blow myself up – a warning he emphatically didn't extend to Creon. Then it was just the two of us in that silent meadow, a few peaceful cows grazing in the distance, and the ink-black doorway to Etele's memorial gaping before us.

Em, Creon signed.

'We probably need to be quick,' I said and barged into the darkness, where I didn't have to ignore the motions of his fingers because I couldn't see them anyway.

The mosaics and stalactites emerged around me, cruel and breathtakingly gorgeous. *Beauty and war.*

I hurried to the pentagonal basin in the centre of the cave and tried to shake off the memories of our last conversation here, the day he'd fled the Underground and left me behind. It didn't matter anymore, I told myself. I'd found him again. He'd survived. If we just got through this day ...

If.

If I hadn't killed both of us with that sentimental heart of mine.

Fear spiked, cold and scorching at once. I swallowed thorns down my throat and managed, 'Do you have the bottles?'

He had the bottles; we'd checked and double checked. But he didn't reply as he appeared next to me, a few loose locks framing his face in the eerie glow of the faelights, and silently handed me one of the two sturdiest leather flasks we'd been able to find.

The pool didn't ripple when I dipped it in. The golden surface continued to throb and shimmer with its strange pulse-like rhythm, enveloping the leather flask as if to suck it into its syrupy depths. Holding my breath, I scooped it as full as I could without touching the blood itself.

Nothing exploded.

I pushed the cork deep into the bottleneck, then wiped the leather with the old rags we'd taken for that purpose, and which we'd turn to dust with red magic as soon as we were out of the cave. Creon stuck it deep into his pockets, and still he didn't die.

'Could be worse,' I said.

Creon smiled and handed me the second flask.

I repeated the same procedure, faster now that I didn't have to fear for my life at every step. Within seconds, we were done. And then there was no escaping his probing eyes anymore – unless I was willing to jump into the blood pool or physically run away from him, neither of which sounded like attractive options.

He was too damn close.

It was a closeness that somehow made everything worse, his scent a reminder of all those hours of training, all that loving admiration. I'd disappoint him, wouldn't I? I'd *hurt* him. He'd know I was nowhere near the person he'd survived a hundred and thirty years of torture for, and people would still die, and—

What in hell is the matter, Em?

'Nothing!' I forced out. My shrieking, quickening breath was evidence of the lie. 'It's just – all of this – Agenor and Ophion and battle and ...' I sucked in a deep breath, gesturing incoherently at the doorway. 'Shouldn't we go? Tared is waiting for us.'

Creon quirked up a scarred eyebrow. *He isn't.*

'Right.' For fuck's sake. 'Perhaps the cows are concerned about our wellbeing.'

A grin curled his lips. *You've been more convincing, cactus.*

Oh, damn him! Amusement made everything more unbearable. Tenderness was worst of all. I staggered a helpless step back, as if two more feet between us would stop those all-seeing eyes from noticing every sliver of agitation, and managed, 'I'm fine. Really, I'm just ...'

Frightened?

'Nervous,' I corrected against my better judgement, shuffling backwards. He followed calmly, slowly, a hunt for which the outcome had been set in stone long before it started. 'We're about to barge into a losing battle, Creon. People have been known to feel nervous under those circumstances.'

He sighed. *I don't care about people. What's frightening you?*

Another step back. My shoulders bumped into the mosaic wall, and I stayed there, struggling for air, struggling for answers. Creon waited.

Somehow, he managed to lock me against the stone with nothing but his presence, his eyes flat, smouldering pools of patience.

Here to save me.

The problem was that for once, I'd really prefer not to be saved at all.

'Creon ...' I whispered.

Why do you doubt yourself?

'*Doubt* myself?' My voice shot from my lips with too much force. Something about that question – so uncharacteristically unaware, so *thoughtless* – was enough to snap the last strings of my self-restraint. 'For the bloody gods' sakes, how exactly did you want me *not* to doubt myself when we're about to—'

You've never been anything but impatient. His quick gestures cut through my rambling. *I had to hold you back from attacking the bloody Mother herself in the bone hall. You once stepped out into a burning town and tried to kill me the moment you noticed me.* A joyless smile flickered around his lips. *There was no shred of doubt on your mind that night.*

I stared at him, swallowing around the dry catch in my throat. Once again he waited, allowing the question to rise in the silence that stretched between us – a question not nearly as ridiculous as I'd thought in that first flare of anger.

What had changed?

Will the girl be ready?

'Perhaps ...' The word came out guttural, my voice dry like grinding gravel. 'Perhaps I was stupid and reckless enough to believe I could handle all of this. Perhaps I've grown wiser in the past few weeks.'

He raised an eyebrow, unimpressed. *You've never been stupid. Angry, but never stupid.*

Hell damn me, why couldn't he just be oblivious for *once* – accept my obvious lies and stop this merciless advance towards that recoiling core of shame and secrets? I *had* been stupid. So very stupid, and now people were going to die because of it, thinking I would do my best to save them while in truth—

Em. His wings flared out a fraction, the only gesture betraying his agitation. The rest of him stood so perfectly still before me, an epitome of flawless control – a male who would *never* make the stupid choice, who would never endanger an entire court and the people in it just for the sake of sentimentality. *What are you ashamed of?*

Oh, to hell with him and his demon powers. I pushed myself away from the wall, tried to duck past his tensing wings. 'We have work to do. Leave it be.'

He caught me before I'd taken a second step, drawing me against his chest despite my snarl of annoyance. The weight of his body forced me back against the wall, his hands tightening on my waist, his scent so insufferably delicious around me that I wanted to burst into tears.

'What are you *doing?*' I hissed. 'We'll be too late for—'

Let them damn well wait. His gestures were not nearly so patient anymore, brusque strokes of his fingers as he moved back a fraction. I didn't dare to attempt another escape. There was an inevitability about him this way – eyes narrowed, features contorted into a sneer of impatient demand. *What worries you?*

'Dying,' I bit out. 'Not everyone considers death a minor triviality, you know.'

Something shut down in his eyes, and I winced as the impact of my own words hit – but he didn't lash out, didn't shove me away in justified fury. Demon senses. Noting what I didn't dare to face, the shame, the regret, the blistering fear.

Em, his lips said.

I flinched.

Still he wouldn't take his eyes from mine. His gaze wormed its way into the very core of me, taking stock of my being with that ruthless, unyielding intensity – an examination as evadible as the advance of night itself. Every fibre of me screamed to look away, and yet I couldn't. Perhaps I didn't dare to. Perhaps I simply didn't want to.

'Please,' I whispered.

His hand came up, as if to form words ... then kept moving, past the spot before his chest, past the endless inches between us. It curled around my nape, the touch of his scarred fingers a command that slipped into every bone of my body.

Don't move, those fingers said. *Feel.*

And then his lips slanted over mine, so roughly that they were a punishment as much as a promise – pressing me back against that wall as my hands scrambled for grip on the cutting edges of the mosaic, demanding my mouth to open with a single flick of his tongue. I obeyed. He swept in, breathing hard as I moaned, hand on my neck locking me against him even as my legs wavered.

Feel.

There was a power in that kiss, a suggestion of violence looming just below the surface of his skin – as if any moment, some dark and ancient terror might awaken within him and reduce the world to ash and dust. But that threat, that night that slumbered in just the *existence* of him ... it wasn't aimed at me. The hungry circles of his tongue were rather an invitation, a reassurance, telling me I could hide in the velvet embrace of his wings while all else burned around us.

Do not ever forget, the pressure of his lips on mine seemed to tell me, *what I would do to keep you safe.*

An apology, that kiss, and a promise, too. The kiss of a male who'd once pulled himself from unconsciousness to find me, demon madness be damned, who'd take down an entire damn army by himself if it was what it took to protect me.

He would not leave me to fend for myself again.

He would *never* leave me to fend for myself again.

I clasped my hands around his shoulders and kissed him harder, tongues and teeth meeting in a clash of passion. He yanked me closer against him. I bit his lip in response, reaching past his torso, finding the velvet of his wings taut under my fingers.

He pulled back abruptly, tore away from me with a silent snarl. His eyes were glazed as he hovered inches away from my face; his left hand tensed even tighter around my neck, suggesting his choices had been to either let go or to fuck me senseless right against this very wall, risk of delay or not.

For a moment, I wished he hadn't been so sensible.

'You ...' The words drifted from my grasp. 'I ... Creon ...'

You're so gods-damned good at playing your roles, he interrupted, his signs fast and urgent. *So good at wanting and feeling what they want you to want and feel. And I know you had to. I know the bastards who raised you gave you no other choice. But ...*

He hesitated, left hand finally releasing my neck. I sagged back against the wall, unable to look away from the blunt motions of his fingers. *The bastards.* Opinions I knew he harboured, and yet he was rarely this forthcoming about them.

'I ... I just didn't want you to think ...'

That I was an idiot. A small, sentimental idiot, not even remotely prepared for the hard decisions saving the world required.

Em. He closed his eyes. *I'm not your bloody audience.*

I stared at him.

Don't make me that. Don't make me someone you have to be perfect for. The gods know I'm imperfect enough, and you still seem to tolerate me for reasons I'll never be able to grasp. There's no need to tip the scales further to my disadvantage.

That shook the life back into me. 'You are *not*—'

He raised an eyebrow. *See?*

'But ...'

I faltered. But *what?* But he might think me a fool and a silly wench? I didn't think him a heartless monster either, and perhaps ...

Perhaps this was what he felt, too, whenever I caught a glimpse of his demon magic – this bone-deep certainty that the truth of me would be wholly and utterly unlovable.

'But all of this is my fault,' I breathed, voice refusing to cooperate as the words broke free. 'This whole attack – this whole fight—'

There's a good handful of people I'd blame for this situation before I'd blame any of it on you.

'No, but you don't know ...' I gasped for air. Now that I'd started, there seemed to be no chance of stopping anymore. 'I let her escape. The fae who warned the Mother. She tried to break out of Agenor's tower and I could have stopped her – I *did* stop her. Got a knife against her throat. All I had to do was just ... just ... warn someone, and then ...'

There was still not a fleck of disapproval in his gaze.

'And then she talked about her children,' I whispered, tears stinging the back of my eyes. 'Said they were still at the Crimson Court. And all I could think was ... if she died, those little ones would never know *their* mother, would never know ...'

Impossibly, something softened in his face. *Em ...*

'So I let her go.' I couldn't let him finish that sentence, whatever words of pity he'd planned to sign. 'Covered her traces and hoped for the best like some senseless twit, and then she betrayed us anyway, and now ... now ...'

There was always going to be a confrontation. If no one had escaped, the Mother would have figured out the truth after a few weeks of suspicious silence from this side.

'Then we'd have had weeks to prepare!'

And so would she, he retorted, still so inconceivably unshaken. How in hell could he not be furious? How couldn't he see I'd betrayed him, too? *It's your presence that's forced her to act so rashly. Do you think she'd send out an army against bloody Agenor himself with just a day of preparation under any other circumstances?*

I faltered. That was a perspective I hadn't considered yet. As large as Ophion's force was ... he couldn't have had more than a night to pack his weapons and set out for battle.

'But ...' My voice wobbled. 'But what if I'm just not ready for any of this? What if I freeze as soon as anyone attacks me and—'

You won't.

'I couldn't kill even one of them! Why would I be better at killing anyone else?'

He shrugged. *What you can't do is kill an innocent bystander in cold blood. Don't you dare to ever feel ashamed of that again. It makes you a far more heroic person than the whole plague-stricken pack of us.*

'What?' I let out a bewildered laugh. 'No, Creon, you don't under-stand—'

That somewhere you seem to have decided I was to be your example to emulate? The thing on his lips couldn't with the best will in the world be considered a smile anymore – a wretched, bitter expression, all walls and thorns. *That you're apparently striving to be like that murderer you despised from the bottom of your heart for a sensible while?*

'But ...' I stammered, feeling suddenly more foolish than even after that ill-advised show of mercy. 'But it's not just you. If Lyn and Tared had found her – or Agenor or—'

We're all rotten inside. He shrugged stiffly. *Centuries of war do that to even the most well-meaning of hearts. You did the brave thing, Em. Saving a life even if it puts you in danger – that's not an easy choice to make.*

'It's a stupid choice to make,' I said sharply.

His smile was joyless enough to break a heart. *What's the sense in winning a war if you've become the evil you were fighting by the time you triumph?*

The shadows – dull, exhausted shadows – in his eyes told me he'd asked himself that question more often than I could count in the past hundred and thirty years.

'No.' The word came out hoarse. 'Oh, fuck. Creon, you're nothing like her. You couldn't be like her if you tried.'

And you're the only damn reason I manage to believe that for a minute every now and then. He leaned forward, resting his forehead against mine. Drew in a deep breath, as if to suck the scent of my stupid, sentimental innocence deep into his lungs. *Don't you ever become like me. Please. If for no other reason, do it for me.*

'You want me to keep putting you in danger for your benefit?' I said bitterly.

He shrugged that slow, cat-like shrug, but there was a sadness to it this time. *I'll handle the danger. I need you to handle whatever is left of my vile, tainted heart.*

'Don't say those things about yourself.' My hand flattened against his chest, seeking the reassurance of his steady pulse, the safety of his strength. 'Creon, I ... I ...'

I faltered there, hesitating habitually on words I'd swallowed so many times before. *Love you.* Because ... something about trust. Something about fear and broken hearts. Something about falling and never getting up again.

With his kiss still burning on my lips, I couldn't quite recall what I'd ever been thinking.

It's alright, Em. His smile barely grazed his lips. *You don't have to—*

'No,' I blurted. Damn whatever I'd been thinking. Damn whatever fears I'd tiptoed around for weeks, whatever lies I'd told myself. 'No, it's really not alright. There's more left of that tainted heart of yours than you'll ever allow yourself to believe. It may just be the most beautiful thing about you.' I managed a laugh, hoarse and choked. 'And you know what it's competing against.'

Effortless elegance or not, the agony brimming in his gaze told an entirely different story. *Don't say that.*

'But I—'

Not now. Brusque gestures, cutting me off. *Please.*

My throat tightened. 'You can't pry half of my truths from my lips and then request I keep the rest inside, Your Highness.'

It's not that. He kissed my forehead, then moved back, wings shifting restlessly. *None of this is going to be pretty. I'm not sure if it will still sound that true to you when I'm done slitting throats and piling up corpses, and I'd rather spare you the trouble of having to take it back.*

I suppressed a shiver. That prospect, the awareness of the blood on his hands ... it should have bothered me, shouldn't it? Once – in what wasn't such a distant past at all – it had bothered me enough to keep me resisting that irresistible pull between us, enough to doubt my own sanity at even the thought of wanting him.

And then I'd nearly died. He'd nearly died. And somehow, somewhere, I'd crossed that line.

I wasn't going to take back a damn thing.

The monster lurking below his skin ... it was mine, too.

But I didn't know how much of his doubt was his own and how much of it had sprung from a few moments too long in the hateful, fearful company of the Golden Court and the Underground. Was I battling his mind or the feelings of others?

We could talk after all of this was over. Probably. If we couldn't, there was little use in arguing my point in my last living hours.

'This is probably a conversation for later,' I muttered.

He closed his eyes. *Yes.*

We stood in silence for five, ten heartbeats. The ominous, overly saturated colours of the cave glimmered around us as lethally as they'd always done, a thousand hues of dread and heartbreak and bitterness.

My own heart slowly, very slowly pulled away from them.

Ready? Creon signed, looking up.

Not even close, I wanted to say. Then again ... 'You're with me.'

A fleeting smile. *Always.*

Even if it were to be the death of him.

But it would *not* be the death of him, or of me, or of anyone else I loved or cared about – because I could play my roles, and today I was playing a warrior. Today I was the little unbound mage fulfilling her destiny for the first time, fighting a battle no one else would be able to win for me.

I wasn't ready. It didn't matter. I was damn good at playing my roles, and I could pretend to be ready well enough.

'In that case,' I said, smoothing my dress as I stood straight and steeled my shoulders, 'it's about time we face our audience.'

CHAPTER 30

THE GOLDEN COURT HAD gone quiet when we returned.

Agenor's small army stood lined up around the pentagon of the high sandstone walls, most of them cleverly hidden in niches and behind the battlements, so that from the outside, the castle looked no more guard-ed than on an average afternoon. On the inside, the walls gleamed with swashes of black paint – a solution preferable, Creon had explained a moment before, to changing the sandstone itself, which was infused with protective divine magic no one truly understood.

Agenor walked his rounds, inspecting and instructing – past the rows of archers just behind the west wall, along the north walls where Lyn and Tared stood waiting, to the east, where most of the court's force had gathered under Doralis's command. There was a reassuring air to him, calm and utterly in control, the sword at his belt a clear reminder that he knew his way around a battlefield. I followed him with my gaze as we waited, watched him make his last adjustments, listened to the boom of his deep voice, and wondered for the thousandth time how in hell it was possible for this creature of gold and glory to be even distantly related to me.

I felt neither calm nor controlled as I stood on the southern wall with Creon, facing the lake that glittered peacefully in the summer sun.

The Silent Death had gone still next to me – not exactly tense but rather tight with focus, his thoughts reduced to a sharply drawn line of which the inevitable end point was death. His eyes didn't swerve away from the lush green of the forest. His wings had drawn taut, ready for flight. An alf steel knife turned and turned and turned thoughtlessly between his scarred fingers, as if every motion might instil some of its wielder's thirst for blood into the white metal itself.

Any moment now.

Oddly, the thought no longer made my stomach turn.

Ophion's people had started moving. That report had been brought in by Irie himself, who sat on the parapet next to me in the shape of a plump squirrel – our only companion on this side of the castle. The pixie busied himself with licking the last traces of cream from his little paws, pausing every now and then to examine the rest of the castle with his clever beady eyes. I'd never know if it was because of the strawberries or because of Agenor's promise to heal every pixie harmed by the fight, but he'd readily agreed to play a part in our experimental first line of defence.

I swallowed and glanced down at the flask of golden blood in my palm, the leather changed into brittle crystal by a single sparkle of yellow magic.

Any moment.

The summer warmth grew stifling, the air heavy with the smells of drying paint and dry grass and fearful sweat. If not for the strong east wind bringing cooler air, it would have become unbearable quickly. I shifted on my feet, annoyed at the trickle of sweat between my shoulder blades, annoyed at the loose hairs tickling my neck, annoyed at my own restlessness next to Creon's single-minded calm. My heart beat too fast in the tips of my fingers, every fibre of my limbs drenched in a sense of dreadful anticipation.

I was starting to wish the bastards would just show up.

Any moment.

It started with a flicker of movement between the treetops.

The knife stilled between Creon's fingers long before I noticed it, those odd flashes breaking through the dappled patters of swaying branches and leaves – wings. Bodies. Flying low, weaving their way through the forest so quietly no one but an exceptionally alert guard would notice them positioning for attack.

I spotted only a handful of them at first.

And then there were more of them wherever I looked, movements brushing in against the rhythm of the forest in the breeze – dozens and dozens of them. More than the full force we'd gathered in the castle behind us, and this was the *small* group Ophion had likely sent first to clear the way.

I'd known there were many of them, but up to that point, the look of five against one hadn't truly fit into my mind's eye.

Next to me, Irie the squirrel squeaked and changed into Irie the crow, shaking his feathers as if to get used to this new shape. On my other side, Creon still didn't move, eyes fixed on the edge of the forest with an intensity that made my heart skip a beat.

The Mother's hunter, marking his prey.

'Now-now?' the crow scratched.

Creon shook his head.

We waited in breathless, motionless silence as those shadows behind the trees moved closer together. Wings slapped out over the trees; one careless cry disturbed the silence. Irie shifted restlessly, and again Creon shook his head.

Behind me, Agenor's deep voice called for calm, for patience.

And from the woods, the vision shimmering in the heat of the summer afternoon, they emerged.

Twelve fae on the first row of their formation. Twelve more behind them. And another row, and another row – a hundred and twenty warriors, black-clad and armed to the teeth, fanning out in a wide crescent shape as they approached.

Fuck.

There were *so many* of them.

But there was no doubt in the faint smile that grew on Creon's lips, a smile that promised bloody demise to every single one of them, as he gestured, *Now.*

I raised the bottle of Etele's blood with trembling fingers. 'Irie?'

He lifted one claw and cautiously wrapped it around the fragile crystal. Hell, what if it was too fragile? What if it was too sturdy and wouldn't break? What if it did nothing at all? But this was not the time to doubt and waver, not the time to check and double check; the plans had been made, the risks calculated.

I stepped back, nodded, and whispered, 'Good luck.'

With a last screech, Irie took off. I followed him with my eyes as he flew towards the forest, a small black silhouette against a stark blue sky, crossing high over the merciless advance of the fae force below. The flask was so small I barely saw it drop. A flash of gold and nothing more.

But as it hit the ground ...

The glass shattered with the sound of a collapsing crystal chandelier.

A mushroom-shaped puff of the finest gold dust shot up from the spot where it had landed, just below the centre of the crescent formation. It clung to skin and wings like dust on a hot day's wind, and fae screamed – *howled* – as they went plummeting to the ground, flinging about flashes of blue magic to no avail. In the blink of an eye, over half of the crescent had gone down. What was left of that perfectly orderly formation flew haphazardly up and down, attempting to rescue crashed comrades and falling prey to wisps of blood dust as well, screaming at others to continue, screaming even louder to fall back. Two or three tried to resume their menacing advance. They soon concluded there was little menace about a handful of lone warriors creeping up on a fully defended castle, and joined their friends on a graceless flight back into the forest.

Some three dozen of them made it back. The majority of the company stayed behind, a large lump of twitching bodies around the spot of the explosion and a trail of those who'd succumbed to their injuries on the way back.

'Gods help me,' I said, unable to look away from the carnage.

Creon breathed a mirthless laugh next to me. *I think they did.*

Wings buffeted the air behind me. I jolted around just in time to see Agenor land on our wall, hair unusually ruffled by the breeze, eyes glued to the gold-dusted spectacle on the other side of the lake. His presence had kept the rest of the castle silent; now that he'd turned his wings on them, a soft but insistent murmur of bewildered excitement rose from the walls behind us.

'Well.' There was a grim chuckle in his voice. 'I suppose she'd have liked the sight of that, indeed.'

I swallowed. 'Etele?'

Agenor nodded, scanning the mess before us, then snapped up his gaze. A small fleck of black came flying towards us from the trees – a crow.

Irie.

I raised my hand on impulse, and he landed gracefully on my forearm, claws digging so deep that I winced. 'Emelin-Emelin!' I'd never heard him sound so excited, and it was enough to make me forget about the pain. 'Did you see-see that!'

'I doubt anyone missed it,' Agenor said dryly, and Irie let out a triumphant screech.

'Did you catch any glimpse of what they were doing?' I asked. 'Did they look like they were about to attack again?'

'They looked about to panic-panic.' Irie hopped on my wrist, wings flapping clumsily, and I winced again at the claws breaking my skin. Creon plucked the pixie off my arm, plopping it down on the sandstone wall with a straight face. Irie barely seemed to notice it. 'They were shouting-shouting about traps. Can we do it again-again?'

I glanced at Creon, who shrugged, and then at Agenor, who was staring at the forest with a slight crease in his forehead, trying to gaze straight into Ophion's vicious mind.

'Do you have any strawberries left?' I said.

He gave an absent grin. 'He'll suspect we'll do something similar again.'

Let them come a little closer, Creon signed, which I passed on.

'I have no desire to let that stuff come near to this castle,' Agenor said wryly. 'But I suppose it could lull them into an illusion of safety, yes. And at least if they're busy avoiding the blood, they may pay a little less attention to our arrows.'

'So we can do it again-again?' Irie squeaked.

Agenor scanned the fields before us a last time. 'Disguise yourself as another bird. Come from a different direction. Drop the blood later – a little beyond the lake.' He turned without waiting for an answer, gave us a quick nod, and shot into the sky again, ready to distribute orders to the other walls.

Irie ruffled his feathers, then rippled and turned into a small grey falcon. I patted him on the head, and he gave a content squawk.

The waiting game started again.

It didn't take as long, this time. Ophion seemed to have decided that if we were prepared for him anyway, he may as well get the matter over with. They rose from the forest without an attempt at stealth, and if I'd thought the previous group large, this army was sizeable enough to stop the breath in my lungs.

There were hundreds of them.

Hundreds.

'Irie.' Oh, fuck. Something to do. I needed something to think about, something to focus on – something that wasn't the line of fae emerging from the cover of trees, growing ominously larger every time I blinked. 'Take the flask. Start flying now, so they don't see you coming straight from the castle. And be careful.'

Creon was already working on the sturdy leather bottle – one quick flash of yellow, and nothing but a thin layer of crystal separated Etele's blood from the fae around us. Irie took it in his claw with more caution this time, squealing a last greeting as he soared off towards the east.

If we were lucky ...

If we were lucky, it would kill a few dozen of them. And then there would still be hundreds and hundreds left, hungry for revenge before they'd even reached the castle.

Breathe. I sucked in the warm summer air, my lungs clinging to the routine Tared had drilled into me – inhale, hold breath, exhale.

Ophion's army approached without mercy. A long, triangular forma-tion, like migrating birds, followed by lines and lines and lines of war-riors, weapons gleaming in their hands. Mere minutes and they'd reach these walls. Looking for me. Looking for Creon. Looking for death and ruin and ...

Inhale. Hold breath. Exhale.

Creon's wings flared out a fraction, and before I could wonder why, his calloused hand closed around mine, the gesture hidden from the view of the court behind that dark shield. I squeezed tight. He rubbed his thumb over my knuckles, a firm caress that somehow soothed the worst of my roaring fears.

Right.

I was ready.

The approaching force had almost reached the lake, and finally a flash of grey broke through the midsummer blue sky – Irie, soaring in from the east. Again I forgot to breathe as the glass flask tumbled down ...

And Ophion's army parted.

They were so fast, so impressively coordinated, that I knew in the first blink of an eye they had discussed the manoeuvre – gods damn me, of course they had. By the time the bottle of blood cracked on the vibrant green grass below, all but a few slow fae had fled out of reach of the dust cloud, and only a few unlucky ones fell crying to the ground.

And two of them broke away from the rest of the group, chasing after the grey bird flying west.

I stifled a cry, grabbing uselessly for my dark skirts – no! No, they weren't going to kill *him*! But the fae didn't cease their hunt as they raced after the falcon, west, then north, then west again, closer to the castle, but always too far removed to even think of reaching them.

Creon let go of my hand.

And with a careless flick of his right hand, a lightning bolt of red magic cracked through the air between us and the two fae, tearing straight through the first one's wings.

The second fae faltered as his colleague gracelessly soared down, desperately flapping his damaged wings to keep himself from crashing. Irie dove to the ground in that small moment of respite, changing forms and slipping away in the grass before his hunters regained their composure. Two seconds, and the danger was gone – but I found myself behind the battlements with a dry throat and a pounding heart, blinking quite owlishly at the unharmed fae male as he hurried back to join the ranks of the others.

'Oh, gods.' Too breathless. At least I was not alone; the feverish murmurs and the faltering ranks of Ophion's warriors appeared equally unnerved. 'That ... hell, shouldn't that be impossible?'

Should be, Creon admitted wryly.

I let out a laugh, squeezing my fingertips into my dress, magic tingling up my arm. Before us, a group of about three dozen fae split off from the main force and soared closer to the castle – closer to our wall.

Oh, fuck.

Perhaps waiting hadn't been so bad.

'Can't you hit them, too?' I managed, hating how my voice came out in a squeak, hating how it trembled at the sight of those approaching warriors. Long, powerful wingbeats. Black clothes, gleaming swords and daggers. All of it aimed at Creon, at me – just the two of us, alone on this bloody big wall.

Fuck, fuck, fuck.

Distance weakens impact. Creon's signs were quick but calm, his fingers taut as he kept his gaze on the attacking force. *Don't move until I do. Also, these were friends of Deiras. Habit of doubling human tributes for their own gain.*

I stiffened. Deiras – the same Deiras who'd trained him, the same Deiras who'd been responsible for a good amount of those inked scars on his fingers? *Doubling human tributes.* Hollow-eyed children, starving elders, women dragged onto the tribute ships to never be seen again, and at once the magic was *hurting* in the tips of my fingers, biting and scorching, wrestling to break free.

Fuck *them,* then.

Everything slammed into motion at the same time.

Agenor's voice rose behind me, yelling commands. Bowstrings twanged. Arrows whizzed. Fae cried out as the alf steel arrowheads bit deep into their flesh, and next to me, Creon moved.

He – Zera help me – *moved.*

Power seemed to swell in him as he flicked the first burst of magic at the approaching army, his motions so inhumanly graceful, so flawlessly choreographed, that there was no sense of violence and brutality to them even as fae went crashing to the ground in sprays of blood. It was a dance. A ruthless, devastating dance of unbridled power, but a dance all the same – a turn around the floor with death.

Red magic rained over us, and I jumped back, mind momentarily frozen between fight and flight. Creon merely whirled to evade that first attack and countered so fast I blinked and missed it; the world lit up in scarlet and crimson around his dark silhouette, and cries of pain rose from the front line as fae again went down twitching and flapping.

The world had gotten too loud, too shrill, too frenzied as weapons clashed and voices howled and colour flashed in every corner of my sight. But he was next to me, a cold knife slash against the dizzying backdrop of chaos and death, and he never even faltered.

This, then, was Creon Hytherion as I'd only truly seen him that first night, amidst the burning houses of Cathra: a blood-curdling, breath-taking instrument of war.

And *mine.*

It was that thought that shattered the paralysis. Not the memories of gnawing hunger. Not the faceless image of my missing mother. Just the pale-haired fae female that raised her hand at Creon as two others clawed at their bleeding throats beside her, the lot of them flying close enough for me to see the white around their irises. She overlooked me entirely, focused on the havoc Creon's magic was wreaking among her company.

Her loss.

The red tore free from my fingertips, drawn from the blackened inner castle wall, and cut a ragged gash across her face, breaking the skin from jaw to eye. She screeched, the sound piercing deep into my guts, and grabbed for her wounded cheek with her right hand, the blue fading from her black coat under her left.

I aimed my next attack at her wings.

Blood sprayed from the spot where I hit her, just beyond the onset of her left wing. She tilted in the air, went down in flailing spirals. I flung another bolt of yellow magic at the earth below her, changing lush grass into a stretch of merciless granite, and she landed face-first with a crack I heard even over the whooshing of the arrows and the battle cries around me.

Dead.

My heart pulsed in my ears, my fingertips, my guts. She was *dead*. I had *killed* her. Which seemed the sort of thing I should think about, or wail about, or throw up about for a bit – but red flashed in the corner of my eye, and I whirled aside just in time for the magic to hit the sandstone where I'd stood a fraction earlier.

Never mind about the wailing.

I lunged forward, pressed my hand to my dress, and aimed for the nearest set of cobalt blue wings in sight. Our attackers were a solid damn *wall* now, limbs and wings wherever I moved, and I stopped thinking, stopped calculating, stopped fearing. An ice-cold, crystal-clear frenzy rose in me through the pandemonium, every sharpened thought focused on one thing and one thing only: *survive*.

Fae flew up at us, flinging deadly red at me from all sides. In that glass-edged blur of focus, I dodged and countered on nothing but reflexes, the rush of fear my only guide. Wings. Eyes. Throats. Fingers. They were no longer part of breathing, thinking creatures. They became inviting targets, begging to be destroyed. I turned and aimed, turned and aimed, colour dazzling lethally around me, magic dancing on my fingertips. My line of sight shrunk to the circle of death surrounding us, blocking out the fights on the other walls; my world was nothing but a sequence of rhythm and instinct and Creon's presence behind me, shielding me. Turn. Dodge. Red. Turn. Something sizzled at my elbow, and I found a long tear in the linen of my dress. When I glanced down, five heartbeats or an eternity later, blood was dripping from a cut in my shin I hadn't even felt.

Worries for later. I didn't have time for pain.

Magic flickered, crumbling stone and metal wherever it hit. Dodge. Red. Dodge. Turn, and turn again. Creon was wherever I moved, catlike and incomprehensibly fast, loose strands dancing around his face as he weaved his web of crimson light against our attackers. His shirt had gone pale green, my own dress a muddy blue, the vast expanse of the painted wall the colour of moss. But red blood splattered across the battlements, ran in trickles around the few who'd made it to the wall and fallen there, and through the heady focus of my bloodlust, I saw nothing but more colour, more magic.

And then suddenly our attackers were gone – suddenly the world went quiet around us.

I gasped in a breath as the turmoil fell away, no new opponents waiting as the last black-clad fae male went down. Creon caught my elbow, and I whirled around, eyes frantically scanning the sky for the next danger to fight.

At the other walls, the struggle continued. But around us, the world was jarringly, blissfully empty.

They were holding back. Only then did I see it, my eyes drawn to the lake shores by a trail of weapons and bodies and blood – some hundred and fifty of them, examining the fight around the castle, waiting. To the west, fae were going one on one, wrestling on the sandstone walls. From the north came the pungent stench of burning flesh, Lyn a small, flaming silhouette dashing through the air on her wings of fire. At the east side, the fight was fiercest, as Agenor had predicted, Ophion's force attempting to break through the defences with the wind at their backs.

Dead and wounded fae lay in the courtyards below, too, the roofs of the castle, the gardens. Our people. Our allies. Ten, twenty of them – I forced myself to stop counting.

My breath was in a tangle. My blood still pulsed feverishly through my veins. Creon didn't let go of my arm, and I didn't waver.

'I'm alright.' I didn't even know if it was true. Alright – what was alright? I was alive. I was breathing. I wasn't a wailing, sobbing mess. 'Are you ...'

He squeezed my elbow, then let go. *Don't worry about me.* His signs were curt, his gaze darting between me and the air around us. *Bastard needs more than this to bring me down.*

Ophion. I glanced at the lake and caught sight of him for the first time, marching through the grass, ordering males and females around. That pale, pointy face, those slick dark curls ... the iron hooks in his hands, and—

Creon shot forward, yanked me into his arms, and whirled around.

I'd been distracted for only the briefest of moments. Somehow I'd missed the approach of a solitary fae male until his burst of red lit up the edge of my sight, hitting the spot where I'd stood. Creon swung one of his alf steel daggers up before I could react, catching the magic on the white blade. Red crackled from his fingertips the next moment, hitting the other's wing just above the shoulder.

A manoeuvre of two heartbeats at most. He hadn't even tensed.

I stumbled back as I let go of him, squinting at the fae male who'd crashed onto the wall and was making frantic attempts to crawl away from Creon with one bleeding, jerking wing. Even with his face contorted in a grimace, something about him looked oddly ... *familiar?*

Sudden dread clogged my throat, and Creon's eyes narrowed at me. *Em?*

'He ... he's the one who took me at the Labyrinth.' The words fell out as the memory returned, that lisping voice behind me, those arms locking me against a stranger's body. *Quiet, or some of us might decide we want more of those sounds you're making* ... 'When Ophion found me there. He was the one who held me.'

The fae male gurgled a plea, wounded wing twitching as he tried to fly.

Do you want him? Creon signed, watching him with tangible repulsion, knife turning temptingly between his fingers.

'No, thanks,' I said weakly. 'Go ahead.'

His smile was as dark as his eyes as he knelt next to the other male, pinning him down with an efficient stab between the ribs. Not in the heart, but the other side of his body, piercing lung and flesh only.

The fae male screeched.

Creon's expression didn't shift while he slowly twisted the knife a quarter turn, then pulled back and slit the other's throat in a single fluid motion. His eyes burnt like blazing embers as he stood up straight again and shoved the dead body off the wall with his foot, tucking his knife back behind his belt.

Fucker, he signed, lip curling into a sneer.

Should I have been repulsed? A last sane corner of my mind suggested so. Told me that the lethal intensity of his gaze shouldn't make my heart skip a beat, that even such a graceful display of violence shouldn't send that dangerous warmth curling around my guts ... but hell take me, it did.

'Much obliged,' I got out. 'Doesn't their pain make it worse for you, too?'

He shrugged, already back to scanning the skies, the battlefields around us, flinging a careless glimmer of red into the back of a fae trying to sneak past the rows of archers. *Fastest way to end their pain is to kill them.*

I managed a chuckle. 'Fair point. And why in hell are they leaving us alone like this? Shouldn't they be aiming for me before anyone else?'

That's what I'm wondering. Of course he had already been wondering. Narrowing his eyes at Ophion's figure in the distance, he tartly added, *Suppose he's planning something.*

'Any idea ...'

Wish I had. He threw a quick look at the other side of the castle, where Tared quickly and efficiently sliced a fae to bite-sized pieces. Agenor was at the east wall, sword circling like a scythe, waves and waves of invaders breaking on his defences. *It's almost like he wants to lure us to the other walls, but—*

The earth moved.

Shifted.

And before he could finish his signs, before I could so much as cry out his name, the wall gave way beneath my feet.

I heard myself scream as the sandstone split open and I went hurtling down, down, down, my stomach in my throat, my body slamming into bricks and beams as the castle crumbled around me. The sound of the explosion reached me too late. A bang so loud it blinded me for a timeless and eternal moment, as I fell and fell and there was nothing to the world but those walls coming down with me ...

Yellow.

Yellow.

I swung my magic wildly, no plan or strategy to it. But I landed in something soft and squishy as I finally slammed against the earth and found the air punched from my lungs for another stunned eternity – down.

I'd gone down.

The wall. Had. Gone. Down.

And then a red flash set the rubble around me afire, and some primal and unthinking thirst for survival took over, moved my limbs when my brain no longer could, raised my head while I no longer had the courage. Every inch of my body hurt like hellfire, and some bone in my left hand was probably broken ...

And those hundred and fifty fae Ophion had held back ... they were everywhere now.

Soaring towards me, towards the castle, towards the breach that had opened in the wall. I rolled back, forced myself to sit up despite the pain flaming in every fibre of me, thoughts rolling through my mind even as my body scrambled for survival. *Planning something.* That first attack had been nothing but a diversion. Just enough to keep us busy, enough to keep us blind, keeping all but that necessary force ready for this true attempt.

Enough to prepare whatever attack had torn through the sandstone and sent me hurtling down.

I hauled myself upright, flinching at the movements of my aching muscles. Fuck. Above me, people were shouting orders, crying in alarm. Before me, invading fae came soaring down, bathing the wreckage and the surviving battlements in a sea of red.

Fuck.

Panic paralysed my thoughts. I didn't have much colour left. The sandstone around me was all peaceful gold, only flecks of black paint to be found. My dress – pale blue. My abrased hands – not red enough.

And dozens of fae came diving at me from above, swords drawn and uniforms black as the night, faces contorted in sneers of furious blood-lust.

Fuck, fuck, fuck.

I staggered back, closer to the wall, stumbling over sharp-edged debris. Far above, someone shouted my name. Agenor? Was that Agenor? But there were so many attackers now, crowding the battlements as others lunged for me, and whoever was trying to reach me wasn't reaching me fast enough.

Hair. Dark brown. I grabbed for the loose locks of my braid with my aching left hand and shot a desperate attack at the nearest fae female. She dodged, zigzagging closer, a dozen others in her wake.

Two dozen others.

So, so many others.

My breath shrieked as I stumbled farther back, clenching a shaking hand around the dagger at my belt. Again someone screamed above me. A hundred feet away, Tared appeared in the blood-soaked grass – too far away from me, too many fae between us. Red so bright it hurt my eyes exploded above me – Creon, that had to be Creon, and it barely cut through the never-ending ranks of Ophion's main force.

Red magic lashed at me. Pain – burning, piercing pain – blasted through my shoulder, and I cried out, mind a blank sheet of panic.

No.

They circled me as I stood there, back pressed against the rough edges of the remaining wall, useless knife in my fist. Like hungry vultures, waiting to tear me apart.

Gleefully so.

I opened my mouth to scream. *Help. Anyone – help.* But my vocal chords seemed paralysed, my lungs already empty to prepare for the inevitable. Only my thoughts still fluttered senselessly through the void – *help.* A tall, one-eyed fae male before me raised his hand, murderous intent obvious in the crook of his smile.

Help.

He grinned. And fired.

I dove aside, scraping over rough edges of stone, splinters of the broken beams digging deep into my shins and arms. More blasts of red rained over me, pain blooming through my arms, my hips, my thighs, and I did the only thing I could think of. Squeezed my eyes shut and wrapped my arms over my face and cried, as loud as the last breath in my lungs would let me, '*Creon!*'

Someone laughed.

A cruel, malicious laugh – and then something changed in that maniacal sound.

A shrillness. A hollowness. And suddenly ... suddenly it was no longer a laugh at all.

It rose into a high-pitched scream as I lay there, curled up on the wreckage, unable to breathe – a primal cry of heartbreak and despair. I winced, expecting a sword to sink between my ribs any moment.

The heavy thud of a body hit the stones beside me. The screaming abruptly ended.

And then another voice took over. And another one. And another one.

I tore open my eyes, unable to make sense of the sight that welcomed me. Fae were screaming. A chorus of heart-rending agony, growing louder and louder; they fell to their knees where they stood, kicked into the air, squirmed in the grass. Next to me, the body of the crooked-smile male lay flung gracelessly over the rubble, his eyes wide open in a frozen expression of horror, his knife buried in his chest.

His own hands lay clutched around the hilt.

What?

The madness spread under my gaze. Before me, a fae female clawed at her own eyes with long, sharpened nails, drawing deep gouges through her irises. Another scrambled for her knife as if to defend herself, only to bury the blade deep into her own throat, screaming and gurgling until the air finally left her.

They went down in waves, like grain blown flat by a gust of wind, taking their own lives with any weapon they could find. Tens of them. Dozens of them. Agenor's fae swooped in from above the next moment, hacking and slashing at the last ones standing, drowning the battle-field in red.

Saving me?

Winning?

What in hell ... what in hell was happening?

I stumbled to my feet. My eyes found Tared's bloodied figure, frozen in the middle of the field, staring wide-eyed at something behind me. Something up on the wall. Something ...

Creon.

Creon.

Oh, gods help me. My heart skipped a beat as I snapped around, thoughts crashing into place with physical force – *power that makes a man kill himself at a twitch of my hand.*

Demon magic.

That ... that couldn't be true, could it?

He was standing on the edge of the wall, inches away from falling. A stark silhouette against the bright azure sky, wings flaring wide, dark hair whipping around his face on the summer breeze. Clenched fists empty, knives gone. Glazed eyes staring unseeing into the distance, an expression on his face that came closest to ... *ecstasy?*

The opposite of what they felt.

Oh, *fuck.*

I needed to reach him. Needed to find some fae to fly me up, to climb that gods-damned wall if I had no other choice. Anything to get my arms around his shoulders and tell him it was alright, tell him I was grateful, tell him to ignore whatever memories the use of his powers dragged up in his mind ...

A dart of red shot past a hair's breadth from my ear, scattering a block of sandstone with far too much force, and I whirled back around.

CHAPTER 31

How in earth the bastard had managed to avoid Creon's sweep of madness, I might never know. But he came strutting through the blood-ravaged grass with all the cocky viciousness I remembered from the Crimson Court, dark curls barely ruffled by the fighting, pale, pointy face contorted into a malicious smile, and the questions about his miraculous survival slid to the back of my mind, never to be seen again.

In their place rose the memory of iron hooks tearing through the velvet of Creon's wings.

I lunged forward and grabbed a handful of the nearest corpse's black shirt, respect for the dead be damned. Ophion whirled away from the flash of red with surprising agility, firing two quick blasts of magic back at my face, and then a third one which hit me viciously in the thigh as a ducked away. I cursed and attacked again. He dodged, retaliated,

449

laughed as I leapt away from my magic source to avoid the bright red that came hurtling for my face.

Hell. I should probably have known his boastful swagger was based on *something*.

And where in hell was everyone?

Agenor's people were chasing fleeing fae. Tared ... I'd no idea where he'd gone and no time to think about it. Ophion chuckled as I scrambled back through the sandstone debris, frantically hunting for a trace of red, and flung another attack at me. I ducked, and a few feet away, a rock burst apart with a thunderous bang. He didn't even look down as he continued his unstoppable advance, stepping nonchalantly on pieces of wreckage and arms of corpses as he sauntered closer.

Another memory stirred – Edored.

I grabbed the golden stone, the ragged edges brittle under my palm, and aimed my desperate blow of yellow magic at the earth below his feet.

Blood-drenched grass became blood-drenched mud, sucking in his right foot with a loud, wet slurp. Ophion cursed, losing the rhythm of his attack for the shortest of moments as he glanced down to pull free.

A ball of fire shot down from the sky.

Lyn hit his back with so much force he tumbled forward, not nearly so brash and brazen as he fell to his knees with another sharp curse. Her chubby arms wrapped around his neck before he could recover, the sharp point of her alf steel ring pressed deep into the softness below his chin. Wings of fire flickered behind her a last time, then sizzled down, leaving her clutching onto his back like a child clinging to its parent.

'Well, well.' There was nothing childlike about her voice. 'I was *so* hoping I'd get my hands on you, Kinslayer. Must be my lucky day.'

He recovered infuriatingly fast. 'Oh, hello, Phiramelyndra. Been a while, love.'

She jabbed her ring into the vulnerable underside of his chin. 'That will look pathetic in the history books, Ophion. Any other last words?'

'Wait!' I blurted, scrambling upright. *Last words.* Which was all agreeable enough – nothing the bastard deserved more than a seven-year-old slitting his throat on an undignified muddy battlefield –

but he wouldn't be able to speak with his throat slit, and as much as I disliked the sound of his voice ...

Was anyone more privy to the Mother's secrets than he was?

'I'm not going to make any attempt to save *him*, Em,' Lyn said, pulling a face at me over Ophion's slender, silk-clad shoulder. 'I need at least a suggestion of underlying morals for that – and stay *down*, fucker.'

I managed a laugh. 'No, no, don't worry. Just ...' A quick glance around. No other fae within hearing distance; those on the walls seemed too busy chasing after the last of the Mother's army. 'I need him to answer a few questions.'

Ophion sniggered. Was it arrogance that left him so utterly unconcerned, or did he have something else up his sleeve? 'What makes you think I'll be happy to answer any of your questions, little dove?'

The sound of that nickname sent shivers up my spine – damn him for that alone. But I clenched my jaw, hauled myself to my feet, and coldly said, 'That bargain for your life I'm offering you.'

His smile paled.

'Em?' Lyn said, amber eyes flashing with warnings.

I ignored her, stuck out my hand to Ophion's kneeling figure, and continued, the words hurtling over my lips before I could think twice about them. 'Answer my questions. Fully and truthfully and immediately, without any attempts to deceive me about your intended meaning. I'll make sure you get out of here alive – that you get back to the Mother alive this once.'

'*Em*,' Lyn snapped, but by the way his thin lips curled up, I knew Ophion had already taken my bait.

'You don't have that authority,' he said, his voice a drawl.

I shrugged. 'Pick whatever better options you have, then.'

He faltered, hand halfway to raised. Lyn studied me with narrowed eyes, puzzled but unwilling to quiz me on my intentions for the Mother's lover to hear; she didn't object.

She can think, Agenor. Bless her little heart.

'Well?' I said. Better to have this behind me before Agenor could fly by and stop me. 'What's it going to be – hell or your faith in my authority?'

Ophion cursed but grabbed my hand, long fingers unpleasantly firm. 'We're in agreement.'

At least I knew what to expect this time, the blistering light blazing between our palms. At least my bargain mark should vanish as soon as I'd fulfilled my promise and safely delivered him back to the Crimson Court. And yet it felt like a filthy stain, that cat's-eye green agate that appeared at my wrist as soon as the bargain magic faded.

Ophion chuckled as I yanked back my hand, rising to his feet despite Lyn's weight on his shoulders. She scoffed but wrapped her legs around his hips without further objection, still holding her alf steel ring pressed tight against his throat.

'Tell me, then, Emelin.' Hell be damned – without the threat of his life hanging over his head, he somehow managed to be even more mockingly arrogant. 'What questions are worth sparing my glorious life to you?'

I sucked in a breath. 'Twenty-one years ago, a human woman gave the Mother a list of human traitors at the Crimson Court. Do you remember?'

Lyn's eyes widened abruptly, her mouth forming a silent *oh*.

Ophion parted his lips, winced as he found himself unable to say whatever he'd been about to say, and tried again. 'I remember a few such cases and am not sure how long ago they occurred.'

'She was pregnant,' I said quickly. 'She bargained for the life of her child. Does that—'

'Oh.' He chuckled, tucking a lock of dark hair behind his pointy ear as if he wasn't standing there with a flaming, furious phoenix on his back. 'The girl with the child that died. Yes, I do remember. What was her name again – Rosie? Something like that?'

'No, but that doesn't matter.' Of course the bastard didn't remember her name. Who cared about the names of lowly humans, anyway? 'What happened to her? After the child died?'

He looked amused. 'She died, too.'

That had to be untrue – but the bargain seemed to give him no trouble. So that was *his* truth, then. Whatever had happened to her ... at least he wasn't keeping her prisoner below the Crimson Court in secret.

'Tell me more,' I said, breath too shallow. 'How did she die?'

'Achlys and Melinoë sent her off to some other island to work in the mines. I think she dropped overboard at night on the way there and drowned.'

Drowned.

Except ... except she didn't drown.

I met Lyn's gaze, her eyes bright and focused, absorbing every word. *Dropped overboard.* And then she'd vanished alive – which didn't sound like an accident, really, but more like ...

An escape?

She'd *escaped?*

It took all I had to keep my face straight, not to reveal the incredulous hope that fizzled up in me. 'Where was the ship going?'

Ophion pressed his lips. 'Khonna, I think – they were undermanned at the time. One of the mining islands in the north, in any case.' He cocked his head, cat eyes too sharp, and pleasantly added, 'Why do you care that much, little dove?'

'None of your concern,' I said sharply. 'Now, do you know—'

'Ah,' he interrupted, tongue flicking along his upper lip as if to taste my agitation. 'Let me guess. The child didn't die at all?'

Oh, fuck. He wasn't *stupid*, the bastard.

'I'm very sorry, Emelin.' He chuckled, sounding delighted despite the fire dancing over Lyn's arms. 'If you're looking for answers on your mysterious origins, I couldn't tell you who she spread her legs for. Or how much it earned her.'

'Shut *up.*' Red pulsed at the edges of my sight – *he loved her, you bastard*, I wanted to spit, but did I even know that for sure? 'I wasn't asking for your thoughts or—'

'Oh, I like to overperform,' he said and winked at me.

Anger got the better of me.

I shot forward, yanking my knife up – to hell with that cocky grin, to hell with that smug confidence. I may have bargained to keep him alive, but I'd never promised to keep him *unharmed.*

Ophion realised his mistake just a fraction too late, staggering back with Lyn curled tight around his torso. 'Emelin—'

And then my dagger sank through the bluish black of his wing, and my name became a muffled cry of agony.

I twisted the blade. Let him know I'd learned from the best.

My breath laboured in my throat as I jumped back and left a ragged hole the size of a silver florin behind. 'Not that much fun when you're the one on the pointy end, is it?'

'Bitch,' he spat, face contorted in pain. Lyn jammed her ring into his chin once again, and he winced, knees dangerously close to buckling.

'I suggest you try to be a little more polite, old friend,' Agenor's deep voice abruptly rose at my left, 'unless you prefer for me to heal the edges of that wound with your wing still open?'

I jerked around. He'd landed soundlessly amidst the remainders of the southern wall, arm bleeding violently, hands covered in blood and gore, shirt torn and dusty, and somehow still utterly dignified. With a quick glance at me, he added, 'Apologies. I was occupied at entirely the wrong place, it seems.'

Ophion bit out a stinging laugh. 'And a good afternoon to you, too, even older friend. Bit of an odd change of mind you've shown here, hm?'

Agenor threw Lyn an exhausted glance. 'Any reason why he's still capable of talking?'

'Oh, I suggest you don't kill him,' I said, apologetically raising my wrist to show the pale green agate. 'Made a bargain to save his life.'

'You did *what*?'

'For questions about her dear dead mommy,' Ophion drawled, the undertone implying I'd sold my soul for a bag of sweets. 'So very sentimental.' He chuckled – so content with this opportunity to blacken me in Agenor's eyes that he failed to notice the other's abrupt look of understanding. 'Unless you want the little vixen dead, you'll have to let me go, I'm afraid. Any message you'd like me to pass on to the court, if we're standing here anyway?'

'Ah,' Agenor said – his voice flat, but too flat, an overabundance of self-restraint that suggested the alternative was something far less civilised. *Her dead mommy.* He'd heard that clue, too, then – heard Ophion's accidental confession he had no idea what had happened to my mother. 'Yes. Let Achlys and Melinoë know they have nothing to fear from me as long as they leave the Golden Court alone. I won't be laying siege to that cursed island of yours. So whatever they want—'

Ophion sniggered. 'What they want is the girl.'

'A shame,' Agenor said, shoulders tightening. 'I'm not entirely inclined to hand over my own daughter to their questionable treatment, you see.'

Ophion's smile fell abruptly.

My own daughter.

That ... that almost sounded *proud*, didn't it?

'Oh, sorry,' I said, my voice unwillingly smug. 'Did I forget to tell you?'

Ophion turned worryingly green as his eyes shot back and forth between the two of us, adding up facts, drawing conclusions – mother, father, magic powers. The next laugh he spat out was even sharper than the last, laced with genuine revulsion.

'A *human*, Agenor? Really?'

How Agenor managed not to punch the bastard in the face was a profound mystery; I wouldn't have hesitated if not for his presence beside me. But his only reaction was an alarmingly mild smile and an equally mild, 'I wouldn't expect that to offend your sensibilities that much, friend. You've had worse in your bed.'

Oh.

He *did* have claws.

Ophion scoffed. 'Do I hear a hint of jealousy there?'

'I know how their lovers tend to end,' Agenor said dryly, his face so unfazed I dared to believe that suggestion had been based on nothing but Ophion's overwrought self-esteem. 'I've never felt the slightest desire to tread in their footsteps.'

'And so you run after *humans* instead,' Ophion sneered, the pulse at his temple all that betrayed he'd heard the thinly veiled threat. 'How many of the little cunts did you—'

Agenor merely sighed, interrupting the outburst that had been on its way to my lips. 'Em?'

'What?' I snapped.

'Would you do me a favour and take care of his other wing, too?'

I stared at him, lost for words. He gave me a quick smile – weary, yet faintly amused.

Well. That was one type of father-daughter bonding, presumably.

Tared appeared out of nowhere just as I buried my knife in Ophion's right wing. The alf was covered in blood and dirt, but none of that stopped him from looking quite amused at the scene waiting for him. 'Are we all invited to take a swing at his wings here?'

Ophion winced and tried to fend me off, groaning as I jumped back and Lyn stabbed him again with her ring. She impatiently clucked her tongue and said, 'We're taking him back to the Crimson Court.'

'Are we?' Tared said, raising an eyebrow.

'After Em is done stabbing him and asking questions, yes.' She threw him a look. 'Bargain.'

Tared rolled his eyes, looking uncannily similar to Edored with smudges of blood covering his clothes and half of his face. 'Damn shame. Any other questions, then, Em?'

I turned back to Ophion, gathering my thoughts. 'Do you know of any other unbound mages?'

'No,' he said through clenched teeth.

'Do you know how to break a binding?'

'No.'

'Is it possible to break a binding?'

'Don't know.' He let out a pained hiss – his bargain pushing him to say more, perhaps – and added, 'Achlys and Melinoë can reverse it. I've never heard of anyone else breaking it.'

I closed my eyes, trying to be sensible through the rush of blood-drenched panic. 'What are her plans for the coming months?'

Ophion launched into a monologue on small tribute revisions and palace restorations he'd heard the Mother mention once or twice.

'Oh, shut up,' I snapped, cursing my sloppy questioning. 'What are her plans for the war, roughly?'

He muttered a curse. 'Protect the Crimson Court, stop other fools from joining you, smoke you out of whatever rat's nest you're hiding in.'

Nothing surprising there. 'How are her eyes?'

'Bad.' His lip curled up. 'She'll figure out a solution.'

'Can't wait,' I said, unable to suppress a small grin. 'Send her my sympathies in the meantime. Last question – do you know what the importance of her throne is?'

Ophion huffed a laugh. 'Her *throne?*'

'Yes. She seems protective of it.'

'Took a damn lot of work to build it,' he said and let his eyes slide over the company around him, mouth tightening into a cruel smile. 'She might just have enough bones for a new one by the time she's done with you all, though.'

I ignored that and glanced at Agenor, who shook his head. No additional questions.

'Well,' Tared said sourly, twirling his sword around as he slid his gaze over Ophion's damaged wings. 'Any other parts of him we want carved up, then, or can we go?'

'Could think of a few parts,' I said, 'but—'

Agenor let out a mirthless chuckle. 'That would offend *my* sensibilities, I'm afraid.'

This time I was the one who couldn't help but grin at him. Gods help me. Perhaps I'd hit my head harder than I thought during that fall – I hadn't suddenly started *liking* him, had I?

'Let's go, then,' Lyn said, scoffing at the male she was holding. 'The faster I can pull my hands off him, the better it is for me. Faewood, Tared?'

He met her gaze as he stepped in to grab Ophion's elbow. A moment later, the three of them had vanished into thin air, leaving nothing but Ophion's muddy footprints behind.

Agenor clutched my shoulder, whirling me around. 'Gods and demons, are you alright?' Blue magic spilled from his fingers as he spoke, drawn from my paled dress; on my arms and shoulders, the wounds grew shut, the sudden absence of pain enough of a relief that I nearly cried. 'I should never have ... This was far too close ... If not for ...'

His voice drifted off even as his fingers tirelessly continued their work.

Creon.

If not for Creon.

I jerked back from his grasp, snapping my head up. Above me, the castle wall was deserted – no menacing silhouettes, no blinding red magic. Where in hell had he gone?

And why?

Those damn powers. My breath quickened. Those powers he'd sworn never to use, those powers he wouldn't unleash upon the world even to save his own life, and then I had decided to start dying. Giving him no other choice. If he'd been far enough gone to leave me on my own with Ophion ...

It had to be bad.

Agenor was saying something. I ignored it entirely. 'Where is he?'

'What?' He blinked at me, genuinely lost. 'Who?'

'*Creon.* Where did he go, after—'

'I have no idea,' he said, glancing over his shoulder as if the Silent Death may jump from behind a few blocks of stone. 'I'd worry about anyone he runs into before I'd worry about him, Em – he doesn't need—'

'You don't have the faintest idea what you're talking about.' I let out a bitter laugh, glancing up and around for anyone to ask. Hell, where could he be? Did he have his own rooms in the castle? Had he locked himself behind the Blood Gate again? *Someone* must have seen him vanish, even in the chaos of those last minutes of the fight. Stepping back, I added, 'I'll ask around. See you later, if—'

'Em – Emelin – *wait.*'

I'd never heard him so flustered; it wasn't enough to slow my steps. 'It won't take hours!'

'But what did he say about ...'

About Allie. He didn't finish his sentence. For two heartbeats, I felt guilty; then I reminded myself that Lyn would be back soon enough to tell him, that my mother had survived wherever she was for twenty years already, and that Creon was gone *now*.

'What's a few hours in a fae life?' I yelled over my shoulder, and I started running.

CHAPTER 32

HE'D FLOWN TO THE northeast, a fae female with a broken leg told me from her deep chair on the courtyard, where she sat waiting for her turn to be healed. Towards the hills, another wounded male confirmed. To the coast, a tall female dragging corpses around corrected them, and she was sure of that because she'd been on the walls and seen him descend in the direction of Sunstone Bay.

'Of what?' I said.

Either she noticed my distress, or she was sick of hauling bodies out of the castle, because she immediately suggested she fly me there.

'Not all the way, though,' she added quickly as we swept towards the summer sky, her minty green shirt and trousers fluttering around us. 'I'm in no hurry to see him again.'

I'd be lying if I said I didn't understand. Watching an army mow itself down at his command had given new depth to the stories I'd heard about him all my life.

'A little closer is fine,' I said.

We flew to the northwest of the island, where I hadn't been before; on this side, low hills fed the thin streams of water that ran down into the lake, the endless stretches of wild grass and flowers interrupted by the occasional copse of trees. My guide descended without a word as we approached the coast, tension infusing her movements.

'I'll just leave you here,' she whispered as she set me down in the high grass. 'The bay is that way – follow the coastline and you'll see it. I'll just ...' She cleared her throat and nodded at the castle. 'Get back to work.'

'Of course,' I said. Too loud; she winced. Voice hushed, I added, 'Thanks so much for your help.'

'You're very welcome.' She smiled wryly. 'Thenessa.'

Oh, hell.

Emelin Thenessa, daughter of Agenor's house. No escaping that title, now that even the Mother would soon know about it.

I glanced at my wrist as the nameless fae female flew off. The green bargain mark had quietly vanished – Ophion had been delivered safely to the Crimson Court, then. A damn shame, but at least now I knew ...

Dropped overboard.

I shook the thought off and began to walk, worry making my guts ache. I'd consider the details of my mother's escape later. First I ought to make sure Creon wasn't following his victims' example.

The cliffs were even higher on this side of the island, rugged rocks rising from the crystalline sea below. I started out walking fast, then fell into a trot, then found myself sprinting along the ragged edge – hell, where was that bloody bay?

And what if he wasn't even there?

Finally the coastline receded, and I all but hurtled over the edge in my hurry to look down. Steep rocky slopes, embracing the quiet beach on all sides. A broad stretch of orange-reddish sand, glowing in the afternoon sun. Cobalt water, frothing and sparkling around the razor-sharp rocks that rose from the surf, and the shallow waves sloshing against the equally sharp-lined silhouette kneeling where the sea lapped the beach.

Creon.

Even the midsummer sun couldn't soften the cold shiver that ran up my spine.

It wasn't *fear*. I still couldn't bring myself to be afraid of him, even if the fae clawing her own eyes from her face would likely haunt my dreams for the rest of my life. But there was a sense of dark foreboding to his slumped figure in the water, trousers soaked, boots and shirt discarded on the other side of the bay, his hands and torso covered in cuts and smudges of blood. His wings lay wilted over the sand, the corded muscles of his shoulders drained of all their strength.

He had to be aware I was here. But he didn't turn to look up, and in the pressing silence of the island, I didn't dare call out to him.

A narrow path wound down the side of the cliff, and I prodded my sore limbs back into motion, more grateful than I wanted to be for Agenor's quick treatment of my wounds. I might have fainted from blood loss halfway to the beach without his help. Now I merely stumbled a few times, but reached the safety of the bay without incident, the orange pebbles crunching under my boots as I walked.

'Creon?'

His wings and shoulders rose slowly as he took an agonisingly deep breath, bracing himself. I kicked off my boots and hurried towards him, over the red-hot sand, into the soothing coolness of the water. Salt stung the unhealed cuts on my legs. With my eyes locked on his still figure in the surf, the sharp profile of his face hidden behind the locks fluttering in the breeze, I barely felt the pain.

'Creon? Are you ...'

Only then, when I reached within a few arm-lengths of him, did he turn. Dark, bottomless eyes met my gaze with the exhaustion of a convict who lays eyes on the gallows and finally accepts his fate.

It was that look that made me falter in the ankle-deep water, feet momentarily unsure of where to go.

There was no death in his eyes. None of that festering darkness I had expected, the self-hate rotting his heart. He just looked ... fatigued. Depleted and tired to the marrow of his bones, but it wasn't *devouring* him.

With five feet between us, we stared at each other, grimy and wounded. Trickles of dried blood stuck to his cheeks, his temples. A long cut ran through his eyebrow, mirroring the inked scar on the other side of his face. His full lips were too tight, tension radiating through his clenched jaws, his taut shoulders, his clenching and unclenching fingers.

The bay was unbearably silent around us, nothing but the whisper of the surf and the summer breeze over the sand and a distant company of crickets.

'Are you alright?' I whispered.

He drew in an uneven breath at that word – *alright*. His gestures came hesitant and erratic; he kept his eyes glued to his fingers as they staggered through the familiar motions, as if he couldn't believe the words he was signing himself.

I thought I'd kill myself if this ever happened.

A chill spread from below my midriff, seeping into every fibre of my body. *This.* Fae squirming in the mud, killing themselves with nails and knives because of whatever horrors he'd unleashed in their minds.

Kill myself.

'Thought,' I breathed.

A near invisible nod. He raised his hand again, faltered, then dropped it back into the shallow water and unfolded his right wing a fraction.

I stumbled forward and splashed down next to him, unable to suppress a squeal at the shock of the cold water soaking my dress. His wing curled around me even though his hands remained motionless by his side, the black velvet warm from the sunlight.

His body was tense as a tightened bowstring, every movement more of a twitch. I moulded my palm to his muscular thigh, and he stiffened at the touch.

'Talk to me,' I said quietly. 'Tell me what's happening in your head.'

He didn't look my way. But he folded and stretched his fingers as he raised his hand reflexively, the motions cramped.

What I did ... Every sign was a struggle, his own muscles resisting the words he was trying to shape. *Draining them – taking all hope and joy in life from them – it was ...*

His fist clenched up so tightly even his scars paled.

'Creon?' I whispered.

Father, he signed – a single, explosive sign, like a wall breaking through.

Oh.

Oh, Zera help me – no.

'This ... this is what he did to you?' My voice cracked. 'When he escaped? When you ...'

He nodded a single strained nod, eyes clinging to the azure horizon.

'But you ... you didn't die.'

Didn't let me.

'Oh, fuck.' My battlefield rage had never been gone. Just temporarily soothed, waiting to erupt again. I wanted to scream. Wanted to break something into a thousand little pieces, wanted to dig the bastard up just to kill him all over again. 'And that was the first thing you learned about your demon magic?'

He didn't nod. But his lips twitched – a wordless, soundless rhythm.

'Oh, Creon.'

Something had fractured in the depths of his irises. Cracked through the poisonous layers of self-hate and bottomless anger and laid bare some far more vulnerable wound at the heart of him, a wound that didn't lash out or push away, that simply, helplessly, bled.

I've never wanted to be his. He still didn't turn towards me, such heartbreaking weariness in every single one of his signs. *Even when I was still very much hers. I was her proud little prince, her murderer, and the gods know I was enough of a prick about it – but I never wanted ...*

He faltered. A story he'd never told any other soul – three hundred and sixty years of brewing secrets, finally burning to the surface.

I swore I'd never be like him, he added with tight fingers. *That I'd never hurt anyone that way. I truly thought I'd rather die.*

And then I'd been the one dying.

Creon Hytherion, the male who could not be tamed, brought to his knees by his own ruthless devotion, defeated by his own damn victory.

'I'm sorry,' I breathed.

His fingers stiffened for the blink of an eye. *Don't you dare, cactus. You were glorious. I could watch you slaughter Ophion's friends all day.*

'But I made you ...'

Yes. A tremor wracked his body, trailing into the tips of his wings. *And now that it happened, I'm finding I don't particularly feel like dying. So I think the offense you're apologising for may not actually exist.*

The offense of ... what? Of standing in the wrong spot at the wrong moment, of nearly breaking my neck dropping off that gods-damned wall? If I thought about it for a moment, perhaps I didn't have much to blame myself for.

Perhaps ... perhaps it was the opposite.

I blinked up from his hands and found him watching me with night-black eyes, drinking in every inch of my wet, dishevelled presence. Even with his muscles gleaming and bulging in the glittering sunlight, there was still that sense of powerlessness to him – of resignation

'What changed?' I managed.

Restraint twitched at the corners of his lips as he averted his gaze again. *Something to hope for, I suppose.*

Something.

Oh, Zera have mercy on me. 'What do you ...'

With a silent groan, he unfurled his wings and lay back into the shallow surf, flattening his wings over the sand as he closed his eyes. Long hair drifted around his face, pulled back and forth in the rhythm of the current. His chest rose and sank slowly, drops of seawater drawing lines through the blood staining his bronze skin.

I suppressed the temptation to splash a handful of water into his face or to strip those soaked trousers off him. 'Tell me what you're thinking.'

It took two slow breaths until he raised his hand above the water. *Thinking about what you said.* He didn't open his eyes. *Before I left.*

'I said a great deal of very wise things before you left,' I said, unable to suppress my chuckle. 'Including some excellent advice to not get in trouble or run into any old fae enemies, if I recall correctly.'

A wry grin curled around his lips. *Not that.*

'Then what ...'

In the ... He hesitated. *Library.*

Oh.

Oh, hell. 'You heard that?'

His throat bobbed as he nodded, eyes still closed.

I love you. Of course he'd heard. And then he'd run off, drenched to the marrow of his bones in the hate of the Underground, convinced I'd change my mind if he just released me from his aggravating company for long enough.

And now …

Now he'd done the exact thing he'd feared most, the exact thing he'd thought unforgivable. And yet he was still with me. Clinging to that little shred of hope – clinging to words I'd never even planned to speak.

He had to feel the feverish anticipation pulsing through me, had to notice the way my heart broke into a dizzying gallop. But he winced as he looked up, so oddly vulnerable even covered in blood and ink.

And you're still here.

I breathed a laugh. 'Yes.'

Still don't hate me.

'No.'

Even though … He winced again. *Even though you saw* …

'I saw you saving my life, Creon.' I shifted to my knees in the wet sand. 'That's not the same as torturing a child, for the bloody gods' sakes. You used the same weapon to do something entirely different, and if that makes you a monster, you'll have to consider me a traitor for ever having used Agenor's magic, too.'

He blinked as he came up on his left elbow, drops rushing from his shoulders in unfairly alluring ways. Thoughts whirled behind his eyes – dumbfounded, apparently, over every immensely sensible word I'd uttered.

'And don't ever tell me again I shouldn't want you because of your own damn father torturing you to near-death,' I added, scowling at him. 'I'll punch you.'

You'll … He blinked again. *Punch me.*

'Hard,' I supplied helpfully. 'I've had practice, you see.'

He stared at me for another moment, then averted his eyes, lips straining to suppress the most joyless of grins. *Em* …

I swatted a handful of water at him and scrambled back before he could retaliate. 'Anything else? If we're discussing all your deepest hurts and secrets, we may as well—'

Without warning, his right wing slammed two buckets worth of water into my face, soaking me to the bone from head to toe.

I shrieked, cowered, gasped for breath. When I shook the drops and sticky strands of hair from my face like a wet stray dog, he sat snickering in the shallow waves, all excruciating memories evaporated in the rush of one far too satisfying victory.

'You bastard,' I sputtered.

I was hoping for a declaration of love, he signed, grinning even broader, *but I suppose I'll make do with this.*

I burst out laughing, splashing my way back to him. 'Oh, to hell with you and your dramatic wishes – I love you so much, you prick. I'd love you even if you hid your dirty socks under the bed, or if you ... if you ...'

He held out a hand, and I allowed him to pull me into his lap, a messy tangle of limbs and wet hair and slippery skin. His chest shook with laughter as he wrapped his arms and then his wings around me; his heartbeat was a dizzying rattle below his ribs.

'I love you,' I whispered against the satin firmness of his shoulder – such a relief, such an unimaginable relief, to finally speak the words out loud. Home. I was *home*. 'And I meant it the first time I said it – I meant it the first time I thought it. I just ... I didn't want to say it while I might still feel the smallest bit of doubt. You deserved certainty.'

He didn't answer. Instead, his left hand hooked around my nape, tilting my head with such savage force that a cry escaped me.

His lips smothered the sound instantly.

He kissed me hard, desperately, tasting of blood and salt and war. Kissed me like he was death and I was life, like he was frost and I was spring, like he was the darkest depths of night and I was the last flickering candle defying the shadows – his lips so full of need that I no longer felt the salt in my wounds or the cold sting of the water.

A kiss like the battlefield we'd left behind, and I was *not* falling again.

I dug my nails into his shoulders, finding his skin slick with sweat and seawater. He snarled soundlessly against my lips. Our tongues fought a vicious battle for control as we tangled up in the surf, teeth nipping and nibbling, the stings of luscious pain just sharp enough to numb the lingering images of torn wings and empty eyes and that little fae boy who'd nearly died at his own father's hands. I moaned his name. He kissed me harder. His mouth was hot and feral on mine, claiming me, devouring me – begging for the reassurance of my desire even after the unthinkable had happened.

He tasted like freedom. Like sweet abandon and merciful oblivion, like problems I could forget for a few more hours.

I wrapped my legs around his hips and locked my hands around his jaw. His muscular thighs strained beneath me, and my body went weak as if by command. I rubbed myself against his crotch, soaked underwear over equally soaked trousers; the feel of his bulging erection shot a sting of lust straight into my core and curled my toes in the wet sand behind his back.

He pulled back with a gasp, lips red and glistening, eyes glazed from the assault of our mutual arousal.

'Don't stop,' I breathed. 'Please don't stop.'

His jaw strained. No more than mere inches between our faces, our entangled bodies tense like scales about to tip one way or the other. One more kiss, one twitch forward, and we wouldn't stop until we'd fucked our minds empty and our hearts full again.

He moved back.

'Creon—'

A finger over my mouth smothered my husky objections. My breath hitched; even as he pulled back, his touch lingered, leaving me incapable of speech or sound.

I just need you to know ... His breath shook as he inhaled slowly and deeply. *I do miss my voice sometimes, Em.*

My mouth went dry. 'What do you—'

I'd kill to tell you just once how senselessly in love with you I am. To be able to whisper it in your ear at night. His fingers moved with breathless urgency between us, his other hand tight on my hip. *This gods-damned silence has never destroyed me the way it does with you. At times I feel like I'm bursting with words and I just ... can't ...*

His gestures slowed, sentence unfinished. I glanced up at his face, unable to scrape my thoughts together to the point of coherence. Even sitting, he seemed to tower over me, a menace of bronze and black against the stark blue sky, fresh wounds and inked scars a tangle of pain over his arms and chest.

All that savage power. All that gods-damned silence.

Bone-deep resolve burst through me.

'First of all,' I muttered, brushing a thumb over his tight lips, 'I'm going to get your voice back for you.' A plan that hadn't truly occurred to me until that moment, but the instant the words left my lips, I was no longer sure why it had taken me so long. Of course I was going to get his voice back. Starting tomorrow, if no one got in my way. 'Give me a few months. I'll take care of it.'

The shadows in his eyes softened. *You don't need to—*

'Second of all,' I continued, unfazed, 'you'll be glad to hear your tongue won't be at all useless in the meantime. As a matter of fact' – I grinned at him – 'I can think of some excellent ways to put it to use right now.'

He blinked, then burst out laughing, all lingering traces of darkness dissolving. *You shameless little viper.*

I prodded the bulge of his erection. 'Clearly you mind.'

He ripped my dress off me in response, flinging the wet linen onto the golden beach. Gone was the tenderness, the gentle care; his calloused hands moulded to my waist with unbridled greed, answered the invitation of my lips with a challenge of their own. I clawed at his trousers as he rose with a jerk, lifting me effortlessly to my feet, water splatting against his wings. His fingers drifted up to the swell of my breasts, then flicked over a pebbling nipple – no more than the *suggestion* of touch, but I gasped at the heat melting all the way through me.

'Oh, gods – Creon ...'

He chuckled. *I have a debt to settle, don't I?*

A debt? And then he sank to his knees in the surf, and all thought rushed from my mind in less than the time it took to blink.

That debt.

He looked up to meet my eyes as he stripped my underwear off my hips, baring the last of my body to the warm breeze. The smile he gave me made my insides curl tighter than a clenched fist.

Give me your words, Em.

An easy request, if the first stroke of his tongue over my drenched flesh hadn't abruptly robbed me of all awareness of civilised language.

I moaned, lost for thought – such an easy surrender to a male who knew every sensitive spot, every secret my body hid. He kissed me again. Unbearable pleasure coiled through me, and my knees wavered, buckled.

His strong hands wrapped around my hips before I could collapse, holding me in place for him to devour – every kiss, every graze of teeth aimed just where I needed it most, exploring the lines of my lips and the inside of my thighs. Slowly, so torturously slowly, he wandered closer, closer, *closer* to that bundle of nerves screaming the loudest for his attention ...

And pulled away before he reached it.

Disoriented curses tumbled from my lips, and I felt him chuckle, his breath so hot I squirmed. 'Creon ...'

He glanced up, a wicked smile threatening war on his lips. Oh, gods help me. He may be kneeling at my feet, but that smile told me I was far from the one in control here.

Words. The gestures looked shamelessly vulgar on his fingers.

'Oh.' Words. What were words? 'You ... *please*. I ... I ...'

The corners of his mouth quirked up as he slid a hand between my thighs and grazed a fingertip over my slit – not nearly enough to satisfy, and more than enough to make me cry out loud. His grin broadened, the twinkle in his eyes so gods-damned sinful he might have sent me climaxing with a look alone.

Words. He mimed it this time.

'I love you,' I breathed. 'I love you so, so much, and you really *are* the most beautiful dastardly villain I've had the pleasure of seeing in all my life, and will you please go *on*?'

He chuckled, mercifully bent over, and pressed a single kiss to the spot where my lips met. I moaned, and he moved back just as quickly.

'Oh, damn you!' I swatted at his head and received nothing but another encouraging grin as my reward. 'You already know. How ... how
much I loved you when you walked in and reduced Agenor to stutters
just to prove me right ... when you ...'

He returned his attention to his irresistible torment, wings spreading
wide before me as my voice wavered again. I didn't dare stop talking –
didn't dare risk an end to the blissful teasing and taunting of his lips
and tongue.

'When you trusted me even though you really shouldn't have,' I got
out, wrapping my hands around his head, brushing my fingertips along
the edge of his ears. A firm twist of his tongue was my reward. 'When
you saved Irie's life for me. When you twisted your knife into that
bastard's back for me. And when ... when ...'

He paused, kissing a slow trail up my belly while I fought to regain
control of my voice.

'When you killed them,' I whispered, the sea breeze playing tricks
with my words. 'When you used your powers to save me. I don't think
... I don't think I ever loved you as much as in that moment I realised
what you were doing, Creon.'

He yanked me closer, restraint snapped. Buried his face between my
thighs again and dragged his tongue all the way down to my throbbing
entrance – no longer pleasuring but devouring, no longer teasing but
claiming. I cried out. He clawed his nails into my bottom and slipped
his tongue into me, delving deep, drinking me like a starving male; I
knotted my fingers into his wet hair and gave in, pleading for more,
sobbing for more as pleasure rose to a breaking point within me.

He gave me more.

Even as my climax rolled through me, he didn't slow down, didn't
give me a moment to gather my breath. His strong fingers parted my
soaked lips as his tongue continued to work that bud of nerves at their
apex; two digits slid deep into my convulsing tightness before the last
waves of pleasure subsided, adding more friction, more sensation to
this intoxicating ecstasy.

I imagined for one dazed, heady moment what we must look like
for any innocent fae passing by, the two of us in the azure surf of the

Sunstone Bay, me naked and delirious with lust, the Silent Death feral and bloodied and kneeling at my feet.

Then his fingers curled inside me, and I blew apart again.

He lowered me into his lap, cradled me in his strong arms, as I moaned and writhed through a second devastating orgasm. The world returned to my senses slowly, the cool caress of the water and the sweet breeze on my skin and the warmth of the sunlight where Creon's wings didn't cover me. Reverent hands skimmed over my body, tracing every curve and line, healing every last cut and bruise they encountered.

I blinked open my eyes, breathing shallowly. He was an untamed animal above me, eyes wild and fierce, lips tight as if my pleasure had awakened something insatiable within him, something that thirsted for blood and craved blissful oblivion.

One hand vanished from my bare hip and appeared between us. He held my gaze as he slowly, deliberately signed, *Debt settled?*

I breathed a laugh and scrambled for the buttons of his drenched trousers, his erection a red-hot bulge below the cloth. His breath went rough as I palmed him, but he didn't move, every muscle drawing taut while I fought his buttons with fingers that wouldn't stop shaking.

His jaw clenched as I finally freed him and wrapped both hands around the bronze length of his shaft, savouring his pulsing warmth under my palms. Heat tightened in my lower belly at the feel of him, and his eyes went darker, more ravenous.

Still want the monster?

Fuck. I felt myself go slippery again, warm wetness throbbing down-wards in anticipation of his touch. He was too damn gorgeous, ruffled and wild with need on that sun-soaked beach; the motions of his fin-gers were an irresistible lure, drawing the breath from my lungs.

'Please.' It was a moan, even my vocal chords long past the point of sanity. 'Always.'

Good. The smile that slipped around his lips could have set solid stone on fire. *Because you're not getting anything less from me.*

My breath caught.

But he gave me no time to gasp, no time to brace myself. With one powerful motion, he flipped me over, settling me on hands and knees in the crystalline water, red-golden sand and rugged cliffs stretching out before me. His weight settled against my entrance an eyeblink later, my only warning before he dug his fingers into my hips and buried himself inside me.

One rough, powerful thrust, and the world went empty save for the breathtaking fullness in my own body, the bliss of his cock stretching me open.

He fucked me deep, then somehow deeper, every blunt stroke another conquest. I bucked my hips back instinctively, meeting him as he drove himself into me; his hard thighs pressed mine apart, spreading me wider for him, baring all of me for him to take. I couldn't see him. I couldn't hear him. All he gave me was the touch of his hands and the merciless claim of his cock, his thighs and balls slamming into me again and again, and it was that powerlessness that had me sobbing with desire as much as the torment of his thrusts.

His arms slipped around my waist and midriff, pulling me farther upright, towards his chest, so that I hung defencelessly in his hold as he pounded into me. And before I understood what he was doing, his wings furled around us, soft velvet trailing feathery strokes over my arms, my shoulders, my breasts.

I moaned his name, eyes rolling back at the intoxicating pleasure of his touches. Those wings were everywhere, embracing me tightly, caressing me like the summer breeze. His hard abdomen pressed against the small of my back as his thrusts grew fast and urgent; a panting whisper of hot breath betrayed his lips against the back of my neck.

My fingers found the smooth surface of his wings and stroked it. In response, he bit down hard on my shoulder, adding a sharp sting of pain to the cacophony of sensations.

I roared.

I had no words left. I had no thoughts left. But he could have my voice – have enough of it for the both of us. He could have this maelstrom of sheer feeling, of his cock and hands and wings and teeth driving all but these most primal sensations from existence.

All of me.

All of *us*.

He hissed against my shoulder as that thought swelled through me, so perfectly right that my insides clenched with the joy of it. His hand on my waist slid to my drenched sex, and calloused fingers rubbed that little centre of my pleasure so roughly that once again I cried out.

One last time, he buried himself inside me.

I erupted at the impact, blinded and deafened, my senses overruled by the all-consuming bliss of my release. For one, two heartbeats, I was no longer just myself, heavy and exhausted. Tendrils of some other consciousness danced along the edges of my imploding mind, a sweep of wonder, of need, of bottomless despair; I was death and the emptiness of night, I was a power that shook the earth below my feet.

And then he was gone and I fell, fell, fell through the whirling ecstasy and nothingness, and I became more myself than I had ever been.

Cold seawater brought me back, the sting of it just pleasant against my naked back and breast. I'd rolled onto my left side, Creon's arms wrapped around me from behind, his hard chest labouring against me as he, too, gasped for breath. His cock lay between my thighs, pulsing softly, my legs and bottom covered in the warmth of his seed.

Every inch of me was sore like hellfire, and I clung to it, to the overwhelming elation of it.

'Mine,' I breathed.

His arms clenched tighter.

I wiggled in his embrace until he allowed me to turn, and then we lay face to face in the shallow water, small waves playing around our knees and hips as we quietly watched each other's faces. A softness settled over his features under my gaze – soothing, for a moment, that immeasurable darkness I'd felt.

'Did you know?' I murmured, lifting my hand to run my fingers through his wet hair. 'You're all mine.'

I knew before you knew. He closed his eyes as I caressed his temple, his neck, a small smile quirking up his lips. It looked genuine – so peaceful and genuine. *And if I get even a tenth of you in exchange for all of me, I'd consider that an excellent bargain.*

I leaned closer, breathing against his lips. 'I don't love in tenths, Your Highness.'

He opened his eyes, a question gleaming in the black of his irises. His hand wrapped around my waist and nudged me closer, keeping that last intimate inch between my face and his.

'Stay with me,' I whispered. 'Take all of me and stop running from it, Creon. I'll beg you for that, if I have to.'

I'll never let you go again. His lips hesitated around the words.

'Is that a threat?' I tangled my fingers in his hair and chuckled. 'I'm not scared of you. Not even if you love me. Stay with me.'

He kissed my forehead, then moved back far enough for his hand to move between us. *I can't ask you to stay in the world above for me.* There was little conviction in his gestures. *It's a dangerous mess up here.*

'Come back to the Underground with me,' I said quietly.

His fingers stiffened. But he didn't look away.

'You did the worst you could think of, and the world hasn't ended.' I slid my hand down his neck, his chest, tracing the lines of his ink scars until he shivered. 'So you can do this, too. Ask Naxi to help you. Stop allowing your magic to control you. Your gods-damned father doesn't deserve that power over you from beyond the grave.'

He shook his head – a mere reflex, the gesture meaningless with the doubt that whirled in the darkness of his eyes.

'Please,' I managed, moulding my palm to his chest. 'Come tell me about the stars again. Come bake me honey cakes and defile libraries with me again. I'll get the alves to let you join our card games, and you'll be there for my birthday, and if we ever get bored, we'll go out and I'll stab a few of Ophion's friends for your amusement. It'll be glorious, you see?'

A grin grew on his face, wistful and heart-stoppingly beautiful. *Em* ...

'Don't say no!' My voice broke. I didn't know what more I could say – what else I could do if he still wouldn't risk it. 'Tell me what you need. Tell me what I can do to make this easier for you. I just ... Hell, I can't save you, Creon. But I can love you to death while you save yourself.'

He abruptly sat up, shaking the droplets off his wings with a quick roll of his shoulders. I scrambled up, ready to grab for him if he tried to run, ready to beg and plead and cry ... but he didn't run. Didn't argue.

Just watched me, naked and messy on that deserted beach, as if I was a goddess rising from the waves.

And you will. There was no question in his signs.

'Yes.'

He closed his eyes, long lashes trembling. I clenched my hands into fists and forced myself to wait, to be patient and sit motionless until finally he drew in a shaky breath and raised his hand again.

Don't be so frightened, cactus. You can't feel that way about me and still expect me to deny you a single thing.

I didn't dare to breathe. 'Do you ... Are you saying ...'

If they allow me back in ... He opened his eyes, fingers stiffening one last time. *If they let me, I'll come with you. I'll try to save myself.*

CHAPTER 33

IT WAS LONG PAST noon when our clothes had finally dried and Creon had repaired the tears in my dress with a few quick flickers of blue magic. It was later still before we finally flew from that quiet bay and faced the towering shape of the castle in the distance again.

We walked most of the way. I wasn't that eager to rush the confrontation with Agenor and the ruins of that crumbled wall.

Fae swarmed over the blood-drenched grass before us, repairing the worst of the damage and carrying bodies towards the mass grave someone had opened west of the castle. Magic flashed around the walls, most of it blue. Now and then, a spark of fire proved Lyn had returned from the Crimson Court, although Tared was nowhere to be seen.

We strolled through the high grass and the wildflowers, neither of us signing or speaking. It took a while before anyone at the castle noticed us, but once the heads started turning, *all* of them turned, watching our approach with what seemed like a mixture of apprehension and unrestrained curiosity.

A traitor prince and an unbound daughter they hadn't yet known about at sunrise. I shouldn't even have hoped for a quiet return.

But no one stopped us as we walked around the eastern wall, and not even the softest murmur followed behind our backs. One by one, even the most curious fae resumed their work with characteristic diligence, leaving us free to walk the last few hundred feet to the open gates of the castle.

As we rounded the last corner, Creon looked up beside me, eyes narrowing.

I followed his gaze. Leaning against the battlements above the gate, Agenor stood watching us, his face unreadable from this distance. I might have thought he considered the repair work beneath himself, if his dust-covered wings and stained clothes hadn't proven he'd done his fair share of the work already.

Might want to go have a word with him, Creon signed, turning towards me.

I thought of the way I'd stormed off a few hours ago and grumbled, 'I'll just go hug a cactus instead.'

A grin slid across his lips. *Even if I tell you he's feeling more doubtful than I've ever known him to be in the past three centuries?*

I blinked, glancing up again. Agenor merely sent me a tired smile, making no attempts to stop me or engage in a fatherly conversation.

Had he come after me, tried to pull me away from Creon's side, I'd probably have run. But something about his slumping shoulders and his resigned distance made me mutter a last curse, warn Creon not to kill any alves in my absence, and climb the many steps up the inner castle wall.

Agenor hadn't moved when I reached the top of the stairs. Elbows resting on the sandstone, dark wings swaying softly in the island breeze, he looked like a statue that had rested in the same place for the last five centuries.

'Evening, Em.' He sounded tired.

I muttered a greeting and sat down on the parapet, throwing a glance at the fields below. The blood had run all the way down to the lake, the crystal clear water gleaming red on the shore closest to the battlefield. Rough blocks of sandstone lay scattered in a semi-circle around the breach gaping in the southern wall – that tear that had opened up around the spot I'd defended.

A shiver ran down my spine as the sensation returned to me, earth giving way below my feet, stomach slamming into my throat.

'It'll get better,' Agenor said, not lifting his eyes from the dozens of fae circling the debris. 'As long as you don't bottle it up. Keep talking about it. It's normal for the fear to linger a while.'

I swallowed. Not the first words I'd expected from him – not after the way I'd run or the way I'd shouted at him before the battle or the way he'd carefully kept his distance even in the days before.

'Thanks.' I hesitated. 'I presume you'd know.'

A joyless smile. 'I'm afraid I do.'

We were both silent for a while. I noticed Tared for the first time, working just around the corner of the castle, fading back and forth between the grassland and the courtyards with the heaviest of loads.

'You found Creon,' Agenor finally said.

It wasn't a question. I would have been more annoyed at the curt undertone in his voice if not for the fuzzy warmth still glowing in my guts – *I'll come with you.*

'I did,' I said, keeping my expression carefully meaningless.

'I ...' He cleared his throat. *Doubtful*, Creon had said, and hell take me – something about the hard set of his jaw looked unusually unsure indeed. Displeased lines deepened around his lips as he considered his words and discarded option after option. 'I seem to have ... misjudged him a little.'

I cocked my head at him and briskly said, 'If only someone could have told you.'

'I suppose ...' He rubbed his dust-stained forehead, avoiding my gaze. 'Considering the circumstances, it would have been helpful ...'

'Oh, for fuck's sake,' I said, huffing a laugh. 'Is it that hard to say? "Sorry, Em, you were right and I was wrong". I promise it won't hurt.'

A sour chuckle fell over his lips. 'Sorry, Em. You were right and I was ... I was not interpreting the evidence in the most—'

'Wrong,' I corrected him.

He hesitated, then groaned a sigh and repeated, 'Wrong.'

'Look at that!' I said, spreading my arms demonstratively. 'You said the word and you haven't even withered to ashes yet. Perhaps you should try it more often.'

'Gods and demons,' he muttered, burying his face in his hands. 'Have you been holding back for days, or are you feeling particularly vexed at the moment?'

'Of course I was holding back,' I said sharply. 'For all I knew, you'd keep him in that cell for five more years and disown me if I—'

He jerked around, wings snapping out in a rare reflex of lost control. 'You thought I'd do *what?*'

'What?' I echoed.

'You ...' He blinked, eyes darting over me as if he was praying for me to burst out laughing and admit to a poorly placed joke. 'You thought I planned to *disown* you?'

'You didn't tell anyone who I was!' Anger got the better of me; hell's sake, he didn't get to pretend *I* was the mad one between the two of us. 'Even Doralis had no idea of—'

'I just dropped a title and an heirdom in your lap!' he said, and again there was that flicker of confusion in his eyes, just enough to lend a hint of sharpness to his voice. 'It seemed to me you could use some time to consider if and how you wanted to spread that news, taking into account the pressure that might come with the position.'

I stared at him.

'You *did* realise that, didn't you?' he hurried to add. 'That being my firstborn—'

'That ... that's all?'

'Why for the gods' sakes would I not acknowledge you?' he said blankly.

'Because I'm not even fully fae!' I burst out. 'And you're an idiot! And all you've done for days is treat me like a toddler and ignore every single bloody word I've spoken, so how was I supposed to get the impression you were at all excited to have some bad-mannered almost-human without those bloody wings walking around your home all of a sudden?'

His eyes flashed down the wall and back to my face, suggesting he considered for a moment whether he might be better off throwing himself off the battlements than staying here and facing me. 'I didn't realise—'

'Did you *ask*?'

He froze, then sagged back against the sandstone wall, eyes closed. 'No. Fuck.'

I had not been aware until that moment that Agenor Thenes, Lord of the Golden Court, would be capable of swearing. For some reason I couldn't identify yet, that single muffled curse made it oddly harder to hate him.

I waited, arms folded and teeth clenched. It took a few more heartbeats before he drew in a deep breath and muttered, 'Your mother would have my head at this point.'

Not what I'd expected him to say. 'She ... she would?'

'Oh, yes.' His smile didn't reach his eyes. 'With the kitchen knives, probably. She was rather fond of those, especially when I was being an idiot again.'

'Like now,' I said wryly.

'Yes, thank you,' he said and grimaced. 'Gods help us all. You're ... a lot more like her than I realised.'

My heart thumped. 'Is that a good thing?'

'Yes.' He rubbed his eyes, wiping soot and dust over the bridge of his nose. 'The only problem is I couldn't make sense of her, either.'

An unexpected chuckle escaped me. He smiled again and looked away, as if he was afraid he'd given away too much with that single little sentence.

It was harder and harder to despise him like this – to even be disappointed in him. Somehow, drained and abruptly aware of his own fallible mind, he lost most of his infuriating polish, revealing something far rougher and far more human below.

'Agenor?' The words were over my lips before I could stop them, his sudden vulnerability so much more inviting than his condescending attempts at conversation. 'If you don't mind me asking – well, if you do mind, I'm still asking it – but did you ... did you actually *love* her?'

'Did I ...' He interrupted himself, blinking at me. Had I told him I was actually Ophion's secret love child, begotten from some humble human lass in between his dealings with the Mother, he couldn't have looked any more bewildered. 'Gods help me, Em. Did you doubt *that*?'

'No, I'm asking invasive questions for the pleasure of it!' I let out a breathless laugh. 'I wasn't sure—'

'I turned my back on the empire after a bloody twelve centuries of loyal duty,' he said dazedly, hand coming up and dropping down in a gesture that didn't seem to know what it was supposed to be. 'I assumed that would tell you something.'

'It does! It does, but ...' I faltered, grasping for words. 'It's just ... you made it sound like such a sensible ethical decision, you see? You didn't know the truth about the Mother, then you figured out you'd accidentally been serving the wrong side, so you made your choices to leave. You just seemed so ... so *rational* about it.'

He opened his mouth. Closed it. Seemed to think better of it, parted his lips again, then let out nothing but another befuddled laugh and shut them once more. 'Em ...'

'Please,' I said, chest tightening. 'I already think you're an idiot. At the very least, give me a reason to think you a sympathetic one.'

'I ... I'm not sure what to tell you.' He sounded profoundly lost – twelve centuries of fae pride, and suddenly some daughter was shouting at him over *feelings*? 'I'm not sure what you want to hear. But I suppose – if you want the full story ...' He averted his eyes, raking a hand through his dark hair, leaving it even more unusually ruffled than it had been after the battle. 'Looking back, it would be a stretch to call me reasonable about anything that happened those months.'

I blinked. 'Is that your way of saying you were being a senseless madman about her?'

'That ...' He released a joyless laugh. 'That would be closer to the truth, I suppose.'

Oh.

A confession I found hard to picture, him being a madman over *any-one* – but it seemed tactless to tell him that, so I stayed silent, head spinning. Agenor hesitated, then slowly raised his right arm and shook down his sleeve a few inches, revealing two bargain marks. Lyn and my mother; Creon's mark had already disappeared.

'I've been frightened to fall asleep every night since she vanished.' His voice was still so very level – but it was a different kind of flatness now, bone-deep fatigue rather than that courteous distance. 'To know I might wake up in the morning to find the mark gone. That one day I'll have to accept she died and I'll never even know what happened to her.'

I stared at him as he stared at his wrist, avoiding my gaze – twenty years. Every single night of my life, even when I'd not had the faintest idea he even existed, when I'd not yet known about the family I'd lost in the hours after my birth.

I'd been frightened to miss Creon for even a few weeks. Agenor had lived through worse for all those years.

'I'm so sorry.' My voice cracked. 'I ... I didn't realise.'

He sighed, lowering his hand with a small, insincere shrug. 'Ophion's version of events at least told us something. My biggest fear was that she would still be at the court. Now that we know she isn't ...'

He didn't finish the sentence, but the silence spoke as loud as his words – a silence of equal parts relief and dangerous new questions. At least it seemed she had escaped ... but if she had, then where in hell was she now? Why wasn't she *here*? It had to be common knowledge that Agenor was spending his days at the Golden Court; why hadn't she managed to make her way to this island in the twenty years that had gone by?

Didn't she *want* to?

I swallowed. 'Do you think—'

'I don't suppose Achlys and Melinoë told her why I wasn't returning as planned in that month,' he muttered. 'She may have decided she'd rather save the world on her own.'

His voice didn't give way; his face didn't tighten. But I saw the way his wings sagged a fraction, and I knew even speaking that possibility out loud must have hurt more than he'd ever admit to any other living soul.

The little spark of sympathy grew into a solid flame – a bright, viable flame, the warmth of it comforting and oddly safe.

'Perhaps when word of your existence spreads ...' He hesitated, his lips a thin line. 'If she's able to, she may show up when she hears about you. She wanted you, Em. She really, really wanted you, enough to defy the bonds of that gods-damned island for it. I can't imagine she will sit back once she knows where to find you.'

Something cracked inside my chest, flooding me with soft, rosy sunlight. All I managed to bring out was a wobbly 'Oh'.

He looked up, eyes narrowing. 'Em?'

Wanted you. I tried to be frustrated at that catch in my voice, tried to care about pulling myself together, and didn't manage it at all. 'Did you ... did you want—'

'Oh.' He sounded too breathless. 'Gods. Yes, of course.'

'Oh,' I managed again.

He looked helpless on the edge of my sight. I didn't dare to look at him, didn't dare to meet that familiar green gaze and risk breaking down on the spot; I stared at his hands instead, at the fidgety motions of his fingers on his sleeve.

He started, 'I didn't realise ...'

'They hated fae,' I blurted out, because I had no idea where to start, and if I didn't start *now*, I may never manage again. 'My ... parents ... whatever they were – they kept me only because they didn't dare get rid of me. As soon as Creon showed up, they kicked me out and told me never to look for them again, and then it was just ... me. By myself. And I'd tried so hard to be what they wanted me to be, tried so hard to suppress that bloody magic, and in the end, none of it mattered a damn, you see?'

Agenor drew in a torturously slow breath. 'I see.'

'So what I'm trying to say is ...' I wrapped my arms around myself, soldiering on. 'I've never had a decent parent before. I have no idea how any of this is supposed to work. It would be nice to not be frightened all the time, I suppose?'

He muttered another curse. 'Do I frighten you?'

'Not you. Just ... just who you're supposed to be.'

'I don't have the faintest idea who I'm supposed to be,' he said bitterly, the confession so easy, so natural, that I almost dropped off the parapet in surprise. He didn't seem to notice, staring stubbornly into the distance. 'I've never had a daughter before. I should probably have warned you I might not go about this very ... adequately.'

I sniggered despite myself. 'Like an idiot, you mean.'

A wry grin grew around his lips. 'Thank you, yes.'

'Well,' I said, and then I no longer knew what to say. I glanced at his feet, which were safe, and then at his face, which was not at all safe, and then at his hands, which were calloused and tense and still slightly bloody.

Which were, also, my father's hands.

For the very first time, that thought felt like it might one day make sense.

'I'm sorry, Em,' he said, his voice too quiet for his stature. 'I'll try to do better. You might have to give me a few nudges in the right direction every now and then, though.'

'I tried nudging,' I said, pulling my knees to my chest. 'If you don't mind, I think I'll just start with punching next time.'

He let out a laugh. 'Figuratively?'

'I'm quite flattered you feel a need to confirm that.'

'I heard something about broken noses and that madman of a cousin Tared has,' he said, a small grin hovering over his lips. 'He was rather descriptive explaining why I shouldn't be too surprised about Ophion's wings.'

Trust Tared to smugly inform the rest of the world of my battlefield prowess, even if he knew damn well I could barely swing a stick around. I laughed and said, 'You'd have to be impressively vexing for me to repeat the Edored incident. I don't think you've been quite *that* bad yet.'

'A meagre comfort, but thank you.' He shook his head, still looking faintly amused as he threw a quick glance at the forest. The direction of the Crimson Court – as if the mention of Ophion's name had reminded him that another ship full of fae warriors might arrive any moment.

Another shiver trailed down my spine. 'They'll be back, won't they?'

'Oh, yes.' He absently rubbed his fingers over his right bicep – the spot that had been bleeding fiercely mere hours ago. 'I have no illusions they'll believe my lies. The only intention was to buy us some time.'

'You mean, if they know you won't lay siege to the Crimson Court tomorrow ...'

'They'll allow themselves more time to prepare. Yes.' He turned to nod at the work on the castle below. 'Which gives us a little more time to prepare as well.'

I swallowed something unpleasantly close to fear. 'You're staying here? Even if she knows you've turned against her?'

'It'll give others in the archipelago a place to go if they hear about this confrontation and decide they'd like to join us,' he said with a shrug. 'Can't collect new allies if we're hiding wherever that Underground of yours is. But I've had a quick word with Lyn and Tared, and we'll have some alves at this court permanently, and preventatively move everything of importance to safer places. As soon as we're attacked in all earnestness, we'll be able to get out quickly and efficiently.'

The Mother's commander again, working out his risks and strategies already ... He'd be careful, I supposed. His reputation at least suggested he was rarely anything else.

It didn't make the thought of it any less unpleasant.

'Do you have any idea how long you have?' I said, my voice too small.

'Couple of months, probably. They're not going to hurry this, and they'll need time to figure out just how much support I have here.'

Months. I breathed out slowly, adjusting to that estimate of the future. If the Mother would attack again in a few months, if she'd force us to take our next steps by that time ...

Well, then what? I'd be ready.

I'd always been ready.

'Alright,' I said, and my voice didn't waver. 'That's good to know.'

He nodded but hesitated as he opened his mouth again. 'Did you ...' He cleared his throat, suddenly quite interested in the cuff of his sleeve. 'Have you spent any thought on your plans for the coming ... time? Weeks? Whatever you ...' An annoyed gesture. 'Well, whatever you prefer.'

Oh, gods help me. 'I was planning to return to the Underground.'

If his wings sagged, it was by such a fraction of an inch I couldn't be sure if I'd imagined it. His voice remained unaffected as he said, 'I thought you might, yes.'

No attempts to convince me. No pleas or promises, no attempts to make what I wanted about his wishes instead. And perhaps it was that unexpected smooth acceptance, no appeals to my guilty conscience or family responsibilities, that made me plant my feet on the sandstone floor and say, 'My birthday is in a few weeks, though. I could probably convince them to let you in for cake.'

Agenor frowned. 'Fae don't usually celebrate birthdays.'

'Well,' I said, rolling my eyes as I got to my feet, 'that's a shame, because I don't celebrate name days, or any other fae holidays for that matter. Looks like we'll have to accept we'll never attend a party together for the rest of our immortal lives. Such a shame. If only something could be *done* about—'

'Oh, hell.' He groaned a laugh. 'Thanks, Em. That was enough punching.'

'Are you sure?' I said dryly. 'I could make a point about changing old habits, if you need it. Or about being ancient and rusty and probably no longer entirely sharp of mind.'

He winced. 'Definitely enough punching. How does one celebrate a birthday?'

'With cake,' I said. 'And family.'

He opened his mouth, abruptly closed it, then averted his gaze with a breath just too level to sound natural. It took a moment too long before he cleared his throat, nodded, and said, 'I'll be there.'

My smile felt more genuine than I'd expected. 'Thank you.'

Then we were silent, leaning side by side against the sandstone, watching fae flow by with abandoned weapons and pieces of alf steel. An oddly *comfortable* silence – too comfortable, really, for it to make sense. I'd gone against his wishes. I'd called him an idiot and a potentially heartless creature. And he still wasn't threatening to cut me off, or telling me I'd embarrassed him, or writing me letters to tell me I should just go find myself another family.

What an odd, unconditional safety to wrap my head around.

'I should go back to coordinating this mess,' he finally said, his voice still a tad croaky. 'Get some rest. You've done enough for the day.'

Almost true – but he had nothing to do with my last mission, and I shouldn't keep him occupied if there were likely more urgent issues to take care of. So I just said, 'Will do.'

'Good. Will I see you at breakfast?'

Right. We probably weren't eating an elaborate dinner in the hall tonight.

I nodded, and he stepped back, smile strained but genuine. 'Night, then, Em.'

'Night,' I managed, and with two steps and a powerful wingbeat, he vanished from the castle wall and soared towards the groups of faé gathered on the battlefield below.

I found Lyn and Tared in a shadowy castle courtyard, surrounded by the rubble of a broken fountain and a handful of torn rosebushes.

Tared sat chewing on a piece of date cake, his sword in his lap, but his face and hands at least mostly clean. Lyn darted around the small space, burning the occasional bloodied arrow to ashes with handfuls of fire. They looked up simultaneously as I emerged from the low gallery that gave access to the courtyard, Lyn with a beaming smile, Tared with a single raised eyebrow that I knew to be just as warm a greeting.

'Still got all your limbs on you, Em?'

'Miraculously,' I said, planting myself down on the edge of the crumbling fountain basin. Lyn singed a last snapped arrow, then wandered towards us, flames still sparkling on her fingertips. 'Did you deliver Ophion safely to the court?'

'Well, safely ...' Lyn said.

'Most of his bones remained whole,' Tared said, breaking off another piece of date cake. 'And if he's lucky, they'll manage to fix his wings just fine. So it would be ungrateful of him to complain, really.'

'Ah, yes. Must have been gratitude that he was wailing about.' Lyn sent him a grin as she sank onto the irregular tiles next to him and stole a crumb of cake from his palm, then turned back to me. 'Long story short, he's back at the court, yes. You found Creon?'

I nodded, and her smile was too relieved to pretend she hadn't been worried sick about him. But she merely stuck her cake into her mouth and added, 'And Agenor?'

I shrugged. 'Had a word with him.'

She hummed a note of approval. Tared dryly said, 'Didn't kill him?'

'He's grown significantly more pleasant in the last couple of hours,' I said, unable to suppress a grin. 'Someone seems to have told him about Edored's nose.'

'I think Ophion's wings made your point convincingly enough before I said a single word about that incident.' The corners of his lips were trembling in an expression suspiciously close to pride. 'Worth a few bonus points. Although, the footwork was sloppy. We'll need to work on that – assuming your ladyship will stoop to take orders from some lowly alf, naturally.'

I snorted. 'Did I ever take orders from you?'

'Regrettably, no.' He didn't look particularly regretful. 'An alf can hope, though.'

'Liar,' I said.

'Brat,' he said.

We grinned at each other; a little knot of tension unclenched just under my midriff. He had to at least suspect what I was here to suggest. And yet there was none of that fear in his eyes this time, none of the panicked apprehension as when I'd shown up with Creon's unconscious body in Faewood.

'What are your plans, Em?' Lyn said, stealing another bite of date cake. Ah. She definitely knew I must have discussed the coming weeks with Creon, and by the look of it, she wasn't sure what the outcome had been. 'Of course, if you prefer to stay at the Golden Court a little longer – with Agenor here and all of—'

'I'm coming back to the Underground,' I said.

She hesitated, lips still parted. 'Ah.'

'And I'd like for Creon to come, too.' I turned to Tared, whose smile paled. 'I don't know what exactly you discussed with him for these weeks, but—'

'That we'd meet again in six weeks' time,' he said flatly, 'and that I'd agree to let him back in by that time on the condition he'd provide plausible proof that the risks of him losing control and harming anyone in the Underground would be sufficiently low.'

I shrugged. 'They are.'

He glanced at Lyn, who sat studying me with squinting amber eyes, and slowly said, 'They are?'

'If it starts getting worse again, I'm pulling him out of the place myself,' I said. Now that I'd seen the alternative – now that I knew how much better he *could* be – there was no way I'd allow him to stay in that mess again. 'But I don't think it will be necessary. And I need him there to figure out how I'm going to break the Mother's bindings.'

That sent both of them stiffening.

'To do what?' Lyn said, as if there was any chance she may have misheard me.

'Break her bindings,' I said brightly. *And get Creon's voice back* – but perhaps that wasn't the point to make now. 'Since Ophion said she can reverse them, I'm figuring we should be able to do it, too. I'm going to figure out how. But since Creon is the one who has been reading up on the subject in her personal library, I'd like to have him in the Underground. Also, I need him to train my magic. Also, he just won you this battle.' I smiled at Tared, whose shoulders hadn't loosened. 'Have I convinced you yet?'

He uttered a joyless laugh. 'You know damn well I'm not getting between you and those cursed bindings, Em. I just hope you know what you're doing.'

'I know what I'm doing.'

He and Lyn exchanged a single quick look, a wordless confirmation of what I already knew would be their mutual conclusion. Tared muttered a curse as he averted his eyes again ... but I recognised that curse, and it signalled agreement he wasn't happy to give.

'Wonderful,' I said, jumping up from the fountain basin. 'Oh, and before I forget – I invited Agenor to my birthday celebration. We might want to convince the Council before that time that they should allow him into the Underground, but that won't be a problem, I take it?'

'Orin help us all,' Tared said dryly. 'The fae nobility is showing, after all. Need us to build you a pretty little throne, too, Thenessa?'

I beamed at him. 'Well, if you're suggesting it yourself ...'

He huffed a laugh. 'Five extra rounds at our next training session, brat.'

It could have been fifty extra rounds and I wouldn't have cared. Finally the triumph was bubbling up in me, a sudden, glowing sensation that made me feel like singing out loud even though I knew very well no one would appreciate the sound of it – a terribly premature but temporarily soothing burst of hope.

The Mother was still out there, brooding on revenge. My own mother was gone, and I might never find her. Perhaps we would get a few months of peace, and even then they'd be the silence before the storm; rationally, I knew that much, knew that war would come and destroy more than I could stand to lose.

But for a few blissful minutes, none of it felt real.

I'd faced my first battle and survived.

I'd found my father, and perhaps I didn't even hate him.

And when I returned to the Underground, Creon would be with me – would sleep with his arms around me again and learn to control his magic and *stay*.

I half-danced, half-sprinted my way through the castle as I left Lyn and Tared behind, past the Blood Gate, past the kitchens, past the tower where I'd allowed the violet-eyed female to escape. Even that place no longer made me wince. All my heart could focus on was the southern castle wall behind, where the gaping breach had healed over without a trace – such quick, spotless work that I knew exactly who to hold responsible for the change.

Creon was sitting in the shadow of the restored wall, in a pale yellow stretch of grass that must once have been a vibrant green and lost its blue in the process of the castle repairs. The smile that crept up on his lips as I bounced around the corner was a languid one, an expression that wouldn't shock the fae tiptoeing around him too much ... but I caught the twinkle in his eyes as he met my gaze, and I knew his demon senses had already picked up on my victory.

Arranged things? he gestured as soon as I skidded to a halt beside him.

'Of course I did,' I said. 'I'm the pinnacle of diplomacy. You should know, Your Highness.'

Apologies. A grin hovered close to the surface of his expression. *I was so busy being impressed by your various other epithets that I forgot about this one for a moment. Emelin Thenessa, daughter of Agenor's house, cactus hugger and pinnacle of diplomacy – anything I'm forgetting?*

'Yours,' I said quietly.

His smile stilled, then deepened as he gestured for me to join him in the pale grass. I fell down next to him, revelling in his nearness even with two feet between us, as around us fae flew by and walls grew whole again. The Golden Court recovering – preparing for worse.

Worse no longer bothered me.

I was Emelin Thenessa, daughter of Agenor's house. Cactus hugger and fae whore. Nosebreaker and little brat. *His.* And whatever the Mother wished to send after us next ...

I was ready for war.

Emelin and Creon's story continues in book 3, *Ruins of Sea and Souls.*
Grab it here: https://mybook.to/RoSaS

And check out the FREE prequel *Heart of Silk and Shadows,* a full-length novel telling Allie and Agenor's story twenty years before the events of the main series.
Find it at www.lisettemarshall.com/heart-of-silk-and-shadows

Acknowledgments

Lord of Gold and Glory was probably my most challenging book to date (which is author speak for "the cause of several breakdowns"), and it would never have become this story without the help of my wonderful author and reader friends.

In particular, I want to thank Steph for helping me through all my emergencies, Emergencies and even EMERGENCIES, and Amber for her general expertise on Gorgeous Yet Mildly Vexing fae princes and our highly enjoyable Agenor therapy sessions. Many thanks also to Sahana for her last minute speedreading and to Colleen, Jay, Rae and Vela for the numerous helpful comments that helped shape this story. And Erin – apologies for the heart attacks; you've been phenomenal as always.

Thank you so much to all coven buddies who have given me advice, celebrated my wins, and listened to my whining when matters didn't go as planned – I'm not going to try to name you all because I'm bound to forget someone and make things awkward, but you know who you are. I love you all to pieces.

Finally, as always, all my love to W., who remains eternally mystified by hate blow jobs and kidnapping-to-lovers romance but nonetheless continues to support this crazy writing dream of mine. Thank you for cooking dinner every time I forgot because my characters were running off with me. You're the best. (Yes, better than a Gorgeous Yet Mildly Vexing fae prince.)

Other books by Lisette Marshall

The Princess & The Spy

She despises his coldness. He loathes her nosy questions. But to avoid a war, they have no choice but to work together...

When a rebellious princess joins forces with her father's cold, bitter spymaster to keep her kingdom safe, there is no denying the forbidden fire flaring up between them.

The Queen & The Assassin

He was supposed to kill her, not to melt her iron heart...

When a common enemy threatens both their lives, a ruthless queen and the assassin out for her life have no choice but to close an uncertain alliance. And as shadows of the past draw them deeper and deeper into a tangle of deceit, sizzling hate turns into something much more dangerous...

For a complete overview of all Lisette's published and upcoming work, visit www.lisettemarshall.com/books.

About the Author

Lisette Marshall is a fantasy romance author, language nerd and cartography enthusiast. Having grown up on a steady diet of epic fantasy, regency romance and cosy mysteries, she now writes steamy, swoony stories with a generous sprinkle of murder.

Lisette lives in the Netherlands (yes, below sea level) with her boyfriend and the few house plants that miraculously survive her highly irregular watering regime. When she's not reading or writing, she can usually be found drawing fantasy maps, baking and eating too many chocolate cookies, or geeking out over Ancient Greek.

To get in touch, visit www.lisettemarshall.com, or follow @authorlisettemarshall on Instagram, where she spends way too much time looking at pretty book pictures.

Made in United States
Orlando, FL
20 May 2024

47041775R00300